"You're no gentleman," she blurted out. "You're a rogue."

"Since you seem convinced I have naught but your worst interests at heart, mayhap you ought to find out the extent of my terrible intentions."

His hands were making little circles on her back.

"Don't—"

She pushed her hands against him, but he wouldn't budge. In truth, it wasn't him she was trying to resist as much as the unbidden throbbing he created in her body.

His eyes turned dark. "You see, when you call a laddie—particularly the one in charge of your safety and well-being—a scoundrel enough times, he begins to think he might as well live up to his name." Slowly, he lowered his head and slanted his mouth against hers.

Other Books in
THE AVON ROMANCE *Series*

CAPTIVE ROSE *by Miriam Minger*
CHEROKEE NIGHTS *by Genell Dellin*
DEVIL'S MOON *by Suzannah Davis*
FOOL FOR LOVE *by DeLoras Scott*
ROUGH AND TENDER *by Selina MacPherson*
RUGGED SPLENDOR *by Robin Leigh*
SCANDAL'S DARLING *by Anne Caldwell*

Coming Soon

DEFIANT ANGEL *by Stephanie Stevens*
OUTLAW BRIDE *by Katherine Compton*

Lavender Flame

KAREN STRATFORD

AVON BOOKS ◆ NEW YORK

AVON BOOKS
A division of
The Hearst Corporation
105 Madison Avenue
New York, New York 10016

Copyright © 1991 by Karen Finnigan
Inside cover author photograph by Butch Williams
Published by arrangement with the author
Library of Congress Catalog Card Number: 90-93604
ISBN: 0-380-76267-6

First Avon Books Printing: May 1991

AVON TRADEMARK REG. U.S. PAT. OFF. AND IN OTHER COUNTRIES, MARCA
REGISTRADA, HECHO EN U.S.A.

Printed in the U.S.A.

RA 10 9 8 7 6 5 4 3 2 1

Dedicated
to my mother,
E. May Wattum,
who has traveled many roads
with me in life,
all of them leading here.
With deepest love and thanks.

Acknowledgments

I wish to thank many people for special help during the writing of this book: Stephen Reid of the National Museums of Scotland and R. M. Harvey of the Guildhall Museum, London, for long distance research of hard-to-find details; also, Brian Perth of the Black Watch Highland dancers, F. W. MacIntosh, Douglas Brackett, Shelly Thacker-Meinhardt, Linda P. Sandifer, and, for their stout moral support, my sons and husband.

And in particular, I wish to thank Charlou Dolan, friend and fellow author, for her generous, insightful critiques of the manuscript and her encouragement of my writing.

The heart has its reasons
that the reason does not know.
—Pascal

Prologue

Scotland, 1721

All day an ominous stillness hung over Castle Fenella MacLean, a silence so heavy that not even the mists dared lift from the loch. The lonely wail of the pipes at dusk at last broke the spell, and the harsh grating of the castle yett being pulled up signaled the awakening of action. Aye, something was amiss, Catriona Ferguson decided, and, ever curious, she could not resist the temptation to move closer to watch.

With one arm around her collie, Shep, the other behind a sharp outcropping of rocks, she crouched and spied on the MacLean chief as he and his kin moved down the path through the glen, past the wee kirk, and into a shroud of mist. With him walked the chiefs of many clans, come from glen and hill afar, and a bonnie sight it was to see the colors of their plaids. But their faces held anger, and she wished now she'd listened to her grandfather when he'd told her to stay home.

Shep laid back his ears and whimpered. To settle the dog, Catriona stroked his head, yet she shared the animal's restless mood. She hated being separated from her grandfather—the only one of her family with the same fiery hair as herself—and so she'd tried to follow him. But she'd lost him, and now she'd have to look for him, which would make her late and her mother angry. Catriona shook her head. Oh, Grandfather shouldn't have come so close to the wicked Castle Fenella MacLean, because even a seven-year-old girl like herself knew this procession promised danger.

Giving in to a daring impulse, she fell on her hands and knees in a patch of heather for a closer look. The chiefs carried a great chest, borne like a coffin, yet Catriona knew of no person in the village who had died, and as the autumn twilight deepened, the men's voices carried up to her. She caught her breath at their words. The Regalia, someone whispered too loud. Catriona knew what that was. The crown of Scotland. They were hiding it!

One by one, she watched the plaids pass by, squinting in the fading light until the MacLean himself walked abreast of her. Suddenly ducking from beneath her hand, Shep bounded out, and, with a cry of alarm, Catriona burst from her hiding place, chasing Shep as fast as her bare feet could carry her.

She was breathless by the time she caught the dog by the fur of his neck. The MacLean halted and stared down at her. Spare and sharp-featured, his face was crisscrossed with lines, and no welcoming smile warmed her.

Signaling the other clansmen to continue, the MacLean, a taller man than her grandfather and a chief, hung back, hand on the hilt of his dirk, his stare marking her as an unwanted intrusion.

He stepped forward, the dirk flashing. "What are ye doing here, lass? What have ye spied?"

"N-nothing." She took a panicked step backward.

"Why are ye no' with yer mother?"

"I-I lost Grandfather."

Before she knew what had happened, the MacLean reached up, caught her shoulder, and tugged her onto the path. "I say ye were spying on the MacLeans. Favor yer mother, ye do . . . except for that red hair."

"Let her go." Her grandfather's voice boomed from the next outcropping, and, using his staff to balance himself, he clambered down the hill.

Catriona jerked loose, ran to him, and half hid behind his plaid. "Grandfather, it's the Regalia." She had heard many a tale of the Regalia's legendary hiding places, but she'd never dreamed the royal crown and scepter might end up right here in Glen Strahan. Her flesh tingled.

"Angus Ferguson," the MacLean sneered. "I should have known ye'd be nearby. Taking secrets back to yer family, I suppose?"

"After the number of times ye've raided my land, I'd be daft not to watch out for pillage. What blackmail do ye exact now to save me from yer thieving?"

The MacLean did not hesitate. "Rid yer manor of its spies. Lousy Jacobite spies . . . If it were no' for yer family, we'd no' be having to hide the Regalia again."

"You lie."

"Go and inquire among your family. My pillage of yer estate is naught compared to the treachery within yer own son's family."

Catriona knew the exact moment when Angus drew his own dirk. "Dinna look for reasons to worsen the MacLean-Ferguson feud," he told the MacLean.

" 'Tis the almighty truth, and Jacobites will make yer life a living hell. Unless ye cast them out. What say ye to that?"

Catriona shuddered at his grim question. She knew the Regalia had to do with kings, but in all her seven years, she'd never figured out this thing called "Jacobite"—yet the word came up whenever her parents argued over the cost of her mother's French gowns.

Shep whined, and the MacLean frowned at Catriona, who squirmed in fear.

"Dinna touch her, MacLean. She's naught but a child."

The MacLean stepped closer. "If she's seen what only the chiefs should know, she must be punished too. Ye must learn to run yer manor as a chief would, Angus, else I'll no' just pillage it—I'll take it over." The MacLean, mighty chief of Glen Strahan, looked down on Catriona. "What did ye spy, lass?" he demanded again. "Are ye going to tell yer mother?"

Shaking her head, Catriona clung to her grandfather and peered around his leg. Oh, no, she'd never tell her mother about *this*.

Angus untangled her grip from his plaid and caught Catriona into his arms. "The lass knows naught. If she's to be punished for running wild, I'll decide her fate."

Trembling, Catriona buried her face in his neck. "G-Grandfather, why is he angry at me?" She could scarcely hear her own voice for its shaking.

"Hush, lass . . ." With long strides he carried her home. He seemed to forget his threat of punishment—until the next day.

Clutching a fistful of white heather she'd plucked on the moors, Catriona pressed close to the library door and listened to the angry voices. Her grandfather was shouting at her father, and her father was arguing with her mother.

"Ye're a disgrace to yer fine Ferguson forebears. Ian Ferguson would roll over in his grave. Leave for Edinburgh." Angus's words carried right through the door. "Do ye ken? Yer brother is here to carry on for me."

When her father spoke, he sounded sad. "You mean to send us back to the Lowlands for good?"

"Spying for the Jacobites is no' looked on with favor in this glen. Ye are lucky to leave alive."

"Ross," said her mother, exultant, "it's the very opportunity we've hoped for. Think of it—Edinburgh. Catriona can become a lady instead of roaming about these godforsaken hills. Do you want your daughter growing up knowing nothing but how to ply wild herbs like some little sorceress?"

"Aye, your wife's only bit of wisdom." For once Catriona's grandfather and her mother agreed.

"Catriona will go with us?" her father asked.

A pause. "Aye."

Unable to restrain herself, Catriona burst into the library, faithful Shep at her heels. Desperate to understand why everyone was angry, she fell at her grandfather's knees. *Spying,* they said. She'd been spying on the castle yesterday . . .

"No . . . I wouldna tell, Grandfather . . ." she whispered brokenly. She plucked his coat sleeve, then wiggled her way onto his lap. "Dinna send me away. Please . . . I'll never spy again." She pressed the heather into his hand and glanced about—at her mother's flushed face and silk gown, at her father's bowed head and shamed expression.

Her grandfather sat rigid and silent.

He stared at her little bouquet. "I dinna ha' a choice, bonnie Catriona," he said at last. "Ye are the bloom of my heart but—"

"Grandfather," she cried, "was it wrong to look upon the chiefs? To spy on them and the Regalia? Why?"

For a few seconds she thought his embrace tightened. "There are many kinds of spying, lass, but ye're too young to ken the difference now."

"No." She clung more tightly, and her tears dampened the plaid at his shoulder. "No, Grandfather. Let me stay . . ."

"Take the bairn away," he commanded. With a rough gesture, her grandfather untangled her arms from his neck and thrust her at her father. "I said take her. I've grown too auld to tramp through the hills wi' a bairn."

Catriona ran outside, tears wet on her face, ears echoing with the sound of her mother's anger and endless chatter—of silly things like assemblies and parties. She wanted none of it. She wanted her grandfather. Oh, it wasn't fair. And she still had no idea what these Jacobites were up to, hiding the king's crown. Why were they all so angry? All because she'd spied on them? But why? She flung herself across a whimpering Shep and wept into his fur.

"Why . . . why?"

Chapter 1

Edinburgh, 1736

Drawing the hood of her cloak closer, Catriona hurried through the low-hanging mist, her footsteps clicking on the cobblestones. As the sky darkened, the tall houses that rose like a stone forest blackened into forbidding shadows. With but a wee imagination, one gnarled fir in the square could pass for a black-clad crone. At least Catriona thought so.

The horseman who trotted out of a wynde and into her path, however, had naught to do with imagination.

"Ha' ye no answer to these missives, Catriona Ferguson?" the fellow called out as he rode across High Street. " 'Tis blasted weary I am of the journeys, lass."

Not bothering to dismount, he thrust the letter into her suddenly shaking hands, then disappeared into the Edinburgh mists, his Highland plaid flying behind him.

Pretending a calmness she didn't feel, Catriona pushed the sealed parchment into her basket of herb mixtures. She didn't have to read the letter to know the message and the signature. And her answer was the same as before.

No. No. No.

A waste of ink and parchment, that's all Angus's missives had become. She shivered. It was gloaming, that time of day when above the tightly shuttered streets of

Edinburgh, the sun had set, leaving the ramparts of Castle Rock cold and the city below it in shadow.

All the more reason to hurry home with the letter. Elspeth would know what to do. Her mother's servant woman had always been there to provide counsel as well as starched and mended dresses. If there was one thing with which Elspeth would sympathize, it was Catriona's anger at Angus Ferguson's insistence that she return to the Highlands.

Because her father and mother were both dead, there was no family to bind Catriona to the Lowlands, and now that her cousin had died last year, she had a duty as sole heiress of the Fergusons. Angus wanted a reconciliation with his last living relative before his own life slipped into the braes forever. Or so he argued in letter after letter.

Angus was tenacious, of that she had no doubt, but he'd banished her long ago. Why should she care if he suddenly needed her now? Besides, she had no desire to play the heiress of a feuding Highland clan. Let Angus himself wed. Some Highland lass could father a new son for his heir.

Quickening her step, Catriona left the street and, taking a shortcut through a wynde, hurried up the hill through the shadows until at last she reached the familiar dark stones of her own tall, narrow townhouse.

In the ground-floor flat she found Elspeth bent over the hearth. On the floor a turned-over bowl spilled brown eggshells and runny yolk, which was being lapped up by the neighbor's tabby cat. A pot of thin mutton broth bubbled in one caldron, and next to it a smaller black pot hung over the fire, the rising steam scented with herbs. Except for the making of herb mixtures, Elspeth did not count cooking among her accomplishments as a lady's maid. Her gray hair half fell out of her snood, and her apron hung askew. Shaking her head, she stood up and removed a batch of black-tinged oatcakes from the hearth. Ever since the cook had left, Elspeth had done her best, but sometimes Catriona thought the herb mixtures smelled better than the food.

She slipped off the hooded cloak, shaking out the tangled red curls that had long been her bane, and, while warming her hands at the hearth, told Elspeth about the poultice she'd applied to a patient. "Spilled the kettle of broth on her arm, the poor woman did, and such a scald. It took the strongest poultice you ever taught me to apply, Elspeth. She cried so in pain."

"Helen cries in pain over everything. But I'll tend her myself tomorrow and reassure her. How did the almighty Campbells pay you?"

Catriona paused. It seemed crass to speak of payment for an errand of mercy. "With a new piece of mutton to come round soon."

"Aye," Elspeth said with obvious skepticism. "Still on the hoof, I wager. Catriona, it seems I neglected to teach you the most important lesson of all. Ye canna treat people in return for promises. Coins are what buy the food and—" With a cluck of her tongue she broke off her usual argument and turned back to the hearth, muttering, "Forgi' me, lass. It willna matter now."

A scrape sounded somewhere. Pausing with a warm oatcake halfway to her mouth, Catriona turned.

"Have we new neighbors moving in above us?"

Before Elspeth could reply, Catriona heard another telltale scrape of furniture coming from the next room. She cast an alarmed look at Elspeth. "Who's here?"

"I dinna think 'tis for me to say till you read the letter, lass. Did the messenger no' find ye?"

The letter. Where was it? Catriona felt a momentary panic before she remembered. The basket on the rocking chair by the hearth. Quickly she rummaged through it, and in the time it took to rip open the parchment, she had already marched toward the drawing room.

Elspeth followed, clucking like a mother hen. "Ye'll be better prepared if ye find out the news from the letter first, lass." She wedged herself between Catriona and the door.

Giving in, Catriona tried to ignore the ominous sounds of furniture scraping across the floor that came from the

LAVENDER FLAME   9

other side of the door. Squinting in the dim light of a candle Elspeth held up, she read.

> *Granddaughter. That kindness which disposed me to favor you with an invitation to reside at Ferguson Manor having been ignored, I feel the want of alternative offers. To that end, I've given orders that . . .*

"An auction of all our belongings!"

"I fear so, lass," Elspeth said.

"Safe escort to Glen Strahan, and with a minister! Angus presumes too much."

"We canna go alone," Elspeth said calmly.

"I don't want to go at all! 'I am, granddaughter, your most humble servant,' he says." Catriona shoved the letter at Elspeth. "Angus hasn't invited me this time." She sounded incredulous. "He has *summoned* me back to Glen Strahan." Elspeth stepped aside, and Catriona pushed open the door.

A complete stranger, an old man wearing breeches baggy at the knee and a mended long coat, was pushing a settee across the room, calculating its price out loud.

"A solicitor!" Catriona accused. Her temper flared. "Vermin. You deserve a shrew's dunking stool."

The man looked up guiltily. " 'Tis only my job, lass," he complained.

"Your job! You're a thief!"

"Nay, an honorable businessman, lass. I have a proper arrangement with your grandfather."

"Angus had no right to arrange my affairs."

"Every right, lass."

Having spent the worst of her anger, Catriona could only stare in shock. The agent had actually taken the liberty of stacking all her furniture in preparation for an auction.

The china cabinet cried out for its porcelain. Faded spots showed on the walls where paintings had hung. The candlesticks had parted company with the mantelpiece. Even the fire in the grate had vanished. It was a wonder he hadn't packed the cat as well. One floor of the tall building was all her family had occupied, but the rooms and especially the furnishings held memories. For the first time Catriona felt an affection for her mother's gaudy belongings.

Her gaze went to the crate that was rapidly filling with her father's books, and her heart skipped a beat. With a cry, she rushed across the room, fell to her knees, and began to sift through the contents. She looked up, mute. Elspeth followed more slowly, wringing her hands in her apron and casting a beseeching look at the stranger, who shrugged.

"Lass, 'tis to be sold through newspaper advertisement," the auctioneer said. "Come Tuesday next . . . so there's no way to prevent it. 'Tis no' my doing." The solicitor spoke in the emotionless voice of one who'd long ago memorized his little speech. As if unable to meet Catriona's stricken gaze, he stared at the buckles on his shoes.

"But I can't give up my father's books," she whispered numbly. "They were to be mine for always." Why, just as if it were yesterday she could recall her gentle father taking her on his knee and making her forget all her woes with a favorite tale. *The Iliad* . . . Yes, that must be saved, but *Tristan and Isolde* had always been her favorite legend. And Shakespeare's sonnets. She *had* to save those. She rooted around and dug out the books, their gilt edges worn.

"I'll buy these back," she said, holding them up.

Quickly standing, she rummaged in the secret drawer of her father's desk for a few shillings. "Here, sir, would this be enough for just three books?" She held out a few coins to the man.

His wig askew, he sighed and looked away, as if this scene of penniless orphans and widows losing their household goods occurred too frequently.

"If it were your daughter, sir, what would you do?" she pleaded.

The man turned.

Catriona smiled hopefully. Please, God, let him have a daughter . . . and a conscience.

With a negative wave of one hand, the auctioneer rejected the proffered coins and sighed again. Then he smiled. "Nay, lassie, what's a book or two? They're hard to resell, so I'll not tell. Go on with ye and hide them with your clothes."

Catriona almost wept at the simple kindness and didn't wait for his generous mood to fade. Indeed, by the time she retreated, Catriona had cajoled the poor man out of half the books. She left him mopping his perspiring brow with a snowy handkerchief and muttering about his five daughters needing husbands.

With Elspeth in tow, Catriona hurried to the bedroom. After dumping the lot on the floor, she ran a tired hand across her forehead. "Well, what shall we do now, Elspeth?"

"I suggest we pack our clothes."

"And whose side would you be on?" Catriona cast a betrayed glance at her woman.

"The practical side, hinny. Catriona, I knew Angus when I was growing up in the Highlands."

"Fie, does he think I'm a goose to run happily to him whenever he summons?"

Elspeth pursed her lips. "I think 'tis a miracle he's sending for ye after all these years apart. I dinna ken why ye were banished, as ye put it, but in the past year since yer cousin died, like it or not, ye've become yer grandfather's heiress. Ye've a duty to go, and arguing about it is only putting off the inevitable." She picked up some sewing and slanted a glance at Catriona. "He's auld, lass. Besides, ye know ye can't do for yerself in Edinburgh by peddling herbs for an occasional coin and a lot of empty promises."

Catriona lifted her chin in a defensive gesture. "I'd manage . . . I could become a Latin tutor."

At Elspeth's pursed look, Catriona relented. "I know, I know. Only men become tutors . . ." Men. A sudden awful possibility occurred to her.

"Angus wouldn't be thinking of finding me a husband now, would he?"

Elspeth looked up from the needle she was threading. "Who can say, hinny?" she said, squinting at Catriona. "But ye are his only hope for the Ferguson line," she reminded her.

"Pish, I'll never wed."

"Catriona, ye canna expect to ignore yer duty." When Catriona ducked her head as if hiding tears, Elspeth added in a gentler voice, "Didn't I teach ye to put one foot in the front of the other? First go and talk to him as the heiress, will ye?"

Blinking back sudden tears, Catriona nodded to Elspeth, then sifted through the contents of the trunk, wishing she could buy back everything and cram it in. She'd long ago decided the Lord in heaven had not had wifely duties in mind when He created her, so she had no need of a dowry, but she did have a streak of sentimentality. These personal possessions would lend comfort to a spinster, and an unloved spinster she planned to be . . .

Vague memories beckoned—of her grandfather climbing through the Highland heather with his hand holding hers, telling her of love, but she pushed the image away. He had banished her, betrayed their love, and with banishment had come another life—one of painful loneliness with a mother and father who were too distracted to pay attention to her. And with schoolboys who teased her relentlessly for looking odd.

Lots of lads and lasses had red hair, but hers was a wilder color. Like fire. And instead of freckles, the good Lord had seen fit to curse her with this pale white skin. Like a ghost, she felt. A tall, skinny, flame-haired ghost. Sometimes she wanted to burrow down into the ground just like a carrot.

And then there were her bookish inclinations, which had caused her immeasurable grief and teasing, especially on the jaunts with her father to university for tutoring. Edinburgh girls were well-educated compared to the English, but Catriona made a fine art of it. No, she might be the heiress, but Angus would be hard pressed to marry her off. One look at her and he'd know it too.

She glanced at her faithful servant woman. "You'll come with me, won't you, Elspeth?"

Elspeth feigned a look of disbelief. "Ye dinna think I'd send ye off alone now, do ye, when ye're the closest thing to a daughter I've got?"

At Catriona's grateful smile, the older woman broached a slightly different subject. "Angus loved ye when ye were a bairn . . . and, though ye're not remembering, ye loved him too. The years mellow everyone—even Angus. Ye'll see."

Catriona made a scoffing sound and busied herself stacking books. "He's had a peculiar way of showing his affection."

Nodding with sympathy, Elspeth poked her needle through a strip of lace. "Even a thistle has its soft nub, Catriona," she said, and without explaining what *that* meant, she handed her Angus's letter. "Here, go on, ye ne'er finished reading this."

"I don't want to. It's clear he cares nothing—"

"Would he provide an escort if he didna care?"

Catriona sighed and lit a candle. She read on a bit before again casting down the letter, this time in resignation. "Now why would my loving grandfather provide a clergyman from a feuding clan as my escort?" she asked, her voice bitter.

"As I said," Elspeth explained, "I dinna think we could go alone—not two defenseless women. Even our two feuding families—the Fergusons and the MacLeans—close ranks against certain dangers in the Highlands—superstition, bandits."

"Pish." Catriona's voice held a note of disbelief.

"Nay, 'tis true. Bandits grow in more abundance than barley—or even members of the Scots clergy."

With a sigh, Catriona sank down on top of the pallet, conjuring up visions of the clergymen she knew—pale-skinned, black-robed, their Adam's apples bobbing, always debating the finer points of theology or else bewailing the Jacobites. She imagined the good Lord must smile down on such tangled debates. "I hope he can converse on subjects other than admonitions to women to be dutiful and obedient," she muttered to herself.

Elspeth clucked and gave her a bracing hug. "Dinna fret so, lass. Who could be a more proper escort than a strong Highland lad going into God's service? I wager he's saying a prayer right now that he can lead us on a safe journey."

In the Crown and Mitre Tavern, Robert MacLean downed the last of his ale and said another silent prayer that a miracle would yet deliver him from seminary at the University of St. Andrews. Simultaneously, his drinking opponent slid off his chair and fell in a stupor under the trestle table.

With the ease of habit, Robert pushed back his chair and stood on it, an arm raised in victory. The watching crowd of students who'd accompanied him on his monthly sojourn across the firth from St. Andrews to Edinburgh let out a roar of approval.

"Bravo, Robbie. You showed them French fops last month, and now the best Edinburgh's got to offer is lying on the floor without e'en the strength to make use of a lass . . ."

Robert MacLean's laugh was deep and hearty. "I dinna see any more challengers waiting for me, and as for France, it hasna yet produced a man who can drink a Scotsman under the table."

"Or be a match for him wi' a lassie," someone chimed in.

As the barmaids tittered, Robert winked at them and continued. "You Edinburgh lads," he boomed. "Aye, you," he said when they looked up in surprise. "Growing weak from carrying your philosophy books about?"

"Not yet, we ain't," declared one young student, knocking his chair over in his haste to stand up. With a lift of his tankard, he challenged Robert to yet another match. "Name the stake—even your timepiece will do against . . . against my father's best wig."

"I've no use for periwigs, laddie. Forsooth, it's too late, ye are. Your Edinburgh cronies have already forfeited. The challenge is over, and I've other matters to attend to."

He didn't have to turn around to know that Jeannie, the serving wench, was standing all too near, dimpling in anticipation, ready to provide him with a diversion. With a hand on her waist, he steered her to the back of the tavern. Restless and dissatisfied though he might be feeling of late, Jeannie, with her bonnie kisses, still gave him pleasure—and a private room where he could meet Lord Kendrick later to discuss politics. Given Scotland's uncertain moods, private meeting places were almost more necessary these days for intrigue than for wenching. But right now, wenching would do . . . more than do.

With hurried movements, Jeannie led him up the stairs and eased off his coat. Back in the main room, the tavern door slammed shut, and Robert heard his name being called by his cronies. He debated putting Jeannie aside, but it seemed an indelicate moment to retreat, what with her crooning, "Robbie, I dinna ken a man wi' hair so thick and golden . . . 'tis been a long month waitin' for ye."

Robert felt a familiar stirring in his loins. Aye, politics could wait.

He kicked shut the door of the little bedroom into which Jeannie had drawn him, and bent to her lips. When he untangled himself, she was tugging at his cravat. "Such a winnin' kiss ye have, Robbie."

"All those corsets and laces were fashioned to craze a man's patience, Jeannie," he observed quietly.

She dimpled and blushed. "Oh, milord. You never keep a lass waiting for a bonnie word then, do ye? I dinna know ought other man like ye." With the quick hand of a practiced tease, she untied the ribbon that held his hair at the nape of his neck.

Giving a tug in turn to the ribbons confining her ample bosom, Robert pulled her down and tasted her sweet lips. "Wench," he said in between nibbles. "Think teasing me can get your way, eh?"

Her arms wove around the back of his neck, and as she molded her heated body close against him, he responded in kind.

"Robbie, always so impatient," Jeannie cajoled, and did tantalizing things to his skin as her hands slid down his back and round to the front of his breeches, to the evidence of that impatience.

"Impudent lass," Robert said at her boldness.

A discreet knock sounded. Immediately on guard, Robert straightened. The Edinburgh taverns harbored too many agents of England and France for a man to give his concentration solely to a wench, lissome though she be. Jeannie's ample figure blocked his view, and then she was busy kissing him again. The door squeaked open.

"Ahem . . ." The low cough held a note of disapproval. Jeannie giggled and pulled up the bodice of her mantua to a more modest level.

Peering up over Jeannie's head, Robert half expected to see his mentor, Lord Kendrick, who was due from England at any hour now, but instead he recognized in the dim light the dour features of his grandfather's Highland messenger. Resplendent in his plaids, Douglas MacIver stood framed in the doorway, the sparest of frowns etched onto his sharp features.

"How long have you been standing there, mon?" Robert's intimate plans for Jeannie thwarted, he straightened and set the wench aside. "You shouldna sneak up on people that way, Douglas," he admonished.

With a rueful smile and a last kiss, Jeannie straightened her apron and hurried out, impudently draping the errant hair ribbon over Douglas's hand. Douglas looked after her, his disapproval deepening.

"State your business, Douglas," Robert demanded, "else I'll hire you off as a neutered English butler. What is it?"

Douglas turned his gaze back to Robert. "Your grandfather sent me, of course. I'd have been here a day sooner, but I didna know you'd left St. Andrews for the pleasures of Edinburgh."

"I trust the boat trip across the firth went

smoothly?'' Robert inquired dryly, knowing that
Douglas suffered like a sick dog if he so much as stared
into a mud puddle.

"I survived."

Robert thought briefly of tempting Douglas with a
tankard of ale or a wench, but the man seemed immune
to the weaknesses of the flesh. Proper to the core, he
was.

"Your grandfather does not know how you spend your
time here in the Lowlands."

"Feel free to tell him." Gamely, Robert tried to retie
his cravat, but the ale had befuddled his head and, impatient, he ripped it off. Despite that, he didn't miss Douglas's look of surprise. "Aye, you heard right. Tell him.
Mayhap then the old goat will decide to get me out of this
place—or has my grandfather sent you here merely to
chastise me?"

Douglas shook his head.

"No, then perhaps it's my Lowland dress that offends
you?" Robert tucked in his shirt. "Did a ruff come loose
from my shirt? Is the lace on my cravat ripped or my
breeches torn?"

Douglas shook his head again. "Robert MacLean, I
didna come to pass judgment, so there's no need to behave
like this."

"Like what? Like a lust-filled man? Tell me, did the
wench make off with my shoe buckle? No? Then toss me
my shoes and coat, Douglas. I believe they're on the floor
behind you."

Douglas handed him his shoes, then bent and picked
up the coat, brushing it back and front and holding it
away from his body as if it might bite, like Robert's
words.

Deftly, Robert slipped into it. It was scarcely wrinkled,
and only one loose button near the hem offered evidence
of his adventures here today. With crisp movements, he
pulled his shirt ruffs from beneath each wide-cuffed sleeve
and stepped into his black brogs.

"Douglas, one more favor, then you may state my

grandfather's latest request.'' He pointed to the hair ribbon, which Douglas still held.

With the neat efficiency that came from having once served as manservant to Alexander MacLean, Douglas gathered Robert's hair at the nape and tied it with the ribbon.

"So . . . what does my grandfather want? Should I write another instructive letter to my cousin Lachlan about how to handle the clansmen with a measure of benevolence?'' Robert turned to face his grandfather's messenger with a wry smile. "Or is it the wenches who are not benevolent with Lachlan? My cousin is hopeless with both, you know.''

With no softening of his expression, Douglas held out a letter.

Hope flared in Robert's eyes. Drawing a deep breath, he gingerly reached for it.

"A candle, Douglas—be quick.''

Out in the hallway, Douglas tipped his taper over the letter while Robert read, so engrossed that he looked up only once—when Jeannie, bosom pushing out of her gown, passed by with a tray full of tankards. He playfully swatted her bottom and went back to reading.

A quick scan confirmed that Alexander MacLean's message had indeed been worth the interruption. "Douglas, do you want to hear the answer to a prayer? Listen.'' Robert's voice rose in barely concealed excitement.

He read, stopping after each sentence to give Douglas the gist of the news. "He says the village needs me more than the Scottish pulpits do . . . the clan is a wee bit restless . . . two young women have died mysteriously . . . mumbles of rebellion . . .'' Slightly alarmed, he looked at the manservant. "Good Lord, why did you no' come for me sooner?''

Reading on, his voice moved from alarm to a rising excitement. "He says letters have come from Lord Kendrick. Letters that have convinced him to agree to my wedding his niece, Sarah Kendrick.'' Privately Robert was exulted. At last.

There followed a list of wedding details that would

have made a clergyman's sermon look short, yet the further he read, the wider Robert's smile became. Hurrah for Lord Kendrick, that clever rascal! Lord Kendrick, as ambitious as he was canny, sought for himself the plum appointment of secretary of state for Scotland, with the task of pacifying the Highlands—a stepping stone on his political climb. But Lord Kendrick knew that because he was English he would need assistance in dealing with the suspicious Highlanders. He intended for Robert to be that help.

It was not surprising then that Lord Kendrick had cultivated Robert's friendship and had pointed out to him that his natural way with people might suit him for diplomatic rather than divine service. To sweeten that thought he had suggested that in return for assistance, the Hanoverians might restore the MacLean family titles, titles stripped after the 1715 Rebellion. Robert's father, whom Robert remembered as a fiercely proud Scotsman, might have died in vain during the Rebellion, but at least Robert could reestablish the family's honor and power.

But what an impossible fight it had been to get that notion through Alexander MacLean's stubborn head. Robert could still hear his grandfather's angry denunciation. What was done was done. After losing two sons, he'd give no more MacLeans to either side, Jacobite or Hanoverian, not even a grandson serving as a peacemaker for an ambitious English lord.

After all, males in the MacLean family—even sons of second sons—did not spend themselves in wastrel behavior with English lords. They filled the pulpits of Scottish kirks—especially a son whose mother had been as pious and loving as Robert's.

But now that implacable grandfather had changed his mind.

Home to the Highlands Robert would go. There he would have a chance to apply the mortar to his case in person, convince his grandfather once and for all that if he could charm villagers and wenches alike, then he could also charm the fight out of the Highland clans, for Lord Kendrick and ultimately for the MacLean honor.

"Etcetera. Etcetera," Robert said, impatiently wading through his grandfather's list of Lachlan's shortcomings, which to Robert was no news at all. Suddenly he frowned, his voice slowing. " 'As heir to Castle Fenella MacLean, Lachlan should long ago have taken a bride. I have perforce settled with Angus Ferguson for a suitable marriage with his granddaughter, Catriona, who . . .' " Robert's voice trailed off.

"So—the price of going home to my own bride is duty as an escort," he said at last, then silently considered. Any woman who'd shackle herself to Lachlan must needs be a docile mouse. The worst problem she was likely to create would be a few squeamish qualms about the narrowness of the trail. Nothing he wasn't already expecting from Douglas.

"Done." Robert crumpled the letter in his hand, a gesture of triumph that did nothing to destroy Douglas's unflappable calm.

Stuffing the crumpled letter into his coat pocket, Robert stalked to the main room of the Crown and Mitre, where he grabbed a tankard of ale from the tray Jeannie held and lifted it high.

"To Scotland," he toasted, and swilled deeply. "Congratulate me, gentlemen . . . my days of practicing sermons are over. I'm to go home and be married."

Even men who'd been cradling their heads on the tavern table raised them and blinked at this announcement, and Robert heard Jeannie's soft, "Oh, dearie," behind him. "To wed?"

He caught sight of her disappointed face and, slipping one arm around her waist, whispered in her ear, "I'll no' forget you, lass, but you know the way of Highland grandfathers. Now, off with you and bring back a second round of ale for my friends—a double for Douglas here." He motioned the messenger onto a bench.

Andrew, the sharpest student of the lot, pulled Robert's attention back to his cronies. "So, you're to wed an English cow. Is she a match for our winsome, bonnie Scots lasses?"

The quick-witted Alastair stood up and raised his tan-

kard. "The question is, is she a match for Robert Mac-
Lean?"—to which everyone laughed and raised his tankard
in a toast of congratulations.

Still smiling, Robert raised his own tankard, giving no
outward sign that other parts of his grandfather's message
weighed on his thoughts. As heir, Lachlan should by rights
be handling clan unrest.

Ever since their youth, Robert, not Lachlan, had been
the grandson of Castle Fenella MacLean whom the villagers loved and trusted and looked to. Even as he drained
his tankard, Robert thought ahead to the calming things
he'd say. As for the mysterious deaths, superstitious villagers could panic easily, especially if a Jacobite agent
were snooping around, whispering rebellion in their ears.
If he were already assisting Lord Kendrick, he could use
those rumors, take those whispers back to London and
curry favor with the English. But that was the future of
which he still dreamed.

Clearly, time was of the essence, and he half wished
he didn't have to escort a pair of females into the Highlands. Especially a Ferguson female. The name played
against his memory. Angus Ferguson was a relative new-
comer to Glen Strahan, his family having used the profits
of a thriving whiskey trade to purchase a wealthy and
oft-plundered manor across Loch Aislair from Castle Fenella MacLean.

The Fergusons and MacLeans had feuded for decades—
mostly over the land Angus Ferguson possessed, land that
had once belonged to MacLeans. If a marriage would end
the feud—and fatten the meager MacLean coffers—why,
all to the good. But the lass, Catriona Ferguson, brought
no memories to Robert.

"Robert. Dreaming of your wedding bed already?" a
shaggy-haired student asked.

Robert shook his head and surveyed his cronies. Andrew. Alastair. William. They sat staring back, as if anticipating his response.

"Who here knows a lass named Catriona of the Ferguson family?"

At Andrew's puzzled look, Robert explained. "Is she bonnie and winsome, or homely and shrewish?"

Andrew frowned. "She was naught but a child when she tagged along to university with her father . . . Ross Ferguson taught here," he finally replied. "A wild redheaded scamp, the lass was. Ye'll have yer hands full."

Laughter echoed off the wooden rafters of the tavern, and to Robert's amazement, his cronies' memories suddenly came alive.

"You aren't taking the red thistle into the Highlands?" Alastair said, his voice a warning. "Ye'll need more'n a bit o' luck wi' her. Apt to scare off your delicate English bride, she is."

"Aye," William confirmed. "She was an unruly bairn when I saw her four years ago."

"Either wild in a fit of temper or else hiding sullen behind a book," Alastair added.

"It's been four years since you've seen her?" Robert asked, scoffing at their descriptions. "Feisty female bairns often grow into winsome lasses."

Another young man finally lifted his head and added his farthing's worth. "Heard some tell she lives wi' a crazy woman. Grows herbs and all that fanciful stuff. I wouldna trust the neither one of 'em."

Not pleased with what he was hearing, Robert stood abruptly. "Douglas, considering the unrest in Glen Strahan, we must leave as soon as this "red thistle" can pack her goods."

Douglas nodded, his ale untouched. "Your grandfather will be most relieved."

Robert set his cocked hat atop his head, and those of his cronies who were still sober enough wished him Godspeed as he and Douglas strode out.

"Prepare for a hard ride," Robert warned the older man. "I'm no' lingering on the road for a squeamish lass of Lachlan's or to pander to your delicate stomach." He eyed Douglas. "And dinna tell this Ferguson lass any stories about Lachlan, no matter what she asks. No sense letting her vent her wrath on us. Let her bridegroom have the joy of her.''

Jacques Beaufort pulled up the collar of his tweed coat for warmth and sat huddled in the dark tavern. Sipping brandy, he considered the rumors floating around Edinburgh. He considered the juicy tidbits he'd heard from the table full of noisy students in light of what the exiled Stuart king had requested he come to Scotland to find—the Regalia, the crown of the realm.

For weeks he'd been watching every suspected agent of both the Jacobite and the Hanoverians. One rumor had persisted—that the Regalia was hidden near Castle Fenella MacLean.

Jacques had discounted it as an old rumor, but now the grandson of one of the chiefs had been summoned home to the Highlands. Not just any grandson, but the one who met frequently with Lord Kendrick, that wealthy Englishman with the rheumatic walk and the ivory cane. A Hanoverian sympathizer if ever Jacques saw one. As for Robert MacLean's sympathies, Jacques was uncertain. He was not a Jacobite, that much was clear.

Perhaps the prize Jacques sought—the crown of Scotland's kings—was hidden in the Highlands after all. The Scots had ensconced it there once before during Cromwell's time. Who was to say they hadn't done so again? Perhaps, as his spies suggested, in the very castle of Robert MacLean's family.

Oui, Jacques had bided long enough in Edinburgh with nothing to show for his time. He had little to lose by following a rumor and seeing what this Robert MacLean led him to.

When the buxom serving wench, Jeannie, approached his table, he smiled broadly. She looked askance at his French brocade, but at least he'd had the foresight to leave off wearing wigs and patches while in Scotland. He felt years younger than his three decades, rather naked in fact, but such was the price of his quest.

''That Scotsman who just departed with the Highland

manservant in tow? Is he a Jacobite or a Hanoverian?"
Jacques asked.

Jeannie, hand on hip, eyed him suspiciously. "And why
are ye caring, Frenchman? Do ye think I waste my time
talking politics with him?"

Jacques widened his smile and showed her a sketch,
a tolerably good likeness of Robert MacLean. Had
Jacques been less anxious to rub elbows with kings, he
might have ended up a portrait painter. Now his talent
with the pencil and brush served well as both alibi and
bribe.

"I'm only curious where he calls home," he said.

He watched the unfriendly expression on the wench's
face dissolve into longing for the sketch.

"Oh, it's so like Robbie," Jeannie cooed. With quick
fingers she reached for it. "May I?"

Still smiling, Jacques held tight to it, and flirtatiously
bargained. After all, he knew his own smile and good
looks were a match for Robert MacLean's.

"Perhaps I should send it by post to the man whose
likeness it bears."

Again Jeannie reached for it, only to have it pulled from
her grasp. "You won't get post all the way up into Glen
Strahan," she said with a pout.

"Is that where he's taking the woman named Ferguson?"

Jeannie realized her slip, but shrugged. "Och, what's
the harm? Aye, it's Robbie MacLean. His grandfather's a
Highland laird, ye ken," she added proudly.

"And how do the villagers support themselves in that
place?"

She rested one hand on her hip. "I'm no' a Highlander—lifting cattle and crops of oats, I suppose. Is that
no' the way of the clans?" She shrugged again. "Mayhap
whiskey. Some latecoming Ferguson laird does well for
himself, but the rest—the MacLeans—they're living
through meager times."

Smiling, Jacques handed the sketch over to Jeannie's
eager hands, and she scurried off with her prize.

Oui, Jacques could do worse with his time than follow

a rumor to Glen Strahan. As Jeannie had just told him, whiskey would be for sale and a buyer welcome. He could easily arrange to be a French traveler looking to import the best Scotch to France. If he were discreet and flirtatious, he could convince anyone of anything. And if he were lucky, he'd find the missing Regalia.

And someday, when the exiled king or his son returned to claim Scotland, it would be Jacques who made certain that king was crowned in all his glory. Yes, this wasn't France by any means, but for the prestige of a king's favor, Jacques could learn to live anywhere—even in a wild and prickly place like Scotland.

Chapter 2

"**V**ultures! If it's money for debts you've come seeking, I've no coins for you." Advancing on the two men who'd appeared on her doorstep, Catriona brandished a brass candlestick over her head.

"Vermin. Get out, both of you. The auction money's not mine. Go hound my grandfather's agent." She tried for a look of haughty disdain, the sort of look her mother had used to scare off creditors, but Catriona had never been able to imitate it and wasn't certain of her success now. Mainly because the younger, taller of the pair didn't look the least bit scared, and his older companion, whom he called Douglas, ignored her.

Indeed, the younger man stalked closer to her as if prepared to disarm her of the candlestick, his shock of golden hair framing a face with disarmingly blue eyes. His roguish smile nearly knocked her off balance. A man accustomed to charming women, this one was. Well, let him try.

"Judging by the flame of your hair and the flint of your tongue, you'll be Catriona Ferguson," he said easily.

"Miss Ferguson to you." She glared, ready to drive him off. "And I don't care if you're the exiled king himself come all the way from France, I have nothing to pay." The candlestick grew heavy in her grasp, but when she tried to shut the door, the brute jammed his foot against the frame and muscled his way inside.

Every movement of his body, even the casual flick of his sensually laden glance, told her this man wasn't going

26

to be as easy to get rid of as the agent had been. She doubted if all her mother's haughty arrogance could have done the trick either.

Indeed, her handsome visitor lingered. Not only lingered, but reached over and plucked the candlestick from her hand.

"Alexander MacLean has requested I escort you to Angus Ferguson," he said, "but I'm no' keen on wondering if you'll bash my skull along the way."

While Catriona struggled to speak, he handed the piece of brass to his Highland companion.

" 'Tis Robert MacLean, lass," Elspeth whispered behind her.

With dawning comprehension, Catriona stared at the man. Vaguely, she recalled her preconceived image of a pale clergyman in a black robe. Instead, she faced a rogue in jerkin and breeches of coffee-brown. In his hand was an elegant cocked hat. Color flooded her face while Robert MacLean—the divinity student—stood surveying her.

This man, with his classic profile and skin like burnished copper, surprisingly dark for Scotland's clime, looked as if he'd walked out of her book on Greek gods. His hair contained intriguing streaks of gold that glittered the way gilt-edged pages did when she rippled them through her fingers. Tied back with a ribbon his hair might be, but the wind had played havoc with it on his forehead, and Catriona found herself wanting to smooth the unruly locks into place.

Her pulse raced. Why, this man had no business climbing into a pulpit. The women of the congregation would never pay heed to admonitions about duty to their husbands. They'd think . . . Well, she wasn't certain what they would think, but it wouldn't be proper.

He smiled. "If I were you, lass, I'd save your staring for the Highland scenery. We're in a hurry." He tossed a soft leather haversack at her feet.

What a conceited rogue, she thought.

"I'm taking everything that hasn't been sold," she announced, and moved to the open trunk.

To her dismay, he looked at her bounty and laughed aloud.

The sound resonated right down to her stomach, then slid to her toes. It was with some effort that she assumed an outraged expression. She might like the sound of his laughter and the way little lines crinkled about his mouth, but she did not appreciate his manner. Patronizing he was. And accustomed to the wenches fawning over him, she'd wager.

She stood with her hands on her hips. "You find this amusing?"

"We're going to the Highlands, lass, not on a ship to the New World."

He knelt down and, to her acute embarrassment, began sorting through her trunk. "You'll no' be taking a trunk," he stated evenly. "We've got one packhorse to share for four of us."

One by one he pulled out the few possessions she'd saved—her father's scholarly books and her mother's mementoes of an idle life. English whist cards. Dice. Bottles of scent. A brass case full of black face patches. Despite the best efforts of the auctioneer, she'd steadfastly refused to let him touch these precious belongings.

But, as she'd already guessed, Robert MacLean wouldn't be as easy to cajole as the auctioneer, nor as moved by her pleas. He cavalierly pawed through her treasures, and for a few minutes she watched spellbound. What was it that bothered her about him? It had nothing to do with his good looks, certainly not the gold-flecked hair or the glacial blue eyes or the way he hunkered down like a lion about to pounce.

No, it was the sin in his gaze. Why, he looked as wild as if he'd just walked out of the Garden of Eden instead of off a wind-blown Edinburgh street.

"Your mother appears not to have been a Highlander," he commented, startling her out of her reverie. He held up a French corset and a fan from Paris. "Tell me—were you raised a Jacobite?"

When his icy blue gaze met hers, she felt as if her heart had been dunked in a dazzling loch. The way his eyes glittered, she imagined he was laughing at her, but she didn't care.

"I wouldn't tell if I was." She whisked the corset away from him. "Mother enjoyed pretty things. She hated the Highlands. And Father—"

"Don't tell me. He favored books." Blithely ignoring her, Robert MacLean began tossing items out of the trunk. "I suppose you can wear this locket," he said, dangling it at her.

She grabbed it from him.

"But this . . ." He shook his head at a dress of velvet and lace, followed by a petticoat of chine. "Too fancy for where we're going."

As quickly as he discarded the garments, she snatched them up and stuffed them back in the trunk.

He threw out more books. Quickly kneeling, she flipped them back into the trunk, one by one by one.

He handed her a lace cap, and that too she immediately tossed back. The corset slipped off her lap and she snatched it up, ready to throw it also in the trunk, when his hand, large and warm and very strong, closed around her wrist, stopping her.

Leaning back on his heels, he narrowed his gaze at her. "I haven't time for a tantrum," he warned.

She glared at him, wishing her pulse wouldn't hammer so. Carrying on a conversation with a man while holding a corset did not lend itself to ease of communication. "Well, how would you feel if you had to leave behind everything you owned?"

Robert stared back at her for a long minute, then let go of her. He saw she was going to be as possessive of her belongings as a Jacobite of his loyalties, yet he also felt a bit sorry for her. It wouldn't do to let her know that, though, not if he wanted to get her up into the Highlands.

"Actually, lass, I can't wait to leave Edinburgh behind."

"That's different. You're a MacLean—one of those Highland wild men."

He bit back a smile as her naivete struck him full force, and for the first time he envisioned the coming trip being difficult in a way he'd not anticipated. The prospect of playing nursemaid to an innocent woman did not immediately please him. He frowned.

"Catriona, for all I care you can take naught but French patches for your face up to Glen Strahan, though I'll warn you it's cold." He steeled himself against the surprise on her face. "You've exactly one hour to choose what you're taking, lass, and you've but one criterion—that it fit into this haversack." His boot nudged the sack that lay between them.

He stood up, towering over her while she continued to place her remaining possessions back in the trunk.

She gave him a fleeting sideways glance. "You're different from what I expected, Reverend MacLean," she said unexpectedly, meeting his gaze head on.

He wished her voice wouldn't wobble so. It unnerved him, used as he was to flirtatious, confident women. "And what did you expect?"

"I—I expected someone in black . . . someone scholarly . . . someone who liked books." She croaked out the last word and turned away to gather up the last volumes he'd tossed out.

His conscience caught then, leastwise that's how he explained the sudden tug in his chest. It was her vulnerability, her innocence, he told himself, not those guileless gray eyes, that so affected him.

"There's no time to read on a journey to the Highlands, and as for the 'reverend,' it's plain MacLean from now on—or Robert to you, lass."

"It's still Miss Ferguson to you. And why should you be so anxious to leave here? Running away from the gibbet?"

He felt sorry for his unnecessary harshness then. He tried his best to sound no more threatening than a stern professor.

"I'm going back to the Highlands to help my grandfather."

In the blink of an eyelash, she fastened a petulant look on him, the sort willful women frequently gave him when they wanted their way.

"Father told me about students like you."

"Catriona . . ." Elspeth warned.

"If you're leaving university," she rushed on, thumping books into a pile, "you must not have given enough attention to your studies."

Robert smiled. "Aye, I had my diversions."

"Master Robert!" Douglas admonished.

Catriona looked up, a tiny frown between her eyes, and Robert, to his surprise, felt a bit weak-kneed. The lass had rather startling opinions. He forced himself to frame a calm reply.

"Affairs with my clansmen call me." He paused, unable to maintain the usual formidable glower. "And my own upcoming marriage holds far more appeal at the moment than a stack of musty books."

"Your marriage?" She blinked those guileless gray eyes, as if amazed that he would pledge his troth.

In those few seconds, he tried to recall the name of his betrothed and failed. He needed a stiff dram.

"Douglas," he called, and, turning, nearly bumped into the man.

"Aye, sir?" Douglas said with disarming calm.

"Mind the horses while Miss Ferguson packs for the journey." Robert slapped his hat on his head. Next he addressed her woman, Elspeth. "She's not got a lot of flesh on her bones, especially about the shoulders. In the Highlands, displaying one's bosom is not as fashionable as preventing death from draughts. I trust you'll dress her warmly."

Elspeth, whom Robert assumed had grown up in the Highlands, nodded. Of the two women, she seemed far and away the more sensible, and he counted on her to smooth out the feisty Catriona before the difficult journey began.

Catriona's words caught him off guard. "You know, you needn't plunder my belongings just because of some silly old Highland feud. My grandfather's had his share of Mac-Lean raids, and I expect you're no better than the rest of the MacLeans."

That did it. Flame sparked in his gut, and he advanced

on her. "A right wee curmudgeon, ye are, eh? Ye'll have to curb yer tongue, lass. I give orders only for the protection of the people I travel with. Do ye ken?" He deliberately strengthened his brogue, taunting her for her gibe about the Highlands.

Catriona saw the flint in his eye, heard the toughness of his brogue, and remembered that despite his Lowland dress, he was a fierce Highlander. A MacLean at that, as she'd had the temerity to remind him.

Suddenly short of breath, she began circling the trunk. For each one of her backward steps, he matched her with a forward one. "I dinna care about an old feud, or your opinions about Highland wild men."

It was too close in the room, too warm, but he seemed not to notice. She put out a hand to the trunk to steady herself and took another wobbly step backward.

"I have naught but selfish reasons for returning, aye," he said. "You see, I promised my grandfather I'd deliver you safe and sound, and whatever else you think of me, I'm a man of my word. I've no intention of leaving without you, but I've every intention of leaving without these books and fripperies."

Still, he stalked her, and on she backed until, dizzy, she bumped against the trunk. The floor fell out from beneath her. When she and gravity made their peace, she was in a sitting position right inside the trunk.

Robert MacLean's stormy expression threatened to break.

"Do ye ken?"

Mortified, she could only nod. Her legs stuck straight up in the air, displaying her ankles for the world and Robert MacLean to smirk at. She felt like a felled moor fowl, a scrawny one, and he stood over her like an exultant hunter who'd bagged an unexpected shot.

A smile lurked in his eyes, and he reached for her arm. With an effortless tug he pulled her up and, both hands on her waist, balanced her on her feet. His hands lingered longer than was necessary before he let go, and, with a tact she wouldn't have expected, he reached down to examine a volume of Plato. Hastily, Catriona rearranged her gown.

Robert MacLean looked at her again, unbuttoned coat shoved from his waist to display a cravat-less shirt, cocked hat pushed back on his sandy hair. A smile cracked his handsome face. "As I said, you've one hour to choose what you're taking," he said, and headed for the door.

The manservant stepped in Robert MacLean's path. "Master Robert, where are ye going?" The fellow's voice betrayed a touch of panic, and he glanced at the two females before fastening a beseeching look on his master.

"To find a stiff flagon of ale, Douglas. Guard the doors and take care they dinna run off from you, mon." He gave further instructions to Douglas to tend the horses, and walked out.

Scowling at Robert MacLean's departing back, Catriona grabbed an armload of clothes and, weighted down by the assorted wool, velvet, and chine, stalked into her bedroom. She dumped it all at her feet and stood there for a moment, hands on hips, planning how to outwit this arrogant MacLean. A sly smile spread slowly over her face, and she began to yank off her dress.

She removed all her clothes except her slender corset. All the while she both shivered and cursed Robert MacLean, from his fancy shoe buckles to his smug smile. She knew his kind, him and his patronizing airs. He might be a Highlander, but he was no different from other men . . . except he left her feeling flustered.

For a long time now, she'd told herself she didn't care if men didn't fawn all over her the way they had over her mother, yet it bothered her immensely that this Highlander, this wild MacLean, treated her like a difficult child instead of what she was—a young woman whose life had been turned upside down.

All women felt upside down around him, though, even the ones whose lives hadn't just been sold out from under them.

Pensive, she tucked a curl of bright red hair behind her ear. Elspeth, looking like a traitor with the bag for the packhorse in hand, entered the room, and together the two women stood looking down at the pile of clothing.

Catriona picked up a treasured lace cap.

"Ye'd be better off taking a head shawl than a cap, lass," Elspeth counseled.

"Don't worry, Elspeth, I'll show these Highlanders I know how to dress for the weather," said Catriona. She bit back a smile. Oh, yes, she couldn't wait to see the expression on Robert's face when he realized she'd out-foxed him.

"Catriona, I recommend the riding habit. It's warmest—and perhaps the cloak with it."

Catriona eyed the more sensible riding costume and then the array of petticoats. "Elspeth," she said slowly, "how much of this do you suppose we could each wear at once?"

Elspeth's eyes grew wide. "Oh, no, Catriona. I'll no' be dressing up in any but my own clothes."

Reluctantly, Catriona examined what the practiced Elspeth wore. A sensible dress of gray wool. Sturdy boots. A long plaid shawl to drape over her head and shoulders.

While acknowledging the outfit's warmth, Catriona dismissed it for a more compelling reason. "Elspeth, you've scarcely any pockets to carry things in." Catriona was already reaching for a brocade mantua. "Why, when I'm dressed I'll carry more than will fit in a bundle on his packhorse."

"Now, child, he'd probably store the trunk for you if you asked politely," Elspeth suggested. "Why not do that?"

She tossed her head. "I'll burn it all before I'll ask a favor of a MacLean. Besides, I can't leave without my books—no matter how short the stay. I have to have them with me."

"Humph," snorted Elspeth. "If ye're meaning to load yerself down, I won't tell. But *I'll* no' dress the fool."

"All right then, go as you want. I'm wearing it all. At least as much as I can. Bring me another armload from the trunk," she directed, feeling smug.

Even with Elspeth's help, it took Catriona nearly the

entire hour to dress. First she donned her petticoats and, despite Elspeth's clucking about discomfort, stuffed about her waistline two lace caps and a pair of gloves. Her mother's whist cards and dice fit under the hem, in between a few loose threads. Next came the mantua of green brocade. Her mother had worn a matching stomacher over the corset, but Catriona reached instead for a slender book of similar proportions—a portfolio of discourses in Latin.

Holding the leather cover against her abdomen, she instructed Elspeth to lace the mantua on top and for good measure fasten green ribbons to hold its two sides in place. Behind the lacings and ribbons showed only a bit of the soft leather book. "Why, it's softer than brocade," declared Catriona proudly, adding, "and stiffer than stays."

"Aye, no doubt, and ye'll regret that after an hour on horseback."

"Pish. Now help me into the riding outfit, Elspeth."

And so on went a skirt of gray wool, a cravat to fill in the low-cut neckline of the mantua, and then her father's riding coat because, as Elspeth noted, that's all that could fit by now. About her neck Catriona draped the locket, and on her head she placed at a jaunty angle her father's black cocked hat.

"Elspeth, find me something else to fit between the layers of my dresses, will you?"

With a look of resignation, Elspeth offered a small muff. Catriona tried to push it between her corset and the strings of her bodice, but declared it made her into a Christmas goose. Yanking it out, she let her gaze fall on a few slender volumes of Shakespearean sonnets they'd neglected to pack. Grabbing several, she stuffed them down the dress and smiled at the result. Like an extra set of stays, the thin books bolstered the layers of clothing in place. Satisfied, she preened for Elspeth.

"There, that ought to keep his Highland draughts away from my bosom," she declared.

Finally, she flung her cloak of lavender wool about her shoulders. At last she stood, costume complete. She felt rather warm and overstuffed, but she could ride, of that she was sure.

Elspeth tilted her head and gave Catriona a doubtful look. "Can you bend over in all that?"

"Of course." She bent to show Elspeth and saw her unshod feet peeking out.

With a rueful smile she leaned against the windowsill as Elspeth pushed a pair of riding boots over her stockings.

And into the haversack, just in time for Robert Mac-Lean's return, went a simple smock, a nightdress, two dozen books, and wooden containers of herbs and herb potions. For while Robert MacLean might be her escort, she had no doubt he was ignorant of the healing arts. And who knew what might befall them before they arrived at her grandfather's?

Catriona glanced one last time into the tiny looking glass Elspeth had salvaged from her mother's articles of toilette. The glass reflected a paler-than-usual version of herself. Twisting sideways, she felt the layers of clothing chafe lightly, promising more havoc once she was at the mercy of a sidesaddle. She dreaded the coming journey, for more reasons than one.

"What if Angus doesn't know me—or still hates me?" she asked.

"You're the Ferguson heiress," Elspeth reminded her again. "He doesn't hate ye, lass. Now stop fretting. He cared enough to provide safe escort."

A spot of color filled Catriona's cheeks, and she reached for the leather pouch. "Robert MacLean is not what my mother would call a 'safe' man." Not that *she,* Catriona, had anything to worry about. Her hair was too red and unruly to be called beautiful, her breasts too small to suit the stylish cut of the low-necked gown. If she'd been presented at the court of the exiled king in France, she'd be smirked at rather than seen as the witty beauty her mother had once been. So why did she expect something different from this Robert MacLean?

"He's got what Father would call too much dortyness," Catriona observed.

Elspeth fussed with a strand of Catriona's hair, trying to pin it back into a knot. With a reassuring pat on the cheek, she said, "Now, now, all men get a bit tetched when they're kept waiting. You'll soon see a humbler side of him."

In the taproom of an unfamiliar Edinburgh inn, Robert whiled away the hour with a tankard of ale, a pocket watch in front of him. He'd give her not one second more than the sixty minutes.

Red thistle. Curls of fire and a disposition prickly enough to scare off a wildcat. Aye, a most apt nickname for the chit, he decided, taking a long pull on his ale. Despite his ill humor, he smiled faintly at the recollection of their minor feud over her trunk. Or, rather, at the memory of shapely legs displayed most provocatively.

Contrary female. He made a wager as to how many heavy books she'd try to smuggle along and smiled again, making another secret wager as to how soon he'd find them and toss them by the wayside.

But it wasn't her books that really annoyed him. It was her beauty. He took another long pull on the ale.

His cohorts at the Crown and Mitre had obviously not laid eyes on this lass since *they* took to ale. The "thatch of carrot-red hair" had grown into a mane of coppery curls that cascaded halfway down her back. The "moonish little face" had matured into cheekbones of sculpted alabaster. The tall skinny girl had ripened into a woman of slender grace. And then there were her eyes . . . The color of a stormy sky they were, but creamy as if the sun hid behind them.

He found himself wondering if the time spent readying for the journey would warm her disposition. Such a wary little thing . . . Fleetingly, he wondered, too, about her connection to Angus Ferguson, and why the old man would leave a granddaughter down here in Edinburgh for all these years with nary a word spoken of her. He shoved his tankard away. It was none of his affair.

When the time was up, and he rejoined her, he sat on his horse, amazed. Taking his order to extremes, Catriona had dressed in enough clothing for three people, from riding habit of gray to cloak of purple. Light purple like thistles. Moreover, his discerning eye detected that her previously slim figure had within the past hour developed an admirably ample bosom.

He ducked his head to hide his smile and pretended to adjust his stirrup. As he looked up, feigning nonchalance, she cast a withering glance at him. "Am I dressed warm enough for your Highland draughts?"

Willful chit. Didna know when she had it good, he thought irritably. Well, she was asking for it now. "Aye, lass," he managed, "but you've overdone it a wee bit."

"Oh? In what way?"

Aye, she was a saucebox, this one. "You've enough clothes on for a regiment." Again, his mouth twitched.

"I fail to see anything amusing about this journey," she snapped.

"I was picturing you upside down in a river with that cocked hat floating away."

"I'm a very good rider."

"This won't be a pleasant jaunt in a park. It's a long, grueling journey."

He was glad when Douglas interrupted with a query about their first night's destination. "Falkirk," Robert announced a touch testily, "and a long trip it is to the manse there. Shall we begin?"

"Don't you want to say a prayer first?" Catriona asked, all gray-eyed innocence.

Of all the things women had requested of him, this was new, and for a moment his tongue was tied.

"Are you jesting, wondering if I know a prayer from an ale tankard?"

Her eyes widened in a guileless manner. "Oh, I've no doubt you know an ale tankard when you see it," she said sweetly. "But I think a prayer might be appropriate before beginning such a difficult journey."

"Indeed, we all have our different concerns." He decided to accept her challenge. "Might I suggest a silent prayer then?"

Without waiting for her response, he bowed his head

and asked the Lord to take away the sudden yearning he felt to divest this woman of her excess clothing.

When he looked up, her head was still down, her silky red curls shining in the sun. She held her hat in her hand, and her lips moved silently. Obviously she had a lot of requests of God.

When at last Robert led them at a brisk pace out of Edinburgh's walls and into the open country of Lowland Scotland, he questioned the Lord more thoroughly than he had in years. Over and over he asked both God and himself just one thing—why couldn't Lachlan's betrothed have been as homely as Lachlan deserved?

Chapter 3

F our days later, all manner of feminine garb draped the mane of Catriona's horse. She looked like an Edinburgh tinker displaying her wares, Robert decided.

By the time they'd spent one night in Falkirk, one in Bannockburn, and two more in lonely cottages along the way to Loch Lomond, their pace had slowed considerably. With each passing day, Robert noted Catriona discreetly shed an article of clothing, so that even today one more layer had come off.

Whenever he glanced back at her, she gave him a brave smile, but he could see the squirm of discomfort in her face. Lord only knew what all she'd hidden within those clothes. Finally, on this, the fifth day, taking pity on her, he stopped half an hour sooner than he'd have liked for their noon meal. A stand of fir trees clustered near some rocks provided the privacy which Catriona would no doubt seek so as to discard more clothes—an entire petticoat perhaps.

They'd arrived at the first vantage point for Loch Lomond, and he always relished the sight of the steep cliffs and sparkling water, as well as the knowledge that at last, at long last, he would wind his way up into his beloved Highlands.

He called for Douglas to break out the oatcakes and cheese and some whiskey. Catriona wasted no time in removing the cravat from her neck, and the glimpse of her smooth white bodice was entirely too appealing for his peace of mind. He turned away to eat, allowing himself to think ahead to the unrest in Glen Strahan.

When he looked back, the view was even more provocative. Catriona's rump was up in the air as she reached under a bush of gorse, her brocade bodice and woolen skirt mingling with Scotland's finest nettles and thistles, and her petticoat as visible as if it hung from her horse. She was pulling something toward her. Alarmed, he strode over.

"What mischief are you into now?" he asked.

She swiveled in place and glared up at him. "I wish you wouldn't talk to me as if I were a child."

Her red curls had fallen out of their plaits. A tender expression touched her face, and in her arms she cradled a hare. The squirming creature looked as if a hawk or some equally ruthless predator had grabbed for it once and lost the contest.

"Elspeth," she called out, "fetch the herbs from our bundle."

Robert stood stock still. Books were wasteful enough. "We haven't time to cook a rabbit stew," he said.

A look of horror crossed her face. "We aren't going to eat this poor wee thing. The herbs are to heal it." Catriona scrambled to her feet, clutching the wretched animal in a protective gesture beneath her breasts.

"That hare will make a gift of food for the manse tonight," Robert said with a Highlander's practicality.

"But it's defenseless," she argued, backing out of his reach. "If you studied for the divinity, you must have some pity for God's creatures."

"God's creatures were put here to feed men."

Her eyes glittered angrily. "You men," she scoffed. "All alike, aren't you? You put God first. Then men. And mayhap your women and animals last."

For a few seconds he was speechless. For days, they'd scarcely exchanged words, and now she was debating theology with all the fierceness of a true martyr.

Without waiting for his reply, she knelt by a gorse bush and, holding the hare, allowed Elspeth to rub a salve—a bottle of which he'd been hauling on his own packhorse—onto the creature's paw. As if that weren't enough, she carried on a conversation with the wild creature.

"We'll no be packin' a rabbit wi' us, lass," he announced finally, his Highland brogue thickening.

She looked up and, ignoring him, asked Elspeth to hurry with the poultice. "It's but a wee beastie," she crooned, holding the paw while Elspeth tended to it. The herbs should heal it quickly," she added, poking and prodding amid the fur in a careful examination.

"There now," she told the hare. "It won't take long . . . I wonder if I should carry it along for a while to make certain it doesn't lick off the salve?" She sneaked a peek at Robert.

He met her gaze, unflinching. He felt as if he were playing a game of chess with her, and knew the satisfaction of a man about to checkmate his opponent.

"Take the hare if you wish, but I assure you, Catriona, there'll be ample time this evening to cook rabbit stew for supper." His gaze fell to her heaving bosom, petite and soft. "You've been losing weight by the day," he taunted, looking up and down her slimmer figure. "It won't do to have you arrive at your grandfather's looking scrawny. That hare should fatten you up."

Before she could retort, he stalked back to the horses, tense and frustrated with lust, aware of how little it would take to lose control of his baser impulses. He turned back, irritated for no plausible reason at the way the hare nestled against her breast. This had gone on long enough.

After all, healing with herbs was all good and well in Edinburgh, but she was going into the Highlands, where people still believed in demons and sorcerers and witches, and he had the distinct impression she'd been away from the Highlands too long to recall the superstitions of the people. Strange her family had kept her naive about the place of her birth . . .

Aye, it was just as well they'd delayed here. He needed to tell her of the dangers of the Highlands. And then there was Lachlan to consider. If Lachlan couldn't manage to keep peace among his own clansmen, how in the world did he expect to manage this headstrong woman?

With an exasperated sound, Robert looked toward the horizon. He'd like to wring his grandfather's neck for insisting he escort her. Automatically, he glanced down the road, searching for the prime danger at the border of the Highlands—bandits.

Instead he saw a lone traveler plodding along on horseback. At the sight, Robert's gut clenched—instinctively and immediately. His hand gripped his dirk.

That lone horseman could be anybody, from a lost Englishman to a murdering blackguard. That's what he had to explain to Catriona before she went chasing after any more "wee creatures." In the Highlands, wildness and impetuosity could lead too often to danger. He walked back to where he'd left her and Elspeth, but the women had vanished.

He stalked down to the riverbank, angry, taut, ready to give the cheeky red thistle an earful. When he spotted her, however, he drew up short. Beyond her, scattered rocks led to the stream, and across that rose rugged mountains. But it was Catriona who made the most tempting scenery, standing in the wild grass at the edge of the stream, a cloak the color of summer heather wrapped about her. The breeze whipped her red curls around her shoulders like a crackling flame, holding him spellbound. As he watched her, the other danger he'd been trying to ignore—desire—struck him full force in his loins, sudden and unexpected.

Damned inconvenient, too, forcing him to cool his heels while he drew in a few deep breaths. He mentally gave himself a shake. She was innocent, for God's sake.

Moments later, he approached her, wary this time because of the way she aroused him.

"We have no more time to waste," he said softly, coming up behind her.

She was still cradling the hare and, when she turned and saw him, tightened her hold on it.

He reached out and stroked its furry head. When his hand accidentally brushed her fingers, he pulled back. "It's time to set it free," he said in a tone that brooked no delay.

To his relief, Catriona knelt and let the hare loose. For

a moment it sat there, twitching its nose, wiggling its ears. It gave one brief lick to the herbal salve that Catriona and Elspeth had slathered on its gashed paw, then scampered off out of sight.

"You have a tender way with wild animals," Robert said softly, grateful she'd obeyed him without a show of temper.

He followed her glance upward to where a blackbird took wing. "I've always loved animals," she said softly, her tone wistful. "There were so few in Edinburgh, but I'd find them in the fields. Birds. Cats. And then long ago I remember riding the Highlands on a pony beside my grandfather. We used to chase the wind, pretend we were riding in pursuit of the English, defending an army of purple heather with birch whips or swords . . ." She stopped, as if embarrassed to have revealed so much.

He gave in to a half smile. He felt a tender spot for the way she'd defended God's creatures—not that he'd let her know. But at least arguing about a wild hare was more suited to his tastes than talk of gaudy possessions and stuffy books.

"There'll be plenty of other animals once we're in the Highlands, but you are no' to stray off searching for them— not without me." When she tried to argue, his words stopped her. "There will be more dangerous creatures than deer or rabbit."

"What do you mean?"

He wanted to reach over and smooth away the tiny frown that creased her skin. "I want you to obey me without question if need be."

She turned her back on him and flicked her flame tresses over one shoulder. "Your horses are surefooted. I've shown that I'm a capable rider."

He swallowed. This wasn't the first time her hair had come loose on this journey, and he had a feeling it wouldn't be the last. The trouble was that every time she flicked it over her shoulder, as seemed to be her habit, he wanted to reach out and feel it. *You'll burn, Robert, in those red locks. She's no' yours to touch.* "Lass—"

"If you mean bandits, Elspeth warned me already."

She turned back to face him. "I have my mother's pistol, and thanks to my grandfather, I have no money for them to steal." Her voice didn't sound as confident as she probably would have liked.

So she wasn't as brave as she pretended. He smiled. "Bandits will take anything—like that gold locket you're wearing. Or this little frippery," he said, indicating the silver brooch pinned to her cloak. "They'll even strip the clothes off your body," he added, and regretted his words immediately. The image of her stripped of clothing intrigued him rather more than he liked.

Her expression held too much vulnerability for his comfort, and he adopted a teasing tone.

"They aren't particular. They even take books." Reaching out to tug a curly lock of hair, he added, "Not to mention long tresses. Fetch a good price from wigmakers, they do."

Despite his better intentions, his fingers lingered on her hair. As he'd guessed, it was silky and soft, and despite its color, it was as cool as the breeze. But touching it, he reminded himself again, could set a man on fire, could make him yearn for a woman who wasn't his to possess.

She stood mesmerized, not moving. "My hair is the wrong color for wigmakers," she said in a soft voice. "And as for my books—*if* I had any with me—I doubt there's a bandit who can read."

Gently, he pushed her hair back over her shoulder and dropped his hand from her. An unwilling smile tugged at his mouth. "I doubt there's a bandit willing to lug the heavy things away—*if*, of course, you had any with you."

"Aye . . . you trouble yourself needlessly. We Fergusons aren't as addlepated as MacLeans have thought. My grandfather wouldn't have the goods for MacLeans to plunder unless he was very wise to begin with."

"The plundering is over. The MacLeans and the Fergusons are ending their feud." It seemed natural to begin walking back toward the horses, and she fell in step with him.

"Does everyone else at your castle share that sentiment?" She slanted a glance at him.

"You mean Lachlan?" He delayed answering, and they walked in silence. Should he come right out and tell her of Lachlan's mean spirit? Then again, perhaps he was being hasty. Several years had passed since he'd left Castle Fenella MacLean. Perhaps time had mellowed his cousin. He could do more harm than good by planting unkind thoughts in the lass's head.

"Perhaps you can heal past hurts as well as you heal animals, lassie." He was staring ahead of them as he talked. "If you're as gentle with Lachlan as with that hare, you'll probably find him the most docile person to live with."

Stopping in place, she turned on him, her eyes wide with confusion.

"What do you mean—live with?" she demanded. "I'll live with my grandfather." A tiny strand of fear threaded through her words.

Frowning slightly, he studied her. "To be sure, but after you're wed to Lachlan . . ." The blood drained from her face. He looked over his shoulder in case a bandit even now crept up on them. But there was nothing to cause alarm, only Douglas and Elspeth tending their horses, and way down the road, the lone horse and rider plodding along, coming closer.

Robert turned back to Catriona, puzzled by what was causing her to press her hand to her mouth. Was she ill? Had she eaten tainted food? "What's ailing you, lass?"

In a strangled voice, she said. "You're lying."

"Don't be daft. After the years of plundering, Lachlan won't dare set foot near your grandfather's manor house. Besides, it's customary for the bride to come to Castle Fenella MacLean."

"I'm no bride to this Lachlan. I'm not getting married. I'm not! You're lying!" Her voice rose hysterically. "I should have known not to trust a MacLean—not even you."

He reached in his vest pocket for the letter and held it out to her. She snatched it from his hands. When she looked up from reading it, tears glittered in her eyes.

My God. He couldn't believe what the look on her face

was telling him. "You didn't know, did you? Angus didn't tell you about your betrothal?"

"I'm not betrothed! Angus can't do this to me." She backed away a few steps. "I don't know this Lachlan. My grandfather presumes too much. I'm not staying in the Highlands, never mind marrying some Highland stranger."

The sight of her stricken face created a peculiar sensation in Robert. He breached the space between them and grasped her shoulders, meaning to lend comfort. "It seems I've spoiled your homecoming. Understand, lass, Lachlan is heir to—"

"No!" She jerked away and flung the letter to his feet, where the wind caught it and tumbled it away. "No! Fie on all MacLeans—on all Highlanders! I won't be betrothed to anyone—heir to a clan chief or not," she shouted. "Angus must think his granddaughter is a simpleton." She stumbled over to her woman. "Elspeth . . ." she cried. Briefly she touched the older woman's plaid shawl. "Fie on being an heiress. I'm no more than a marriage pawn to Angus." Her voice shook. "Go without me." She picked up her skirts as if to run.

"Catriona—"

"The devil and the plague can both take him—and the MacLeans as well!"

Elspeth gasped. "Lass, ye canna mean such blasphemy . . ."

Catriona was stumbling away now, running down the road in the direction of Edinburgh, as wildly as the frightened hare had darted away.

Robert stood motionless, watching her desperate flight. He felt a twist of sympathy for her and wished he could let her escape. She certainly didn't deserve Lachlan as her fate. But honor-bound to his grandfather, he knew what he had to do—capture her and force her to continue the journey.

Whisking off his hat, he handed it to a shocked Douglas and headed after Catriona, running as nimbly as if he were on the hunt. He'd never chased rabbits or angry lasses before. But he'd taken his share of swift red deer, and he knew he could take her. Damn, but she was a wild little scamp, and despite himself he felt a surge of reckless abandon.

His breath came hard. Scurvied tavern cronies had her looks all wrong, but her fiery nature—aye, they'd been keenly accurate.

He was gaining on her already, and she didn't seem to have noticed the stranger whose horse was blocking her path. Good. She'd have to slow down, and that would give him the time he needed.

"Stop, you little idiot," he called out to her. "You're going to trip and break your fool neck."

Catriona chanced a quick glance over her shoulder. Pursuit by a man was new to her, but Robert MacLean had stopped in his tracks and was peeling off his coat. Good. She knew he hadn't the stamina to outrun her. Still holding her skirt in her hands, petticoats falling out of her grasp, she stumbled on a rock and looked back to the road. At once, she spotted the lone rider blocking the narrow road. She had no choice but to slow down and only seconds to consider her options.

Lifting her skirts higher, she darted off the path, up the hill and into the gorse. But even as she ran, she knew her hesitation had been fatal. She heard Robert coming closer again, heard his deep breaths at her back, the pounding of his boots on the hard ground, and the crackling of brush behind her. She should have untied her cloak. It flew out behind her like a flag. A prickly bush caught at it, and more precious seconds passed before she could jerk herself loose. She felt a second strong tug at the purple cloth— so strong that she was jerked to a stop. She reached for the ribbons at her neck. Just as she would have shed her cloak, Robert, his grasp strong, caught her arm.

She squirmed this way and that, trying to pull away, and somehow they both ended up on the ground. Her struggles continued as, more desperately than ever, she tried to break loose.

"Ouch, ye're harder to hold than a bloody nettle." He treated her to a string of Highland curses.

Rolling her onto her back, his hands spanned her bodice. With no apology for his forwardness, his fingers pushed and probed through the layers of her clothing.

"Books?" he said. "Ye've padded your clothes with books? I'd hoped I wouldna see another one. Ye're a dangerous woman to embrace, Catriona Ferguson—not at all soft like Jeannie," he said between short breaths. "And not to be trusted either."

She pressed an arm to her face and fought silent sobs while the books cut into her small breasts. Sitting up and wrenching away from him, she fumbled with the ties of her bodice, then reached down the neckline of her dress and pulled out the books, flinging them at him one after another. Who cared about her books anyway now that she was betrothed to a man she'd never met? "Take them!"

Finally, she sat there, bodice ties dangling over her exposed corset, breasts heaving. "If you'd read your own books closer, you'd be doing some good instead of chasing me back to Edinburgh." To her mortification, she began to weep. She bent her head to the ground and sobbed harder.

He moved up behind her and, pulling her to her feet, turned her around to face him. "I don't want your books, lass," he said roughly. "I only want to keep you safe."

"No, you don't," she sniffled. "You only want me to marry Lachlan—a man I don't even know."

His hold on her shoulders tightened. "I've not yet met my betrothed either. That's the way the world is, Catriona."

Bereft, she sniffled again. "You might be willing to wed a stranger, but I'm not, so this—this Lachlan can look elsewhere for a bride." Her chest rose and fell against him with unchecked sobs.

He held her away from him, just far enough so he could look into her eyes. "Run away from me again, lass, and I'll not be responsible for what I do—I'll tie you to the mare if need be. I dinna care how grand an arrival you make for Lachlan, for he and I have ne'er been close, but it does matter that I deliver you safe and sound. 'Tis a point of honor between my grandfather and yours. Do ye ken?"

Wide-eyed, face wet with tears, she could only nod. With Robert's anger he'd lapsed into a thicker brogue. She was suddenly too aware of his hands on her, and the warmth curving up her body. His eyes echoed the color of wild bluebells and sparkled with anger like a cold loch. She wanted him to touch her hair again, gently as he had earlier. Idly, she wondered who "Jeannie" was. His betrothed?

Before she could gather her wits, he reached for her waist and with one swift movement hauled her up, tossed her over his shoulder, and carried her back toward the path. Her feet dangled against his waist, and she grabbed on to the back of his coat and held on for dear life. She bounced, swayed, and pleaded with him to put her down. All to no avail.

"I warned ye, lass. The Highlands are full of more danger than an angry MacLean who might give chase."

She was utterly humiliated. It was bad enough having been caught by him, but to be dragged back to Elspeth like a freshly shot stag? It was unseemly. Her mother would faint if she were alive to see this.

He stopped and shifted her weight so her buttocks were higher up in the air, her stomach pressed tighter against his shoulder. She felt like a sack of oats.

"Put me down."

"Do you take me for a fool?" he said, continuing to walk. "And from now on pad yourself with something softer than books. You're a menace to a man, wearing hard volumes where the good Lord meant you to be bonnie and soft."

"I'm dressed for your Highland draughts." Her voice was muffled against his coat, which smelled vaguely of wind-whipped wool, and she felt the rise and fall of his chest.

He paused, and she thought with relief that he intended to put her down. Instead he spoke—to someone else.

"Good day to you, sir. Do you need directions to your destination?"

If the blood hadn't already rushed to her head, embarrassment would have done the deed now. A total stranger—

someone with a young, cultured-sounding voice—was a witness to her humiliation, and Robert was conversing as if she weren't even there.

"How far are you traveling along this road?" he inquired.

"Far enough, *monsieur,* to find suitable scenery to sketch and to fill a journal with my impressions."

Catriona wanted to scream. How could she have thought Robert MacLean was charming? The closer they got to the Highlands the more barbarically he behaved. She wondered what the stranger, apparently a Frenchman, thought about this new glimpse of Scotland, where a Highlander greeted a foreigner with a lass slung over his shoulder. As for Catriona, she'd never forgive Robert MacLean—or her grandfather—for this betrayal.

The talk—about the scenery, the weather, the whiskey available in Glen Strahan—continued until the stranger suggested they ride along together. Immediately Catriona felt an increased tension in Robert's grip and wondered why.

"We'll be traveling a . . . touch slower than I'd anticipated. You'd make better time to go on past us," Robert replied, a harsh edge to the polite words.

Without waiting for a response, Robert stalked down the path to where the horses were waiting and unceremoniously dumped Catriona to her feet. Douglas and Elspeth both stood silent, looking as if they'd not noticed anything unusual.

Robert glowered at Douglas. "Ready the horses." He turned to Elspeth. "Tend to her scrapes, please."

With chin high, Catriona climbed up on her horse and, after brushing bits of gorse off her skirt, allowed Elspeth to rub some salve onto the knee where her stocking had torn. Out of the corner of her eye, she watched Robert gather the reins from Douglas and tie her horse's reins to his.

The French traveler caught up with them before they set off and, instead of passing, pulled even and smiled. Catriona had her first clear look at him and blushed in mortification at the way he'd first seen her, for this traveler was undeniably young and handsome. A touch effeminate perhaps compared to Robert, but nonetheless striking in a dark way. Dark eyes, dark hair. And he had had the gallantry to retrieve Catriona's purple cloak from the brush and return it to her. It was folded neatly, and through it she felt her books—mercifully hidden so Robert couldn't see them.

She felt overwhelming gratitude to this kind stranger. *"Merci, monsieur—"* She didn't know the man's name and quickly made introductions.

The stranger lifted Catriona's hand to his lips and lightly brushed a kiss to her wrist. *"Bonjour,* Mademoiselle Ferguson. Forgive my omission in not formally introducing myself earlier. You seemed . . . preoccupied. Jacques Beaufort at your service."

Catriona blushed. She couldn't help admiring the stranger's richly embroidered long coat, the breeches of fine cloth, the cravat of French lace—an item banned from Britain. Most of all she admired his suave words.

"Catriona, enough chatter. We're leaving," Robert said.

"Monsieur," the stranger said, "it occurs to me you have your hands full. I would be happy to slow my pace to match yours if I could cheer the *mademoiselle* out of her travel fatigue."

"The *mademoiselle* does not suffer from fatigue. You'll fare better on your own. Stay on the road. Falkirk and Bannockburn are straight behind you and here Loch Lomond leads to the Highlands. Any passing Scotsman will willingly trade further directions. *Adieu, monsieur,"* Robert said with unusual abruptness, and picked up the reins.

Catriona had to bite her tongue to hide her temper. Robert had had his own way for entirely too long.

"Oh, no, on the contrary, we'd be delighted to have you ride with us," she told the Frenchman.

Robert uttered a strong oath. "He's going on around us," he told her, locking his gaze with hers. His mouth formed a straight, unyielding line.

Angry, Catriona stared back, then turned to Jacques and smiled sweetly. "I apologize, *monsieur,* but you know how it is with these Highlanders—the veneer of civilization is very thin."

Jacques smiled ruefully. *"Merci bien.* Perhaps our paths may cross at one of the inns along the road, *mademoiselle.* It shall be my fondest dream. *Au revoir.''* With a suave smile, he doffed his cocked hat and rode on.

Robert glared after the Frenchman, then with a jerk on the reins of her horse started their little procession on its way. Catriona could do nothing but stare at Robert's back and silently promise him many storms ahead. As day dwindled into dusk, the path wound its way up into the rugged Highlands, but Catriona was not willing to admire the wild beauty around them. Her thoughts were focused on the betrayal by her grandfather.

One thing seemed certain. This journey was turning into a contest of wills, one she intended to win. Robert or her grandfather might assume she would go like a lamb to this Lachlan, but they had both sorely misjudged her.

With merciless abandon, a Highland wind whipped the wet flag above Castle Fenella MacLean, and a steady drizzle drenched the cottages of Glen Strahan. The keepers of the castle and the villagers—tacksmen and tenants alike— would be clinging close to their peat fires, Lachlan knew. But he thrived on the wild weather, and today his mood matched that of nature.

Standing in the castle's inner ward, he threaded his fingers through a shock of straight blond hair, and, scowling, watched crippled old Cameron limp by on his crutches. Worthless parasite. But it was his aging grandfather—the clan chief, the MacLean—who weighed on his mind. Alexander MacLean's stubbornness sat like a rock between them. That his grandfather had insisted that Robert escort Lachlan's betrothed all the way from Edinburgh was yet another example of his grandfather's favoritism.

No matter how Lachlan had argued, his grandfather thought Robert could do no wrong. "Who better than your own cousin Robert to escort the Ferguson woman here from Edinburgh?" he had asked.

Hah! Had his grandfather been blind all these years to

Robert's way with women? No doubt Robert would brag about how easily he had charmed this Ferguson lass—all before Lachlan even got a fair look at the wench.

Catching sight of his sister, Lachlan frowned. The perfect person on whom to vent his frustration. Ever since they'd been children, Lachlan had hated his cousin Robert, but he tormented Grizel because, unlike Robert, she could not fight back. Lachlan stalked across the sodden grass toward her, the plaid at his shoulder billowing behind him like a clan flag.

Encased in her thick hooded cape, Grizel couldn't possibly see him coming, which was as he wanted it. Stepping quickly in her path, he captured her against the rock wall of the keep and tugged her into a low doorway.

"Robert arrives soon with my betrothed, the Ferguson lass."

Grizel looked up, her plain features clearly melancholy. "What ails you, brother? Are you feeling the nervous bridegroom?"

Quick as lightning he grabbed her wrist.

The surprised expression on her face faded at once to petulance, and she tried to tug away. "Let me be, Lachlan. 'Tis time the feud ended and you forgot your hatred." She twisted away and rubbed her wrist.

"Mayhap."

Grizel looked up at her brother. "What would you have me do? Ready the wedding chamber?" she said with a little smile.

Lachlan's lips curled, and he caught her fast against the rough planks of a door. "In a manner of speaking, sister . . . In fact, you can find out if Robert brings the wench here pure or if once again he has stolen a woman's heart."

"You hate him still?"

"You admire him, the son of our grandfather's other family?" he said sarcastically.

Shrugging, she moved sideways, and just as quickly he pressed her against the wet moss that clung to the castle bricks.

"Naught about Robert matters," she said. "I've never championed his favor."

The wind whipped the shoulder plaid out behind Lachlan and blew the short knee plaid against his bare legs. He had to shout against the rain to be heard. "Robert's nothing but the son of a second son. He's naught but an arrogant nuisance, and don't ever let him forget his place."

She shrank from him. "Lachlan, let me be. Let Robert be. He can never be chief."

"No, but he's charmed the villagers until you'd think they prefer him as chief. Even now they ask when he comes. Robert. Robert. Robert. That's all I hear."

"But Lachlan, the deaths of the young lasses in the village have them frightened," she said in a quiet voice. "I'm frightened too," she added suddenly. "Robert knows how to make the villagers—all of us—feel calm."

He pushed her hands away. "A trifle. Death is the way of the Highlands. Only an imbecile thinks otherwise."

"But can I help it if the villagers look to Robert for consolation? They fear you, Lachlan." She darted a quick glance at him.

He sneered. "As it should be. They need to fear. A chief doesn't look for love."

Grizel's eyes widened in comprehension. Rain ran off her straight black hair and down her scared face. "Well, you can't be surprised," she said. "It was always Robert whom Grandfather favored—him and his mother's precious Presbyterian piousness."

Lachlan's face hardened. "I want your help when Robert comes."

"To distract Robert so the Ferguson lass won't be wishing it was Robert instead of you she'll be wedding?" Grizel laughed, a scoffing sound. "You're no match for Robert with the wenches and never were. Feel fortunate that she'll wed you at all—especially if she finds out that two of your wenches have died mysteriously."

Lachlan closed his fingers more tightly on her jaw. "Mind the tartness of your tongue."

"She'll think you killed them," Grizel whispered.

Without warning, he struck her across the face so hard and so fast the blow stung his palm. "You silly wench." He shut off her brave talk as effectively as if he'd slammed a ticking clock into silence. With one hand to her cheek, her eyes burning, she sidled along the wall. But again he caught her arm and held her still.

"You owe me your loyalty, dear sister—no one but me."

When he let her go, she fell slack against the wall, then like a coiled spring she leaped at him. "Do I? What have you ever done for me?"

Lachlan grabbed her wrist and twisted it. "It was I who offered you comfort, sister, when your lover betrayed you and took another and then died in battle. Surely, you worthless little jade, you've not forgotten already how you grieved for Ian Ferguson?"

She whimpered. "If it hadn't been for you and the feud, Ian would have come back to me."

"Ian died, Grizel, and he wouldn't have come back." He tightened his grip. "Because of what he did to you, I don't trust this Ferguson wench's loyalty on the journey with Robert."

With a rough gesture, he shoved her away. "Now go on wi' ye, and weave awhile with the village women. And as you're about it, spread some lies to dilute Robert's famous charm. Tell them he's a traitor. That he seeks to wed an Englishwoman and spy for the English court. Make them hate Robert. And later . . . later, find out how pure my bride is."

Jerking her up by her cape, he shoved his sister through the deepening gloaming in the direction of the great hall. By the very devil, she was a bothersome wench, lurking near him all the time, mourning a man who'd been dead since the '15. It was time she earned her keep here. In fact, if she hadn't been his sister, he'd have long ago locked her away in the chapel tower just to spare himself the expense of her care.

Gloaming had come and gone, and full darkness lay over the fells. In the little guest room of the manse near Loch Gilse, quiet held dominion over the night. A very short night at this time of summer. For hours, while the hallway clock slowly counted off the minutes, Catriona had been waiting for full darkness to fall. And for the inhabitants of the manse and their visitors—including Jacques, who'd joined them—to settle down for the night. Rehearsing her escape had seemed the most practical use of her time.

Over and over she reviewed the details of her plan—to steal out of the manse, to saddle her horse and ride through the night back down the road. Naturally, she'd be welcomed in every inn, cottage, and manse which had previously given her shelter, because in each one of them she'd left a gift of excess clothing or fripperies, as Robert called her mother's pretties.

Yes, that part would be easy.

It was leaving here she dreaded. Specifically, escape from Robert MacLean, who'd said he'd be sleeping in an outbuilding near the stable. The thought of Robert prone in the sleeping position scarcely bore thinking of. An arrogant man like that surely didn't succumb to the vulnerabilities of the body and need sleep. But if he did, she wondered how he did it. On his side? His back? Did he sleep in his clothes? If not . . . A vision of tousled golden hair brought her to her feet.

Oh, fie, she had to put these thoughts out of her mind.

And she could delay no longer.

Touching first one foot and then the other to the floor, she groped in the dark for her boots, wrapped herself in her cloak, and started tiptoeing toward the door.

Elspeth rolled over on the narrow bed, and Catriona stood in the middle of the room, scarcely breathing, hoping Elspeth would continue her usual sound sleep.

As the moments passed, Elspeth did not move, nor did Catriona—not until she'd satisfied herself that the only thing awake was the wind in the chimney. She tiptoed to the door which led to the second floor landing of the modest manse. She eased it open a mere inch, then paused, listening for the normal noises of the night—a mouse gnawing at a wall, the steady ticking of a clock at the bottom of the stairs.

More worries plagued her. Would the stairs creak? Would a child wake up and give her away? Would she escape from Robert MacLean only to fall into the clutches of bandits? But even the threat of bandits worried her less than marriage to a stranger. No, marriage was too dear a price to pay for reconciliation with Angus. Far too much to ask in the way of duty.

Taking a last breath for courage, she opened the door wider and stepped forward. At the same instant the clock bonged the hour, and a cat brushed past her on its way into the room. Involuntarily, Catriona jerked back, her heart in her throat. Behind her, she heard Elspeth mutter in her sleep.

At last, as both her pulse and the house settled again into the rhythms of the night, she eased into the darkness of the hall.

Carefully, she let out the breath she hadn't realized she'd been holding and then took another step forward. Her foot hit something soft, and she stumbled. The soft obstacle had a voice. A voice that cursed.

She gasped and inhaled, prepared to scream bloody murder, but before the scream could form in her throat, a strong grasp pulled her down and someone clamped a hand to her mouth.

Chapter 4

The body on which she landed contained undeniably male contours, the same brawny contours of the male who'd earlier today slung her over his shoulder. Though the endearments he whispered in her ear were French, the whisper belonged to Robert MacLean.

"*Chérie,* I told you if you ran away I'd capture you."

She struggled, but he held her fast.

She kicked, but he laughed.

She moaned in protest, but he kissed the hollow of her throat and pressed a string of tiny kisses to her skin.

And then she moaned in shocked pleasure. Which only made him lengthen the kisses. This was not going at all as she'd planned. She felt light-headed, a symptom she'd never expected kissing could cause.

Until now, the only kisses she had known had come from her parents, and with them she'd felt a cool acknowledgment of kinship. To her utter surprise, Robert MacLean's kisses ignited a spark deep inside her.

"You said you'd be asleep," she accused, her words a frightened whisper.

"I was, lass, until you walked on top of me."

"You said—" His hand, warm and gentle, covered her mouth.

"I'll have to remind you to whisper, lass, else our hosts, the minister and his family, will wake up and find you on the floor in my arms." He removed his hand. "You were saying?"

"You lied about where you'd make your bed."

"Unscrupulous of me, I agree," he whispered. He rolled them over so that she lay beneath him on the floor, and with one leg casually thrown over her, his taut thighs held her in place.

She panicked. "But—" She lowered her voice to a whisper. "But what are you doing to me?"

"Trying to keep you from waking everybody up." He lowered his head toward her, and she felt his breath warm against her skin.

"You can't do this. I'll—"

His lips covered hers in midsentence, and she forgot whether she'd been about to scream or cry. She tried to pull her mouth away, but couldn't. He continued to exert subtle pressure until finally, despite herself, she relaxed and let him move his mouth against hers. She'd never felt a man's mouth on hers before. In fact, she had expected such kissing to be . . . vulgar. But this felt wonderful, and even though only their lips touched, her entire body tingled as if an invisible flame moved down her. Why, this surpassed anything she'd imagined or read about.

One of Robert's hands supported the back of her head, and she felt his fingers in her hair, felt his breathing deepen. She tasted his lips, his tongue—and then she heard a woman's moan. Herself. She was kissing him back. It wasn't difficult, which surprised her since she'd never read an explanation of it in any book or play. Not even Shakespeare had been able to explain exactly what it was that Romeo and Juliet . . . well, *did.* Catriona moved her mouth against Robert's, and that made him move his mouth all the more. She shifted her body and felt his shift in response.

Robert lifted his mouth from hers just a wee bit. *"Chérie,"* he whispered, "your insubordination is almost as unpredictable as your kisses."

Her mind spun. Guilt washed over her. What was she doing on the floor of a manse kissing a man? What would come next? She had to force herself to think. Why, in all of her books, had the authors never described a kiss? Was it because no words could convey it? That had to be it. She felt more exhilaration than when she and her grandfather had galloped across the glen on ponies long ago . . .

But what a strange time to remember *that*. She thought she'd forgotten almost everything about Angus. She closed her heart on the bittersweet memory and pushed against Robert's broad chest.

"Let me go."

"I dinna think that would be wise."

Oh, aye, this was the MacLean barbarian Robert who taunted her. "You have no right—" she pleaded again.

"Shh." The admonition preceded another kiss, during which his tongue silenced her.

She felt his brawn and the span of his hands on her waist, and beating him on the shoulder caused only a wickedly deep laugh to form in his throat. She was awash in new sensations—the smell of the damp wool of his coat, the taste of whiskey, and the stubble of his face burning her cheeks. Undone, she stopped struggling and let him have his way, but his way was long, it turned out, and she felt the fire turning inward, burning somewhere deep inside her. His hands moved down her back, pressing her to him until she thought she'd lose her senses.

Suddenly, he raised his head, but before he could speak, he clamped his hand over her mouth, and then she heard a faint rustle from somewhere in the house. Was someone awake among the minister's family? It would serve Robert MacLean right if the good minister himself came out and caught his guests in this compromising position. Her hands came up to push him away, but she couldn't budge an ounce of his muscled brawn.

His other hand gripped her tightly by the waist, and he pulled her to her feet. She struggled, and the next thing she knew he had swept her up in his arms. As effortlessly as if she were a wee bairn he carried her downstairs, his boots barely clicking on the bare wood.

His boots? If he had his boots on, he must have been expecting her to come out of that bedroom. Expecting her and lying there waiting to—to seduce her? How dare he? She'd tell Angus about this!

At the bottom step, he set her down and lit a candle before propelling her into the privacy of the darkened study. Here their voices would go unheard, but if he thought she intended to discuss the episode upstairs without an argument, he underestimated her stubbornness. Not for nothing was she the granddaughter and heiress of Angus Ferguson.

She stalked in ahead of him, her way lit by the soft glow of the candle he held, and headed for the fireplace. Emotions in a turmoil, she stared down at the grate, where the earlier roaring fire was now banked for the night.

Now that she had a chance to talk, she didn't dare tell him how she felt, not after what he'd just done to her. When he moved up behind her, she held her breath.

She flinched at his hand on her shoulder, but she wouldn't give him the satisfaction of turning and ending up in his arms again.

"What were you doing sleeping in my doorway?" The frigid drawing room held more warmth than her voice. "What *were* you doing?" she demanded.

"Did I no' make that obvious, lass?" His voice held a wry irony, and she remembered the sensation of his lips first touching hers. Something moved behind her, and she jumped, but looking around she saw only the tall shadow Robert cast against the heavy draperies.

"There is nothing obvious about you," she said, turning back. "*Why* are you interfering in my life?"

"I thought to keep you quiet, lass, while I talked you out of running away," he said dryly. He began to pace back and forth, his shadow moving with him, tall against the walls. "You wouldn't want to wake up the entire household now, would you?"

She almost didn't care. Almost. Looking around nervously, she said in a stage whisper, "You can go ahead to Glen Strahan without me. I have no wish to keep you from your own wedding. I can hire a guide to take me back to Edinburgh."

"Lass, lass," he cut in, "I don't feel I've explained the situation fully. There's the matter of honor. I made a promise to my grandfather, and if I don't honor that promise and bring you to Glen Strahan, *my* wedding may not take place."

She could not prevent the smile that turned up the corners of her mouth. "Then prepare to live the life of a bachelor, because I'm not going to marry—ever—and certainly not to guarantee you a bride. Do ye ken?" she said, mimicking his brogue.

His soft laughter mocked her. "A hardhearted wench you are, Catriona, denying me my bride."

Her sharp retort died on her lips, and she felt a strange twist in her chest to imagine him holding some other woman. Appalled at her thoughts, she summoned the most righteous voice she could find.

"What would happen if your betrothed found out you kissed me?" When the candlelight fell on him again, she could clearly make out the roguish smile on his handsome face.

He began casually walking about the room, moving in and out of the circle of light. "A difficult thing to predict, lass, for I've no' met her yet."

Unaccountably, Catriona's heart pounded.

"But I doubt," he went on, coming to a stop and smiling at her, "that she'll hold a wee kiss against me, not until after the wedding."

"Who is your betrothed?" Catriona asked, deliberately trying to change the subject. "Jeannie?"

He moved even closer until he stood towering over her. "No—her name is Sarah, and she'll be coming from Carlisle."

"English? Why would her family want her to wed a Scotsman? And why would you wed an English?"

"Bluntly, lass, it has to do with the way of politics. An alliance. Sarah Kendrick's father wants a husband for her. Her uncle, Lord Kendrick, wants appointment as secretary of state for Scotland. I want to help Lord Kendrick keep peace in the Highlands in exchange for getting my family titles back. We'll all form a most pleasant alliance, I believe.''

Catriona blinked, trying to take in the complicated relationships that would tumble apart if he did not wed. Indeed, if *she* did not wed.

''And in case ye're wondering, aye, 'tis a double wedding our families have planned. Why all the curiosity? Have you had a change of heart about attending your own wedding?'' he asked hopefully.

''Of course not.'' Catriona swallowed hard. ''You've made it all—your wedding day, I mean—sound like a political convenience instead of . . . of . . .'' At a loss for words, she peeked up at him. So big a man he was, so brawny and fair of face.

''Instead of what?'' he prompted her.

''A matter of the . . . the heart.'' Blushing, she turned her back on him and concentrated on the single candle flame. She could almost feel his warm breath on her hair. In the back of her mind, the legends of Tristan and Isolde ran rampant. But plain and scrawny as she was, with carroty-red hair, he'd not be seeing her in a romantic way. He must be laughing inside at how she'd kissed him back.

Without warning, Robert MacLean placed his hands on her shoulders and, more gently than she would have expected, turned her around to face him. The candlelight illuminated the gilt-tinged mat of hair at the open throat of his shirt.

''Matters of the heart?'' he questioned in a soft voice. ''Next you'll be telling me it's romantic to have the Scottish Pretender living in France plotting with the likes of Jacques Beaufort. Lass, lass, life is not a romantic legend, and marriage *is* a convenience.''

''Then I pity your future bri—''

''Shush, lass.'' His silencing finger touched her lips. ''Would you wake the house debating the merits of my own betrothed with me?''

She nodded and could taste the slightly salty texture of his skin. ''What happened to your titles?''

''My grandfather's title,'' he corrected, ''went the same

way as too many other Scottish titles after Sheriffmuir. Earl of Strahan he used to be until the title was stripped from him after the '15 . . .''

She shut her eyes, enchanted by his deep voice.

"Are you listening?" he asked.

Her eyes flew open and again she nodded.

"So you see," he went on, "I'm no less mercenary in that sense than Lachlan and no less patriotic to Scotland."

"Patriotic!" she scoffed, pushing his hand away.

" 'Twas a Scottish title, lass, bestowed on the chief of MacLean by James IV. We value it, and if I have to give my talents to England as the price of getting it back, then so be it."

"A noble sacrifice," she observed, still skeptical.

"I owe my grandfather much. Besides, such is the lot of non-heirs like me . . . to find their own way in the world. Why worry your pretty wee head over what I do? If I succeed, you shall be Countess of Strahan someday."

Her mother would have loved it. "I don't want to be a countess," she declared.

He paused, as if biting back a smile. "Did it disappoint you to find out it was me tonight instead of Jacques with his bonnie words?"

"Yes," she lied, unwilling to let him know how his kiss had affected her.

"I dinna believe you."

"And I dislike easy flirtation, Mr. MacLean. In fact, I detest it."

She heard soft laughter and felt his gaze flick over her. "Why, lass, ye dinna kiss like ye detest," he said with a stronger brogue.

She wanted to scream. How had he managed to turn this conversation back to kissing? "Why do you insist on teasing me?" she asked, her voice threatening to break. "Why?" she asked, half turning to him.

Staring down at her delicate profile, Robert considered her question. "I don't know, lass. Must everything have an answer?" Truth be told, he didn't know the answer himself, yet ever since he'd kissed her, he'd felt the layers of civilization falling away. He was shedding piece after piece of his self-control and throwing it by the wayside like so much excess clothing. He wanted to hold her again, to feel the pliancy of her uncorseted breasts through her nightdress. A clock on the mantel ticked, the only sound in the room.

He moved away from her, but Catriona moved too at the exact moment and collided smack into him. A low laugh escaped him at the way she jumped.

Lachlan held first claim on this lass, Robert reminded himself. The kiss upstairs had been meant only to keep her from screaming, and he had done no more than any robust man did when a pretty wench landed in his lap. The difference was, most women he knew were just that—wenches, not naive little rabbits like this one.

Despite that, he wanted to kiss her again. He wanted to be the one to show her things he knew Lachlan never would—like the sweetness of a kiss prolonged, the mingling of a man and a woman's breath until it became one. Before his impulses could get the better of him, he put some space between them. He walked over to one of the windows, pushed aside the heavy draperies, and stared out at the night.

"Tell me more about Lachlan," she requested.

Her voice caressed him as gently as heather on the breeze, and he cursed himself for his soft thoughts. He let the draperies drop and turned back, but he kept his distance.

"I've not seen him in several years. I've been at university, you know."

"I know, but what was he like? Is he like you?" Her words tugged at him.

"The resemblance is there, but not exact," he said. He wondered what she might think when she met Lachlan and saw the same light hair and similar blue eyes. Granted, Lachlan's features appeared cut with a sharper, less kind knife, but the family resemblance could not be denied.

"How then are you so different? Is he larger than you?"

"No." What would she do when she learned that the resemblance between the cousins was most different in other ways—temperament for one? Would she blame him for delivering her into the hands of a—? He cut his thoughts short and asked her to repeat the question.

"Is he wiser?"

"Ten tutors resigned from teaching Lachlan."

"Stronger?"

"It's been many years since we fought each other. I can't say."

"But he's the heir?"

"His father was the eldest son. E'en though I'm older, he inherits. Things like that do not change, not even in the Highlands."

"Is he . . . kind?"

He paused, at a momentary loss. "Highland men dinna think in terms of kindness, lass. They think in terms of survival. Your family is no different, or are they? Tell me," he said with a slow smile, "why has your grandfather never mentioned you?"

"He banished me."

"For bad temper?"

"For knowing too many Jacobite secrets," she retorted, adding, "My family, you see, lost more than titles and land. Cousin Ian . . . the English killed him in the Rebellion. Uncle William died in 1723 of apoplexy, my father of consumption, and my last cousin was run over in a carriage accident a year ago New Year's. Which is why I'm the heiress." The tiny line of confusion on her face deepened again.

"Which is why you must marry."

"Never."

This conversation had not gone at all in the direction he'd hoped it would. He felt uncomfortably aware of her lips, her voice, her vulnerability to *him*—her guardian so to speak.

Had she figured out that this trek into the Highlands was not the sentimental journey he'd hoped it would be?

And that the difficulty had little to do with bandits or the rugged terrain or the wild weather?

He forgot his place, the dangers about him, his plans for a future at the side of King George's secretary of state for Scotland. He forgot his own betrothal, for God's sake.

Moving to her, he looked down into her eyes again. "Only promise me two more things, lass." She was still standing there looking at him, as innocent as if he were going to ask her to say her bedtime prayers. "Not to run away again tonight . . ."

"Of course I won't," she said rather too airily to suit him.

"I want you to swear on a Bible you'll not run away."

"You don't have one."

"But we're standing in the manse study, Catriona." Holding the candle high, he directed her along the minister's shelves of books. The faint light illuminated dusty copies of Latin and Greek texts, tattered copies of sermons . . . and at last a Bible, which Robert pulled from the shelf.

"Your hand on it, Catriona."

Ignoring her impatient sigh, he blew the dust off the cover, and the candle went out too. They stood in pitch blackness, the Bible their only tangible link.

"Now, repeat after me, please. On my honor, I, Catriona Ferguson, do solemnly promise not to run away tonight . . ."

In a petulant voice, she repeated him word for word. He paused, wondering what her sacred word was worth.

"And the second—?" she prompted him.

He smiled. "Promise not to scare off my English bride. My friend, Lord Kendrick, has convinced her family that Scotland is not as wild a place as it sounds. I'd not want them to think otherwise when they see the red Scottish thistle."

She placed her hand on the leather cover. "I promise," she said quickly, and headed into the hallway. He followed and caught her arm.

"Catriona, you're not forgetting the dangers of the Highlands, are you? You're to beware of the likes of Jacques Beaufort."

She stopped at the bottom of the dark stairway. "Why don't you like Jacques?" she asked softly. "He's not dangerous."

Robert moved closer. "It's his motives I'm wary of, lass. Whyever he's here in Scotland, it's not to fill his sketchbook with pretty pictures or his cellars with good Scottish whiskey."

"Why, you're daft. He's a harmless traveler."

Robert wanted to shake some sense into her, but then she'd be back in his arms. As it was, with one hand on the banister, she was close enough to touch. He clenched his hands into fists before he lost control. "You've been away from the Highlands too long," he admonished simply.

"Not long enough. I've seen ample heather and thistles and gorse and—" She paused. "Red thistle?" she asked.

Even through the darkness he could almost see the frown on her face.

He smiled to himself. "With red hair and a prickly disposition—who do you think it could be?"

"Me—!" She sounded outraged and whirled from him. Even in the darkness, he could see her curls flying. "You're an unholy barbarian," she accused. "I hope you end up in your own dungeon."

"Be careful, lass, about throwing easy curses around in the Highlands. Someone might think you mean it."

"I do mean it."

To his bemusement, she dashed up the stairs. He heard her light footsteps and then the sound of the bolt on her bedroom door being shoved home. Mercifully, no one from the clergyman's family stirred.

He drew a deep breath, but he relaxed too soon, for almost simultaneously a flint sparked in the dark and a mysterious third person held up another candle. From the shadows of the staircase a figure stepped out.

Instantly, every muscle in Robert's body tensed, poised to fight. Then the smooth voice of Jacques Beaufort cut through the darkness. "What is it about me you do not trust, *monsieur?*"

Chapter 5

With a languid gesture reminiscent of someone who'd idled about the royal courts, Jacques Beaufort placed the candle on a tiny table beside the stairs. His cultured French accent filled the silence. "Is it fear that after we arrive in Glen Strahan I might tell your bride-to-be about your midnight rendezvous with the beautiful *mademoiselle* who is betrothed to your cousin? Such tempting hair she has. Makes a man feel he could touch a sunset, perhaps even hold it in his hands, *n'est-ce pas?*"

"What is your point?"

"Merely an observation I make. *Mon Dieu,* such tangled affairs of the heart." Jacques laughed softly.

Robert moved to Jacques's side, taking his dirk in hand. Before the laughter could die in Jacques's throat, Robert had the point of the blade at the Frenchman's neck.

Jacques held perfectly still, but by the flickering candlelight, Robert saw only amusement in his eyes. Robert never trusted a man who smiled in threatening situations. It reminded him too much of a wolf bearing its teeth when cornered.

"Such violence is not necessary between gentlemen, *monsieur.* Is it my fault I spend the night in the same manse and am awakened by voices?"

"Tell anyone about my affairs, and you'll wish you'd taken a different road into the Highlands. What exactly do you seek in Glen Strahan, Frenchman? A lost relative? Eternal youth? Or eternal rest?"

Jacques gulped visibly. "I told you—whiskey."

"I hope you're telling the truth," Robert said between gritted teeth, "else instead of taking your lace cravat back home you'll wear a necklace of red." Teasing Jacques's ear with the tip of the dirk, Robert added, "Do you ken what it feels like to live with but one ear?"

Jacques swallowed hard, visibly nervous, his earlier calmness deserting him. "I prefer a pair, *monsieur,* the better to hear your commands. Tell me one thing—are all Highlanders so protective of their womenfolk?"

"You've a keen wit, Frenchman. Interference among the clans of Scotland is not tolerated—especially by bandy-legged Frenchmen." He sheathed the dirk down the waistband of his breeches and moved back upstairs to guard the door to Catriona's room—this time to keep intruders out, rather than prickly thistles in.

By midmorning of the next day, it occurred to Catriona that she'd missed seeing Jacques Beaufort at breakfast.

She was surprised he'd not lingered and waited to ask again if he could travel with them. After all, he'd supped with them last night—swallowing the rather horrid chops and coarse turnips with an alacrity that surprised her.

He was an intriguing man. The sort who would have made her mother's fan flutter all the faster. Robert, on the other hand, was an enigma to Catriona. Not one given to the flirtatious games of men and women, yet a man who invariably knew his way around a woman's thoughts. She ought to be glad he was making every effort to ignore her today.

Yet Catriona recognized a subtle truth. After last night, she'd become aware of Robert in some deeper, more primitive sense. Which is why she would have welcomed some of the Frenchman's suave conversation—as a diversion from the memories of Robert's mouth initiating her into the wonders of a kiss.

Desperate to put the episode from her mind, she forced herself to savor the changing scenery as they wound up into the Highlands—the golden eagle that took wing in the misty sky; the steep hills broken by patches of heather, rust-colored now, waiting for its season. Close by the road, a wild thistle waved in the wind, its purple bloom near at hand. She pulled her cloak more closely about herself and wished for warmth.

She'd been warm in Robert's arms.

It was no use. No matter how wildly beautiful the sight of snowcapped mountains and sparkling lochs, her gaze kept coming back to one sight—Robert riding ahead of her on horseback . . . to one memory—her body entwined with his on the floor.

She thought the day would never end.

When at last it did, and she found herself at yet another inn, lying in yet another bed-cupboard, she couldn't let herself relax as Elspeth did. Instead, Catriona lay there watching a particularly lazy spider weave a web above her head and considered her next course of action. Her body ached so from all the riding that she yearned to sleep, yet her honor demanded that she escape and head back on her own to Edinburgh.

Honor would have its way. She'd be less than a Ferguson if she didn't try to escape from Robert MacLean again, and if there were rivers to ford or rocks to climb, she'd simply put one foot in front of the other.

But first, of course, she had to put her feet on the ground and get out of this hostelry. She rejected the bedroom door at once, fully expecting Robert to be sleeping there again. Idly, she looked up to see how the spider fared with its web, and from the web, her gaze went to the window. She could crawl out of that window—provided it wasn't rusted shut—climb carefully down the roof, avoiding skinned knees, if possible; and then . . . With a little moan, she buried her head under the blanket.

Escape attempts were such a nuisance. Her body ached at the monumental work *this* escape would involve—climbing out of windows, saddling her horse by herself, sending all four other horses down the trail to make it more difficult for Robert to give chase. Just the thought of pulling on her boots made her want to roll over and sleep. Leaving the single candle burning, she closed her eyes, wanting to drift off . . . just for a few minutes.

The bedroom door squeaked open, startling her, and

she rose up on one elbow to see what new guest had been assigned to the room with her and Elspeth. But it was no stranger who approached. With a sleeping pallet tucked under one arm, a chipped crockery cup in his other hand, Robert MacLean in all his masculine glory sauntered over to her bed and stood looking down at her.

He held out the cup to her. "I regret having to disturb ye, lass."

She accepted the cup and stared down into it. "What is this? Your idea of a potion?"

"It's your doch-an-dorris."

After another baleful glare at the cupful of amber syrup, she sniffed it. Brandy. As intoxicating as the sight of the man who stood spread-legged just a hand's touch from her.

"Our hosts are Jacobite," Robert explained, "and keep more French spirits in their larder than they do good Scotch whiskey."

That announcement didn't shock her. What did shock her was the sight of Robert MacLean calmly dropping his pallet to the floor.

She pinned a condemning look on him, then leaned over the bed to glare pointedly at the pallet.

"What's that for?" Even to her own ears, her voice sounded unnaturally high, and she tried her best to hold the cup steady while clutching the bedsheet up under her chin.

"This," he said, indicating the pallet, "is exactly what you're afraid it is. I'm spending the night in this room with you."

Openmouthed, she stared, looking from his gold-flecked hair down to the tan breeches that sculpted his taut thighs. He was coatless, and his jerkin hung unfastened to reveal an open-necked shirt.

"You can't. It's not proper."

The gleam in his eye had acquired a wicked sheen. "Catriona, I keep forgetting your mother was a Lowland lady with an inordinate fondness for French fripperies and the prissy rules of court. Up here in the Highlands, we dinna have as many rules about what's proper. We're more concerned with what's safe—and with keeping impetuous lasses from running away.''

It took her a moment to realize her mouth was open, then she pressed it shut. If he thought she was pouting, who cared?

Why did Elspeth have to fall asleep so easily, especially when she needed her? But she'd not wake her up, for though Elspeth never complained, she was as weary as Catriona herself.

And then it hit her, the single calming thought. If Robert slept by her, there'd be no need for all that work of running away. She could actually sleep.

Or could she?

The sight of Robert MacLean stretched out so nearby was enough to keep the most determined spinster awake.

As if he knew exactly what she was thinking, he rolled over and faced her, and she found herself filled with sights much more dangerous to the pulse than glistening lochs and craggy peaks. Even Catriona, who'd paid scant attention to beaux, had to admit he was a fine specimen of a Scotsman.

His face could have been sculpted from stone. By candlelight his hair echoed the very color of the rocky cliffs through which she'd ridden—golden-brown and splashed with gilded streaks of sun. His eyes rivaled the depthless blue of lochs, and as many muscles contoured his torso as the Highlands had fells and glens. Aye, as rugged and beautiful as his Highlands he was.

She had the shocking urge to feel his embrace again, and the temerity to wonder what it would be like if he shared her bed and she explored him more thoroughly. She blushed to realize she was staring, and he was . . . well, not undressing, but loosening his clothing in preparation for sleep.

With a hasty movement, she lifted the cup and gulped down the brandy. She choked on it, and he had the nerve to laugh, a deep-throated husky sound.

A smile still lurked all over him, she decided, even when he leaned over the candle sconce. She heard his breath extinguish the flame, and then darkness fell over them both like a shared cover. For a moment all was silent, except for the steady sound of his breathing, the shift of his weight as he turned on the pallet, the rustle her blanket made against the sheets when she tried to curl up. Sleep was an elusive bedfellow, Robert all too near.

"I can't sleep with you lying so close to me," she said in some desperation.

"Aye, 'tis a dilemma," he agreed, but didn't move.

"If you were a gentleman, you'd leave."

His soft laughter was almost a caress. "I'm a MacLean, and a Highlander, and I've pledged an oath of allegiance to an English king, but I've never worked out this thing the Lowlanders call "gentleman." It sounds like something a foppish Frenchman would worry over."

Was he teasing? She was never certain around Robert MacLean. She rolled close to the edge of her bed and peered down at him. "How can you possibly be so hateful toward the French? Even if you're not a Jacobite, you can't deny it's Scotland's own king who finds support in France, and someday—"

Unexpectedly, he touched a hand to her face. "Someday, if we're fortunate, you'll quit romanticizing over lost causes—like ballads of love and the Pretender—and go to sleep."

"I can't believe you'd talk that way of the exiled king. What kind of Scotsman are you? Where's your fighting spirit?"

"Perhaps I lost it while chasing you through the gorse, lass," he replied dryly.

"That's different. I meant the—"

"I ken what you meant, lass, and since you're the bookish sort, I ken ye won't be satisfied till you've had your serious answer." With a restless thrust of his torso, he sat up and leaned so close to her that she could feel his warmth. His hand cupped her neck, his fingers tangled in her curls.

"My fighting spirit," he went on, "is with my great-great-grandfather, who died in a pool of blood at the hands of the English, lass, so there's no need to disparage my loyalties. But times have changed. The Pretender is wal-

lowing in French luxury while my Highland villagers fight
the enemy of famine. The need to fill their bellies decides
my allegiance . . ." He paused, as if he'd lost the trail of
his thoughts. "Is that enough?" His voice had grown oddly
husky.

Actually, she didn't think she'd ever tire of the way the
rich burr of his Highland words warmed the darkness. "I
don't think I can sleep tonight," she said in a small voice.

"Catriona," he said softly, "I'm *not* leaving you tonight. If the ghost of Queen Mary walks in here, I'll bow
to her memory, but I'll *no'* leave."

"What makes you think I'll run away?" she whispered.

"Like some Highlanders, I've second sight." His reply
was soft. "I see you, lass, running back down the road
like a foolish chit."

"Well, it would be just as foolish of me to let my grandfather wed me to this—this stranger Lachlan."

"That's for ye and your grandfather to work out." He
sounded exasperated, so the gentle touch of his lips against
the side of her face took her by surprise. "Why is it ye
canna behave and let me deliver you to him so that I can
meet my betrothed?"

Unaccountably, she trembled. His touch evoked responses within her body that were more acute than memory. And then the shameful memories did rush back—his
arms pinning her down, his kiss searing her, Robert
MacLean's hands teaching her what no book ever had.
Even now, his chaste touch was like that of Midas, turning
her insides to molten gold.

"If Jacques Beaufort were here in your place," she said
hoarsely, "he'd be the perfect gentleman. He'd trust me."

"Aye, but I'd *no'* trust him." Robert pulled away and
lay down.

"Why not?"

"When I know the reason, lass, I'll tell you."

She leaned over the bed in the dark, looking for his
warmth. "Are you worried he might help your 'red thistle'
escape? Then you'd lose your wedding." Now the brandy
was loosening her tongue, making her head heavy, her
desire shameless.

"Catriona," he said softly, "I'd no' waste a second of sleep troubling yourself over me."

With an exasperated sigh, she lay back down, feeling strangely light-headed. "I doubt I'll sleep at all," she murmured. "The idea of meeting this Lachlan is far more likely to keep me awake."

"Last night you asked me about Lachlan—" he began, then stopped abruptly, as if he'd changed his mind.

"I have the feeling I failed to ask the right questions about my betrothed," she said.

A pause. "Your questions were fair."

She ran her tongue over her lips, tasting brandy, and touched her fingers to the place where his lips had just brushed her. "Would Lachlan mind that you kissed me last night?" she asked.

The unnatural quiet from the pallet was answer enough. "Was that your first kiss?" Robert asked.

"Why do you think it was?" she said, grateful the darkness hid her blush. "Why does it matter?"

"You kiss with innocence," he replied, then after a moment added, "Perhaps it'd be wise not to let Lachlan know I kissed you."

"I see." But she didn't see and lay awake a long time wondering what he'd wanted to tell her about Lachlan before he'd befuddled her mind with talk of kisses.

The next morning Robert stood looking down at Catriona in her sleep. A touch of dawn lit the room, highlighting her alabaster skin. She didn't stir an eyelash.

Some feeling he couldn't identify tugged at him. He might be an unwilling caretaker of this girl, but she roused protectiveness in him the way the wounded hare never had. Wild and slightly wounded. That's what made her different from all the other women he knew. For a few minutes, Robert watched the rise and fall of her slim shoulders. His fingers ached to reach out and brush a curl from her cheek, but Elspeth's presence kept him from temptation.

What was he thinking of anyway, wanting to brush curls off the cheek of the red thistle? If he let down his guard for just a second, she'd likely threaten him with a dagger and be off down the road, where all manner of ruffians could be lying in wait for her. Or where the likes of Jacques would be all too willing to ply her with suspicious flattery.

Still, he couldn't forget the way she'd felt in his arms. It had been a mistake to kiss her, he realized now. If she didn't understand the danger of what he'd done, he did, and no doubt Elspeth did as well.

He lightly shook her shoulder, surprised at the fragile feel of her. "Catriona."

It was Elspeth who lifted her head, and so Robert backed away and gave the maidservant swift instructions. "I'll settle the account and expect Catriona downstairs in a quarter hour. Tell her if she takes longer, 'tis cold oatcakes for her instead of porridge."

Already out of bed and wrapped in a blanket, Elspeth leaned over the younger girl's bed. "Catriona," she murmured softly, shaking her. "Wake up. It's dawn."

"Dawn comes too early in summer," Catriona moaned, stretching like a cat. She opened her eyes, saw Robert, and clamped them shut again.

Robert stopped with his hand on the door latch, a vague amusement tempting him to tease her, to linger and listen to her moans of protest at awakening. But that was a dangerous idea.

" 'Tis morning, and Highland women dinna sleep past dawn," he said.

"Let them get up then," she murmured flatly.

Obviously, Catriona was not going to cooperate, and he debated whether to indulge her or reprimand her. For a long moment, he looked at her. She lay on her side, and the blanket outlined the curve of her hip. After dismissing his summons to get up, she now lay with her eyes shut, long red curls fanned out behind her, her hands tucked next to her cheek.

When Elspeth would have nudged her awake again, he ruefully shook his head, and instead Elspeth pulled the blanket over Catriona's shoulder. She stirred, and he had a memory of her lying soft and shocked beneath him while he kissed her, and suddenly he had no choice but to leave.

If Elspeth wondered why he slammed the door, he didn't

care. He stood outside in the hallway trying to gather hold of himself. This entire journey was turning into a battle of wills between him and a too-tempting female, and it was all his grandfather's fault. Still unsettled with his thoughts, he headed downstairs to find Douglas and get the horses saddled for the day.

At the foot of the stairs, the hostess of the inn—a harsh-faced woman of thrift—met him with their clothes that had dried by the fire. When Robert glanced over her shoulder to see who was up and about already, he silently caught his breath.

In the dining room, already positioned at the trencher table close by the fire and tucking into a steaming bowl of porridge, was Jacques Beaufort. Before the Frenchman could look up, Robert backed into the hall and returned upstairs. He wanted at least an hour between Jacques and himself on the road. Robert usually liked people. Only one kind of person bothered him—the sort who said one thing and meant another. Jacques's sort.

When he returned to the room, Elspeth was up and dressed. She sat close by a candle and, with head bent over Catriona's lavender cloak, busied herself mending a tear near the hem. With a few words to her, Robert handed her the dry clothing and bid her remain upstairs in the room. As for himself, he moved out into the hallway to allow the women privacy and to watch out a window for Jacques Beaufort's departure.

At first sight of the river to be crossed, Catriona reined in her horse and caught her breath. She didn't dare complain, not after lying abed so long and causing them to get a late start. Sighing, she pushed back the hair from her face and assumed a stoic expression. Inside, her courage was failing.

They'd dropped down into yet another glen and ridden past a waterfall. Surrounded by mist, it resembled a veil, the froth of white spray falling into a rushing river. The road came to an end at the riverbank, and Catriona could see where it continued again on the other side. She didn't have to ask to know what came next.

Already Robert had moved his horse down to the river's edge, looking for a shallow place for them to ford, not an easy task given the water level this late in the spring season.

Downriver, men labored over a half-built stone bridge. Future travelers would have the luxury of dry passage, but as Robert shouted up to the green-gilled Douglas, the only way across the river today was the wet way. He selected a level part of the riverbank, one where the imprint of other horses' hooves promised a shallow crossing.

As he guided Catriona across the river, the bone-chilling water crawled up to her saddle lap. Icy water splashed against her skirts, soaking her boots, her stockings, and half of the hem of the last outfit she still possessed—the gray riding skirt and her lavender cloak. She wasn't the least surprised when her hair—unruly as ever—fell out of its plait and onto her shoulders yet again.

Robert gave no quarter to her femininity except to ride downstream with one hand on her reins. Though she'd seethed at him earlier for tying their reins together, now she welcomed that hold, for a raging eddy sucked at her boots and threatened to topple her into the icy current. When the poor horse finally staggered onshore and wheezed water from its nostrils, Catriona wanted to slip off and fall to the ground. Her every muscle cried out in protest, and exhaustion owned her.

Her pride, however, refused to let Robert MacLean know that, else he'd taunt her again about her late sleeping habits.

At the sound of a horse approaching from down the road, Robert looked back, and his eyes narrowed in dislike.

"Why, it's Monsieur Beaufort," Catriona exclaimed, her face lighting up. "He's been riding behind us all morning. How lovely that he's caught up to us."

She reined her horse around to go back and wait at the riverbank for the Frenchman to ford the water.

Robert watched her ride off with guileless abandon toward Jacques Beaufort. He compared her figure now to the stuffed duckling with whom he'd begun the journey.

Slim and vulnerable she was beneath that lavender cloak now that she'd shed her excess layers at every stopping point along the journey. The dark-haired foreigner and the beautiful red-haired lass made a pretty picture.

Because Robert naturally liked people, he truly wanted to believe the Frenchman was no more than a sociable traveler with a predilection for Scotch whiskey . . . and for turning up when least expected.

But he didn't trust the man. Jacques had deliberately turned from the trail and waited until they'd caught up and passed him. Now he had the suave Frenchman at his back again. A bad sign, Robert decided, for Scotland grew as many Jacobite agents as it did thistles these days. Under Lord Kendrick's tutelage, Robert had learned not to trust easily. Lord Kendrick, Robert would wager, would scoff at Jacques's flirtations with both Catriona and the sketch-book, and agree that Jacques had ulterior motives.

Robert's knuckles tightened on his horse's reins, and he wondered again what Jacques Beaufort wanted—the lass or something else? If it was something in Glen Strahan, Robert would find out in time and handle Jacques with a bit less subtlety than he reserved for the villagers.

But if it turned out to be Catriona the Frenchman wanted, Robert realized with a flash of white-hot rage that he just might kill the man—and not for Lachlan's honor.

Chapter 6

Robert frowned. Damn that French bastard. The entire day Catriona had been constantly wondering out loud if the "oh, so charming" Frenchman would catch up to them again.

After their encounter at the river, Robert had refused to let Jacques join them. Instead, he had taken his party and ridden ahead, leaving Jacques Beaufort standing soaking wet next to a lonely crag. Now, no one was gladder than Robert that today's journey was almost over.

"I never promised you a bed tonight," he warned Catriona over his shoulder. "Remember that. Only a roof above your head. If you're lucky, you may be sleeping in one of the castle's embrasures."

"You mustn't go to so much trouble on my account, Robert," she replied archly. Ignoring Elspeth's warning look, she continued her verbal sparring. "The dungeon will do nicely, thank you. You can lock me in and save yourself a lot of worry."

"A tempting offer, lass. First let's see whether there's a dungeon strong enough to withstand your clever escapes."

She yawned. "Actually, I'm rather tired tonight and think I'll skip the escape attempt. After all, we've only one day before we reach my grandfather."

"Your thoughtfulness overwhelms me, lass," he said before turning his attention back to the narrowing road.

Catriona let him have the last word. There was no besting him. All day she had stared at his back—except when he'd turned to her and she'd pretended to examine the craggy scenery. The few times they had exchanged words, the mood had been one of a storm about to break.

As Robert guided them around yet another bend in the path, Catriona looked up and saw outlined against the late afternoon sky the ruins of a castle. It perched high on a hill overlooking a jewel-colored loch that looked more inviting than the castle.

"This is where we're staying?" she asked in a dubious voice. There was definitely no hostler to greet them.

"I said it would be primitive."

"Jacques will never find us here, but I suppose you're glad of that," she retorted tartly.

"I count it a blessing."

The mention of the Frenchman's name clearly piqued Robert, and Catriona felt a perverse pleasure. After Jacques had forded the river with them that morning, Robert had left him behind and, for no reason that Catriona could fathom, ordered him to stop following them. For the rest of the day, she'd pretended to worry about the Frenchman, just to taunt Robert. He was so arrogant.

"You were rude to Jacques this morning," she added out loud. "He's a fellow traveler. Why don't you want him with us?"

"Jacques Beaufort spends too much time turning your head with flowery words," Robert said, his tone laconic. "Lachlan would not like his bride-to-be flirting so outrageously."

Catriona glared at Robert's back, but ignored the comment. The day had been too full of banter. She was exhausted.

The iron gateway of the ancient fortification was gone, allowing them to ride into the outer ward without waiting for the raising of a yett. Except for the soft clip-clop of the animals' hooves, only a breeze, weaving like a ghost among the irregular stones, broke the silence. The inner buildings, meager of windows, rose up in mute testimony to an earlier century, to a time of damsels in distress.

Catriona might not be a damsel in distress, but, as she looked around the courtyard now, her spirits sank. When

Robert had described tonight's accommodations, he had not been exaggerating. What roof there might have been on the towers lay in a heap of centuries-old stone at her feet, and the wooden doors had long ago rotted away. Only the old moss-encrusted keep looked intact.

Robert and Douglas slid off their horses and began to prowl the perimeters of the crumbling stones.

Ignoring an earlier admonition to stay put, Catriona slipped off her horse as well and circled in place, slowly but surely captivated by what she saw. What strange bedfellows devastation and beauty could make, she thought. Wild daisies and foxglove poked their way up amid the weather-beaten stone, and Catriona's imagination began to run rampant. Had a clan feud set off this destruction—an earlier, more tragic version of the MacLeans versus the Fergusons? Or had it been an English raid?

In her mind's eye, she saw orange flames shoot up into the night, half-dressed men and women running out into the frozen white of a winter's snow, the silver flash of swords, the thrust of pikestaffs turned crimson with blood . . . the hum of bows, flinging off their arrows like angry hornets; the skirl of bagpipes like wolves closing in for the kill; the screams of the dying calling out for hell's release. Catriona felt all the terror and despair and helplessness as if she'd lived them herself.

"Are you all right, lass?" Elspeth asked, startling her.

"Just a wee bit weary," she replied, and if this journey did not end soon, someone would surely accuse her of turning fey.

Such wildness, she reminded herself, was of the past, and suddenly she missed Robert's teasing banter. He might be a rogue, but there was something reassuring about having him nearby.

She ran across the courtyard to where he was exploring a tower.

"What are you looking for?" she asked.

"The water well." Robert pointed to it.

"There's nothing here but us." Catriona could not hold back the nervous tremor in her voice.

Robert gave her an appraising glance. "You never know

in a place like this. You have a dirk hidden on your person, don't you, Catriona? In case bandits are lurking nearby, waiting to murder us in our sleep?''

She thrust out her chin at him, unnerved. ''Well, you are going to post sentries, aren't you? Isn't that how it's done in a castle?''

A thoughtful look replaced his smile. ''Aye, an excellent idea. You get first sentry watch.'' He turned his attention to Douglas, who was unsaddling horses, and Elspeth, who stood with portmanteau in hand, looking weary.

''What should I watch for?'' Catriona asked.

''Watch out for intruders while the rest of us sleep. The keep looks as if it should do as a shelter . . . Douglas, take Elspeth and check the lower floor.''

''And how long is first watch?'' Catriona persisted, deciding to play along. She didn't know if he was serious or not, but she was not going to let him tease her for naught.

The sudden gleam in his eye was not reassuring. ''Until the half moon slips down the fells, hinny, and then you come and wake me—if you can.'' He began to climb some broken stairs that led up to what was left of the ramparts. ''Up here is your post,'' he said.

''You jest. I don't know why you've been in such a foul mood all day, but it's naught to do with me, and if you want a sentry you can be one yourself. I've got exploring to do.''

With a defiant step, she set off toward one of the other towers. Oh, how she hated his arrogance, his calling her ''hinny'' with such loathsome familiarity.

''Exploring is forbidden, Catriona.''

His voice stopped her in her tracks. Her back stiffened, and she turned only her profile to him. ''Are you going to tie me up and throw me in the dungeon if I disobey?''

''As we discussed earlier, the thought is not without merit.''

''With bread and water, I suppose.''

''You would be dining on as fine a fare as the rest of us, hinny. Our supper is no' as elegant tonight as it has been on other evenings.''

"At least in the dungeon I'd have a roof over my head," she taunted.

"Catriona, ye're deliberately provoking me."

"You provoke too easily, Robert. I'm tired of being forbidden to do this, forbidden to do that." She resumed walking. "What do you think can possibly happen to me?"

The words were no sooner out of her mouth than she tripped over a stone hidden in the nettles.

"You might trip and fall?" Robert suggested, his mouth quirked in the hint of a smile.

Catriona glared up from where she'd landed. The nettles stung her hands something fierce, but she gritted her teeth and fought back tears. "Whatever gives you that idea? I *like* sitting in a patch of Highland weeds."

Scrambling up, she ignored Robert's outstretched hand. She'd hang from a gibbet before she'd give him the satisfaction of rescuing her again. Lifting up her skirts, she ran for the next tower.

He caught up to her just outside the open doorway. When he swung her around and pulled her against him, she saw the dangerous look in his eyes, and her heart beat a little faster.

"I told you no' to defy me, lass."

That was the absolute last provocation. "Do this," she blurted out. "Dinna do this," she mimicked. "I'm weary of you ordering me about like I'm some witless lackey. I'll have you know, Robert MacLean, that I'm not following your orders anymore." Lowering her eyes, she confessed, "Besides . . . the nettles prick." She rubbed the backs of her hands against her skirt.

He moved a step closer, if that was possible, and took her hands in his. Her back was against the rough stone tower, rubbing against the moss and wet ivy. Looking at the I-told-you-so taunt in his eyes, she felt her pulse race all the faster. His body radiated warmth, and her face flushed.

"Let me go find Elspeth," she pleaded, trying to break away. "She'll have a salve for the sting."

"A remedy better than this?" He raised her hands and kissed first one, then the other.

She shut her eyes, not against the sting but to prevent herself from being drawn against him. He had no business charming the sting out of nettles . . . though his lips felt ever so marvelous. She shut her eyes, savoring the cool rapture of his mouth on her skin.

"You were saying something about not liking the way I treat you, lass?" He rolled one hand over and kissed the palm. "You forget, I'm the guide your grandfather entrusted you to."

Her treacherous body turned limp, even while fire licked through her veins. Alarmed, she opened her eyes. A sweeter sting than mere nettles was enveloping her. Caught in his embrace, she could only shake her head. Perhaps, she wondered, she'd gone too far in taunting him this time.

He was shockingly hard, from his chest to his thighs—especially his thighs. No fairy-tale character from her storybooks, this man was made of real flesh and blood, not paper and words. He looked and felt menacing, yet irresistible.

He smiled—if the twitch threatening his lips could be so termed. "Go on," he said with mocking undertones, "tell me to go to the devil, as you're yearning to do. We dinna stand on the niceties of polite speech up here in the Highlands."

"Don't do this." She tried to move, but he held her firmly in his embrace, twisting one of her curls about his finger.

"Ah, but you dinna play fair, hinny. Refusing my commands but expecting me to obey yours."

"What's wrong, Robert?" she asked, a catch in her voice. "If I've made you angry, I'm—"

" 'Angry' is no' the word for it, lass."

"What then?"

He looked at her for a minute, amusement in those deep blue eyes. "Mayhap I've had to watch you slip off one too many of those fripperies and gowns you dragged along . . . and once too often been forced to sleep guard by you, lass . . . never touching a finger to ye."

At his implication, her eyes widened. "I never realized—"

"I ken how much ye dinna realize, lass, and mayhap it's time ye were educated where your books left off."

Effortlessly, his hands spanned her waist and she felt lost in his size, his potent power.

"Don't do this, Robert . . ." Tears threatened. It was the worst possible time to try and reason with a man, but she saw no option. "How else do you expect me to behave when none of this journey was my idea, when my home is sold out from under me, and . . ." Heaven help her, she could no longer string rational words together.

He was regarding her with unexpected tenderness. She felt his hands move up her back until he pushed them into her hair. "Now dinna weep all over me, Catriona," he said in a husky voice. "It's no' as bad as all that."

Weeping was the last thing she intended to do. She stared at the sleeve of his jacket, anything to avoid his eyes. "Well, I don't want this Lachlan person, or my grandfather's favors, or—"

"Ye dinna mean that."

"Well, I certainly won't kiss you again, and you're an arrogant scoundrel if you think I will. Besides, it would be untoward."

"Untoward," he mimicked. "Such fancy words, lass. But your book learning canna sway me. It's time you learned what daring does to a man and how eventually you have to pay the piper."

She gasped as he pulled her against the full length of him.

Desperate, she said the first thing that came to her head. "My grandfather will not like this."

"Your grandfather expects you to wed and bear heirs, lass. I think he would like this just fine, wee red thistle."

"Don't call me by that absurd name. Do you hear me?"

"Aye, I hear ye, lass." His hands moved to rest just below her breasts, right where her heart beat wildest. While her chest rose and fell, he teasingly fingered the lacing that concealed her stomacher, and beyond to the suddenly tingling peaks of her breasts.

"You're no gentleman," she blurted out, appalled at

the sensations coursing through her body. "You're a rogue."

"Since you seem convinced I'm no' a gentleman but a rogue who has naught but your worst interests at heart, mayhap you ought to find out the extent of my terrible intentions."

Now his hands were making little circles on her back, and those little circles were setting her on fire.

"What are you going to do?" Her breath came in short gasps.

"Exactly what some man should have done instead of leaving you to your fairy tales . . ."

"Don't—"

She pushed her hands against him, but he wouldn't budge. In truth, it wasn't him she was trying to resist as much as the unbidden throbbing he created in her body. She felt the insistent pressure, the heat of him between their thighs.

His eyes turned dark. "You see, when you call a laddie—particularly the one in charge of your safety and well-being—a scoundrel enough times, he begins to think he might as well live up to his name." Slowly, he lowered his head and slanted his mouth against hers.

At once, she caught fire. Briefly, her hands came up to push him away, but then rational objections fled and she was kissing him back, her hands spreading against the solid muscle of his chest. She was shamelessly leaning into him, quivering at the subtle play of his tongue against hers.

He was pleading with her, teasing her tongue, boldly advancing, retreating, advancing again, sending sweet flames through every crevice in her body. And then quite suddenly his tongue retreated again and he was simply kissing her lips, his mouth caressing hers gently. He tightened his arms about her and deepened the kiss at the same time that she did. For long moments time seemed to stop. There was nothing in her world but the sensation of his lips and her thudding heart.

He released her as suddenly as he'd pulled her to him, and they stood looking at each other. His breathing seemed to come as deeply as hers, and there was a strange expression on his face. He resembled a schoolboy puzzling over the answer to some unspoken question.

"You kissed me differently the first time," she said.

His mouth crooked into a smile. "Aye," he said after a moment. He leaned one arm over her shoulder to imprison her against the wall. "Aye, that I did. Did your books no' tell you that either?"

She shook her head. "And so you kiss each lass differently?" she asked.

He looked momentarily startled, then tipped her chin. "Rule one in kissing, Catriona. Ne'er tell how you kiss other lasses . . . But as for ye, aye, you've got a fine passion to your kiss. It goes with your tart tongue, lass, and with your name." He tucked a strand of hair over her shoulder, and his hand lingered on her temple where a curl blew in the night wind.

"In fact, you're fortunate we're nearly in Glen Strahan, Catriona," he said at length. "The Lord only knows what I'd be driven to do if you kept on daring me. I might not even turn you over to Lachlan."

"I don't think I intend ever to speak to you again."

"An entire day without hearing you," he mocked. "Dinna be so noble, lass. After so many days of vitriolic words, I can handle one more day of your threats and curses. I can even," he added with a slow smile, "forbear and restrain my desire."

She glared and ducked under his arm to move away from him. "You're an arrogant cur."

"I'm a Highlander," he corrected her, "and dinna forget it."

Smiling, he caught her by the arm and led her toward the keep. For Elspeth's sake, Catriona put on her bravest face before walking inside. She headed straight for the haversack that contained the salves.

"You took a fine time, lass," Elspeth observed. "Beginning to think ye were lost, I did."

"I fell in some nettles," Catriona said as airily as possible, as if that ought to explain the delay.

With doors and windows on the tower long gone, the cold night air blew right through the place. For a few moments, nobody spoke. Robert remained in the doorway. Aware he was watching her every move, Catriona rubbed salve on her stinging hands and inspected the place as if it were a royal palace.

Even by the slice of half moon that shone through one narrow window, it was clear the spiders held court here, weaving tapestries all around the brick hearth. A piece of oatcake forgotten by some previous traveler lay on the stone floor. As for furniture, it didn't exist. Not even a coat of arms decorated the place. Cold suddenly, she stood before the empty hearth shivering in her cloak, arms hugged about herself.

After too much silence had passed, she decided that talking might dispel the sense of dark isolation.

"You were right, you know, when you said not to expect luxurious accommodations," she said, hoping Douglas and Elspeth would assume that a long conversation about the sleeping conditions had detained her and Robert.

She could still taste Robert's kiss, feel the slightly swollen texture he'd given her lips. And the longing he'd awakened deep in the core of her still throbbed.

She was glad when Robert began giving Douglas directions about the horses, and, despite Elspeth's close scrutiny, she finally relaxed.

"Elspeth, we could have an herbal broth for our supper," she said hopefully. Actually she cared not a whit what she ate.

Elspeth smiled wearily and reached into her bag for a very small pot, which she held up.

"Now what ideas have you got for a fire, lass?"

Robert came to a stop behind Catriona. "Books make fine kindling," he said, his breath uncomfortably warm against her hair. "If you've any more hiding about in my packsacks."

She whirled. "I'd sooner freeze."

"Surely no' before you eat your last meal."

"What meal?" Her gaze dropped to the small bundle she'd seen him take from Douglas. He handed her the package, and, suddenly ravenous after all, she dropped to her haunches beside Elspeth to inspect the contents—salted mutton and bannock, a gift from the lady of the manse this morning. Catriona said a blessing for the good woman and helped Elspeth divide the food.

They ate in silence. Too much silence. It was a welcome distraction when at last Douglas returned bearing an armful of precious wood. As soon as a small fire had begun to warm them, Robert stood up.

Catriona stood hastily also. "Where are you going?"

"To find you a bed," he said matter-of-factly.

"But there aren't any beds outside." She glanced up at him and found him looking at her as if the passionate interlude outside had never happened. "Just wild animals," she added, "and ghosts and—"

"And heather, which Douglas and I can cut for a bed. If you dinna want a heather bed, I suggest your maidservant needs one."

Catriona looked at Elspeth and recognized the weariness in the older woman's face. "Of course."

Robert lingered in the doorway. "Are you afraid of staying here alone?"

"Certainly not. I just don't want you to get lost on a wild goose chase."

"I appreciate your sudden concern, lass," he said with a smile. "Scream, of course, if you see a ghost."

"I'm not afraid." She turned her back on him, and when she glanced over her shoulder a moment later, he had vanished.

Again silence fell over the darkening room, and she turned back once more to look at the empty doorway.

"What ails ye, lass?" Elspeth's voice had a knowing quality, and Catriona wondered if this was the sort of subject she could discuss with her companion. She touched a finger to her lips and felt again Robert's mouth, hard and demanding against hers.

"Robert took an uncommonly long time in pulling you out of the nettles," Elspeth prompted.

"One minute he acts like he hates me, and the next minute he . . . he . . ." She turned and gave Elspeth a helpless look.

"Aye," Elspeth said, adding another chunk of peat to

the fire. "Provoke a man in a tempting setting, lass, and he'll give ye temptation," she said softly.

"How do you know?"

"Just because I'm a spinster doesn't mean I dinna know a thing or two about the laddies."

"What else do you know?"

"That a lusty man and a bonnie young woman canna live together in close quarters for long without nature taking its course. Why else do ye think young women need chaperones, hinny?"

Catriona stared blankly.

"In other words, as your books might say it, ye tempt him, Catriona."

"I don't." Despite Robert's earlier accusation, she'd never done a single flirtatious thing. Besides, who'd be tempted by a scrawny redhead with a sharp tongue like hers?

Elspeth looked amused. "Oh, not deliberately ye don't. And 'tis no' deliberate the way he reacts to ye, lass."

Catriona felt curiously deflated by that piece of information. "Why then?"

Elspeth shrugged. "By defying him, ye inadvertently ask him to prove himself. 'Tis the way of men."

The words were small comfort to Catriona. She felt as if her heart still pounded in her chest and thoughts of Robert were always with her. Why, she felt as many sparks between them as if they were flint and steel caught together in a tinderbox. It made no sense.

Suddenly she realized Elspeth had picked up the kettle and was moving toward the door.

Catriona hurried to take the kettle from the older woman. "I'll fetch the water, and don't be giving me any admonitions about me waiting on my own maidservant. After all you've done for me, I can do this one small thing."

A wind had begun to howl about the ancient castle, and in the Highland braes a mist had dropped in like an unexpected guest.

Catriona wrapped her cloak more tightly about her and pulled up her hood. Feeling decidedly reluctant to tempt the castle ghosts, she stuck her head out the door and peered first right, then left. When nothing moved except the rustling weeds, she took a deep breath and hurried across the ward to the well tower.

With the help of a rope she dipped the little caldron down into the well's darkness and drew it up overflowing. The water sloshed out, puddling onto the ancient stones and wetting her boots. She was still fumbling with the knot in the slick rope when she heard footsteps. Not deliberate footsteps as when Robert had come up behind her earlier, but softer, stealthier. Her fingers slid off the cold rope. Feeling slightly undone, she straightened.

"Robert?" She said his name softly, hopefully. Despite her earlier complaints about his maleness, that very maleness did have its practical uses. He was, for one thing, strong and capable with pistols and dirk.

"Robert, is that you?" she called out again, and was not surprised when no one answered. The doorway leading out of the tower was empty of anything save a lone thistle.

It was her imagination, she told herself, and turned back to the knot. Then from a rafter in the tower she heard another sound, a whir of movement as a bat flew down past her. Ducking, she gasped, barely stifling a scream. Robert must not discover her screeching over a bat, one of God's wee creatures. He would laugh at her all day tomorrow, and she didn't want him to make fun of her. Deep down, she wanted him . . . well, to like her. But getting Robert to like her, she decided, would doubtless require bravery.

Just as she'd decided that, the wind howled louder, moaning about the tower like a ghost, and again she heard the sound that reminded her of footsteps. Yes, somebody was walking outside, crushing down the weeds, one footstep at a time.

Bravery required decisive action. She moved to the doorway and stood hands on hips. A sudden suspicion, a not unpleasant one, had formed in her mind.

"Please come out from wherever you're hiding," she

called. "I know you're there." Her voice shook rather more than she liked.

A familiar figure stepped from behind the back of the tower and into the murky light provided by summer's lingering twilight and the half moon. She could make out the rueful smile and the way the figure tugged at the lace of his sleeve, which was slightly the worse for travel by now.

Her face lit up with undisguised relief. "I should have known you'd find your way here too," she said softly, relaxing. "How good to see you, Jacques."

Chapter 7

"*Mademoiselle*, I did not mean to frighten you, but I deemed it wise to avoid Monsieur Mac-Lean."

"Obviously you succeeded. He looked over the entire castle grounds but claims he saw no one . . ."

Jacques's smile only deepened, and he held out his empty hands, palms up. "Your bad-tempered Highlander did not see me because I hid beyond the castle."

"But there's no need for you to hide like that merely because Robert's manners are lacking. We have a fire going. There's some food. You'll share with us. I insist."

Jacques took a step backward. "No, no, *mam'selle,* your Robert will not like it."

"He's not *my* Robert," Catriona declared.

"As you wish," Jacques said. "In any case, in one more day I expect to arrive in your village, and I'll eat hearty there."

Catriona was determined to have her way in this matter, if only to show Robert up. "Nonsense, I won't allow it."

"And I won't allow *you* to anger your escort, *chère mademoiselle.* It is best if I do not make myself known to him."

Before Catriona could retort, Jacques backed out through the doorway. Immediately, she hurried to the door and looked around. Which way had he gone? She heard footsteps behind the well tower. After climbing over the broken stones of the wall, she headed in that direction.

"Jacques," she called. "You're being foolish." Her

voice turned smaller. "Jacques, don't do this. It's too dark to be playing hide and seek."

Ahead of her the brush crackled louder in a stand of birch trees, and she moved toward the sound, expecting to tug at Jacques's cuff at any moment.

Without warning, an unkempt man jumped out of the brush. Her heart stood still. By the light of a half moon, she took in only quick impressions. Long tattered hair. A raggedy plaid. The flash of a dirk. She turned to flee and bounced off the chest of another raggedy creature.

As if from a great distance, she heard a scream and realized it was her own. She tried to run but couldn't. Caught in a trap, she was between two frightful creatures, one short and squat, the other tall and lean. A dwarf and a giant about to carry her off to their cave—just like a nightmare she'd had many times. Only this was too real. The metallic whisper of a knife teased her back.

Guttural words shot back and forth between the men. She'd never heard the brogue spoken so fast and with such a thick accent. She could not make out a word. Then in a panicky moment, she realized this was not brogue at all, but the Erse.

She'd heard a few Scots-Gaelic phrases as a child, but now she could barely understand a word. All she understood was the frantic pounding of her heart. Knives at the ready, the creatures circled her, waiting for an opportunity to grab her.

Hugging her arms to herself, she whimpered. "Oh, dear God, Robert, why did you have to choose now to go off and cut heather?" By the time he returned she'd be boiled alive. Or at the least have caught the plague.

Like nasty claws, the creatures' hands reached out for her, and she swatted them away. "Don't touch me," she said over and over. Front and back, hands reached for her, and, whirling, she again tried to push the filthy things away. Desperate, she ducked and started to run, but her cloak caught on a tree limb. With a few frantic tugs, she managed to jerk it loose, only to fall into the arms of a third man, a hairy man who laughed through his bearded face. She had only one recourse.

She took a deep breath, as deep as possible, and screamed again.

Instead of releasing her, the three men looked at her in astonishment, then, laughing, they picked her up and hauled her off through the trees.

Moments later, Jacques Beaufort stepped from behind a bush and looked in the direction the men had taken Catriona. Cautiously he edged his way to the site of her struggle. He picked up the little volume of Shakespeare that had fallen to the ground.

Idly turning the book in his hands, he debated what to do—follow the screams and rescue the damsel himself, or put aside his reluctance to confront Robert MacLean and let the girl's escort claim the honor of being rescuer? Jacques had a pair of pistols and could have shot at least two of the bandits dead, but what would it profit *him* to rescue the impulsive *mademoiselle*—especially since he lacked experience with these creatures whom the Highlanders called bandits? And dueling was such messy work. He far preferred using malicious words to accomplish his ends.

The solution came to him like the sun after a storm. He would take the book and risk Robert's wrath by explaining Catriona's dilemma to the bad-tempered Highlander. True, Robert might be displeased to see him, but if he timed his return just right, he could earn Robert's gratitude for a deed well done.

He was not disappointed. At the well, Robert's hand shot out and grabbed him by the lace at his throat. His eyes blazed coldly, and Jacques wasn't sure but what there wasn't murder in the muddy, peat-smelling hand that tore his cravat.

"Where's Catriona, you French bastard?"

Catriona huddled inside the tiny hut and shrank away from the speculative leers of the three men. Frantic, she looked about for a way to escape. The hut, crudely built into a hill, was little more than a lean-to, the open sides facing a small clearing in the birch forest. In the center of the hut, a peat fire sent a spiral of smoke up through a hole in the roof. Nearby, an old woman with matted gray hair stirred a caldron of some vile-smelling concoction, and Catriona dearly hoped this unlikely Highland family did not plan on offering her a meal.

The father bandit and one son guarded the woods with pikestaffs while the other son, the squat fellow, fingered her red curls and locket. Forever it seemed, she endured his touch, waiting to die.

Gradually, through her fear, she became aware of running feet and crashing branches in the woods. Opening her eyes, she nearly wept as her heart soared. Robert. Striding through the trees, his chiseled features frozen into stone, he held his own dirk at the ready. The things he'd do to fulfill his bargain and deliver her to Glen Strahan, she thought. Even this. Oh, but he did look furious. To her surprise, Jacques followed—but he hung back a bit, as if he'd seen too close a glimpse of his own funeral gibbet.

Immediately, Catriona stepped forward, but the older bandit blocked her way, grabbed her arm, and dragged her outside. The father bandit, yanking her up by a handful of hair, held a dirk to her. Catching sight of her, Robert stopped suddenly in his tracks. Their eyes locked, and, with lightning speed, an unspoken message of danger passed between them.

With the tip of his dirk, the bandit sliced off a tendril of Catriona's hair, and she nearly stopped breathing. Not that she valued her hair, but her neck was so impractically close to it. Then, holding his knife like a metal salver, the bandit displayed the lock first for her pleasure and next for the admiration of Robert, who stood unmoving.

"Go back, Robert," she whispered between clenched teeth. "They'll kill you."

She risked death by even calling out a warning, but Robert must be given a chance. She shut her eyes and, moving her lips silently, said her last prayers.

Robert's voice cut through her pleas to God. He was conversing with the bandits in the Erse. Of the hasty words he spoke, Catriona understood only two phrases.

"Dinna touch the lass," Robert said. "She's my woman."

She's my woman. It was a lie, of course, but Catriona remembered the male warmth of his body close against hers and decided it was as pleasant a thought as any to die with.

Carefully, she opened her eyes to see what effect Robert's words had on the bandit's dirk. Not much. If anything, it was positioned closer to the frantic pulse in her throat. Catriona was sure that if she so much as swallowed, the blade would draw blood. And all the while, the bandit woman calmly stirred the contents of her caldron. The fire glinted off the metal and cast terrible shadows on their faces.

Though Catriona held perfectly still, her gaze sought out Robert, pleading with him silently. *I've changed my mind. Don't go back . . . Help me, Robert, and I'll never run away from you again.* He had the strangest look on his face—half angry, half . . . well, she couldn't explain it, but if she didn't know better she'd think he was afraid. Afraid of what might happen to his arranged marriage if he failed to rescue her, no doubt.

It was the bandit woman who moved next. She spoke to one of her sons in the Erse, and, like an overgrown child, the fellow argued. She snapped back, and with a petulant expression the fellow released Catriona.

"William, ye're behavin' like a heathen," the woman said to her husband—in English yet, to Catriona's profound surprise, and she couldn't have agreed more with the message.

"Take yer dirk away," the woman said in a mixture of English and Erse, "and the locket as long as the lass is offering it so nice."

Catriona hadn't realized till now that she was holding her locket in a death grip. She gasped when someone sliced the gold chain from her neck.

Then, while she watched in frozen fascination, the woman hobbled over to stand directly in front of her. She shook a spoon to motion her son away, raised a gnarled finger, and pointed it directly at Catriona. Then she cack-led, just like a witch.

"Beware, lassie," she intoned. "Beware of entering our glen and these hills. Once ye've entered these hills, ye'll ne'er return to your own home alive, not unless you be-come an outlaw like us . . ."

"Marcail," the old man said, followed by a string of Erse. The tone clearly chastised. With the tip of his dirk, he traced the outline of the silver brooch on Catriona's cape, and she leaned back as far as she could, a whimper escaping her throat. The old woman's words rang over and over in her ears, like an eerie echo. Out of the corner of her eye she saw Robert step toward her.

"Ye'll ne'er return to your Lowland home alive . . . I've the sight, ye see. I know these things." The bandit woman kept on chanting.

"No!" Desperation made Catriona react. She wanted only to close the space between herself and the safety of Robert's arms.

But as soon as she moved, so, it seemed, did everyone else—the bandits, Robert, even Jacques.

The Frenchman raised a tiny pistol and aimed it at the bandit nearest her.

Instinctively, Catriona moved between the bandit and Jacques. "Don't shoot him!" she screamed.

A shot rang out, slicing through the mist. Catriona felt a painful grip on her arm, a hard shove, and the ground came hurtling up to meet her. She landed on her stomach, Robert's body covering hers.

Someone uttered a curse, and all four of the bandits scattered to the winds, vanishing into the darkness.

Catriona lay where she was, once again pinned beneath the brawny contours of Robert MacLean's body. She knew they were both still alive because she felt his heartbeat against hers. She clung to his warmth, the way a drowning person clings to a piece of flotsam.

The strident tones of Jacques's voice broke the silence.

"Dammit, I could have shot one of them, MacLean. I've not won my share of duels in France without pos-sessing a sure aim."

Robert rolled off of Catriona and sat up. "You could have killed Catriona, you French swine!" He pulled himself to his knees.

"I suppose this means the offer of hospitality is rescinded?"

"Get back to the castle grounds," Robert ordered in a taut voice. "You're better at flirtation and lying than you are with a pistol."

"But, *monsieur*—"

"I'd rather know where you are than worry that you'll come sneaking up on us again . . . Get going!" Robert bellowed.

Jacques scurried off, calling moodily over his shoulder, "I don't want to share the castle with you barbarians. I'd rather travel all night by myself."

Catriona sat up, dusted off her bodice, rubbed a bruised elbow, and considered whether an apology would be in order for causing Robert all this trouble. Or a thank-you for rescuing her. She never got the words out because Robert was pulling her up, then tipping her face up to his and pushing a flyaway strand of hair off her face, as if examining her for injury.

"Hush, lass, they're gone. The bandits have run off. They'll no' be back this night, and neither, it seems, will Jacques."

When she could not fathom why he persisted in reassuring her, he finally solved the mystery by pulling her to him. "Catriona, hinny, do you think you can manage to stop shaking? I'll make sure you get another locket."

"I don't want another locket. I want to go back to Edinburgh." She fell against him. One of his arms came up tight around her back. Silent tears wet his shirt, and his jacket sleeve was damp from the fall to the ground. "Fie on you and your beds of peat. Fie on my grandfather and his arranged marriages." She vented all her fear and anger onto his shoulder, and he held her until the storm abated.

His hand came up to push tangled curls off her wet face, and warm fingers wiped away traces of her tears, first from one side of her face, then the other.

"If you'd only screamed louder, I'd have come sooner, lass."

She sniffled. There was a smile in his voice, the rogue. She ought to be angry at him, but Robert was holding her close again and calling her all sorts of endearments, telling her over and over that she was safe.

With an effort, she pulled away from him.

No, she wasn't safe at all. The memory of this afternoon's kiss still pulsed through her.

They looked at each other, as if both became aware of their desire at the same time. Robert spoke first.

"I posted you as sentry, lass," he said in a rougher tone of voice. "Not as the entire reconnaissance force. I suppose if I sent you out looking for Jacobites, you'd return with the Pretender himself and we'd have a full-scale rebellion on our hands."

He continued in a teasing voice. "Can you no' do anything the simple way, Catriona Ferguson? Do you have to be braver than all the men?"

Hands on hips, she glared at him. "I was minding my own business at the water tower when I found Jacques hiding from you—not trusting your Scottish hospitality."

"The Frenchman's got some sense after all, it seems—except when it comes to using a pistol." He began to peel off his jacket.

"Robert," Catriona said evenly, "if you'd been civil to Jacques, none of this would have happened. That's the only reason I followed him into the woods . . . to reassure him that he'd be welcome to share our fire and then . . ."

Catriona let her words trail off. Robert was not listening. He was reaching with his right hand to touch the coat sleeve of his left. A dark stain spread through the fabric. She glanced at her hand, the one that had clutched his left arm. Blood.

"Oh, Robert, how could you let me go on and on, clutching your coat when you were bleeding so?"

"The coat was done for anyway. I didn't see that a few tears could do much more damage, lass."

Catriona moved to inspect the wound, but Robert pulled back.

"I'm no wee creature to cosset, lass," he objected, "so dinna be suggesting one of your poultices."

She reached down for her petticoat. "No, you'd rather die from the shot. And leave *me* to find my own way to my grandfather's." She tore off a strip of cambric. "Believe it or not, I'd prefer to finish the journey with you, Robert MacLean." Moving back to him, she gave a tug to his coat sleeve, which had stuck to the drying blood, and then pulled it off.

He grimaced. "Nuisance wasting a good coat like this. Whatever possessed you to step between Jacques's pistol and that ne'er-do-well bandit?" Robert's voice sounded a bit ragged.

Catriona refused to argue with him. Gently, she rolled up his shirt sleeve to reassure herself the shot had merely grazed his skin.

Robert, however, would not be distracted.

"Answer me," he demanded between clenched teeth.

"First of all, I didn't like the old woman's prophecy. Cheeky of her to tell me I would not return home. Otherwise, they just looked rather hungry . . . once they took the dirk away from my neck."

With a gentle touch, he tipped up her chin and forced her gaze to his. "Liar. You were scared witless."

The smile in his voice warmed her to her toes. Who but Robert would ply his roguish charm on a woman while standing there wounded?

"All right," she confessed. "Yes, I was scared."

She still was. Except this time the danger came from being close to this man. The light from the fire danced off his face, cast shadows in the crags and valleys of his aquiline features, and she felt something primitive turn over in her.

"You did say the Highlanders suffered from famine," she reminded him in a small voice, tying the bandage. She looked up to find him watching her. "Elspeth will know exactly how to care for this wound," she added quickly, then paused. "May we go back now?"

Robert watched the way the firelight flickered across her face, and remembered how it had felt to hold her and comfort her. Rather nice when she was not in a fit of temper. Too nice. Nodding curtly, he turned and led the way back through the birch trees to the castle.

If he took long strides, it was because of his anger. Anger at himself for not watching over her more closely. The chit had no sense when it came to Highland dangers. Hadn't she proven that enough times already? It was his own fault she had fallen into the hands of bandits. His thoughts went back to the way he had held her and kissed her earlier. A mistake, a stupid mistake. He lengthened his strides.

Later, after his wound had been fussed over by Elspeth, Robert finally sat in the keep, tending the fire. His arm throbbed, but not as much as his conscience, and that not as much as the parts of his anatomy that had been pressed against Catriona. He flipped through her thin book of Shakespearean sonnets, as if seeking there a hint of what made her different from other women he'd kissed.

The answer wasn't in the book, so he glanced at her where she lay on the floor of the keep wrapped in a plaid. The ache intensified, an ache to feel her slim body melt into his. He buried his head on his arms, fighting back the stirrings of his body. Did he forget the lass was no common wench? A virgin yet. And he never bothered with virgins, especially one promised to Lachlan.

When he looked up again, she had opened her eyes and with a wide gaze was watching him. The firelight flickered off her face. For once she looked vulnerable.

"I saw a bat this evening," she announced in a whisper, so as not to wake Elspeth or Douglas.

"Castles are full of bats, lass," he said softly.

"I only meant that it's because of the bat that I found Jacques and because of Jacques—"

"That you found the bandits and because of the bandits—"

"You got shot . . . Oh, Robert, I'm sorry."

"We're lucky, lass, that we're nearly in Glen Strahan." Where a marriage bed with Lachlan awaited her, he thought.

She stood up, and he groaned inwardly. Twice today, he'd held her in his arms. Could he resist a third time? Such noble restraint was more than Lachlan deserved.

"Where do you think you're going, lass?"

Catriona crossed from the crude bed on the floor and came to where he sat propped up against the stone wall of the ancient castle. Her trembling hand reached down and found his. Would he spurn her or tease her?

He surprised her by pulling her down and gathering her against him. " 'When in disgrace with fortune and men's eyes . . .' " he began to recite, and didn't stop until he'd murmured the last line. " 'That then I scorn to change my state with kings.' Shakespeare and I disagree on a few fundamentals, but he's got an ear for rhythm."

"I would have expected you to recite Bible verses, not poetry."

"I live by a rogue's code of honor rather than the Ten Commandments, hinny."

"I'm sorry I called you a rogue."

"Don't be. Never apologize for the truth. Rule number one in the rogue's code. Besides, as your guardian, I suppose I ought to blame myself for the events of tonight. That's rule number two: A rogue always takes the blame."

"Oh, no, Robert, that's far too noble of you. After all, I found the bandits all by myself."

He laughed, a deep, masculine sound. "Unfortunately, lass, there's no Highland medal bestowed for such distinction, and I am feeling decidedly ignoble."

"Why?"

He was silent a moment, then: "It would take a long demonstration."

Smiling, she nestled closer to his warmth. She liked the feel of his arms, the sound of his voice reverberating through her, playing on her soul.

"If I were your grandfather," he said, "I'd lock you away in a library, with nothing but books for comfort. Far more conducive to a man's peace of mind, you ken."

"But you're much warmer than a book."

It was on that thought that she fell asleep. When she awoke in the early morning Robert was gone, but his plaid covered her still, and the book of sonnets lay near her hand.

Chapter 8

The travelers stopped their horses at a natural vantage point for their first look at Glen Strahan. Glen Strahan, the place where in one week Robert would be wed to another woman. Catriona felt her chest tighten.

If the expression on his face was any indication, Robert was pleased to be home. His eyes practically devoured the village. He'd probably forgotten already that he'd held and kissed her, Catriona decided. But then, no doubt rogues took kissing more in stride than she did. Swallowing the lump in her throat, she turned her attention back to the bird's eye view of the village.

Her first glimpse of Glen Strahan brought unexpected memories—a little glen nestled below the fells, the heather-covered hills where she and Angus had once ridden ponies. Now cattle dotted the hills like black currants. Loch Aislair, a sapphire jewel, nestled in the middle, and at one tip of the loch on land's end stood that unforgettable feudal guardian, Castle Fenella MacLean, more dark and forbidding than she remembered, a giant rock fist. Fields of oats and barley fit in wherever a Highlander could scrabble some topsoil and level ground.

Far across Loch Aislair, nestled back among the fells, sat a familiar manor house, the home of Catriona's childhood. Lacking the feudal fortifications of the castle, the stately manor house stood on open unguarded ground, its dark stone walls punctuated by casement windows.

Memories rushed back. Herself as a wee lass caught between two feuding Highlanders—one a chief, one her grandfather. Because of them she'd been banished, her life turned upside down. Amazingly the pain was still there, keen and bitter.

"I never realized how far Ferguson Manor was from the rest of the village," she said out loud to Elspeth, trying to staunch the old wound with idle chatter.

"The manor house had to be separate from the castle, ye ken. 'Twas a rival chief who built the manor before Angus bought it. It was safer to be separate."

With a start, Catriona realized she was watching Robert instead of the scenery. She pulled her attention back to Elspeth's lecture.

"The Fergusons came late to Glen Strahan, and the MacLean of the castle was the chief of the village." Elspeth pointed at the village lane far below. "See how it runs in a straight line right toward the castle? And then look across Loch Aislair at how Ferguson Manor depends on itself."

"Completely cut off from the village," Catriona said softly. "The manor house is open to plundering by the MacLeans, or so I've been told." Catriona was thinking of the way Robert's mouth had plundered hers.

"Well, Angus could afford to be independent of course." Elspeth's face was animated. "Oh, he's surrounded by his own clansmen, mind, because he needed protection from MacLean raids in the early years, but as for wealth, he brought it with him when he sold his whiskey trade."

"It's strange Robert and I didn't know each other," Catriona said softly. "After all, we lived in the same village, didn't we, Robert?" She looked at him.

He tore his gaze away from the glen, his expression thoughtful. "Not strange at all. As Elspeth said, our grandfathers were always feuding. My grandfather was the clan chief but poor, your grandfather the interloper with wealth. Given those circumstances, a bit of jealous rivalry was bound to fester."

The horses moved restlessly, and in the process of catching the reins to Catriona's mount, Robert allowed his thigh to brush her leg. She could feel the taut strength of masculine muscle.

Reining his horse back a few steps, Robert looked directly at her. "You were also much younger than I, lass," he said. "On top of that, I was discouraged from calling on playmates at Ferguson Manor."

"I was afraid of the wicked chief of Fenella MacLean," Catriona confessed. "All I did was play with my collie and—"

"You were the little girl with the dog," he said suddenly, a disarming grin on his face.

"Yes." Suddenly she could scarcely recall her dog's name; all she could think about was Robert's smile. His expression was unguarded—and more appealing than ever.

"Aye," he said, "I remember once the dog knocked over a sack of barley, and a little girl climbed up a tree just outside the kirkyard and threw green pears down on the lad who was trying to punish the collie. That was *you?*"

Suspicious, Catriona asked, "Were you the boy who was tormenting Shep?"

"Me? Cruel to a defenseless animal—to one of God's wee creatures?" Robert asked. He sounded insulted, but it was his way of teasing. "What do you take me for? I chased the rude fellow away."

"Then was it Lachlan?"

As he considered that, his brows dove into a frown.

"As like as not," he admitted.

Another reason not to wed Lachlan, she thought. Anyone who would poke a stick at a dog was unsuited to be her husband.

Catriona turned back to the view and squinted down through the soft rain at the glen. "Why did you help me?" she asked.

Again, Robert's brows knit together, and he shot a quick look her way. "It happened a long time ago, lass. No doubt I stood in mortal fear of getting hit by one of your green pears if I didn't. And who knows what Angus Ferguson will do now if I dinna deliver you there posthaste?"

She wanted to scream at him. Didn't he care a bit that

they were about to part? Yet without another word, he set
his heels to his horse's flank, and she had no choice but
to follow him down into the glen and along the dirt lane
of Glen Strahan.

Catriona had been so young when she'd left that she'd
forgotten what a Highland village looked like—a humble
stretch of homely cottages, some of simple sod, others
whitewashed with thatched roofs like so many unpow-
dered wigs. A pony cart with a load of dripping wet peat,
driven by a lad in homespun clothing, rattled by on its
way to the castle. It was all so different from Edinburgh
with its tall black buildings past which strutted sleek horses
drawing fancy carriages belonging to silk-clad ladies and
gentlemen.

"Robert!" A homey figure, a woman with hair coiled
on her head, darted around the cart and crossed the street
to greet them, and Catriona's thoughts were pulled back
to the village. "Robert!"

"Fiona Grant!" Robert replied, slowing his horse.
"Where's that farrier husband of yours? Still tending to
the village horses all night and day?"

Despite Robert's jovial greeting, Mrs. Grant frowned;
her face was as dour as soured milk. "Robert, you've got
to help—"

She never finished her sentence. Someone else ran out
into the street. "Master Robert!"

"Agnes Drummond! I've outgrown the last shirt you
stitched for me," Robert said with a smile, and before he
could engage in conversation more villagers claimed his
attention. One by one he gave a kind word to all who came
to greet him. They were plainly dressed and barefoot, the
men in saffron shirts and short plaids or trews, the women
in homespun dresses. The farrier's wife, Fiona Grant. The
seamstress, Agnes Drummond. A tenant crofter, Fraser
Robertson. The butcher, Thomas MacKay. Oh, but it was
a horde of people surrounding Robert, a variety of emotions in their faces.

"God's wounds, if it's no' Robbie MacLean."

Catriona turned to see whose voice had boomed the
latest greeting. A man strode out of the farrier's shop and

with quick footsteps crossed a mud puddle to the center of the street.

"Colin Grant, a sight for sore eyes. I wouldna know ye with yer beard. But your voice still rumbles like Highland thunder!"

As the farrier shook Robert's hand, still other villagers appeared in their doorways and came forward to encircle the travelers, smiling and reaching up to touch Robert, as if his handshake alone would bring good luck. Over and over they chanted his name like a litany.

Robert. Robert. Robert.

Women held woolen shawls over their heads and tittered in gossip while others handed him gifts—a black bun from one, a handful of damp, drooping daisies from another. Children came running, dogs yipping in their wake, wagging their tails. Despite the Highland rain, they all made it a welcome homecoming, with cheer upon cheer and the same words echoed over and over in the tone of proud pipes:

"Robert's returned. Robert's come home." Soon, though, the exchange of greetings gave way to an onslaught of excited questions.

"Given up university for a bride and bairns, eh?" Colin Grant asked. "I predicted so when ye left."

With a nod, Robert smiled, oblivious to the rain glistening in his hair. "I'd forgotten the haste with which the village likes its news. Tell me this—is there a stranger lately arrived in Glen Strahan, a Frenchman?"

"Aye." A veritable chorus of voices responded, and then Colin Grant stepped forward as spokesman and recounted how Jacques Beaufort was not only there but was spending his time at the wee kirk, sketching it. "And he's fond of the Stuarts," the farrier said, as if Jacques were some nasty insect.

Robert nodded. "The very fellow. Talk is easy and I know the land is hard, but dinna let him lead ye into another rebellion yet."

"Robert, ye've grown too serious down in Edinburgh with yer books," Agnes Drummond pronounced, shifting a straw basket to her other hip. "Introduce us to yer bride," she said, looking hopefully at Catriona. At the same time her own husband slung an affectionate arm around Agnes's shoulder.

"Is this the lady?" Mr. Drummond asked.

Robert's expression betrayed not a nuance of his thoughts.

"No," Catriona answered quickly, pushing wet curls off her face. It was a natural assumption, she supposed, that Robert might ride home with his betrothed. "I'm not his lady."

At her quick denial, Robert's mouth tilted. She knew what he saw. A red-faced, too scrawny lass, pushing back a tangle of curly wet hair. She had the most awful suspicion that she resembled a wet rat . . . and she hadn't even known how to kiss. She could well imagine he found the Drummonds' question amusing. Most amusing.

"This is Lachlan's lady," Robert offered.

A stillness fell over the villagers. Robert might as well have announced that Catriona had grown three thumbs or had arrived bearing the plague. She felt a dozen pairs of curious eyes on her, all waiting as if for her to breathe fire. By now the mist had turned to rain. A most inauspicious homecoming indeed.

Robert reached for her horse's reins, which had fallen slack, and at that moment a toothless old lady pushed back the plaid from her head and squinted up at Catriona. Wet hands, stained with dye and callused from weaving, reached out to touch the edge of her cloak. After Catriona's encounter with the bandits, it was a natural reflex for her to shrink away from a strange old woman.

But this one smiled, and her eyes sparkled. "Ye're the little bairn from the manor come home at last, ain't ye?" The toothless smile widened.

Catriona nodded, though she had no memory of this woman. Reverend Macaulay's widowed mother, someone said.

The woman rubbed her hands together in glee. "Aye, I thought as much. I remember ye well on yer pony rides around Loch Aislair. A little redheaded bairn who would pluck herbs from my cottage with Angus watching. Catriona was your name?"

The old lady was rewarded with a nod. Aware of Robert watching her and smiling Catriona smiled too, a bit uncertainly.

"Come home to wed Lachlan," the old woman continued. "Oh, that Angus. First he sends ye away wi'out a word and now he brings you back all growed up. A fine peace offering for ending the feud, lass. Too fine for the likes of Lachlan."

"Hush your mouth, old woman," Colin Grant said. His voice was stern but held a measure of affection.

"You're all prattling too much." Robert's suddenly stern tone startled everyone into a respectful silence. Even the rain suddenly let up. Only a light mist hung in the air, while men suddenly doffed their caps and women smoothed their aprons.

"Now then," Robert said, "what's this I hear about unrest in the village? What's happened?"

The farrier stepped forward. "Two of our lasses have died suddenly, Robert. Found in the rocky crags above the loch, not a mark on either lass. Two fresh graves bide in the wee kirkyard, and the womenfolk are afraid."

Robert looked around at the faces of the villagers. Their expressions, which moments earlier had been exuberantly welcoming him, had become shuttered like petals closing at darkness.

"You're certain it's no' some malady?"

"It's possible," Mrs. Drummond said. "E'en now my lad lies ill."

All through the crowd, heads were shaking and eyes shone with veiled hostility. "That's no' the same, Mrs. Drummond . . . Robbie, ye've got to help us. It's no' natural the way the lasses died without mark or warning . . ."

One of the women lifted her apron to her face and began to weep, while old Mrs. Macaulay moved to embrace her.

"The mother of one of the lasses, Robert," the farrier said.

Catriona's heart went out to the grieving woman, and she noted with relief that Reverend Macaulay joined his mother in offering words of comfort as well. He looked, Catriona noticed, exactly the way she'd assumed Robert would. Spare and garbed in black and with a prominent Adam's apple bobbing as he talked.

"Has Sheriff MacIvie looked into this?" Robert asked.

Catriona felt a tangible hardening of the mood.

"He's done what he can," Colin Grant said, scowling.

"I'll talk to him as well," Robert said. "Keep your eyes and ears open, and I'll do the same." To Mrs. Drummond he had a special word. "May your lad be well and on his feet soon."

Before the crowd could press in again, he handed Catriona back her reins. The travelers continued to wind their way through the village and on about the loch to the very borders of Ferguson land, land that had in centuries past belonged to MacLeans.

When Robert stopped, Catriona's heart began to pound. And so the moment had come—farewell to her strong-willed escort and reunion with her grandfather. Robert had fulfilled his promise to deliver her to Ferguson Manor intact, and that's all she meant to him, she reminded herself—a bargain completed. Delivered virginal and alive, just as her grandfather decreed. Strange then that it hurt to breathe.

"To be certain you'll no' run away, I should escort you right into your grandfather's hands," he mused, and moved as if to spur his horse nearer to the house.

"No! Don't set foot on Ferguson land," she snapped. Then, in a gentler tone, said, "When I meet my grandfather, it will be *alone.*"

She bit back the threat of tears and stared up the rocky lane at the grand house. For a minute, neither of them moved. At last she urged her horse forward.

"What will you do first?" Robert's voice behind her sounded almost tender.

Catriona decided she must be hearing things and, after reining to a stop, glared back at him. "First of all," she replied, "I intend to tell my grandfather what I think of his plans for my marriage."

Robert smiled. "That would be a conversation to eavesdrop on."

She was on the point of smiling back when suddenly he turned serious again. "Will you be all right from this point on?"

To tell the truth, she wasn't sure. She had an awful premonition of danger, which of course was silly. It was her nerves, still shaken from the bandit woman's curse . . . or mayhap from the fear she'd seen in the villagers' faces just now . . . or the memories of the Regalia that being back in Glen Strahan had stirred up.

Robert waited, his glance flicking over her across the several yards that separated them. A veritable Highland chasm.

"What will *you* do next?" she asked timidly. Even from this distance, she could see the lines that creased his face when he smiled, though he managed a tender look. "Do? I'll go to the castle, of course, and warn Lachlan that his bride-to-be is a fiery lady dragon and not to be trifled with."

She gathered up her reins to turn about, pretending to bristle. "You may tell Lachlan that I'll not be showing up for any wedding in seven days, or ever."

A curious expression crossed Robert's craggy features— a cloud, but chased off in short order by his easygoing words. "I shall miss seeing you at the betrothal banquet then, Catriona. You do, however, have a few days in which to change your mind."

All formality had returned to his face and voice. No calling her "hinny" or even "lass."

"Never," she said. Unaccountably, she found herself wondering if this Englishwoman he intended to wed was pretty.

"Your mind is made up then. I wish you well in convincing Angus."

"And I wish you a long and happy life," she said, equally formal. Tit for tat. Then why did her words sound so stiff and wrong? As if the two of them had never touched, never argued, never kissed?

"I'll tell her when I meet her," he said at last. "Have you any other messages for my bride?"

"Aye . . . tell her . . . that she must change the dressing on your wound every day." Her voice sounded different, as if she might do something silly like cry, though heaven knew he'd seen enough of her tears on the journey up here. And she so hated the weepy heroines in her books.

He turned his horse to go.

"Robert." The word slipped out and there was no taking it back.

When he reined in and looked over his shoulder, she added, "I forgot to thank you for rescuing me. Angus will surely thank you as well."

This wasn't as easy as he'd expected, Robert thought. After days of anticipating being rid of her, he felt curiously wooden. "Dinna be too tart-tongued with your poor old grandfather now, lass. Do ye promise?"

She bit her lip and finally nodded. It was a forlorn gesture from a proud little eagle, suddenly trapped and clipped.

Watching her wheel her horse and ride away from him, Robert fought off an even stranger mix of emotions. Already he regretted what he'd said and what he'd left unsaid. He wanted to gallop after her and kiss the silly pride out of her stiff words, but they were in Glen Strahan. She was on Ferguson land. And she belonged to Lachlan now. With a swift kick of his heels, he spurred the horse forward and headed for the castle.

Castle Fenella MacLean stood as he remembered it, a dark stone fortress, medieval in appearance, jutting out above Loch Aislair, towers and ramparts inviting only those without faint heart to enter. Robert had always admired its structure and its history, but he had never let himself feel too attached because, after all, he was not the heir. Lachlan was.

And now Catriona would be coming here to live—here to this very castle. The thought of her in Lachlan's bed, innocent and vulnerable, made him feel the same fear he'd just seen on the villagers' faces.

Passing beneath the raised iron yett, he pushed his horse into the inner ward, then dismounted and handed the reins to a bowing ostler from the stables. With Douglas at his heels he strode up a few worn stone steps and past more bowing lackeys until he reached the heavy oaken door to the great hall.

He pushed open the door and entered, pausing just inside until his eyes became accustomed to the gloom. On the surface, not much had changed. The place was still lit by a meager supply of tallow candles, and on the stone walls hung a vast array of banners, swords, tapestries, and blindly staring stag heads. Oh, without a doubt, it was familiar, yet after the years he'd spent in civilized Edinburgh, the room seemed formidable, harsh, no longer a place that invited boyhood games.

Looking across the great hall to the massive fireplace, he saw his family—what was left of it—and moved to greet them.

Alexander MacLean, the aging chief, sat polishing the fowling piece that lay across his lap—a docile greyhound at his feet. When Robert had been here last, it had been a falcon he was training and broadswords he sharpened. So it seemed Alexander was slowing down.

As he caught sight of his grandson, the old laird's eyes lit with pleasure. His face had more lines now than an Edinburgh map, and his hair had whitened to winter snow. Cousin Grizel sat talking at the trestle table near his grandfather. With jerky strokes she moved a needle and thread in and out of a stretch of tapestry, embroidering what appeared to be a serpent. At her elbow sat a bird cage in which was perched a lark. While he watched, Grizel set down her tapestry and picked up a cracked walnut with which to entice the bird. As soon as it flitted close to the bars, she poked it with her needle and laughed to see the hurt flutter of its wings.

"Grizel," Robert called, "if ye dinna have anything better to do with that needle, go and find Lachlan."

"Lachlan doesn't want you back, Robert," she said without looking at him.

God's wounds, but Grizel had never possessed a measure of tact or warmth. No wonder she remained a spinster after the death of her sole beau. Pity. Ian Ferguson might have made a softer woman of her.

Robert turned his attention to the most honored of Glen Strahan—his grandfather . . .

The MacLean of Strahan, still tall, stood and came toward Robert. Never having been a demonstrative man, he did not embrace his grandson, but a keen pleasure shone in his eyes.

He turned to a servant. "Bring us each a dram. This is a welcome-home for my grandson. Make haste."

While they waited for the refreshment, Robert allowed his grandfather to circle him, as if examining him for any changes time had wrought. "The Lowlands have no' weakened ye, lad. More braw than ever." The aging chief possessed a shrewd glance, yet his stooped shoulders were clear evidence to Robert that the years were taking their toll on the older man.

"So ye have escorted Angus Ferguson's granddaughter here?"

"Aye, I saw her to the edge of her grandfather's property."

"Ferguson land, bah! That has been MacLean land— ever since the days of Robert the Bruce—and we shall have it back again. The Fergusons are no more than temporary interlopers."

"Is that why you betrothed Lachlan to a Ferguson? Because she brings land as her dowry?"

His grandfather's white eyebrows shot up in surprise. "Ye've grown wise as well as braw down in Edinburgh, laddie. Aye, we're too poor to continue the feud. We need both peace *and* the lass's dowry."

Robert accepted a mug of whiskey from a scraping servant and took a long pull. "Catriona is not the sort of lass to let herself be used as a pawn," he said suddenly, surprising even himself.

His grandfather laughed. "She has no say in it, and why

should ye care?'' He studied Robert. ''Is there something wrong with the wench?'' his grandfather asked. ''Something that Lachlan will find unappealing?'' Shrewd blue eyes—much like Robert's own—stared back, waiting.

''There's nothing about her that Lachlan—or any man—would not find appealing,'' he said at last.

''Ye dinna act glad to be home,'' Alexander observed.

Robert ran a weary hand through his hair. ''There's no need to be at cross purposes. I'm most grateful to be out of Edinburgh.''

A servant handed him a fresh pewter tankard of whiskey. After taking a sip, Robert sank down onto a wooden bench. He stared at the lark in its cage and suddenly stayed Grizel's hand before she could poke the hapless creature again.

He turned to study her while he drank. Black-eyed and black-haired, Grizel never missed a thing that went on around her. Even now, as he stripped off his sole remaining jacket, her black gaze took in the bandage on Robert's arm.

''Did the Ferguson lass bite?'' Grizel asked.

''Bandits,'' Robert replied carelessly, hoping to deflect her sarcasm. ''Catriona and her woman put on some herbal potion and bandaged me, so dinna get ideas of teasing her—''

''Teasing her?'' Grizel ran the tips of her fingers over the serpent she stitched, as if petting it. ''Why, Robert, you sound so protective. What happened on the journey? Lachlan will kill you if you bedded the wench.'' She said the words as coolly as if she'd announced that dinner was served.

His grandfather banged down his tankard. ''Ye were to bring her here intact. That was understood.'' With bolder strides than Robert would have expected, he came after him.

Robert tossed his cocked hat onto the table and stood. ''Dinna question my honor.'' He was on the verge of losing his temper, he realized, and softened his voice. ''She's no' a common whore,'' he added, and moved around the table, restless at the direction of this conversation.

Struggling to hold his tongue, he stared at a fine old tapestry on the wall—Adam and Eve entwined—and fought down the searing urge to entwine himself about Catriona and burn himself with her fire.

"Go on then, Robert," Grizel urged with exaggerated sarcasm. "Tell us what happened that makes you so worried about Lachlan's dear betrothed."

Robert set down his mug. He placed the flat of both palms on the table and leaned toward his cousin. "I told you, Grizel. She was captured by bandits. I had to rescue her."

"Gi'e o'er, Robert. If it was naught but bandits she'll get over the scare. The lass was born a Highlander, wasn't she?"

Robert had not come all this way to play Grizel's games. "Where's Lachlan?" he demanded.

"I'm right here, listening," said an imperious voice. Lachlan moved out of the shadows by the stairwell. "I'm waiting to hear whether you will try to charm our grandfather out of my own lawful inheritance. He's favored you in most other ways."

Stunned at the bitterness of the words, Robert watched Lachlan stride into the great hall, his expression one of ill-concealed loathing, a well-remembered cruelty in his eyes.

"Is the wench worth bedding?" Lachlan asked.

Robert's hand closed on his tankard. It took all of his willpower not to pull his dirk and drive it into Lachlan's black heart. His cousin's jealousy was more unreasonable than ever.

"Aye," he said at last, "and I saved her maidenhead for you," he added, reasoning that the best way to deal with Lachlan was on his same crude terms.

"I didn't think you'd be so eager to see me, cousin," Lachlan observed, circling the table and reaching for the whiskey, which he drank straight from the bottle. He set it down and wiped a dribble off his chin. "Somehow I assumed your first care would be for this Englishwoman you're so intent on wedding. Instead it's my Ferguson bride who concerns you.'' Sarcasm laced his words. He shoved the bottle in Robert's direction.

Robert ignored it. ''Catriona sent you a message.''

''Indeed? Catriona, is it? And has she come to call you Robert?''

He ignored the insinuation. ''She's no' wanting to wed. If she can talk Angus out of the bargain, you'll mayhap no' see her at the banquet. She's filled with temper so you may have the better bargain if she refuses you.''

Lachlan tossed back his head and laughed. ''Did they no' teach you how to lie better than that in your fancy Edinburgh?''

''She's more innocent than any lass you've known, Lachlan.''

''Tell me more of my bride-to-be, Robert. A temper you say. Tell me, will I like her?''

Too much, Robert feared. ''She's no' what you'd expect, Lachlan.''

Lachlan raised his eyebrows in mock horror. ''Trying to talk me out of her? You'd no' be having an eye on her yourself, would you, Robert?''

With a rough movement, Robert slammed a hand against the plank table. He would lose control if Lachlan rubbed one more grain of salt in the wound that had festered between them since boyhood.

Lachlan's smile held a caustic edge. ''Grandfather needs the land that comes with her dowry. To please him, I can manage to deflower an innocent. I'm not entirely without practice here in the village—''

Scarcely aware of what he did, Robert moved around the table and grabbed Lachlan by his plaid and yanked it to his throat. ''Hurt the lass and you'll live to rue the day you put a hand to her.''

Quickly, Alexander MacLean stepped between his two grandsons. ''Unhand each other!'' he commanded, a veined fist shaking where he restrained each of his grandsons' collars. ''Not back a half hour and already fighting over a woman—and over this poor castle.'' He turned to Lachlan. ''If I have seemed to favor Robert, it is because he leaves me more often. Nothing more.'' Letting go of

Lachlan, he turned to his other grandson. "Robert would rather have his own marriage of alliance than my favoritism, wouldn't ye, Robert?"

Robert stood there, struggling for control. "Of course, as I also want our titles restored." He stared directly at Lachlan. "I do it for my father's honor, not to curry favor with Grandfather." Somehow he forced enthusiasm into his voice and deftly changed the subject. "Does the Englishwoman's family arrive tomorrow?" he asked.

Alexander nodded.

"A message came that her family refuses to travel to the wilds of Scotland," Grizel said with a laugh. "So she comes with her uncle, your fancy English lord . . . aye, tomorrow, if you can bide that long."

Sneering, Lachlan tipped the whiskey bottle to his mouth. "Betrothed to an English and smitten with Catriona Ferguson, are ye, Robert? Now I'm more curious than ever to sample the Ferguson wench." With malicious laughter, he gulped the whiskey again, while Robert stalked from the room.

Chapter 9

C atriona rushed up to the housekeeper who opened the door of Ferguson Manor.

"Is my grandfather about? I need to see him at once."

Even to her own ears, her voice sounded dictatorial, as if a Highland regiment had arrived to see Angus and she were the commander-in-chief.

The housekeeper, Mrs. Burns, a rawboned Highland woman of plain face, blanched and ducked a curtsy, the keys at the waist of her dark blue dress jingling. "Begging your pardon, Miss Catriona, but Angus Ferguson asked that you be settled in before he spoke with you. I've orders to show you to your room first."

"But I don't want to rest—"

"Catriona," Elspeth warned, "a wee rest sounds just the thing before ye talk to Angus."

Catriona considered the merits of that suggestion. During a "wee rest," she could examine the porcelain in the house and decide, should it come to a throwing match, which would create the dandiest smash. She could torture herself with thoughts of Robert's wedding night. Or she could go over in her head for the umpteenth time the little speech she had prepared for Angus and add saltier language to it. "A rest does sound useful," she conceded.

Entering the hallway, she slipped off her wet cloak, but refused to part with it.

"Aye, and the place has scarce changed a bit," Elspeth was saying, her eyes shining. "Compared to Castle Fenella MacLean and the village, 'tis a new manor house,

125

ye ken, hinny—scarcely a century's passed since these
rooms were laid out and plastered. A chandelier in the
dining room fell down once, so the story goes, and ever
since only candelabra are used.''

Catriona listened to Elspeth in a daze. The instant she
had set foot inside the manor house and laid eyes again on
the glossy wood of the hallway, feelings of homecoming
had overwhelmed her. Never mind that Edinburgh had
been her residence for the past fifteen years. She was aware
of vague memories tugging at her, urging her down into
some dark painful recess she didn't want to see. Like bad
dreams from her past in which the heroine got caught by
the dragon.

"It might have started out as a castle," Elspeth was
saying. "A rival to Fenella MacLean. But Angus's forebears did away with all the defenses and made it a cozy
residence. 'Twas yer father knew all the history.''

They were heading up the staircase to the upper floor,
and Catriona let her hand glide along the polished balus-
trade, while beneath her feet worn wood groaned its welcome.

Elspeth's voice echoed on the stairwell. "Why, he told
us that Cromwell himself marched up here trying to claim
more than his due, but the Fergusons held tight to it.''

Mrs. Burns led Catriona to her old bedroom, the one
with a view overlooking Loch Aislair. At once she saw it
had been redecorated. Gone were her childhood play-
things, and a profound disappointment gripped her.

She stood in the middle of the chamber and looked
about, imagining herself an auctioneer about to evict Angus Ferguson for the high crime of betrothing his granddaughter to a family of Highland rogues.

The bed hung with tartan designed fabric would fetch a
tidy price, especially if she claimed Queen Mary had slept
here. Prints of Highland scenery decorated the walls, and
they'd be dear to buy. On a chest beneath the casement
window sat a vase of daisies and dried heather. Worth a
bit, especially if the chest were antique. She ought to be
able to scrape up enough in this room alone to have her
grandfather transported.

Mrs. Burns opened up an armoire, finer even than the one Catriona's grandfather had auctioned out from under her in Edinburgh. It was well nigh empty—except for a gown of velvet and brocade, and a plaid in the Ferguson colors. A pair of woolen shifts completed the wardrobe.

"New gowns are being stitched now in the village for your dowry, miss," explained Mrs. Burns. "The seamstress, Mrs. Drummond, only needs to take your measure."

"I won't require them," Catriona informed her abruptly, collapsing face down on the bed. The lump in her throat was so big it felt like a pear. She hadn't known she'd miss Robert so much. Rolling onto her back, she pressed a hand to her eyes, a dramatic gesture calculated to forestall questions.

"Mistress Ferguson is weary from her journey," Elspeth said by way of explanation. "And I also. Mayhap we can discuss gowns later. Will ye show me where I shall sleep and then find some household duty for me? I dislike idle hands, especially my own, and I need some work to keep me busy."

"Elspeth—"

"Dinna air yer grievances in front of the servants, hinny," Elspeth whispered.

Catriona removed her hand and glared mutinously at her maidservant.

"Wait to speak to Angus." Elspeth met Catriona's glare with one of her own and slipped out behind the housekeeper to the small anteroom which held her bed.

"Mrs. Burns," Catriona said, calling the woman back, "when exactly did my grandfather say he'd meet me?"

Mrs. Burns peered in the doorway at Catriona's prostrate figure and shrugged. "I dinna ken. Your arrival's no' been announced to him yet, miss."

"Why not?" She feigned a yawn, as if the matter were of scant importance.

"He's ne'er disturbed at this hour of the day, miss," Mrs. Burns announced mysteriously, then left.

At the click of the door latch, Catriona sat up and pounded a fist into her pillow. How could she rest with an unwanted marriage looming? But nothing would be gained by losing her temper. Not yet.

Slipping out of her bedchamber, she began to explore the nooks and crannies of the manor house, looking for Angus. She'd announce her own arrival.

Searching through room after room, she explored first upstairs and then down, the creaking stairs announcing her to every spider. She peered in the dining room, then the parlor. At last she pushed open the door to the library and saw a vase of dried white heather. She remembered that a rare bush of white heather grew up in the moors behind Angus's manor house. She'd not seen it since childhood. She looked around more carefully.

The library was filled with book-lined shelves, while damask draperies had been pushed back to let in a fine Highland sun. The upholstery in the library gleamed as only scarlet leather could, and a carpet cushioned her feet. A game table dominated the center of the room, and on the fireplace mantel sat an hourglass for keeping time. A favorite childhood object of hers it was. She turned it over and watched the white sand rush through the narrow middle. As tears sprang to her eyes, Catriona touched the furniture, the finely filigreed plaster of the walls. Oh, yes, this room was as familiar as if she'd stepped out of it just yesterday. In *this* room her grandfather had banished her.

She was bent over the vase of white heather again, a finger barely brushing the brittle blooms, when footsteps paused at the door. Catriona whirled.

"Excuse me, miss," Mrs. Burns said, "but I believe your companion is no' well. A bit of the headache. There's a sickness in the village, ye ken."

"So I heard."

"Asked me to brew a potion she did." Mrs. Burns's voice sounded dubious.

Catriona looked at the leather pouch of crushed herbs and the stillroom book of handwritten receipts Mrs. Burns held. "Yes, it's quite all right. Heat the milk and add a teaspoon of leaves and stir it. It's quite simple and safe."

"Aye, miss," Mrs. Burns said, still dubious. "As you say."

Catriona followed her to the kitchens in the back of the house. "Mrs. Burns, I've looked all over and my grandfather is nowhere to be found."

"The staff ne'er disturbs his game," Mrs. Burns said over her shoulder.

"Game?" Catriona was truly astonished. "He has the audacity to have me dragged halfway across Scotland and threatens to marry me off to a MacLean barbarian and when I arrive he's busy playing a game?"

"I'm sorry, lass. He's given strict orders."

Summoning the last bit of patience she possessed, she said as calmly as possible, "I don't care if he's in the stables playing dice. I shall see him—now."

Mrs. Burns bobbed her head. "He'll be frightful upset with me for interrupting his golf."

Golf! "I won't let him be angry at you. I'll pretend I found him myself. Now tell me, if I were going to play golf, where would you suggest I go?"

A sly smile lit Mrs. Burns's plain face. She pointed the way behind the manor to a field bare of trees.

Moments later, Catriona watched in silence from the wild grass while a stocky man swung a wooden stick at a clump of thistles.

"It's golf, Miss Catriona," explained the stableboy who had intercepted her and followed her to the back of the Ferguson estate.

"Yes, so I see," she said, a bit more brusquely than she intended.

"He sold the ponies off years ago—after your parents left—and dug holes all over the field. He spends hours trying to stuff that little ball into the holes. Dinna ask me what it's about, for I dinna ken." He lowered his voice conspiratorially. "If it were me, I'd hold the ball over the little hole and drop it straight down, but it's not me place to advise him. Meself, I prefer a good game of cards. Warmer, you know."

"Aye, you've been most forthright." Actually, she'd heard much about the game of golf from friends of her father in Edinburgh—at the Leith links men neglected their duties to chase the wee ball from hole to hole all day long.

And though she'd never wielded a golf club herself, it looked to be an admirable way of venting one's frustration. Someday perhaps she'd try it, but for now, she watched her grandfather and let the memories have their way.

Angus Ferguson was dressed in the familiar saffron shirt and blue bonnet that she remembered so well. The short plaid that swung about his spindly knees was woven in the familiar dark green colors of the clan Ferguson. As for Angus himself, he was much older than she'd remembered. Smaller too. But then, no doubt he'd find her older as well—and taller.

He swung the stick, and a small round object went flying through the sky. The golf ball. An enticingly tight little bundle of feathers bound in leather.

She shaded her eyes to watch it land, and when she looked back Angus had turned and was staring at her. For a second, some familiar emotion flashed in his eyes, but then it vanished.

It was painful to swallow. She strode forward, purpose in her steps. "Hello . . . Grandfather." The familiar term sounded foreign.

Moisture glistened in his eyes as if the wind stung them. He turned away, busying himself swinging the golf stick. "Ye've grown older, lassie," he said, and then tramped away in the direction of the ball.

Catriona had no patience with him. Lifting the hem of her cloak against the wild grass, she headed with determined steps in the wake of her grandfather. Damn him! After all those letters, he had no right to ignore her as if she were a weed grown too tall.

"Grandfather—"

"Stand back."

She stopped in her tracks, watching while he swung yet again. With a whack the little round ball went arcing through the air, landed with a hard thump, and finally bounced to a stop. Angus stood poised, plaid swinging about his knees in the wind, golf club still positioned over his shoulder, while he peered ahead at the ball, which lay somewhere in a nest of wild grass.

"I'm not going to marry Lachlan MacLean," Catriona said in desperation.

Very slowly Angus lowered the club. Cradling his hands over the club handle, he leaned into it and looked at her. The lines about his eyes deepened. "So ye grew up to be as stubborn as yer mother and father combined, lassie."

She walked closer to him. "Perchance you could have asked my opinion of my bridegroom first," she countered, not about to be waylaid by sentimentality.

"Ask ye, lass? Marriage is a family duty. Besides, I've given my oath."

"And how is this alliance with a MacLean barbarian going to help the family? I deserve to know that at least."

"When yer last cousin fell under a carriage wheel a year ago, that made ye my only kin—heir to all the Ferguson holdings."

"I found it hard to believe you even remembered my existence, let alone that I was your heir," she said, not even trying to control her caustic tongue.

"I'd not forgotten ye, lass. I had my reasons for sending ye away."

"I remember," she snapped. "I want to discuss what's happening to me now." Her words were muffled by the wind.

He paused. "I have decided it is time the feud between the MacLeans and the Fergusons ended. They get back the land they lost a hundred years ago, and Alexander has agreed that yer second son will bear the name of Ferguson. That way our Ferguson line will no' die out. A perfect solution."

Catriona set her hands on her hips. "For everyone but me. I don't know this Lachlan. I'd sooner toil in a kitchen over the oatmeal pot or grind meat for your white puddings than wed a man I've never met."

"Still as prone to melodramatics as when ye were a wee lass, I see. If ye must know, such a marriage will also buy ye protection from Jacobite agents."

Blinking in confusion, Catriona pushed a strand of windblown hair from her eyes. "Well, I don't know why I'd be of interest to Jacobite agents."

"But ye said ye remember why I sent ye away, lass."

"I know," she said in renewed exasperation. "The Regalia. I stumbled across some clan chiefs hiding Scotland's greatest treasure. But I was only seven, and it was only a chest. If a Jacobite agent came straight from the Pretender and put me to the rack, what could I tell him? Nothing. Not about the Regalia. I have no real knowledge of its hiding place . . . I know *nothing*—except the receipts in Elspeth's stillroom book, which could be useful to no agents unless they've the ague . . . or fancy a cure for a bout of melancholy." She was being facetious and didn't care.

"Catriona—"

"Or would it be an old receipt they might fancy?" she continued, ignoring her grandfather's pained look. "My Lord Lumley's Pease-pottage? The Queen's Barley Cream? Who will pay the highest price for those? The Hanoverians or the Jacobites?"

"Catriona, yer temper is most unsuited to the game of golf, lass . . . and to a husband as well."

"Good." She could not contain her anger. "Mayhap Conserve of Red Roses would interest a Jacobite." She began to recite from heart. "Boil gently a pound of red rose leaves for about the time it takes to recite the Lord's Prayer ten times, keeping the pot covered while it boileth and—"

"Catriona, listen to me—"

"Ah, my favorite grandfather does not want to hear how much sugar or juice of lemon? Or does the physick here in Glen Strahan have a better receipt? Mayhap the Jacobites fancy an amulet to frighten off demons and witches . . . except I believe a potion of mandrake or periwinkle is far more effective against the demons—"

"Good God, lass, dinna let the servants hear such talk. Ye ken how superstitious they are."

"If the agents do not want my knowledge of the stillroom book, then mayhap a few ghost stories of the old bards—from my loving father's collection," she finished, chin tilted defiantly.

Angus's face flushed in impatience. "Most women, lass, would welcome an easy marriage."

"I'm not most women."

"Catriona, I had no choice after . . ." His words trailed off. "It was yer happiness at stake."

"Happiness! I remember being happy before I had to leave here." Her voice wobbled, and she checked herself. "But as much as my mother loved Edinburgh, I hated it," she went on. "It lacked the fells and rocks and mists to play in, and instead I had soot to breathe and chamber pots to dodge and carriage wheels to dart about. When you never even wrote, I decided I had no grandfather."

"Catriona." His eyes were filled with pain, as if she'd whipped him, but she remained firm in her resolve to let nothing sway her.

She stood straight, chin up, biting her lip, willing herself not to give in to feminine emotions. There was too much at stake, and all could be lost by a woman's tears.

"I've given my oath to the laird of Strahan," her grandfather said in harsh tones, "and ye'll abide by my word." He turned his back on her and strode off toward where the golf ball had landed.

Enraged, Catriona ran past him and, arriving at the ball first, scooped it up and hid it behind her back.

"Put that down. Ye've ruined my shot," Angus said.

"And you've ruined my life!" she cried.

He stood there, as if considering how far to test her temper.

"Nevertheless, ye'll attend the betrothal banquet, and the day after that ye'll wed."

"I won't."

"Ye'll meet Lachlan MacLean like a docile lass."

"I'd sooner wed a scurvied hunchback."

"There's no other ready mate for ye, granddaughter. Wedding ye to a MacLean was the only practical solution."

"Then I shall remain a spinster."

"Ye have a duty to provide heirs," he reminded her.

"Mayhap." She'd begun to enjoy the verbal sparring and decided to see if she could outwit her grandfather.

"I'll have the privilege of deciding for myself when I wed."

"There's naught to decide. I've given my word." He held out his hand for the golf ball.

Catriona held it up, just out of reach. "Am I allowed no courtship?"

"Stuff of books."

"I want it."

"Are ye defying yer grandfather?"

Catriona shut her eyes and pleaded for patience. "May I please at least meet Lachlan and have the privilege of saying yes myself?" she asked gently.

After a moment he nodded. "Aye. If the illusion of courtship makes it a softer bargain. As long as ye accept yer duty."

"Very well," she said at last, holding out the golf ball, which he snatched with a gruff *harumph*. "I agree then," she said, pretending to relent. "I'll go to the betrothal banquet."

"Cheeky chit," she heard her grandfather grumble behind her.

Indeed, he didn't know the half of her intentions. She would run away again. Surely one of the invited guests might be traveling back to England and would gladly give her a ride. As for money, well . . . she could earn her keep as a governess. There. Life didn't have to be arranged by some man, after all.

As she strode back to the manor house, she pondered in her heart how much of her life had changed, and so fast. Except for Elspeth, Robert seemed to be the only constant left. Which was why she'd see him one last time and have a look at the woman he would marry. Other than that she expected the banquet to be stuffy and formal and reeking of haggis.

Much more appealing would be a climb for old time's sake up the tree by the wee kirk. What fun to be up in the tree with a hefty branch full of green pears at her disposal. She would throw one after another . . . little ones, just to scare Robert's bride.

Robert would, of course, be very angry. He would call her names. "Bothersome wench" and even "red thistle." But it would be worth it to see his eyes turn dark blue like Loch Aislair.

Chapter 10

It had been a mistake to come to the castle. Catriona knew that as soon as Lachlan MacLean reached up to help her off her horse. She looked at his outstretched hand, then at his leering face, and hesitated. She saw the same golden hair as Robert's, but lanker in texture; the same blue eyes, only filled with a naked cruelty. Lachlan's sharp features and scowl belonged, she realized, to a man of temper, a man who would not take kindly to a broken betrothal. He bent over her hand; his lips were cold, and Catriona pulled away.

She watched the ostler lead her horse to the stables. The inner ward held naught but cobblestones and one lone Caledonian pine under cover of which stood a gnarled old man, balancing himself on knobby sticks. Rain was beginning to fall, and the wind blew a piece of goatskin across the ward.

Beyond, high up on the ramparts, she could see a single sentry, plaid flying in the wind, pacing back and forth, back and forth. He reminded her of something caged.

Herself.

Taking a deep breath for courage, she looked Lachlan square in the eyes. "Before we go in," she announced, "you may as well know that there'll be no wedding tomorrow."

Lachlan looked momentarily startled, then suddenly threw back his head and laughed. "Robert was right, it seems," he said.

It was Catriona's turn to look askance. "About what?"

"A woman of temper, he said you'd be."

She felt the blood drain from her face. "Robert said *that?*" Robert had told her the rogue's code precluded telling about the lasses he'd kissed. She prayed he'd confined his talking to her temper.

"Aye, Robert warned me you'd be reluctant." Lachlan gave a queer smile. "But that's all to the good. I like a wench to have a measure of fight and fire in the bedroom, so if ye play the reluctant virgin, I'll no' mind at all," he said. "I'll never even ask if my cousin took liberties with you on the journey up here," he added.

She was outraged. Did the man have no tact? "Your cousin behaved as a gentleman." She felt her cheeks turn crimson from the lie.

Lachlan smiled slyly, as if he didn't believe a word. "Mayhap you'll tell me in detail some of your adventures on the trip, eh?"

Recognizing a checkmate when she heard one, Catriona decided to postpone any more talk about the betrothal. Ignoring Lachlan's outstretched hand, she swept past him to the doorway and waited while he sauntered over and led her inside.

He escorted her into the great hall—a vast room with a wooden ceiling and weapons hanging on the walls. While a fire burned brightly in the enormous fireplace, servants scurried about putting the finishing touches on a banquet table laden with pewter and flickering candelabra. In the middle of it all sat the MacLean in his great chair, a greyhound at his feet.

Catriona had not seen Alexander MacLean since he'd pulled a dirk on her years ago. She couldn't help trembling, fearing he'd bring up the subject of the mysterious Regalia. Instead, he smiled gently at her. He looked not half as fierce as all her childish memories of him, but rather very tired and yet very much the patriarch of his castle. He did not look as if he even remembered the Regalia. Yet he seemed to remember *her.*

"Ye've grown bonnie," was all he said, and she dipped a curtsy.

She followed Lachlan down the length of the great hall.

Over her shoulder, she looked back once at the MacLean, just to reassure herself, but Alexander was occupied in talk, stroking his greyhound's head. She allowed herself to relax a bit, until Lachlan stopped the wine servant.

He took a swallow and scowled. "It is the wrong wine, you stupid jackanapes." He sent the fellow scurrying off. "Swine," Lachlan muttered.

He continued to berate yet another servant, sounding, Catriona thought, like a petulant child. She could almost see him as a boy. A naughty boy, overshadowed even then by Robert, she guessed. Embarrassed by his boorishness, she moved a few steps away, examining her surroundings.

She tried to look upon this place as Robert's boyhood home, tried to picture him running through the winding, twisting corridors, playing cudgel with Lachlan, the winner earning first ride in a new pony cart. Robert would have bested Lachlan at that and at everything else—hunting, fishing, foot racing. She knew it in her heart.

And then she heard him, recognized the rich timbre of his voice. A safe sound it was, and, like a falcon returning to its home, immediately her gaze snagged his. Fortunately, Lachlan chose that moment to waylay yet another harried servant with his demand for a different wine. Catriona stood unashamedly staring at the handsome Robert—awed at his transformation from the rugged man she'd come to know. It was the first time she'd seen him dressed in anything but breeches and jerkin, and the sight took her breath away.

He was leaning against a casement, one leg pulled up against the other in a casual pose. A portrait painter would have paid him to stand still while he captured his fierce nobility on canvas. Catriona's gaze started at his buckled black shoes and moved up past the knee-high hose. The short red plaid swung about his knees, and his black velvet jacket hung open to reveal a lace jabot. From his shoulder, confined by a brooch of silver, ells and ells of red and blue plaid draped down to his waist. Robert, she decided, was the lion of the Highlands, golden of mane, proud and handsome. She swallowed hard, afraid everyone in the room could hear her heart pounding in her ears.

Slowly her gaze roved upward to his face, where one lock of dark gold hair spilled over his forehead. A most handsome bridegroom-to-be. But bridegrooms came already paired, like brogs and earbobs and carriage horses, and so quite naturally she looked for the other half, the bride-to-be.

Indeed, his attention was completely given over to a lovely woman in silk who stood at his side. They made a match, a beautiful golden-haired match. Robert's deep blue eyes gleamed in naked appreciation of Sarah Kendrick—the English bride who stood batting a fan back and forth, blushing at his masculine attentions.

Sarah Kendrick looked, Catriona thought morosely, like a satin bluebell, all bright and voluptuous. And though Catriona's mother would have said it was indiscreet, her glance lingered on the woman's decolletage. With a twinge of envy, Catriona observed that Sarah would never need to fill out her corset with books.

"Do you wish me to introduce you to Robert's bride?" Lachlan asked abruptly, coming up behind Catriona so stealthily that she jumped and nearly bumped into the goblet of wine he held out to her.

"It isn't necessary—"

"But of course it is. When we are married, she will be your cousin—like Robert."

He pushed the goblet into her hands so fast that it tipped and several drops of wine spilled onto the stone floor, like blood; the heady scent of musky grapes assailed her.

His cold glance repulsed her. She tried to pull back. "I don't expect I shall see her after tonight."

A sly smile cracked Lachlan's features.

"You sound so certain . . . All the more reason to make sure you meet Robert's bride before he whisks her away to London or God knows where." With a relentless grip on her arm, he forced her forward.

Robert turned at their approach, looking more handsome than she remembered, compelling as a magnet. His cool blue eyes and face full of Highland crags made it hard for her heart to beat normally. He smiled at her, and she ached for more.

But what did she expect? A welcoming embrace? After all she'd put him through on their journey? He'd made it abundantly clear she'd been nothing but a nuisance. Suddenly she knew what to do. She'd surprise him and be the model of graciousness. He'd wish then that he'd been nicer to her.

She coolly extended her hand to Sarah, pressed the other woman's limp fingers, and spoke the sort of words her mother had been wont to mouth. "I've heard so very much about you, Sarah, from Robert." She glanced quickly at Robert and saw his mouth twitch suspiciously. "Why, he never stopped talking about you on the journey up here," she added.

Robert coughed and bent to adjust the garter on his stocking.

"It's truly a pleasure to make your acquaintance at long last," she finished, and silently begged God's forgiveness for yet another lie.

Sarah's gaze flicked dismissively over Catriona's green gown and plaid sash. She eyed Catriona a bit suspiciously and then smiled. Her cheeks dimpled prettily, but her words sounded stilted. "You're the one Robert escorted up here?"

"Aye, and he's a most braw guide." Catriona used her mother's gushing tone. Sarah, she noted, turned a touch paler.

When he stood, Robert looked at Catriona, a reluctant smile on his lips, an amused twinkle in his eyes. "Catriona made the journey easy. As a matter of fact, Lachlan," he said to his cousin, "Catriona rarely stopped talking about how anxious she was to end our journey and meet her betrothed."

Lachlan smirked.

Catriona flashed a mutinous glance at Robert. How dare he try to outwit her? But he wouldn't dare tell everything.

"My grandfather's plans came as a surprise," Catriona said, ever so sweetly.

"So did many of the people we met on the journey up here," Robert said, "especially the—"

"Bandits," Catriona said, finishing for him.

"I was going to say runaway travelers."

Their gazes locked.

Lachlan suddenly lifted his wine goblet. Sarah, Catriona realized, was staring at the hem of her dress.

Catriona's heart thumped. "The journey was long."

"It went fast."

They spoke at the same time.

Then nobody spoke.

"Grizel says that you were wounded by bandits," Lachlan commented to Robert, as if demanding details. "Did you chase them off single-handedly?"

"I had a lot of running around to do," Robert admitted, turning his amused blue eyes on Catriona once again.

The memory of being chased through the gorse by Robert did not amuse her. She wanted to clarify his remark, but Sarah was staring at her with a frosty smile. Catriona felt hot all at once, the way she had the day Robert had pulled her into his arms in the castle ruins.

"Did I hear a mention of bandits?" a male guest asked.

Nodding his head, Robert signaled for more wine. At once three servants hovered at his elbow. And then, no doubt sensing a good story, more guests crowded about them. Within seconds, Robert was surrounded by fawning Highlanders, all of whom eyed the handsome young man with admiration.

"Robert tells me you doctored his wound with herbs. Him and a hare . . . how quaint," Sarah said, fanning herself. "Of course, I've never been one to touch a wild animal, not even a hare. They could be dangerous to one's health, you know. At least they certainly were to my uncle, who died bagging a wild boar, but not before he amassed one of the finest trophy collections in all of Carlisle."

Sarah had suddenly turned talkative. Catriona smiled woodenly and secretly considered on which wall of the great hall she'd like to mount Sarah's head.

While Robert entertained a circle of guests with his

description of the Highland bandits, Sarah bragged about her uncle's prowess with various types of weaponry. Nearby, Lachlan engaged in monosyllabic conversation with a paunchy man named Sheriff MacIvie. As Robert's tale grew more exciting, Lachlan's scowl deepened, his monosyllables becoming louder and more abrupt until he demanded the attention of another hapless young servant.

Catriona wished she could hear the version of the bandit episode Robert was relating to the guests, but like a bird in a snare she was frozen in place. Behind her, servants were carrying covered dishes to the table, steamy odors wafting out behind them. In front of her, Sarah blocked her view of Robert and held her captive with her own chatter. Catriona could only nod and smile politely at the Englishwoman, beside whom she felt too bare, too plain, too scrawny. The air was growing hotter and stuffier, and errant tendrils of hair escaped her plait, clinging to her neck.

All Catriona could do was sip her wine and try to concentrate on Sarah's vapid conversation. Why, oh, why, couldn't the woman's coach have overturned in a river and been swept away?

"The Highland weather is so cold," Sarah said. "How these Scotsmen go about in these odd knee plaids is beyond me. They must freeze."

Robert had pulled her so close in the castle ruins and warmed her, Catriona remembered.

"Castle Fenella MacLean looks so ancient."

But nothing compared to the castle ruins—where Robert's lips had teased and tantalized hers.

"Isn't the wind dreadful to one's skin?"

Robert's hands did wonderful things to her skin, even just a gentle touch to her shoulder . . . in the inn when he'd touched her to awaken her and when he'd kissed away the sting of nettles.

"Are you quite well? You're so quiet," Sarah observed, a touch suspiciously.

"The journey was long," Catriona said apologetically. She wished she could do things differently. She'd respond to Robert with politeness, not harsh words . . .

"Tell me," Sarah whispered in a familiar tone, "what is Robert really like? Will he make a fine husband, as I've been told, or was his behavior on the journey heathenish?"

At a loss for words, Catriona felt the blood rush from her head, as swiftly as if Robert MacLean had pulled her down to the hard floor and was taunting her with his practiced kiss. "He's—"

Mercifully, just then, Grizel motioned them all to the banquet table.

Lachlan's fingers bruised Catriona's arm as he escorted her. When he pulled out a chair for her, she sat, gaze fixed on the pewter ware in front of her. A servant distracted her with fresh wine, a steaming bowl of leek soup, and bannock. She sipped the wine, sweet and potent, and over the rim of her goblet chanced a glance at Robert, who had assisted Sarah to her chair. Catriona's fingers tightened on the stem of the goblet. Surreptitiously, she watched the lithe grace with which Robert sat down, the edginess with which he toyed with his knife, drawing imaginary circles on the wooden table. He seemed to be making a point of not looking at Catriona, instead staring intently at some fascinating beam on the ceiling.

Beside her, Lachlan noisily drained his wine goblet and bellowed for more. And still Sarah Kendrick chattered on, as if the wine had loosened her tongue. On and on she went, discoursing on the ways Scotland could be more like England. "This place is so medieval. Has your family never thought of redecorating?"

Lachlan sneered, but Robert patiently turned to her and explained that his grandfather preferred the medieval decor; he reassured her that once they wed she would not spend much time here.

Sarah blushed and smiled. "They told me you were charming, you know. That's why I agreed to this marriage. Better a charming Scotsman, I told my father, than a boorish Englishman. He was determined to arrange my marriage, and that of all my sisters too, of course," she added. "At least I'll marry into adventure," I told my father after my uncle, Lord Kendrick, came and told Father about this handsome Scotsman.''

Robert smiled patiently. ''I count it my fortune that some charming Englishman did not lay claim to you first.''

Sarah's smile deepened, and her bosom heaved from the sweet words.

A lump lodged in Catriona's throat. Her fingers grew clumsy, and she dropped her bannock beside her soup bowl. Crumbs scattered, and Robert glanced her way, his gaze lingering on her. She busied herself brushing crumbs into a little pile until she felt Robert turn his attention back to Sarah.

Sarah was gamely chewing and swallowing, reminding Robert with every mouthful that she was only eating this strange Scottish food because she was a guest. Beside her, Lachlan ripped a drumstick off a roast grouse. Ignoring her own food, Catriona glanced around the table.

At the far end, dressed in black, sat Grizel, dark hair plaited and pulled up. The severe style accentuated her sharp, straight nose. Grizel wasn't even making a pretense of eating, but instead her beady-eyed gaze darted back and forth among the guests, as if savoring the mix of people.

The flickering light distorted the features of the other guests at the table—a motley assortment of castle retainers and villagers, from sheriff to minister. Jacques Beaufort, who had managed to wrangle an invitation to spend a few nights in the castle, looked hopelessly out of place dressed in the silks and satins of his native France. And across from him Lord Kendrick, in breeches and a wig, looked as uncomfortable as a bulldog in a lion's den.

At the end of the table nearest Catriona sat Alexander MacLean, who alternated between glaring at his plate and staring at both the Englishwoman and Catriona, weariness etched on his spare features. All in all, it was a discordant assembly. And it didn't help one whit to have Sarah chatter on.

''You do know how dreadful the landscape becomes once you cross the English border, don't you?'' Sarah said to no one in particular. ''Really, after the last skirmish the loser ought to be made to repair the rubble of all those sad castles. Of course the loser has been Scotland most often, hasn't it?'' She paused, soup spoon poised in midair. "I'm hopeless when it comes to history. My governess knew so little about Scotland, but I promised to write and tell my family what I saw with my own eyes.'' She took a sip of soup. "Tell me, how does one post a letter out of here?''

Robert's reply was polite but terse. Silence followed. Knives scraped across plates like fingernails against bone. Near a stained-glass window, rain blew in, and the wind fluttered a banner that hung on the wall. Catriona welcomed the cooler air, but a servant moved to slam the casement tight.

Other servants arrived with yet more courses. Now platters of haggis filled the table. Tatties and turnips. And again, more wine. In the background, a piper's melody began, at first a steady drone, then wilder, more melodious.

With ill-concealed impatience, Catriona stabbed a piece of grouse, but she could not bring herself to eat it. It was too hot, too noisy, the food too rich, her emotions too tangled. Lachlan watched her, like a fox about to pounce. She blew candle smoke out of her eyes.

Suddenly standing up, Alexander MacLean leaned his shaky hands against the table edge for balance and took the goblet that Robert extended to him. Conversation immediately died down. The MacLean smiled at Robert and then, raising the goblet, proposed a toast. "To Robert's return to the Highlands,'' he said dramatically, "and to the betrothal of my grandsons.''

Scraping back his chair, Robert stood too. "To journeys that end and journeys that begin,'' he said enigmatically, looking briefly at Catriona and then dipping his goblet in tribute to Sarah. Catriona drank a sip, but the wine was more potent than she'd realized, and she felt dizzy. She pressed her fingers to her temples.

Finally Lachlan stood. "Eat, drink, and be merry,'' he mumbled. "We don't need any more platitudes or charm.'' Sarcasm edged his words. While everyone watched, he guzzled his wine. The guests stirred self-consciously. Sud-

denly everyone's attention turned from the MacLean toasts
to Sarah Kendrick, who had let out a screech.

Holding her hands to her mouth, the wide-eyed Englishwoman viewed with horror the arrival of a cooked boar's
head on a platter, borne in by a proud Highland servant.

"Take it away!" Sarah cried. "Mother warned me about
haggis and I did my duty there, but surely you don't expect
a well-bred Englishwoman to eat something as revolting
as this." Pushing back her chair, she stood and backed
away.

With his knife, Lachlan was scooping more haggis onto
his plate. "Now that you are in Scotland," he said testily,
"you must grow accustomed to our food."

"You sound inhospitable, Lachlan," Robert said under
his breath.

Without warning, Lachlan rammed the tip of his knife
into the wooden table and leaned forward as if to pull
Robert from his place.

"Cease!" The MacLean spoke the single word, and everyone at the table started and then fell silent.

Catriona held her breath while the cousins glared at each
other across the table. The MacLean's command hung in
the air.

Robert pulled the knife out and laid it down, gave his
cousin a warning look, and then moved to Sarah.

"You needn't eat it, my dear." He started to lead her
back to her chair, but she pulled away.

"I don't feel well. I want to go to my room." She was
trembling, Catriona noticed with sudden sympathy.

At once, Grizel moved from her end of the table,
waving her hand to shoo Robert away. "Bide here,
Cousin Robbie. Stay here with the people who have
come to celebrate your wedding." She placed a comforting arm around Sarah. "Your betrothed needs her
rest before her wedding day, else she'll take ill, and that
would be too unfortunate." Grizel drew her away into
the shadows, and Catriona watched them go, her emotions mixed.

Returning to the table, Robert sipped his wine for a few

minutes, then set his goblet on the table a touch too hard so that it banged. A servant moved to refill it.

The pipers played on, and dancers began to entertain with a reel. Catriona could only watch the fine play of Robert's fingers, drumming a tattoo against his goblet. Long and tapered his fingers were, she noticed. Warm to the touch they were, especially when he placed them against her face . . . She looked up to find him watching her, thoughtful, and the memory of all the times he'd held her in his arms rushed back to her. Feeling color rise to her cheeks, she turned away.

Abruptly, after a brief nod to his grandfather, Robert scraped back his chair and stalked out of the great hall.

Lachlan stood and watched Robert walk out, then, towering over Catriona, he reached down with a cruel hand and pulled her from her chair. "I've been remiss in not showing you the rest of the castle. Robert would be annoyed with me for neglecting such an obvious duty." He said it loudly enough for everyone at the table to hear.

"I've seen enough," she objected, trying not to cringe from him, desperately casting about for a way to escape.

"You have much more to see than how Robert holds his wine goblet," he said.

She followed him before his insinuations could worsen.

As the massive door leading from the great hall closed behind them, the noise vanished, and her footsteps sounded softly on the stone passageway.

Outside the wind blew against the narrow windows of the castle. Not another soul was in sight. The blood pounded in her ears. As the winding stairway up which he led her narrowed, her uneasiness deepened.

"Where are you taking me?" The best she could hope for would be a private chapel where other guests might be meditating, but somehow she could not picture Lachlan kneeling at an altar, praying for a happy marriage. When his hand moved from her arm to her waist, she recalled too late how much wine he had consumed.

He forced her into a great room in which a single candle flickered.

With a strength born of desperation, she wrenched from his grasp and backed into a dark corner, intending to inch her way to the door.

"You are my betrothed," he reminded her, and advanced out of the shadows. "I see no reason to wait for wedding vows. We can say our own vows to each other now and, as our grandfathers have decreed, begin to make an heir."

Darting out of his reach, Catriona ran for the door, but Lachlan was there, blocking her. She backed away and looked around the room for another avenue of escape.

"I told you . . . I have no intention of wedding you," she informed him. She drew in a ragged breath. "Mayhap you need to speak to my grandfather again."

"Your grandfather and mine have made a bargain, you silly wench," he said. "As for your objections, I care naught for the opinion of a woman." He made a sudden lunge toward her and, catching her arm, hauled her toward him, then quickly reversed positions by twisting her around and backing her against the wall.

His body, rough and fleshy, pressed intimately against hers, and she stiffened in disgust at his touch.

"The Fergusons have no' been welcome here in the past, no more than the English, but you see that is changing," he said smoothly. "I look forward to the *joining* of our two families." He emphasized his words by pressing his loins closer against her.

No! She wanted to scream the word at him, but he caught her face and held it. His leering mouth came nearer. My God, he was actually going to kiss her. Revolted, she twisted her face away.

She wanted to feel only Robert's touch, only Robert's lips, only Robert's body against hers. "Robert . . ." The name slipped out of her, half cry, half plea.

Lachlan's lecherous grin twisted to a sneer, and she felt his hot breath on her. "Robert canna help you now, lass," he taunted. "Why should he care what happens to you when he's got his own Englishwoman to deflower? Besides, from all I've heard, you were naught but a nuisance to him on the journey up here. He's glad to be rid of you.'' When she tried to bite his arm, he laughed. ''The more you struggle, the more pleasure I shall take from forcing you to submit.'' With his free hand, he shoved her skirt up above her knees and clamped a suggestive hand to her thigh.

Desperate, Catriona jerked up her knee and struck him as hard as possible between the legs. Leaving him doubled over and cursing, she fled for the door and flung it open, but Lachlan's voice, rough with pain and anger, held her there for a second longer.

''You little bitch!'' he spat.

''A curse on you,'' she choked out, backing out the door. ''I curse you to the death. May you and your castle burn in the fires of hell!''

Behind her someone gasped, and Catriona whirled to see a hovering servant standing with mouth agape. Before Lachlan could enlist his aid, Catriona fled along the upper hallway in the opposite direction from the great hall, stumbling along twisting corridors, looking for any escape, hoping against hope to find Robert. Her satin slippers whispered on the hard stones and matched the beat of her heart in her ears. Behind her, she heard the curses and shouts of Lachlan calling orders to servants.

At the end of the corridor, she slumped against a door and caught her breath, then, heedless of where the door led, she rattled its latch and twisted it open.

The windswept castle ramparts faced her. She stepped out, and the storm blew the door closed behind her. Wind whipped her hair out of its plait and tangled her skirt about her legs. Whirling, she tugged at the door, but it wouldn't open. The wind carried her name to her and, looking over her shoulder, she saw a dark shape coming toward her along the ramparts. Lachlan must already have found another way out here. Terrified, she began to pound her fists on the door.

''Catriona.''

Her heart soared at the familiar deep voice and she whipped around, scarcely daring to hope she had heard right. Robert. The one person in the world she wanted more than anyone.

Flinging herself into his arms, she clung to him, like a drowning person in a storm grabbing on to a lifeline. Swallowing down tears, she cried, "You left me alone with him."

"I dinna make it a habit to eavesdrop on another man's courting, lass," he said dryly. Untangling her, he pulled her back along the ramparts into the seclusion of a wind-protected alcove.

"You call what Lachlan does courting?" she said, and clung to him again. Big and brawny Robert was, and it was not difficult to find a part of him to hold on to.

Humiliated, terrified, Catriona buried her face against the soft velvet of his jacket, savoring the musky scent of him, wanting nothing more than to stay in his arms until she forgot Lachlan ever existed.

He stood there stiffly, hands at his sides. "Ye dinna ken Lachlan very well yet, lass. He's no' one for romance and flowers."

"You're too kind to your own kin, Robert."

"Lass, shh, you'll have the sentries over here. Shall I take you back to the manor house?"

Despite her terror, she managed to shake her head. "No, Angus is like a stranger. He says he promised on his oath as a Scotsman to give me away. He's giving me to Lachlan as a . . . as a peace offering."

"A most unwise choice," Robert observed dryly. "There's nothing the least bit peaceable about you."

"And there's nothing the least bit romantic about your cousin. Why, he wouldn't know a rose from a thistle." She raised tear-filled eyes to Robert. "But I do, and I won't marry him. I . . . can't." Robert was her rock and she clung all the tighter.

Tipping her chin up, he swept the curls off her face. "So you let him feel the sting of the red thistle, eh, lass?" The back of his hand caressed her cheek and he was smiling at her, a little sadly. To her surprise he enfolded her hand in his and kissed her fingertips as gently as if she were a rose herself. She had to remind herself to keep breathing.

Oh, God, Robert. She leaned her forehead against his chest and shut her eyes. Out here on the windswept ramparts, she suddenly realized an impossible truth. Sometime on the journey she'd fallen in love with Robert MacLean.

The realization began as a whisper. The touch of his breath against her fingertips swept over her in drugging waves and left her breathless.

His arms finally came up around her, tentative at first and then steady and reassuring, tender even, not at all like Lachlan's coarse touch. Oh, how could she ever have accused Robert, who was holding her so gently, of being a barbarian? More to the point, what could she do about loving him? Brew him a love potion? As if it were that easy. Tell him of her love? She thought not. This, after all, was not an appropriate problem to lay on the doorstep of a soon-to-be-married man. Tomorrow he would wed another. Despair overwhelmed her.

"You lied to me about Lachlan," she said suddenly.

"Not precisely," he corrected her. "Lachlan's changed more than I expected."

"I'd sooner have had the bandits take me," she sobbed. "Oh, Robert, how could Lachlan be your kin?"

"Many's the time I've asked the same question, lass."

"Will you help me?" she pleaded, pulling away just far enough so she could stare up at him. The wind was whipping his golden hair about his forehead, and he looked truly startled at her request. "I won't interfere with your plans for wedding Sarah. All I need is a little aid in getting back to Edinburgh . . . A horse. Someone to guide me. A map. Will you help me?"

While she spoke, his eyes had darkened with some emotion she couldn't name, and now he tipped her face up.

"My services involve rescuing lasses, not aiding in their escape."

"Then you're saying you won't help."

"I dinna know if I can help myself anymore, lass," he said in a voice she'd never heard before.

And then to her surprise, he bent to kiss her. Utterly. Thoroughly. This was not the teasing Robert of the castle ruins, but a man who was dry, hot, and parched for her.

Suddenly the horror of the evening vanished and she was safe again in his arms, kissing him back with more fire than she'd known existed between them. He tried to break away, but his lips didn't quite leave hers, nor hers leave his, and she succumbed to the force that they'd been resisting all evening . . . ever since she'd met him.

Finally he pulled back, as if mindful of his place. "Forgive me, but we canna stay out here like this."

"I'm compromising you, aren't I?" she asked.

Robert laughed darkly. You naive little saucebox, he thought. You never obey me. Never understand how you've been baiting me all along.

"I'm long ago ruined," he said aloud. " 'Tis why they have to wed me off to an English. No self-respecting Scots lass of good family will have me," he said, self-mocking.

That made her laugh. At least she wasn't totally naive, he thought.

"Elspeth says it's because we spent so much time together, that it's natural."

He smiled. "Elspeth is a fountain of advice, lass, but I'm afraid it's never quite as simple as that. In the morning I'll speak to my grandfather about Lachlan, but—"

She grabbed the lapels of his jacket, panic building again, seeking the Robert who had just kissed her. "I can't go back in there now. Lachlan will have his way before the wedding."

"He won't." Robert's hand lingered on her cheek. "Remember, I'm your guardian till you wed, lass."

The stark passion in the promise made her catch her breath.

"And after the wedding? You won't be able to defend me then. You'll be married to Sarah." Her voice broke.

"Do you think I need reminding, lass?"

The door onto the rampart burst open. Instantly, Catriona broke away from Robert, but not before Lachlan had seen them. He leaned against the stone of the rampart, his stance casual, but his eyes gleamed coldly.

"This is unseemly, Robert, what with your own betrothed mere steps away in the castle. But then, you never were satisfied with merely one wench at a time, were you? You stole the first lass I ever wooed and now . . ." Straightening up, he advanced on them.

Catriona felt Robert tense like a powder keg which one spark could ignite.

"Can I help it if you frighten the lassies, Lachlan?" Robert replied, his voice still ragged with desire.

"Always ready with the fancy answer, aren't you Robert? Why don't you take your cold Englishwoman to England and chase after our title like a trained dog?" Lachlan reached for Catriona and jerked her out of Robert's arms. "This one's mine, and I'll console her."

"No!" Pulling away, Catriona fled through the door, leaving the men to their anger.

Grizel stepped out of the shadows, a knowing smile on her face. She placed an arm around Catriona. Her role here, Catriona deduced, seemed that of one waiting to console. Pity that she had found no other man of her own after Ian Ferguson's death so long ago. Dressed all in black as she was, she seemed to be in perpetual mourning, withdrawn and sad.

Suddenly exhausted, Catriona allowed herself to be led away. She couldn't solve Grizel's lack of love. Her own emotional state was too precarious. Robert followed them, her guardian shadow. They stopped at the door to a bedchamber while Grizel fumbled with the key, and Catriona felt Robert come up beside her. Lachlan, thank God, was nowhere in sight.

"Bolt your door tonight, Catriona," Robert said quietly, and then, as soon as she crossed into the room, he walked away, as if the kiss on the ramparts had never happened. Robert, the consummate rogue, ignored their indiscretion as if he were a wizard who made desire vanish.

''Sleep well, Catriona,'' Grizel said with her sad little smile, and closed the heavy door behind her.

It had been worse than a mistake to come, Catriona decided, leaning her forehead against the door. It had been a disaster. And it had been an even bigger mistake not to run away as she had planned. Now she'd have to wait till morning.

Chapter 11

❦

*S*arah was dead. Conjuring knaves, blasphemous sooth-sayers who hid in the castle turrets and towers, had consumed her. The castle clansmen had wrapped her in the red MacLean plaid and laid her out on the trestle table of the great hall. The bandit woman, Marcail, stood across from the corpse, gnarled finger pointing, and in a keening voice intoned her prophecy. "Ye see, lassie, 'tis as I told ye. Once ye enter these hills ye'll no' leave again."

Guilt-stricken, Catriona stared at the body, horrified because her curse on the castle had brought out the demons to do their dark deeds. She wanted Robert's forgive-ness, but he had vanished. Gone to London to see the king, Marcail said. And right before Catriona's eyes Mar-cail dissolved into a bubbling caldron of lavender-scented potion. The steam from it swirled around the red plaid corpse of Sarah, choked Catriona until she couldn't breathe. Lachlan stepped out of the heathery mists and, laughing, pounded his fist against her heart. Pounded and pounded and pounded while she screamed.

"Holy Savior! Help me." Sucking in deep breaths, panting from the nightmare, Catriona sat bolt upright in bed and hugged a thistledown pillow to her. It *had* been a nightmare, hadn't it? Perspiration soaked through her chemise, and she ran a shaky hand through her hair, trying to pull herself up from the murky darkness of the dream. But the pounding wouldn't go away.

Pushing tangled curls from her face, she blinked away the cobwebs of the dream, and real memories, darker than

155

her nightmare, came back in a rush. She was sleeping in Glen Strahan in Castle Fenella MacLean. Robert's castle. Like a line of garrisoned soldiers, the memories kept marching at her, shoving the dream farther and farther into retreat. Lachlan's lust. Robert's embrace. His kiss. She touched a finger to her lips, remembering. Too easily she recalled the feel of his body pressed close to hers, and her unbidden response.

She wrapped her arms about her waist to stop herself from shivering. And still the banging continued. Through a narrow slit of window, a sliver of moonlight fell upon the oaken door. The pounding was real. Someone was banging on her door.

"Catriona, wake up," a deep voice said. The latch rattled. "Catriona, do you hear me?"

It was Robert. He hadn't gone to London.

She swung her legs over the side of the bed so fast that when she stood, she tripped, and a bowl of dried herbs crashed to the floor. As she caught her balance, the sweet scent of lavender choked her.

"Catriona!"

Dragging a plaid from the bed, she wrapped it over her shoulders and hurried across the cold stones to the door. Still shaking, she drew open the bolts on the door.

Mayhap Robert needed her. Mayhap he desired her and couldn't sleep out of longing. But that seemed as improbable a wish as that he whisk her back to Edinburgh. Robert's emotional defenses were as high as this castle. He too seldom let down his guard and was too strong to give in to longings. For a minute tonight when he'd kissed her he'd yielded to temptation, but then he'd slammed the door of his heart on her. Robert believed in marriages of alliance just as some castle builders favored moats. Never mind that both were terribly unfriendly. She drew a deep breath and opened the door.

Robert stood there, still dressed in his plaid, except for the jacket which he'd shed. He held a candle up close to his face. "Are you all right, lass? I heard you cry out."

It took only the reassuring tone of his voice to undo her. "Am I all right? Oh, Robert, there were soothsayers in the castle and . . . and . . . I want to go back to Angus now.''

'' 'Tis the middle of the night, Catriona. You must have had a bad dream.''

She rubbed her hands up and down her arms, desperate to throw herself into his embrace. "Please, Robert, I must leave." Her voice choked.

He blew out the candle and swept her up in his arms and carried her to her bed. His hands were caressing her shoulders, moving in tiny circles on her back. "It was a nightmare," he said gently.

"It was more than a dream, Robert. I swear it on my mother's grave. The bandit woman was here casting another spell on me . . . and Sarah, oh, Sarah . . .''

"Lass, lass," he said, moving a hand up to caress her cheek. "You'll anger Lachlan."

"Let him huff and puff like the wicked giant, for all I care. If he's the only husband my grandfather can find for me, I shall remain a spinster."

Robert looked out at the piece of misty midnight sky that showed through her window. "You're upset."

"You'd be upset too if someone turned into a bubbling caldron right in front of your eyes, if soothsayers held you down and gagged you, and—dragons . . . oh, God the dragons . . .''

Robert wore a faint, rather tired smile. He sighed and reached out to fondle a lock of hair.

"The thought of gagging you has occurred to me, but that isn't why I came."

His teasing calmed her. "It's impossible, you know, to sleep in this place. You said so yourself. I wager dragon ghosts do roam here." She felt his hand entwine again around a strand of her hair. Around and around and around. She closed her eyes, and the ghosts receded, further and further away, dissolving and becoming part of the mist.

"It was a dream, lass," he said softly. "Trust me."

"All right," she conceded in a small voice. "It could have been a dream." But her dream had more truth to it than nightmare. For all her book learning, Catriona did believe in premonitions.

"I shall have to leave Glen Strahan, of course," she added in a calmer voice.

"A drastic step, lass."

"I'd sooner peddle herbs than spend another night in this place."

"And what unlucky guide will be escorting you?"

"Fie on guides. They do silly things like drag you back when you decide on a slight detour." Lying on the bed, she felt light-headed. Mainly because now Robert's hands were doing warm things to her shoulders. She curved closer to where he stood, so close her cheek touched his plaid, and she felt the tensile strength of his thigh through the wool.

Briefly, she agonized over her alternatives. Hide in the pear tree. Watch Robert wed Sarah. Wed Lachlan. Oh, fie! When one actually laid out the choices, her course of action was obvious. Run away, of course.

"You dinna have to wed Lachlan, lass, or run away," Robert said. "I'll convince Angus that he should break your marriage contract."

Catriona half sat up. "You'd do that? Why?"

He half smiled. "To keep peace in the Highlands. If I assist Lord Kendrick, 'twill be my first duty to put down the rebellion of Catriona Ferguson. 'Twould seal my place in Lord Kendrick's favor."

"Oh, it would, would it?" She looked up, ready to tease him further, but paused. For the first time she noticed the agony in his eyes, and she didn't need the second sight to realize that Robert may have had good reasons to be walking the castle corridors.

"Robert, something's the matter, isn't it?" Suddenly sitting up, she grabbed his wrists. "What is it? You didn't come just because I screamed in my sleep, did you?"

He shook his head.

She felt a sneeze tickle her. Her shoulders quivered.

"It's the lavender," she explained breathlessly, her voice muffled by his plaid. "I knocked over the bowl . . . You didn't come to ask me why I . . . I . . ." She raised her hands to her face and sneezed. "Robert, I realize it's the middle of the night, but would you have a—?"

He handed her a handkerchief.

She buried her face in its cotton folds and sneezed, leaning against his rock-hard midriff. The intimacy of their situation once again struck her full force. She could feel the crisp fabric of his shirt. She ran her hands up it, grabbed hold, and used him for an anchor to pull herself up until she could hear his heartbeat.

He got up to leave. "I should never have come here."

Before he could cross the room, she followed him and caught his hand. "No, tell me."

Unexpectedly, he pulled her close against him.

"Tell me," she whispered.

"The castle has too many ears."

His breath was warm against her hair, and she could have stayed in his embrace forever.

"Trust me, Robert. Please."

"It's Sarah."

The spell broken, she backed away from his arms, guilt-stricken. She'd dreamed Sarah was dead, almost as if she wished it. Her mouth went suddenly dry. It had only been a dream, she reminded herself, yet a dark premonition coursed through her.

"You need me because of Sarah?" Her voice sounded unnaturally high.

Catriona went to light a taper. Holding it up, she came back to Robert. Faint lines of weariness etched his mouth and eyes.

He put his hands on her shoulders. "Sarah's ill, lass. Lord Kendrick demands a physick, but there's none in the village, and Grizel is ready to bleed her. I hoped that with your knowledge of herbs there might be something, some way . . . Catriona, I need your help."

I need your help. Standing there, crunching dried lavender beneath her bare feet, she knew jealousy. Jealousy that this lovable blackguard should refuse to help her and then with supreme almighty gall ask *her* for help for his betrothed.

Footsteps ran down the corridor, echoing in the night,

and, distracted, Robert glanced at the door. It could have been a servant or even Lord Kendrick. Judging from the worrywart of a man she'd glimpsed at the banquet, Catriona supposed Lord Kendrick must be frantic for his niece, ill in a strange land on the eve of her wedding. The premonition of disaster clung to her like a dark shadow.

"I need you, Catriona," Robert said.

She had no choice.

"I'll try," she said quietly. "I'll do what I can." For of course she'd do anything for Robert.

She grabbed a thin wrapper that did more for modesty than warmth and, pushing her feet into the slippers that went with her dinner gown, she followed Robert in silence, the stones of the floor icy cold through the thin satin soles. Despite the late hour, candles blazed full in their sconces and cast long shadows along the corridor, glinting off the occasional shield and pikestaff that decorated the walls.

They turned a corner and Catriona heard moans coming from an open doorway. Outside in the corridor, Lord Kendrick paced. Suddenly she felt utterly selfish, wrapped up in her nightmares when a poor lass lay ill. She followed Robert inside the room. An overpowering smell of sour wine filled the air.

At once, Grizel stood up and blocked their way.

"Why did you bring Lachlan's woman here, Robert?" Grizel whined, and Catriona's attention was drawn to the bed.

While Robert explained Catriona's ability with herbs, Catriona moved around the bed opposite Grizel and looked down at Sarah, who writhed in a feverish twist of bedclothes.

Grizel continued a litany of complaints. "Can't you see I've too many people in here already, Robert? What does a green lass from Edinburgh know of healing?" Her voice shook.

"You asked for help, Grizel. Catriona knows remedies you've no knowledge of."

Grizel smiled crookedly. "I wager Lachlan does not

know you're visiting his Ferguson betrothed in the middle of the night, does he?''

"I went to ask her help."

"So you say, but try convincing Lachlan. He's already convinced you have stolen her virtue."

"Cease your maligning talk, Grizel," Robert snapped. " 'Tis no' the time to be airing our personal grievances. Now move away and let Catriona see to Sarah."

Grizel's expression turned acid, and she flung herself down upon a chest against the wall. "See if your Edinburgh lass can heal then," she said tartly. "I care naught for your Englishwoman, and as to this Ferguson . . . I'd no' trust her with *my* life. Her cousin Ian betrayed me. This one will find a way to betray us all too."

"Enough," Robert ordered in a quiet voice, and Grizel dropped her head to her knees. Once again, Sarah moaned.

"Lachlan will be as angry as a serpent whose tail is stepped on," Grizel whispered.

Robert knelt beside Sarah and said over his shoulder, "If you dinna cease your complaining, Grizel, I'll be forced to send you outside."

As if a stick had suddenly snapped, Grizel became quiet, though she nervously caressed the round silver brooch at the neck of her dress. "Lachlan will find out that you went to Catriona's bedchamber tonight," she mumbled to herself, barely audible. "You ought to let him have *one* woman to himself, Robert."

Across the bed, Catriona met Robert's gaze.

"Ignore her," he whispered.

Catriona turned her attention to Sarah who, hours earlier, had been imperiously criticizing all things Scottish, and who now lay contorted by pain, a fine sheen of moisture on her face, her blond hair tangled.

"Take the knives away!" Sarah cried. "The knives are slicing me in two."

"Hush," Catriona soothed, running a hand over the woman's brow. But she kept seeing the nightmare: Sarah as still as stone and laid out in the MacLean plaid in the great hall.

Bedclothes damp with fever, Sarah continued to writhe,

her knees drawn up to her chest like a child. Catriona took her clammy hand in her own and knelt beside her, just as she had done so many times with other women in Edinburgh.

She dearly wished Elspeth with her greater knowledge of herbs were here, but the older woman was recovering from a sickness of her own and needed rest. Deciding against disturbing her, Catriona considered the possible ailments that could have befallen this young woman.

Ague? Sarah Kendrick had no fever. Despite the damp bedclothes, her skin felt cold to the touch.

Cough? There was none.

Tainted food? Drink? As far as Catriona knew, they'd all partaken of the same dishes at the banquet.

Mayhap, though, it was a simple case of indigestion brought on by a nervous attack. Everyone knew Englishwomen were prone to highstrung temperaments. Arriving in the Highlands from a more civilized home could well have shocked her delicate system.

While she smoothed the hair back from Sarah's forehead, Catriona thought through the receipts in Elspeth's stillroom book, mentally sorting out the complicated from the simple. Aye, a potion of chamomile would be safest.

She looked up and into Robert's worried gaze. "Bring me my portmanteau," she said, and Robert sent a hovering servant scurrying to Catriona's chamber.

"It won't work," Grizel said idly, still stroking the brooch. "She no doubt drank too much wine. I can still bleed her if you want. I've a cup, or mayhap a good purging is the thing."

"No." Ignoring the way Grizel's dark eyes darted back and forth from her to Robert, Catriona refused firmly. She'd seen too many deaths following purgings and bleedings.

Sarah opened her pain-glazed eyes and looked at Catriona and began to sob. "Why is the red-haired witch here? Take her away from me." Another spasm engulfed her and she drew up her knees. "Ooh . . . I want to go home . . . back to England . . . Can't you get me away . . . away from the knives?"

Catriona had seen death and had no herb for it. For pain yes, but for death, nothing.

"She's out of her mind with pain," Grizel observed. "A potion will be useless."

Ignoring Grizel, Catriona caught Robert's haggard gaze. "I'm not a physick, but the herb mixture works for pain. Whether it will cure her is another matter."

The potion was easy to make. Milk and crushed herbs stirred together. She and Elspeth had prepared similar potions dozens of times. What was hard was watching Robert lift his betrothed and help her while she sipped it, watching while he stroked Sarah's pale blond hair, watching while he said consoling words. But at last, the potion took effect, and Sarah lay quiet.

Even as Robert stared down on his sleeping bride-to-be, Catriona wanted to move up behind him, wrap her arms about him, and take some of the frustration from him. She stared at his bent head, the queue of golden hair that was caught inside the collar of his shirt, the powerful muscles of his back.

"You've done your part," Grizel snapped suddenly. "I don't see that there's any reason for you to tarry here with Robert."

The coldness of the words broke whatever spell had held Catriona in thrall. She turned away and paused. There, hanging over an armoire, was a blue brocade gown, finely wrought.

Sarah's wedding gown. The gown in which she would wed Robert. Or else be buried.

Overcome by guilt and helplessness, Catriona rushed out into the corridor and bumped smack into a masculine body, someone in breeches and ruffs. He dropped a book. Assuming it to be Lord Kendrick, she started to explain how Sarah fared, then as the glow from a candle sconce highlighted the man's features, she gasped.

It was Jacques Beaufort. Shadows etched his face so that his handsome countenance resembled a gargoyle. He stretched his mouth across his teeth in a fair imitation of a smile, a smile exaggerated by the flickering wall sconces.

"*Mademoiselle*, you wander the castle late at night like

a ghost.'' He made no secret of craning his neck to see beyond into the commotion in Sarah's room. "Do you need assistance?''

She put a finger to her lips, a warning to talk softly. "Sarah is ill, seriously ill,'' she explained, and reached down for the book he had dropped.

It lay open to a sketch of a royal crown and a scepter. A blotch of moisture, a single raindrop, blew in through a casement window and sparkled on it in the light of the sconces. The royal Regalia of Scotland. Her breath caught in her throat, and she felt the blood pound in her ears. With sudden insight, she realized Robert had been right not to trust Jacques.

"We never saw this on our journey,'' she commented casually, "or did I miss something?'' She stood up and held out the book to him.

"An old sketch, *mademoiselle*. Done years ago.'' Jacques snatched the book from her hands and, shrugging, tucked it firmly under his arm. "Few have seen it, but many would like to find it, *n'est-ce pas?*''

"I don't know.'' She was shaking. "Why should they?''

He shrugged and smiled in that flirtatious way of his. "Can we French not have an interest in Scottish history? The exiled Scottish court intrigues me with its tales, you see, especially of the Regalia, which was so cleverly hidden once and then, after the Act of Union, vanished. Poof.'' He snapped his fingers. "Truth to tell, *mademoiselle*, I would give anything to obtain this treasure for the exiled king.''

"I see.'' In fact, she saw more than the Frenchman knew. Memories were coming alive again for her. Clan chiefs and a dirk threatening her. Angus's oath of silence and then . . . her banishment.

Her hands trembled. "Have you contacted my grandfather about your whiskey imports?''

Jacques nodded.

"Then there is nothing more to keep you in Glen Strahan, is there?''

"I am only waiting to see if you find your betrothed to your liking.''

A drawn-looking Robert stepped into the hall, stopped at the doorway, and stared at Catriona, his mouth white. His gaze moved to Jacques, and there was no mistaking the dislike between the men.

"You are industrious, Frenchman, learning your way around my grandfather's castle so quickly, not to mention worming your way into his friendship. Surely you do not expect to find a royal crown hidden somewhere, do you?"

Jacques gave a little bow. "Did I leave you with the wrong impression, *monsieur? Mais non*, your cousin, Lachlan, plied me with the good Scotch whiskey which I fear he does not hold well. And then like a dream come true I literally crashed into the fair Catriona here and learned your betrothed does not fare well."

Wearily, Robert looked at Jacques. "Where is Lachlan?" he asked, his tone baleful.

"He sleeps in the great hall," Jacques said, moving to an open window in the corridor and leaning against the stones, his chin propped on his folded arms, the picture of innocence. "As for me, I have been searching for a fabled Scottish ghost but ended up admiring the mist. I have a romantic soul, I fear."

Robert stared at Jacques, as if utterly disgusted with his honeyed words. "I lack your sentimentality, and I doubt, Frenchman, that you'll find any ghosts here. Get on with you. It's a poor night to be about in the castle."

Robert turned on his heel and headed down the corridor toward the great hall while Catriona slipped away, wanting only to say a prayer for the hapless Sarah and banish thoughts of the evil soothsayers that roamed this castle. She couldn't bolt her door fast enough.

A scream awoke her.

Instantly alert, Catriona sat up and shivered, listening. She was alone, and the castle echoed with a shrill wail that pierced the dawn and might have made the candles flicker in their sconces. Her heart began to race so fast she could have jumped out of her skin.

It couldn't possibly be Sarah who'd screamed like that. Not a weak, sick woman. Another wail rent the still dawn, and Catriona hid her head under her pillow, pulling it over her ears to block out the sound.

Merciful silence. Suspicious silence.

No reaction. No running feet. No shouts. Nothing.

Unnerved, Catriona huddled beneath her blanket. Robert would come for her.

She waited. Five minutes passed. Ten. Finally, she lifted her head out from under the pillow.

Then she remembered. He would be making preparations for his wedding day. He had Sarah to console. Not just console, but take to his bed as his bride. Unless Sarah was still ill. She thought for a long time about her dream of Sarah. That dream must be her punishment for not attending kirk in so long. Elspeth had warned her that things had a way of coming round.

Someone rattled the latch of her door. Instantly, Catriona swung her legs off the bed, ready to greet Robert, hoping against hope he would tell her that her imagination had gone fey.

Like a living nightmare, Lachlan strode in. And Catriona knew. She'd already dreamed it. Her legs were buckling, her world swirling.

Indignant, she drew back. "Get out."

Brows raised, Lachlan replied evenly, "As your betrothed, I can walk into your chamber without waiting on your invitation."

"I've signed no marriage contracts yet."

"Your grandfather signed them," he said simply. "If he changes his mind, he'll forfeit his gain."

"Who was screaming?" Catriona asked tiredly. She dreaded hearing the words, having the dream become reality.

"Grizel is hysterical," Lachlan said rather matter-of-factly, then smiled slyly. "Then Robert has not come ahead of me to tell you?"

"Tell me what?" Her voice sounded oddly flat.

Lachlan's face cracked into a look of sly pleasure, and outside, far down the corridor, Grizel's wails changed to broken sobs.

"Robert's wedding is canceled," he said. "Dinna expect him to come and see you,'' he added quickly, following her hopeful glance to the doorway. ''He is in mourning. The Englishwoman is dead.''

Catriona's world swirled. Dream and reality merged, and she sank to her knees in front of Lachlan.

''I know,'' she whispered hoarsely as the floor rose up to meet her. ''The old woman told me.''

Chapter 12

"**W**ho?" With ruthless purpose, Lachlan hauled Catriona up off the floor. "Who the deuce are you talking about?"

Catriona fought her way out of a fog. "It's the bandit woman."

"Talk sense. What woman?" His fingers dug into her flesh.

Catriona felt cold, numb. In a shaken voice, she forced the words out. "On the journey we met bandits. The old woman Marcail gave me a curse. A prophecy."

"Rot. You sound fey."

"I'm not."

He sneered at her as if he didn't believe a word she said. "Your talk about prophecies and curses ill becomes you, Catriona Ferguson. But then, I should have expected such nonsense from a Ferguson."

Fighting disbelief, she advanced on Lachlan and his smirk. Catriona still reeled from the news of Sarah's death. Dear God in heaven, she might have been jealous of Sarah, but never, never would she have wished her to die. It couldn't be true. It couldn't.

"I tried to help her with herbs," she said. "She was sleeping peacefully when I left her." She wiped tears from her cheeks. "She was sleeping," she repeated so softly she could scarcely hear herself.

"Believe what you will." With an evil gleam in his eye, Lachlan moved to stand over her. "The Englishwoman's body will be laid out within the hour in the great hall. As soon as Grizel calms down, she will attend to the dressing of the body. Lord Kendrick is in a snit because we have no black gloves for Sarah—as if we're supposed to provide an English funeral here in the Highlands.'' Lachlan grabbed Catriona again and pulled her close to his face. "My point, dearly betrothed, is that we need no more hysteria.''

The tone of his voice did not augur well, she thought, for the peace of the castle.

"I would speak with Robert,'' she said, her voice reflecting a calmness she was far from feeling.

"Nay, my betrothed. Lies willna get you closer to him. If it's fear you feel, you will turn to me for comfort and to no other man.''

"Don't you have a castle to tend to?'' She tugged away.

"Aye, and I have my own kin to look out for. You will not see my cousin Robert today. He needs none of your soothsayer talk.'' Lachlan's lank hair fell over his forehead in wild disorder, and his eyes gleamed coldly. Catriona thought him an evil dragon, worse than anything she'd ever dreamed, and she sank back down on the counterpane, feeling as if the breath had been knocked out of her.

At the sound of footsteps moments later, Catriona swung round to the door, hoping it was Robert. Her heart fell. Grizel walked in, red-eyed, but the sly smirk on her face belied her tears. In her hands she clutched her serpent tapestry, the full length of it trailing behind her like a veil.

"Grizel.'' Catriona jumped up and hurried to the woman. "What happened?''

"As Lachlan has no doubt told you, the Englishwoman is dead. It was not the pox or the plague that killed her. And obviously your herbs did not give her ease.'' She swatted a spider off the chest and sat down, the tapestry stretching out in front of her. She stroked the embroidered serpents. "Mayhap your herbs harmed her.''

"What do you mean?'' Catriona moved to confront Grizel, but with a hand to her shoulder, Lachlan stayed her.

"Lachlan was wondering what you put in that potion you gave her,'' she said, looking up. "Weren't you, brother?''

"Are you suggesting that I fed her tainted herbs?" Catriona demanded, feeling weak.

Grizel smiled. "Tainted? Perhaps . . . or poisonous? How do we know that you didn't slip in some arsenic or some other fatal substance from an alchemist's laboratory in Edinburgh?"

Catriona felt the blood drain from her face. Sweet mercy, she had actually blurted out before she was told that she knew Sarah had died, as if she'd performed the deed. No wonder they thought the worst.

"I-I have no knowledge of poisons," she stammered. "All I know of herbs I learned from Elspeth, and we use nothing that is not natural—berries, leaves, roots."

"Poisons come from natural sources too," Grizel pointed out with a tight smile.

Lachlan stepped over and, wadding up Grizel's tapestry, tossed it all onto her lap. "Cease your babbling, sister," he said. "We have a funeral to prepare for. There'll be time enough later to vent our suspicions."

"Suspicions?" Catriona whispered, her horror mounting. "Of what? I didn't harm Sarah. I only dreamed that she died, and that's not at all the same as . . ." She couldn't bring herself to say the word.

Grizel rubbed the embroidered serpents against her cheek, as if caressing them.

Heart pounding, Catriona backed up until she bumped into the bed. "I may have dreamed Sarah died, but that doesn't mean I wanted it. Not at all . . . Where's Robert?"

"Grieving . . . *alone*," Lachlan said with heavy emphasis. "Listen, my lovely betrothed . . . Grizel is a bit tetched with fear. But you need pay her no heed." Advancing on her, he smiled smugly. "You're to return to your grandfather's house now."

"How can you smile on a day of death?" she asked.

"I was pondering Robert's dilemma now that his own betrothed is dead and you are promised to me."

Reason fled. Without thinking, Catriona grabbed a pillow and threw it at him. "You pig! I shall never marry you."

Lachlan ducked and pulled her into the cold corridor. "And why not, you fiery little vixen? I'll no' make it that easy for Robert to have you."

She kicked out at him. "Robert's betrothed is not yet cold and you make vile insinuations. Have you no respect?"

He laughed and gripped her all the tighter.

A sentry stopped and asked if he could assist, but Lachlan waved the man off.

"The unexpected death has quite naturally upset my betrothed," he said, then turned to Catriona. "To wed today would be inappropriate. I regret that, with a funeral to arrange, our wedding shall have to be postponed, but only . . ." At the hope she knew must show on her face, he scowled. "But only for the minimum period of decent mourning. Sarah Kendrick was, after all, only an English."

An hour later, after all her pleas for a moment with Robert had fallen on deaf ears, Catriona was escorted back on her horse to Ferguson Manor. It was, she considered, the one small mercy Lachlan provided.

Lachlan watched Catriona ride away and sighed. Of course he'd lied about postponing the wedding. There'd be no wedding at all, but he wouldn't give Catriona the satisfaction of knowing that.

Still, in a way he regretted giving her up. Catriona Ferguson would have made a bonnie bride. He could have agreed to end the feud by claiming her as his own. But who wanted a bride who'd be pining for Robert even while he himself took her to bed? And even if Robert was leaving Glen Strahan, Lachlan guessed Catriona Ferguson would be the sort to pine away after the man forever. So instead of bedding her, Lachlan would ruin her. And ruin Robert while he was at it, him and his damnable charm.

Forfeit the truce. Let the feud continue. Aye, the instant the funeral ended, he'd use the villagers' stupid superstitions and fears to his advantage.

They buried Sarah Kendrick at gloaming surrounded by the mists of the glen and the dirge of the pipes. In the village all work had ceased, and as the MacLean chief and his grandsons, together with Lord Kendrick, strode out of the great hall bearing the coffin on their shoulders, dour-faced villagers stood in the outer ward of the castle to watch.

Pulling the hood of her cloak up against the rain, Catriona stood with her grandfather apart from the others and watched the coffin being carried across the courtyard. The pallbearers passed through the gates, then paused in the midst of the crowd.

Tears sprang to Catriona's eyes. Clutching the customary sprig of heather, she bent her head. What had been the bandit woman's curse? *Once you enter these hills* . . . She shivered. Poor Sarah. There would be no marriage bed with an ardent groom for her. Instead a hole, a gaping hole dug in the sod and sprinkled with sleet.

Catriona raised her gaze to where Lachlan stood. Unlike the other pallbearers, who stared straight ahead, he was watching *her,* triumph and carnal desire in his eyes. Catriona shivered. Who was to say but what a cold grave would not be better than marriage to Lachlan?

Catriona crumbled the dried heather between her fingers and watched it drift to the ground and land in a puddle of rain. She turned to find Robert, but he stood immobile holding his corner of the casket—a plain wooden box with the MacLean plaid draped over it as a pall. Bits of dried heather that had been strewn over the pall fell to the shoulders of his jacket and plaid, and she yearned to brush them off, just to touch him. But, unlike Lachlan, he never once looked at her.

The last few days had been a blur of emotion and veiled suspicion. Only today, while paying her respects to poor Sarah Kendrick who was being buried so far from her family, could Catriona begin to think clearly.

She forced herself to concentrate on the piper who was prepared to play again. His movements had a decided order to them, a comforting predictability that life lacked. First the piper cradled the bag in his left arm and took the mouth tube between his lips. Next, his right hand reached over to position his fingers on the chanter. As he began to blow, from the drone pipes came a steady pitch, mournful and solemn, and finally as his fingers began to move, came a funereal melody.

That's what life needed, Catriona decided. A *first*. A *next*. A *last*. With no surprises, accidents, or tragedies to involve the emotions.

As the somber strains mingled with the rain, the villagers cleared a path to the castle gates, and the pallbearers moved out. The village mourner began keening as she fell in place behind the coffin. Other older women followed in turn, all garbed alike in black dresses with white lace on their heads. Their singing echoed the melody of the dirge. As was customary, the younger women remained behind.

When the men returned an hour later, Catriona was still standing there. Robert glanced at her and paused, but instead of speaking to her, he moved on to the funeral feast with the others. Later, she watched Robert escort Lord Kendrick to the Englishman's carriage, tie his horse's reins to the back, and climb in after the older man.

At first, Catriona was surprised that the two men would leave so soon after the funeral feast, but as she'd heard Lord Kendrick say, he wanted to leave the village. It gave him the willies, he said. Still, Catriona wished for just a word of reassurance that Robert did not hold her to blame for what had happened. Whether he intended to go all the way to Carlisle with the English lord, she had no idea, but she was afraid suddenly, as if the dark mood of the sky had reached her soul.

The carriage rumbled off down the lane leading from the castle. Catriona still stood where she was, listening to the clop of hooves that took Robert farther and farther away. Away from the village . . . across the lonely moors and fells of the Highlands . . . away from Scotland . . . and away from her. In the distance the bell of the wee kirk tolled, and still the pipes played on—haunting, wild music.

The coach had no sooner vanished from sight than Grizel, her dark eyes bright, crossed in front of Catriona. "Had to have Robert for yourself, eh? So desperate for him that you'd wish Sarah dead?"

"No, that's not true."

"Lachlan thinks otherwise."

Then Grizel smiled her sly smile and, lifting her cloak away from contact with Catriona, sauntered over to a gaggle of whispering village women.

Catriona wondered where Angus was. He had planned to return directly to the manor after paying his respects. She had already told him she wished to walk home along the banks of Loch Aislair, once she was certain Grizel no longer required her help with the funeral feast. Now, she wasn't so sure. She had just turned to look for her grandfather's coach when she felt something hit her.

It was naught but a pebble that was still rolling across the stones of the outer ward. But when the second pebble hit in short order, a cold dread stole over her heart. Turning to see who stood behind her, she saw only the village women.

She was facing them when another, larger rock struck her leg from behind, then rolled to the wild grass beneath the Caledonian pine that grew in the ward.

She whirled again, hoping to see a naughty child hiding behind his mama's skirts. Instead, she saw only a cluster of more women, the same villagers who had welcomed Robert home and chattered of his coming marriage.

Another pebble hit her, again from behind. She flinched as another followed in close order. "Stop it!" she shouted, whirling yet again. She met only blank faces or suspicious eyes that darted sideways the instant she looked at them.

From behind came another rock and this time a voice. " 'Twas an evil potion, lassie. Coveting another man was no reason to murder."

She turned, but only a close-mouthed cluster of women faced her.

Another pebble hit her from behind. Spinning so fast that her skirts became tangled, she saw now that the women were beginning to close in on her, encircling her.

"You're a witch—that's what Lachlan said," someone accused.

"No." A whisper of denial was all she managed.

"Cast a spell, ye did, Lachlan thinks. He's talking to the MacLean about ye this very moment."

Again Catriona whipped around, trying to pinpoint the source of the voice. Grizel looked back, blank-faced.

"Betrothed to Lachlan and caught in Robert's arms," someone cackled.

"Lachlan will make her pay."

Catriona whirled in time to see Fiona Grant, the farrier's wife, speaking.

Another pebble struck her. "Cast a curse on Lachlan in his own castle, she did. A servant heard."

From front and back came the assaults. A pebble to distract her, followed by more ugly words. Hatred from women who only seconds ago had been regarding her with innocent faces. Bitter words. Shrewish words. *Witch . . . witch . . . witch.*

Clear as the kirk bell that still tolled came Grizel's voice, vitriolic and whining. "I saw her herbs with my own eyes. Deadly looking. Smelled of sorcery and black magic, they did. Told Lachlan, I did."

"You can't mean that, Grizel." With rain blinding her, Catriona started toward the woman. "You don't know what happened to Sarah any more than I do, Grizel. Lachlan can't do this."

Back and forth she turned until finally she froze in place, and the pebbles and words came in one steady, stinging blur, ending with a stone that hit so hard she tasted blood where it stung her lip.

Catriona slammed her hands to her ears to shield herself from the words. "I'm not a witch!" she finally screamed. "I'm not!"

The pebble throwing ceased as abruptly as if a white-hot iron had been snuffed. Catriona could practically smell the acrid sizzle of hatred, could feel the dark emotions surrounding her.

"Murderess."

"That's not so." Dropping her hands, she stood in place, surrounded, paralyzed with fear. Her hair blew loose about her face like fire. "No . . . no." Tears slid down her cheeks. She had no defense against such hate.

"Angus," she called, panic-stricken, but then she remembered that he had returned ahead of her.

Wildly, Catriona whirled, looking for any friendly face. Angus was gone. Elspeth lay ill. Robert had abandoned her here.

And Lachlan had turned the village against her.

"Angus banished you once, Catriona," Grizel said. "Who's to say he won't banish you again?"

"Or mayhap the village will burn you."

The word stung worse than the stones.

"No . . . no." Catriona buried her face in her hands and sobbed.

Chapter 13

"Egad!"
Lord Kendrick reached up and straightened his wig after the coach lurched in and out of a particularly wicked rut.

"I still cannot believe your grandfather had the audacity to suggest I haul Sarah's body home with me," he grumbled, rubbing his red-rimmed eyes.

Robert shot an impatient glance at his mentor. Like a frightened hare, Lord Kendrick had insisted on leaving the Highlands the instant the funeral feast ended.

"In the Highlands, Lord Kendrick, it is customary to be buried close to one's kin. The suggestion was well meant."

"Foolish sentimentality. As if I'd ride in here with a corpse. Why, I'd have to sit on top and endure the abominable weather. There is a limit to a man's forbearance, Robert." He cleared his throat. "Well, things ended differently than we expected, but your family is to be commended on the funeral preparations. Not up to English standards, of course, but adequate in a pinch."

At that moment the coach lurched sideways again, in and out of a rut that might have rivaled Loch Aislair in size. Again, Lord Kendrick's ivory-tipped cane rolled to the floor, and this time Robert bent to retrieve it.

"Worst roads in creation," Lord Kendrick grumbled by way of thanks. "I should have taken the flying packet."

"How long did the journey from Carlisle take you?" Robert asked, caring little for mundane conversation, but

177

grabbing any chance to divert Lord Kendrick from Sarah's funeral.

"Too long," came the acerbic answer. "Stopped every two days to rest the horses. No proper posting houses along the way, you realize. I had to make do with naught but my own team. Sarah held up admirably well, considering, though she did her share of complaining."

"Doubtless." Robert's lips tightened at the memory of Catriona complaining on their own journey to the Highlands. Robert still reeled with guilt. What a godawful disaster. He'd actually been in another woman's chamber, dallying with Catriona's hair, comforting her from some maidenly nightmare, while Sarah, his betrothed, lay dying.

Lord Kendrick was droning on. "Mayhap it's just as well you aren't shackled to Sarah. I've a suspicion she might have been a whining sort, not really suitable for a politician." He heaved a sigh. "But that's neither here nor there now."

Robert listened in growing dismay. He had whiled away some pleasant hours in the Edinburgh taverns discussing the merits of wenches with Kendrick, but this callous talk appalled him.

"Your lordship," Robert admonished gently, "your niece is not yet cold in her grave."

"And a wretched Scottish one at that," Lord Kendrick said, straightening his wig again. Powder drifted onto the shoulders of his velvet coat. "Buried like a peasant, actually, with none of the proper amenities a funeral in England would have given her. Not even black headbands and gloves for the guests. No invitations. Not even a proper embalming, or a black pall. *Plaid* on the coffin. Damndest thing I ever saw."

"Have a care, your lordship," Robert said, trying to suppress his irritation. "That is, after all, a Highland village, not London. What did you expect?"

Pursing his lips, Lord Kendrick made a tired sound. "You're right, of course, as usual. When in Rome, do as the Romans do. Is that the saying?" Casting a hasty glance Robert's way, he added, "You must pardon me, Robert.

I'm just an old man who enjoys fussing. I can smooth over the death with Sarah's parents—as long as they don't hear the details of the funeral. I'll embellish it a bit. Leave out any mention of the bagpipes. Dreadful noise. Enough to scare away the angels.''

Robert bit back a smile. "Actually, at one time they were intended to scare away the English," he pointed out.

"Were they then?" Lord Kendrick snorted in amusement. "You Scots have the gall. But then I think that's why I like you, Robert. Your direct approach is just the thing for the Hanoverian court. Too much backstabbing and scheming down there as it is now. No, give me a forthright man any day . . . How did we get on this subject now? Ah, yes, Sarah. Well, that's all water under the bridge."

Robert bristled. "Naturally, I'll pay my respects to her parents—"

"No, needn't trouble yourself," Lord Kendrick interrupted. "Actually, if I thought a condolence call would help, I'd suggest it, but because you're a Scotsman it's best left to me. Believe me, when I'm done explaining the situation, they'll no doubt write *you* a condolence letter for the inconvenience their daughter's ill-timed demise cost you.''

Robert could no longer keep the testiness from his voice. "You might allow us the illusion of grieving for my betrothed.''

"Pshaw! No need to play the martyr, Robert. Everyone knows it was a marriage of convenience, and bear in mind, Sarah's father is only an impecunious relative. Fathered too many daughters as it was.''

"Lord Ken—"

"Hear me out now." Lord Kendrick held up a hand for silence. "Sarah's father will accept the idea of sudden illness. Demned nuisance when a bride-to-be dies on her wedding eve, but not unheard of. I shall blame her death on the rigors of the journey and a sudden chill . . . and, of course, discourse a bit about the ways her Scottish bridegroom tried to help her in her hour of direst need. The family will accept it easily enough. More of a nui-

sance for me, actually, having to make this jouncing coach
ride for naught.''

Robert was outraged. And the English had the nerve to
sneer down their noses at the Scots for being barbaric.
Good God!

"You suspect it was murder, don't you, Robert?" Lord
Kendrick asked unexpectedly.

Robert felt a jolt of surprise. He didn't reply immediately. Wily old sot, Lord Kendrick.

"Well?" Kendrick prompted.

"Aye, I have my suspicions."

"Yes, well, take heed to keep people from talking when
you return to Edinburgh, else your ambitions may be jeop-
ardized.''

"I appreciate your concern over my family's titles,"
came the acerbic reply.

With a smile and a languid gesture, Lord Kendrick
reached for his snuffbox and, flipping it open, offered some
to Robert. "So . . . tell me who you suspect as the vil-
lain.''

Robert shrugged, feigning a casualness he didn't feel.
The nagging worry that had been in the back of his mind
suddenly came into focus. Catriona. He'd left her alone
with Lachlan.

With no warning, the crowd of hysterical women parted,
and through her tears Catriona saw Lachlan pushing toward her. He grabbed her arm and pulled her away, not
letting go until he had brought her inside the great hall.
She stood there shivering while he stared at her, his eyes
as cold as stone.

" 'Twould seem suspicion lingers over the way Robert's
betrothed died. Mayhap at the hand of a jealous rival for
his bed? Robert always did have the wenches fighting over
him," Lachlan went on, "but none has yet resorted to
murdering her rivals." He stood there smiling at her, as
if he'd just handed her a compliment.

"You made the villagers say those vile words."

"The villagers trust my opinions. You, they don't even

know. And the unknown is frightening to the superstitious.''

Revolted by his insinuation, Catriona could only glare. Lascivious. Sarcastic. Vile. Evil ingredients brewed in Lachlan's soul, and Catriona wouldn't be surprised but that the devil himself owned the receipt. In any case, he was a bitter brew of a man, one she had no taste for.

There was no reasoning with this man, so she tried flattery. ''You're too wise a man to start such ugly gossip, Lachlan. I tried to help Sarah. And I gave her nothing but harmless herbs, at Robert's request.''

Lachlan's eyebrows rose in a look of skepticism. ''At Robert's request?'' he said sarcastically. ''The man had you in his arms out on the ramparts just hours before.''

''You misunderstood what you saw.''

He held her as if his grip had claws. ''Dinna play the naive chit with me.''

''What you saw meant nothing.'' Her heart was hammering in her ears. ''Even if what Robert and I did looked compromising, that doesn't mean I'd hurt Sarah Kendrick.''

Lachlan's lip curled. ''You wanted Robert for yourself, didn't you?'' he accused. ''What better way to get him?'' His fingers bit deeper. ''Or mayhap it's Robert we should suspect.''

''No. He'd never have harmed Sarah. I—''

She almost blurted out that she loved Robert, but this was a time when the truth could only worsen suspicion.

''Robert and I are friends,'' she said. ''We shared the journey up here. He kept me alive more than once, and naturally I feel . . . gratitude.''

''Liar.'' The single word cut like a whipstroke. ''The embrace I saw on the ramparts was not one of gratitude but of desire. Forbidden desire. Is that not what the foppish poets call it, Catriona?''

Her throat tightened. How could this be happening? Her family had lived in Glen Strahan for four generations. She had been born in this village. Had her years in Edinburgh made the villagers forget?

''I tried to help Sarah,'' she whispered over and over,

filled with a new kind of fear. Not a fear of words or even of stones, but the fear that there was not one person here in this glen, save Elspeth, whom she could trust.

Perhaps meekness would serve where resistance had failed. "I want to go home," Catriona begged.

"I think not," Lachlan said. "I've already allowed you to return to your grandfather once, and to no good purpose."

"Well, surely you can't just keep me here."

"Why not? I'm a hospitable Highlander."

"The villagers will expect me to return to Angus."

"No, they won't. Not if I make them think you're a threat to the village. They'd want you locked up here."

"You can't do that."

"Can't I? It's as simple, Catriona Ferguson, as reminding the villagers of when you were a wee bairn. Running wild, plucking herbs. Healing animals. Always in a temper. Even as a child you were capable of unruly emotion. Some of the good villagers will have even more memories. Memories of a fey child who turned into a beautiful witch . . ."

His gaze ran up and down her, almost as if he were undressing her. "I should like to bed a witch, I believe."

Instinctively, Catriona jerked away from him. "You can't do this. My grandfather will bring all of his men here and take me away."

"He would be a sentimental fool. I, on the other hand, have no room for sentiment. I have villagers who look to the castle for protection. I would have to fight your grandfather off."

She turned to run then, but in a trice he caught her to him again and pulled her closer.

"I don't want your hands on me," she hissed, pushing back from him.

"You prefer stones?" Lachlan's voice was icy calm, his eyes laughing. "Or mayhap you'll let your woman Elspeth be charged in your place," he said in a threatening voice.

"She was ill."

"No matter. She's old and ugly, and the villagers would

find it easy to believe she's in league with the devil. Such, my dear, is the way with superstitious Highlanders.''

"You have no soul at all, do you?''

He smiled. "I haven't looked recently, but the oafs in the village will never doubt the word of a MacLean.''

And so Catriona saw her choice. Reluctantly, she allowed Lachlan to lead her deeper into the castle, thinking that if the Fergusons and the MacLeans sat down and talked, she could explain her innocence. She'd plead with all the logic she'd learned from her father's philosophy books. Somehow she'd *make* these people see the lack of reason behind their medieval suspicions.

"So, who do you suspect?'' Lord Kendrick urged, pulling Robert from his reverie.

He shrugged. "Anybody could have been paid to slip some poison into Sarah's wine. Even a sentry.''

"And those herb potions the little redheaded wench poured down her?''

"Harmless. Naught but some chamomile brew.''

"So she said. And you do assure me it wasn't yourself, Robert? Before I arrange another alliance, I need to know you're blameless.''

"You invited me to ride with you to question my honor?'' Robert scoffed. He had a mind to halt the coach then and there, mount his horse, and ride the short way back to the castle. Running a weary hand over his forehead, he realized how very little sleep he'd had in the days since Sarah had died.

"Robert, Robert,'' Lord Kendrick was saying in soothing tones. "I've never questioned your honor. Why else would I have taken you under my wing? I *want* you to help me with Highland affairs when I become secretary of state for Scotland. But Robert, Robert, I had to ask.''

"No, you didn't.''

"Robert, I could lose my own post for befriending a Scotsman who's involved in any kind of skullduggery, and you know it. Besides, anyone could see you've an eye for the Scots wench. One could draw some unfortunate conclusions from that observation.''

"Such as?"

"Such as that she might have fed you a love potion."

Robert stared dumbfounded at his host. "You exaggerate what you saw."

"Do I?" Smiling, Lord Kendrick ran a lazy fingertip over the gold leaf design of his snuffbox and reached inside for another pinch, lifted it to his nostrils, inhaled, and sneezed several times.

"As you say, Robert."

The conversation had turned down a rockier road than the carriage traveled, and Robert had been put on the defensive. "I feel responsible for Catriona, nothing more. Wouldn't you if Lachlan were your kin?"

Lord Kendrick nodded, his grimace exaggerating the bulldog wrinkles of his face. "Bit of bad luck there all right. How you and he could have sprung from the same line is beyond me, but there's nothing for it but to keep him hidden away up in the Highlands. Wouldn't want him prowling about London, claiming himself as your relative among the haughty English, if you follow me."

"Too well . . . As long as you understand about Catriona?" He'd grown more used to looking out for the wee red thistle than he cared to admit. He couldn't shake the feeling that he shouldn't have abandoned her to Lachlan.

"I understand more than you give me credit for, Robert." Lord Kendrick used the ivory head of his walking stick to snag the drapery on the window nearest him. For a few minutes he gazed out at the rugged scenery, then said, as much to himself as to Robert, "Can't say as I blame you, lad, wanting to have your cake before you shackled yourself to your bread and butter, shall we say? What's her name again? Catriona? Pretty enough, if a bit lacking in flesh, and a bit garish, what with the red hair and all. Pity she's your cousin's betrothed, eh?"

When Robert didn't answer, Lord Kendrick kept on. "But then, she'd never do for a political alliance. Mending feuds between clans carries little weight in London. No, you'll need another Englishwoman for your marriage bed." His forehead furrowed in thought.

Robert studied the passing landscape. The political situation was easy to handle. It was the chaotic situation at Castle Fenella MacLean that troubled him, and he let his thoughts drift back over the past week.

In the days since Sarah's death, the castle and village alike had been paralyzed with shock. Scared-faced servants had tiptoed around looking as if the devil himself had paid the castle a visit, and villagers had shuttered their cottages. Torn as he was between the role of a bereaved bridegroom and his concern for Catriona, Robert had no time to visit the villagers in person and gauge their mood, let alone reassure them.

The one time he had gotten near Catriona during the wake in the great hall, always Grizel had kept her black bird's eyes trained on both of them. The most he had managed was a reassuring hand to Catriona's shoulder when Lachlan and Grizel were diverted by Lord Kendrick demanding why in all of Scotland a man could not find some decent snuff or a black headband.

He had also noticed Catriona just after the burial, her alabaster skin looking paler than ever, her cloak pulled up so that he could scarcely see her hair. By then he had ached to take the little red thistle in his arms, to bury his own face in her silken curls, to take comfort from her softness. But with the entire village watching, how could he?

"Odds fish, Robert," Lord Kendrick said for the third time, "you've not paid any heed to my suggestions, have you?"

A long pause followed, during which Robert realized he was staring at his fists and that his knuckles had turned white.

"These tragedies happen all the time," Lord Kendrick said at length. "I can find you another Englishwoman who will serve the same purpose—" He stopped and chuckled. "Now, I've several suitable candidates in mind. Not all conveniently related to me, mind you, so it may take some doing to arrange it, but any one of them would leave us both well-connected in London with the Hanoverian court."

"Do you think I'm wanting to leap from betrothal to

betrothal like a man moving between doxy houses?'' Robert pulled the drapery across the window to shut out the sight of endless rain.

Lord Kendrick's eyes snapped open, and he half turned to face Robert. ''My dear lad, a future such as yours must not wait . . . nor should mine.''

For the first time Robert realized the depth of Lord Kendrick's selfishness. ''It's too soon,'' he said.

''Robert, you stubborn Scotsman. Surely you realize all the implications of this tragedy with Sarah. An English-woman murdered in Scotland? Do you want some toady to cross the Channel and take this news to the Pretender? It would be fodder for his rebellion plans.''

''Charles Edward is too old to lead another rebellion,'' Robert said.

''Ah, but there's his son, don't forget. James. Nigh on sixteen and vainly ambitious. As for King George, his Hanoverian advisers are itching for a reason to stomp on Scotland.''

''They'll never dare.''

''Nevertheless, Robert, the point is that an incident like this suspicious death can be used to advantage by many people. It must be kept quiet, at all costs.''

Robert shifted uncomfortably in his seat. ''And I suppose you see me as someone who can be counted on?''

Lord Kendrick beamed, his bulldog face fairly lighting up. ''Absolutely. Face facts, Robert. If things are left to drift along by the Hanoverians and Stuarts, I see the devil of a mess down the road.''

At last, Lord Kendrick moved from the subject and began droning on about the changing state of affairs in the Hanoverian court and the desperate need for decent envoys between London and the Highlands.

A chance to make a difference, to alter the history books. That was what Lord Kendrick offered Robert. What ambitious man would not be tempted? Robert stared back out at the rain, trying to see himself moving at ease at the royal court, but instead he kept seeing the vision of a spritely redheaded lass beckoning him, calling him back to Glen Strahan.

"Come along with me to Carlisle—or Edinburgh if you please—and we'll arrange something new," Lord Kendrick cajoled. "There's nothing of importance to keep you in a little Scottish village."

Robert shook his head, his uneasiness turning to dread.

"Come, come. We can be there in a matter of days."

"No. I shouldn't have traveled this far with you as it is." Robert rapped on the roof of the carriage, and with ponderous movements it slowed to a stop. "I only came to talk in privacy. It's past time I returned."

His mentor clucked his tongue restlessly. "All right then. Go back and solve your little murder if you must. Just keep it secret. Meet me in Edinburgh in a fortnight."

"A month," Robert countered.

"It won't do to put it off too long, Robert. Many men are vying for the post of secretary of state to Scotland. With your assistance on Highland matters, I could appear the strongest candidate. Don't let me down."

"Don't worry. You know how much I want my family titles back."

"Well, then . . . ?"

"I need a bit of time up in Glen Strahan." For what, Robert could not explain, only that his sense of foreboding had worsened. Without further ado he took his leave. After untying his horse, he mounted and headed back down the road toward Glen Strahan.

He had gone only a short distance when some demon made him dig his heels into the animal's flank and send the animal galloping on a hellbent pace.

As Lachlan and his sheriff rode out of the castle gates, mud splashing in their wake, a dark drizzle continued to fall.

Reaching the first cottage, he slowed, aware that people thronged the lane near the kirk, their rapt gazes focused on a white-faced minister with a bobbing Adam's apple. Lachlan was weary of their complaints. Paltry nuisances. Always begging for favors. For food. For clothing. For a larger scrap of land on which to sow their wretched barley. This time he intended to use their superstitious ways to avenge himself. Catriona was going to regret dearly ever letting herself fall prey to Robert's charm.

Reining in his horse at the outskirts of the crowd, Lachlan listened to the talk directed at the minister. For days after Sarah Kendrick's death a stunned silence had lain over the village, but now their silence was giving way to panic. He smiled as he realized just how nicely they were panicking. Like ripening fruit ready to be plucked.

"Three mysterious deaths . . . all young women . . . Two young girls and now a wench in the castle itself!"

That English blood had coursed through the veins of the last woman mattered not, Lachlan noted. Aye, they were fearful.

A child suddenly fell out of the pear tree, and the villagers jumped as one. Like a scared animal. To Lachlan's utter delight, one name kept being repeated left and right.

Catriona Ferguson.

Hysterical voices cultivated all the seeds of doubt that Lachlan and his retainers had already planted. Aye, the villagers had fertile minds. Feed them a rumor, and they ripened immediately into panic. He dismounted and stood in the shadows, listening.

"She was sent away once years ago by Angus. Who knows but what she wasn't fey then?" It was the shrill voice of the farrier's wife, Fiona Grant.

"You're wrong," Mr. Drummond argued, and Lachlan tensed, waiting for him to say his piece. Stubborn man. Lachlan never had liked him, not even when they were children. "She gave me wife some herbs for our son, and they healed the laddie."

"A ploy to avoid suspicion," the farrier shouted.

Fiona Grant joined in. "If she was seen outside the castle with Robert at night, after dark, then that's proof enough she's a sorceress because—"

"Shut yer mouth, woman," young Fraser Robertson shouted. "She couldn't have murdered the first two lasses. She wasn't even in the village then."

Idealistic young lad, Lachlan thought. He ought to see what he could do to make his lot more difficult.

"But a blackbird was seen flying up from both bodies," Fiona Grant argued back. "She could have changed herself into a bird."

Now that was more like it, Lachlan thought with a smile. Fiona had remembered Lachlan's words well.

"A servant at the castle says she laid a curse on the castle itself," said red-haired Thomas the butcher.

Aye, a laddie after Lachlan's own heart. Remembered word for word what Lachlan had paid the man to say.

"Heard it with his own ears," Thomas shouted. "If she'd curse the castle and cause a death, what next? Are all the lasses in our village to die before she's stopped?"

"Please. Please," the minister said, raising his hands. He might as well have been trying to part the waters of Loch Aislair.

Colin Grant jumped up on a cart. "There's no end to her wiles. The Frenchman let fall that she cursed our own Robert MacLean on the journey here—more than once— and showed a marked fondness for herbs, which Grizel says is what she used to bind Robert's wound. If we don't act now, who knows but what she'll bewitch our beloved Robbie as well . . ."

Lachlan had heard enough to satisfy himself that the majority of the villagers had been properly swayed by the rumors he'd had his henchmen whisper in the ears of the most gullible. Choosing that propitious moment to dismount, he strode into the middle of the crowd and climbed up the steps of the kirk, where he pushed aside the quavering minister. His sheriff followed in his wake and stationed his considerable bulk nearby.

"My villagers," Lachlan said, his tone for once benevolent. "Your fears must be put to rest. What would you have me do for you?"

It had been a long while since Lachlan had deigned to ride down and ask what he could do for a villager, so for a stunned moment the crowd stood silent. As Reverend Macaulay gaped, Lachlan cast what he hoped was a mournful look up at the rainsoaked heavens.

Then the farrier's wife moved forward again. "Burn her. She's a witch for sure, so burn her."

"No."

Scowling, Lachlan snapped around to see who had pro-
tested. It was Mrs. Drummond. Angus Ferguson em-
ployed her as a seamstress. She'd resisted Lachlan's tales,
much to his frustration, and still she defied him.

"I told you, the day after she arrived the Ferguson lass
gave herbs to my lad and cured him."

"You lie!" Fiona Grant shot back.

Lachlan looked at the women. Of the two, he'd always preferred Fiona Grant. Such a marvelously passionate woman, ruled by her emotions rather than by
intelligence. He'd been impressed by her ever since she
had initiated him into the delights of the flesh some
years earlier.

"The heir of Glen Strahan would never wed her now
and sire the devil's spawn to reign over us," Fiona
added.

"Hush your wicked thoughts," Agnes Drummond
snapped.

Lachlan scowled at the self-righteous seamstress.
"You'd do well, woman, to direct your thoughts to your
own cottage."

She blanched. "Why?"

"It's uninhabitable."

"Nay, I've kept fine care of it."

"That, my good woman, is a matter of opinion. In *my*
opinion, your cottage needs to be torn down. The land
would raise finer barley than it does tenants."

At that Mrs. Drummond shrank back, tears in her eyes.
"No, please . . ."

Fiona Grant stood smirking at Agnes Drummond, and
the minister tried to push forward. "Wait, wait, we cannot
condemn the Ferguson woman out of hand. We'd need to
try the case in a proper manner."

Lachlan pretended to be surprised. "And did you sur-
mise otherwise, sir? What sort of heathens do you think
reside in your parish? Of course we'll conduct a proper
trial," he said smoothly. "You and Mrs. Drummond can
relax on that account."

"How?" the minister asked.

Lachlan looked at his sheriff, a paunchy castle retainer whose father and grandfather before him had held the post of sheriff. So far, his job had involved nothing more arduous than collecting taxes and settling occasional village disputes. It was time MacIvie earned his keep. "You know what we need to do?"

MacIvie gulped, his eyes bulging, as if fearing for his daily allowance of bannocks and ale. He nodded.

A silence fell over the crowd as if they realized the enormity of what they had started.

Striding down the steps of the wee kirk, Lachlan managed to keep his satisfaction from showing on his face. Motioning the minister and Sheriff MacIvie to follow, he mounted his horse and headed back to Castle Fenella Mac-Lean. He went directly to Catriona, who sat shivering in a bedchamber, guarded by a pair of hungry-looking clansmen.

"Bored up here, my dear? You missed all the excitement."

Shivering, she glared up at Lachlan, not trusting his smile or his kind words. "May I go home now, please?" she asked.

He didn't answer her. She realized then that Lachlan had not come alone. The minister and the sheriff moved forward to flank him. Then all three advanced on her, the man of the church, the man of the law, and the man of the clan. She felt blood pound in her ears.

"Catriona Ferguson," intoned the sheriff while a white-faced minister looked on, "for acts of black magic against this village—"

"No, please . . ." *Hope is a waking dream.* Please let me wake up.

"And against this castle's good people—"

"You can't do this to me." She tried to stand, but her body wouldn't move. As if in a nightmare, the words washed over her.

"And for causing the death of three innocent women, I accuse you of murder by witchcraft—"

She felt as if she'd been struck physically. Someone was pulling her to her feet, and her legs were broth.

Lachlan caught her elbow and dragged her from the room, then pushed her into the arms of the quaking sentries.

"Lock her in the storeroom. Chain her to the ale barrels. Put her where not even her grandfather can find her."

Chapter 14

Angus Ferguson learned the next morning from Elspeth that his granddaughter had never returned from the castle.

"Something's wrong," Elspeth insisted.

Angus was standing on the first hole of his golf links, ready to hit. "Mayhap she's decided to stay and acquaint herself more intimately with Lachlan," he said with resignation. His own departed wife had shyly given him her virginity before the wedding ceremony. " 'Tis the way of many a betrothed couple to march ahead of the vows."

Elspeth frowned at his cavalier answer. "Catriona told ye there would be no wedding to Lachlan MacLean, and if ye didna hear it, I did all through the journey up from Edinburgh. Led Robert a merry chase, she did. Nay, she'll no' be biding in the castle with Lachlan. Robert's another matter, but Robert's gone off with Lord Kendrick."

For a long moment, Angus stared down at the wee golf ball. Elspeth had a knack for chastening and properly worrying a man. Sighing, he turned away, staring in the direction of the castle far across the loch.

The auld maidservant was right, and Angus knew it.

For the first time, he allowed himself to acknowledge the uneasy undercurrents at the funeral of the Englishwoman. A mood more of hostility than grief between Robert and Lachlan. A sense of guilt from Catriona, though he'd not known the reason. But now the memory of too many deaths in the village worried him. Deaths of lasses. Suddenly he was afraid for his granddaughter.

Abruptly striding back to the manor house, he sorely regretted allowing his willful granddaughter to have her way when she'd announced she would walk home alone along the loch. He should have insisted a groom stay with her.

At once, he sent a servant to Castle Fenella MacLean to bring her back now. Richard was the youngest and ablest of the Ferguson retainers, the groom who had delighted in showing Catriona where Angus played golf. He was a strong-willed young man, but likable. If anyone could cajole information from the castle, it would be Richard.

For the first time in years Angus postponed his morning golf game while he paced in front of the manor and awaited his granddaughter's return.

Too soon, Richard arrived at a gallop. Alone.

"She's in the dungeon, sir," he gasped as he slid off the horse. Clearly winded, Richard had to bend over and grasp his thighs to catch his breath.

Angus thought he must be hearing things. The dungeon. What the deuce was going on over there?

"Speak up, mon, explain all this dungeon nonsense. I left her there to assist with a funeral feast. Mending fences with the MacLeans, she was. Where's Catriona?" His voice rose, reflecting his barely contained panic. Even as he posed the question, he was half afraid to hear the answer.

Having caught his breath, Richard began to relate to Angus what a sentry at the castle had told him. With each word, Angus shriveled a bit, and the blood drained from his face until he suspected he must resemble a ghost.

Catriona. In the dungeon. His heart cracked and the pieces shifted out of place.

" 'Tis sorry I am to bring these bad tidings—"

"No." *Catriona. My bonnie bairn.*

Aware of Ferguson retainers standing nearby, Angus managed but one word, hoarse and whispered: "Why?"

"The death of Sarah," Richard said quietly, and moved to place a comforting hand on his master's arm. Too familiar a gesture in normal circumstances, but Angus welcomed the feel of a human touch now.

"When?"

"They threw the first stone right after you left yesterday."

Angus flinched.

"Lachlan sent his most loyal men to whisper rumors in the village. Mrs. Drummond tried to defend her, but . . ."

"Aye, a message came from her." Angus held up a hand. "No more." With dark foreboding, he recalled the message from Mrs. Drummond late last night. But, worn out from the funeral, he had taken to his bed early and sent the servant away, telling him to leave the message in Catriona's room. Who else would the dressmaker be sending a message to but the lass for whom she was sewing a trousseau?

Now, while they all waited, tense and silent, Elspeth retrieved the message and brought it to Angus. A terse message: *Catriona is in danger.* No more.

Why hadn't he read it? Why? He cursed himself for a stupid old oaf.

"Mrs. Drummond was threatened for her words," the groom said sadly.

Oh, aye, Lachlan would punish those who defied him, Angus thought, and, even though he'd read it too late, he was grateful for her brave message.

"Why?" There was no reason behind it. Suddenly he slammed a hand against the messenger, but Richard's muscled girth absorbed the blow and his arms came up to steady Angus. "Why?" His single word was a half sob.

Richard shrugged. "I grabbed as many sentries as would talk, but none would give more than hasty words. Lachlan's doing, they say. Stirring up the villagers ever since his grandfather departed for a funeral far to the north."

"Alexander is gone!" With a gasp, Elspeth moved close to Angus and echoed what he was thinking. "Lachlan is ruling the castle."

"Lachlan is a bitter man, methinks," the groom said. "He is spreading rumors about Catriona and Robert. And saying that even as a child she was fey. There's even talk that she was banished."

"No!"

"Aye, I fear so . . . and worse."

"How?"

"Lachlan talks of murder."

Angus's shoulders slumped. He and Alexander Mac-Lean had come to an understanding over the years, but it was Lachlan, always Lachlan, who had continued to bedevil Ferguson Manor.

Oh, but he'd been an auld fool for trusting Lachlan. To have signed his grandddaughter's life over to the man all because his pride demanded an heir. Aye, pride had clouded his judgment. Well, plundering land was one thing, but locking away his granddaughter was another.

No, this time Lachlan MacLean had gone too far.

There was one shred of hope left. "Are you certain Alexander is left already for the north?" Mayhap, just mayhap, he had been delayed and could set his grandson to rights.

But Richard only shrugged.

"Fetch my horse," Angus called out but, instead of waiting, grabbed the reins of Richard's mount.

With surprising agility in a man his age, Angus vaulted onto the animal's back.

Moisture pricked at his eyes. Catriona. His dearly beloved granddaughter. His wee bairn, languishing away in a castle like a trapped rabbit. All these years it was the Jacobites he'd hated and sought to protect her from, and now the man he'd wanted for her bridegroom—a Highlander—had imprisoned her. He could have wept like a woman.

By now the word had spread, and without having to be ordered, two dozen loyal Ferguson retainers had mounted behind Angus. They set off at a gallop for Castle Fenella MacLean.

A sentry brought news to Lachlan that Angus Ferguson stood outside the castle wall shooting through the lowered yett with his fowling piece. Incredible, thought Lachlan with mild bemusement, more incredible even than the lace-ruffed Frenchman poking around pretending to be an artist when he had Jacobite written all over him. Jacques's obvious questions had amused Lachlan, but the sight of Angus Ferguson trying to storm the castle with naught but a paltry army of men—that would be a spectacle.

Lachlan was so curious that he actually deemed it his duty to investigate the news himself. He enjoyed the easy authority he held in his grandfather's absence, though he did call for Sheriff MacIvie to accompany him.

Reluctantly, his paunchy sheriff followed in his wake. "I believe Angus means to storm the castle, milord."

"With two dozen men? Don't be a fool, MacIvie. Besides, the castle is impregnable . . . but bar the wooden gates behind the yett. Just in case. Neither he nor any of his men are to pass through these castle walls."

His grandfather's greyhound followed them along the rampart toward the enclosed gatehouse that looked over the yett. Inside, Lachlan stopped, well protected by the thick walls, and watched unobserved through a small slit in the stone.

In the musty darkness, the greyhound paced and whined.

Incredible, Lachlan thought again. The sentry had not exaggerated. Below them, Angus Ferguson and his humble following of men pounded on the wrought-iron gate and demanded admittance, uttering vile curses. Such marvelously vile curses, in fact, that Lachlan had to secretly applaud the old man's mastery of the language. Suddenly, gunshot peppered the sky. Sentries out in the open rampart ducked behind the most readily available protection—the jagged stone parapet that shielded the rampart. Braver sentries made for the safety of the enclosed gatehouse.

"Where's the sheriff?" Angus yelled up at the gatehouse.

Lachlan caught one fleeing sentry and pushed him back out onto the rampart. "Answer him!" Lachlan commanded.

"He was having a wee dram the last I saw him," the sentry called down, backing toward the gatehouse.

"Well, tell him to get his wee arse out here because Angus Ferguson of Ferguson Manor wants to see him."

"A-about what, sir?"

Angus's face turned fierce. He grabbed the grillwork of

the yett and shook it. "Ye know damned well it's about my granddaughter. Where is she?"

"Calm him down," Lachlan said to the sheriff. "I can't talk to him while he's in such a state."

MacIvie looked helplessly back at Lachlan, who motioned him out onto the rampart. When MacIvie hesitated, Lachlan pushed him onto the stone walkway.

"Do your job. Calm the man."

Indeed, when MacIvie, peering around a jagged opening in the parapet, called down, Angus dropped his fowling piece. But the Ferguson men drew their pistols.

"Now, now, Angus, 'tis regrettable this incident regarding your granddaughter, but 'tis no' me who makes the laws." MacIvie continued talking, prodded by Lachlan's hisses. "She'll have her day in court."

"Ye pox-ridden rogue!" Angus shouted up. "If yer ancestor hadna pullèd a MacLean from Flodden Field, ye'd be starving like the other peasants."

"God's teeth, Angus, there's no need to set up such a din," MacIvie called down. "I've always looked out for your estate." With a nervous gesture MacIvie wiped his hand across his upper lip.

"Looked out for my estate?" Angus shouted up. "Ye mean ye've looked the other way when the MacLeans thought to lift a few cattle for their table. Well, they can't have my granddaughter. Get her out of whatever dungeon she's in."

"Now you know this castle contains no dungeons, mon."

A few more shots peppered the sky, creating a lot of smoke and a great din down in the castle ward as MacLean clansmen raised their voices.

"I would speak to Alexander about Catriona. Alexander MacLean, if ye're hiding in there, I demand an explanation!" Angus shouted. "Come out from behind yer castle sentries, ye thieving excuse for a laird."

"Alexander is gone away," MacIvie shouted back.

Angus's face purpled. "Then I'll pay ye for help—more than Alexander ever did."

"That will be all, MacIvie," Lachlan said. "Clearly, if

he's bribing a sheriff of Shire Strahan, he's tetched beyond reason." A simple hand signal sufficed to bring a pair of rugged Highlanders out of the shadows of the gatehouse.

"Open the murder hole," Lachlan ordered. Muscles straining, one sentry heaved back the floor timbers that enclosed an opening directly over the castle entrance— that narrow space between yett and wooden doors. From that overhead opening, Lachlan could position his pistol at just the right angle and shoot Angus dead. But that, he reasoned, might anger his grandfather, who had hoped for a reconciliation of the clans.

Instead, Lachlan shouted down at Angus. "As you well know, my grandfather is gone from the village. Nothing so cowardly as hiding, but a funeral in the north took him. I care for the village in his absence."

Angus craned his neck to try and find the source of Lachlan's voice. "My granddaughter is no' deserving of a dungeon. Give her to me." He reached simultaneously for his fowling piece and began reloading it.

Flanked by a pair of armed clansmen, Lachlan tried a few more calming words. "Now, Angus, ye ken how volatile the villagers are. She's safer here until her trial."

"Trial! Bah! 'Twill be a sham." Through the yett, Angus's face grew more purple with rage.

"Do you have another murderer in mind to explain the death of the lasses?" Lachlan demanded.

"You think I ken what goes on in yer own castle? Any sentry would do for yer dark deeds. Catriona was not even here for the first two deaths."

"Witches perform their deeds across great distance. Any villager knows that."

"Witch? . . . Witch?" Lachlan watched Angus's face contort in some unseen pain. He slumped against the iron bars.

Never the sort to say one hurtful word when two were available, Lachlan continued. "She gave herbs to the Englishwoman."

"That means nothing."

"The villagers believe she is fey. Why, even you banished her, and when you sent word for her to return, people began to die . . ."

Angus's face mottled with anger. "By all that is reasonable, Catriona is no witch, and she is no longer yours to wed. Give her to me. I want to see her."

"Dinna fret so, Angus. Grizel is caring for your granddaughter."

"Your sister is awa' wi' the fairies," he said in disgust.

"Insult my good family all you want, but Catriona is still my betrothed. I have a right to protect her."

"I cancel the marriage contract."

"It is too late."

Angus grabbed the iron bars of the yett and shook them. "Get me my granddaughter before I set my men to climbing the castle walls and kill ye bare-handed, ye lying . . . cheating . . . cowardly blackguard."

Lachlan stood up and moved away from the murder hole. Angus's rage was so tangible he almost felt it grab his throat and, nervous, he moved back to the relative protection of a slit in the wall.

Clinging to the iron bars of the yett like a caged man, Angus tried to rip apart the yett. "Catriona!" he hollered over and over again. "Catriona . . . Cat . . . Cat . . ." He gagged on his words, and Lachlan frowned. What the deuce was wrong with the old man now?

"Cat . . ." Angus tried again. "C . . . C . . ." Without warning he slumped to the ground, where his body jerked as if an unseen hand shook it. The throes of seizure, Lachlan realized, and a smile came unbidden to his lips. Providence was kind. While Lachlan watched in fascination, Angus's eyes rolled up, and his body quivered. Ferguson men crowded round, some kneeling, others standing, all horrified. When they moved back enough so that Lachlan could see, Angus lay there limp, looking dazed and sleepy. His left arm and leg were positioned crookedly, so awkwardly that someone just coming upon him might think him crippled.

At last, Lachlan deemed it safe to leave the gatehouse and show himself on the open rampart.

"Well, dinna stand there like ninnies," he called down

to the dumbstruck Ferguson men. "Carry the old man back to his manor and send me word how he fares."

"For you, we send curses," a Ferguson retainer hollered back. Then he bent to pick up his unconscious master's form.

"Leave my castle—unless you are in need of assistance for the old man."

"He'd sooner burn in hell."

"Then he's a fool."

Turning to Sheriff MacIvie, who had waddled into the safety of the gatehouse's stone walls, Lachlan explained in a magnanimous voice, "Feud or no feud, one must occasionally offer some Christian kindness toward one's neighbors—even if, out of stubbornness, they reject it."

"But what happened to Angus?" the sheriff asked, blinking in confusion.

Lachlan looked at MacIvie and strove for patience. Too often, his sheriff's head rivaled his girth for thickness. "A stroke of luck, that's what, and if we're very lucky, that seizure will keep the old goat out of our way for some time to come. Now get on down there and make certain that no Fergusons bide and sneak about. I want them all gone. Not a one prowling about looking for Catriona Ferguson."

Alone on the rampart of his grandfather's castle, Lachlan slumped back against the parapet. The work of a clan chief was not as easy as his grandfather made it seem. Angus's anger had shaken Lachlan more than he cared to admit. Angus knew how flimsy Lachlan's reasons for holding Catriona captive really were. And so would Alexander and Robert.

Angus had fallen ill. And Alexander MacLean would be gone a fortnight. It was Robert who was unpredictable. Aye, the sooner Lachlan proceeded with the trial, the better.

After climbing down a stairwell from the rampart, he strode angrily across the outer ward to the great hall. He sought out Grizel and found her working on her everlasting tapestry. With a quick twist of her wrist, he made her drop the needle.

"Go and see how our Ferguson spitfire fares, dear Grizel, and dinna moan that ye're too fine to play the lady's maid. I want Catriona Ferguson to appear well cared for at her trial."

The door at the top of the stone steps creaked open, and again footsteps descended down the spiral staircase toward Catriona.

Seeking to escape the sentries' ribald comments, Catriona curled back up and feigned sleep. If they tossed her a crust of bannock and left her in peace, she would count herself fortunate. She ate little and never touched the ale they often brought. Only ale barrels hid the chamber pot in which she must relieve herself, and she'd rather go thirsty than use it so publicly. Only out of desperation would she crawl back there, and then at night when the sentry nodded off.

She would have sold her grandfather's golf clubs for a soft warm scone to stave off hunger, and her last book for a goose-feather pillow to ease the hard stone floor. She didn't even consider what she'd be willing to pay for a swim in a cold river to cleanse herself. Only the arrival of her flux could make her situation worse, and she prayed she would be rendered barren rather than have to admit such a female failing to one of Lachlan's leering guards.

With a fervent prayer she asked the good Lord to send tonight the sentries who whiled their time at cards and dice. Better by far than the pair who had fondled her breasts and waist, claiming Lachlan wanted to be sure she wasn't losing weight.

Closer and closer the footsteps scratched across the stone, scaring away the rats, and suddenly a taper flared to life, casting eerie shadows in the darkness.

Grizel stood over her, dressed in black. Her hair was plaited, but here and there lank strands fell out of place. A pity she had not at least half of Robert's looks and charm, thought Catriona. An even greater pity that she'd been assigned to Catriona's care.

"Awake, then, and saying your prayers, are you, Mistress Ferguson? If it's cousin Robert you're hoping for, he won't come to rescue you, you know. Not after what you did to his betrothed. She may have been English, but that doesn't mean—''

"Leave me be, Grizel." Catriona rose to her feet, the chain that bound her left ankle scraping against the floor. "How many times do I have to tell you I didn't murder Sarah?" Her voice sounded ragged, even to her own ears. Heaven knew, she felt raw all over.

"Grizel," Catriona pleaded, reaching out to touch the other woman's sleeve, "I belong to this village. I'd never do anyone harm here, no more than you would. Why won't you believe me?"

Shuffling closer, Grizel pushed her lank hair out of her eyes. "Because you're a Ferguson and Fergusons can't be trusted."

"You're still hurt because Ian Ferguson died in battle."

"I'm angry because he betrayed my love with a simple maidservant. Fergusons can't be trusted."

"You could trust me, Grizel."

"Don't be trying to bribe your way out of here, Catriona Ferguson. Lachlan will never let you go."

"Why do you listen to everything Lachlan says?"

"He is my brother."

But that still didn't explain the hold he seemed to have over his sister. "You don't need him, Grizel. He is keeping you here doing your bidding. Why, if you were to go to Edinburgh—''

"Lachlan will release my dowry when the time is right."

"That's not fair," Catriona said under her breath. Lachlan was keeping Grizel a spinster; worse, threatening her with physical harm. "You don't have to do what he says. He's not treating you fairly."

"And did you treat the Englishwoman *fairly?*" Grizel taunted. "Her death was not God's will, and shame has befallen our castle."

"She did not die by my hand," Catriona insisted. "If Sarah's death was deliberate, it was the vile act of someone else."

Grizel sidled closer, circling Catriona. "Well, you fancy

Ferguson baggage, Lachlan and I have never stooped to murdering our own guests in their beds. Peace reigned at the castle until you and Robert arrived.'' Grizel's voice was sweet as honey. "Do you fancy Robert is so infatuated with you that he would commit murder the same night as his own betrothal banquet?"

Robert a murderer? The thought did not deserve life. "He's innocent," Catriona said with stark simplicity.

"Just so. Even now the villagers riot in fear and call for *your* death. They're already setting the stake."

Catriona shrank back, terrified. Once in Edinburgh, there'd been a burning at the stake below Castle Rock. With little imagination, she could still hear the screams and wailing. She still remembered the smell of smoke and of flesh burning.

"Stop! . . . Please, stop."

But Grizel was not finished. "Robert hates you too, you know. You've ruined him. If you see him at your trial, he'll be watching and waiting for you to receive your just punishment."

Catriona felt sickened. "Go away. You are not my judge."

Grizel smiled. "Aye, I'll leave you to your sinful thoughts of Robert. All the lasses have lusted after him, so don't think you're anyone special to him. Especially now. He'll be the first one to light the faggots that set you burning at the stake. Or mayhap he'll put his bare hands round your neck and strangle you first."

Catriona crossed her hands at her throat in a protective gesture.

"Is something wrong?" Grizel asked sweetly. "Are you sleeping well? Is the food satisfactory?"

Catriona nodded.

"Lachlan will be pleased to know how well I am caring for you." She left then, and Catriona slumped down to the floor.

Curled up on the blanket that served as her bed, Catriona tried not to shake, tried desperately to find a shred of hope to hang on to. A few words from St. Augustine provided more illumination than comfort: "Anger is the weed, hate is the tree."

She shut her eyes, feeling as though she were trying to wade through waist-high weeds to find Robert. Instead she imagined the pear tree at the kirk, bare of leaves and fruit, except for one luscious pear high out of reach. Stretching high, she grabbed a branch, but it turned into a vine that twined around her, binding her to the tree.

Hate is the tree. She smelled hatred. She swallowed down the taste of hatred. She imagined that she scanned the horizon beyond the pear tree and saw nothing but empty mist.

Robert must hate her too. Otherwise, why hadn't he come?

Robert stormed around the keep to the chapel tower and headed for the door that led down to the storeroom. Storeroom! The place was more like a dungeon. Lachlan must be mad! Bloody stark, raving mad.

Robert had learned of Catriona's fate just a short time ago and cursed the fates. He'd have been back in the village a day ago, but his horse had turned up lame. A day. That was all it had taken for Lachlan to stir up the villagers and imprison Catriona. Angus Ferguson had been consumed with grief to the point of seizure and Robert's own grandfather, the much honored of Glen Strahan, was ignorant of it all, having had to travel to the far north of Scotland for the funeral of a clan chief whose friendship with Alexander had been of long standing. All this in the span of one sunrise and sunset. It was a living nightmare, and Robert sorely regretted the time wasted in talk with Lord Kendrick.

He also intended to spend no more time acquiescing to Lachlan's demented schemes. Right now, Robert's footsteps took him to the chapel tower and Catriona.

Lachlan was there before him, waiting to intercept him on the top step of the storeroom entrance. His cousin's sharp features and gleaming eyes were exaggerated by the light of the single taper he held.

"Ah, dear cousin," Lachlan said. "How good of you to

come rushing back to aid me in the clan's time of distress."

"Mocking words do no justice to your evil schemes."

"Evil schemes? What can you mean? It is no' my fault that your betrothed is dead. You must still be tetched with grief for your Englishwoman, Robert."

"I want to see Catriona."

Lachlan put out a hand to bar Robert's passage. "Nay. As heir to the castle, I have responsibilities, and I canna have every kinsman with a grievance seek his own vengeance."

"You misuse your authority."

Lachlan arched his brows meaningfully and drew a pistol. The muzzle teased Robert's ribs. "I ought to put my betrothed on trial for adulterous behavior as well . . . but witchcraft, methinks, will suffice."

Robert felt the blood drain from his face, and a white-hot curtain of anger descended over him. His hand slid across the handle of his dirk, and he realized how close he was to murdering Lachlan where he stood.

From boyhood, when Alexander MacLean had presented that dirk to him, Robert had memorized the engraving on the blade. "A soft answer turneth away wrath." Soft words, he told himself.

"As her friend, I would ask to see Catriona."

Lachlan shook his head. "I do not think it fit for another man—even my kin—to visit in intimate privacy."

"You call that filthy storeroom intimate? It's as bad as any dungeon." The white-hot heat began to shatter the core of him. "Have you touched Catriona?" he demanded.

As soon as Lachlan smiled, Robert knew what manner of answer he'd hear. "I dinna ken that it is any of your concern, Robert, but your curiosity amuses me. Like Grandfather's falcons of earlier days, you keep circling back to the subject of Catriona," Lachlan observed.

Robert would not be put off. "Have you touched her?"

"Have I sampled her virginal charms?" Lachlan practically licked his lips. "Of course."

The white heat ignited into a flame, and Robert struck

Lachlan on the left jaw. His cousin staggered, and the taper rolled to the floor amid the strewn dried heather, igniting immediately. At Lachlan's cry of "Fire," sentries came running and stomped out the flames while the strongest ones grabbed Robert. These men had been hand-picked by Lachlan, Robert knew, for their fierceness rather than for their intellect, and trying to reason with them would be as useless as struggling against them.

Like a relic of the castle itself, the old man shuffled over to where Robert sat on a rock at the edge of the loch, deep in thought. Loch Aislair lapped at the foot of the cliff on which perched Castle Fenella MacLean with its soaring chapel tower. It was night, and new moonlight played off the water.

"There ye be, laddie, just as I thought, moping outside over the fair lassie locked in the tower."

Glancing up idly at the unfamiliar voice, Robert took a moment to focus on the wizened man in plaid, so disfigured that at first glance Robert thought he might be a roaming leper. The man balanced gnarled hands and one foot against knobby crutches.

Then Robert's gaze softened in recognition of the old clansman who'd befriended him in his childhood. "Cameron," he said. He stood to assist him to a nearby rock. "You keep yourself well hidden in the castle, old man. I didn't know you still bided here."

"Didn't know I still had breath in me body, you mean? Aye, Robbie. A relic of the auld rebellion with a body not good for much of anything, so they hide me away in the castle, a forgotten soul, with nothing to do but watch from the shadows." He smiled fondly. "Missed you, I have."

"My grandfather has turned over much of the clan to Lachlan," Robert observed. A thistle bloomed nearby, and he reached over to rub his thumb across its nub. It was soft, like down, like Catriona's hair . . .

"Aye," Cameron said, drawing a line through the wild grass with one of his knobby sticks. "I may have lost a leg, but no' me eyes. Lachlan is itching to take over from the old man, though if you ask me, it'll be a sorry day when he does. Lacks the compassion of Alexander . . . or of you, Robbie. Ever since Lachlan shot Ian Ferguson in the back in the Rebellion, he's been dorty, mean.''

"Shot Ian?'' Robert wasn't sure but what the old man was crazy. At eighty-odd years, a man's memory was likely to confuse events. Indeed, Cameron looked out across the rippling dark waters of Loch Aislair as if he were lost twenty-one years back in time.

"So many men have died uselessly,'' Cameron said. "If not in a castle siege, then fighting over a king. When I was young, 'twas the way of the times, but this witchcraft talk, now I don't hold with that.''

"I doubt it matters to Lachlan whether we hold with it or no', old man.''

"Aye, you're right there, but let me tell you, laddie, if I were a young lad again like you and that bonnie lassie languished in a dungeon for no good reason, I'd steal her out of there.''

Robert gave a mirthless laugh. "Tell me, Cameron, if ye were a laddie, how would you secret your lassie past a hundred or so sentries and kinsmen of Lachlan's?''

"I know a way,'' he said. "A secret way in and out of that tower that I never showed you and Lachlan. Never showed your fathers, either.''

Robert's head jerked up. "Where?'' He was on his feet and pulling Cameron to a standing position, thrusting his knobby sticks at him.

"Where, old man?'' he repeated. This could be a trap on the part of Lachlan . . . but no, Cameron had always favored Robert. He'd not betray their years of friendship.

"We're practically sitting on the very rocks that hide the door. Came in handy during sieges, so my grandfather told me, but those days are long gone, so most folks have forgotten all about it . . .''

Before the old man had finished talking, Robert was ripping the brambles from the stones, looking for an opening of any kind.

"A man can do surprisingly noble things for the softness of a lassie,'' Cameron observed. "More to your left, lad, if my memory doesna fail me.''

Soft. Aye, Catriona, for all her slenderness, was soft. Soft where it counted. Then again, Cameron, for all his sentimental talk, had never chased the weé red thistle through the gorse.

"I've never rescued a damsel in distress before, Cameron, so I'll take your word that come morning I'll still feel noble."

Chapter 15

*T*he dragon was chasing her through the burn. Suddenly from high up on the fell came the crack of a pistol. "Robert!" she called, and at the same time a wild explosion of desire reverberated deep within the core of her.

Catriona sat up, shaking off the dream, her thin gown damp with perspiration, the moth-eaten bit of plaid she'd been given as a blanket tangled about her feet. A dream. That's all. Another of her dragon dreams. Somewhere, rats scrabbled in the dark. She felt the cold and the dank, and remembered where she was. The dungeon of Castle Fenella MacLean. A worse place than any dragon lair.

And the shot she'd heard in the dream, she realized now, had been the door into her dank dungeon slamming shut when the sentries changed duty.

Footsteps crossed the stones. She squeezed her eyes closed, ready to scream.

"Catriona." The familiar voice was but a gentle whisper, and at first she thought she'd dreamed it. But she'd felt this man's hand on hers before, knew his scent, and she especially knew his whisper. "Catriona, lass, what fine nuisance have you made of yourself now?"

"Robert!" In a single fluid motion, she flung herself into his arms.

His own arms came up around her back, and she pressed herself to his brawny chest, so glad to have him there that for once she was unable to think of a single curse to heap upon him.

When he spoke, his voice vibrated through her. "It seems, lass, I canna let you out of my sight for even a day, but you create a skirmish for me. First you try to escape your escort. Then you find yourself hosted by bandits . . . and now thrown into a dungeon? Your grandfather expected me to watch you closer than this."

"I missed you," she said unashamedly. With one hand splayed across his chest, she let her fingers slide down the fabric of his shirt, not stopping till she reached the place where his heart beat. He captured her hand in his.

"If you keep up this behavior," he continued, "Angus will have to give you away, dowry free."

She bit her lip, unsure whether to laugh or cry at his outrageous attempt to cheer her. "Aye." It came out a sob.

"I thought you believed them—that I murdered Sarah. I didn't do it." She tightened her hold on him. "Oh, Robert, tell me you believe me. I didn't hurt her."

"Shh. I know that. I had the devil of a time getting down here—my friend Fraser is masquerading as a sentry—and we canna stay long, lass." From inside his plaid, he pulled out a bundle. Food—meat, fruit, and cheese. A little leather-bound book. He dumped it all in her lap, and, laughing, she lifted it up in her skirt, like an apron full of treasures.

Grabbing the pear, she took a bite and let the juice roll off her tongue. It was slightly green, but she didn't care if she got a stomachache. She turned the book over in her hands, her fingers caressing the embossing. A Bible? She peered closer at it, felt the engraving on its cover. The copy of Shakespearean sonnets.

She looked up to see Robert's friend Fraser pacing. He kept casting nervous glances at the door above the stairs. "Hasten the greetings, Robert. If Lachlan finds out I helped you come down here, he'll throw me in the stocks again." Fraser had a rich burr to his voice. Catriona had a fleeting memory of having seen him upon her arrival in the village—a young man with auburn hair and freckles. A childhood friend of Robert's, she'd gathered. Bless someone in this village for helping.

"Robert, make haste," Fraser urged.

"Why did you come back?" Catriona asked between bites of pear. After all, Robert could have kept on going with Lord Kendrick all the way to London if he so desired.

With just his fingertips, he touched the small of her back, and she arched against his hand while he caressed away the ache left from too many hours lying on stones. "Mayhap it's the second sight," he said lightly, avoiding an answer. "Is there anything you need?"

"I need a guide to take me back to Edinburgh." She couldn't keep the bitterness from her voice.

His laugh was the best sound she'd heard in days. "I said I'd help, not grant miracles, lass."

Silence hung between them. She felt Robert's hands skim up her back and thread through her hair.

"I'm in a terrible scrape this time, aren't I?" she asked softly.

"I fear so. The justice of Shire Strahan is here already for a trial."

Trial! She swallowed down the lump in her throat. Robert risked a lot coming in here like this. She hurried to ask the question uppermost on her mind.

"The other sentries told me Angus had a seizure. Is it true?"

Robert hesitated, then with his thumbs traced the outline of her cheeks—feather-light and comforting. "Aye," he said softly.

She put down the pear along with the other food. "I . . . I'll never see him . . . again." Her voice choked, and suddenly she was in Robert's arms again. At first his body stiffened from her teary assault, and then with a mild curse he brought a hand up to stroke the nape of her neck.

"Of course you'll see him. He's mending," he said hastily. "If he's not well enough to attend the trial, perhaps that would be a blessing."

"But you'll be there."

"Aye, I'm expected . . ."

Naturally, she thought a bit foolishly. It was, after all, his English betrothed who had died. The Kendrick family was supposed to have helped Robert with his ambitions.

Oh, but Robert's hopes must be dashed. But he'd been too much the grieving gentleman to express any disappointment on that account.

"Now listen to me, quickly," he said softly in her ear. "At the trial, there'll be many false witnesses. If I am called on, however, I will say whatever I can to defend you, and you must also speak the truth . . . except this one thing. Do not admit, Catriona, that I came to your room the night Sarah died. Break a commandment if you must, else Lachlan will add a second charge and make the trial far worse for you."

She nodded, her heart sinking. "Why do you care what happens to me?"

She felt him go perfectly still.

"You want reasons at a time like this, lass? You're one of God's wee creatures. I value life. There, will that do? There's no time for more."

What else could she have expected? Professions of undying love? That he rescue her like a damsel in an ivory dungeon? Robert was a practical man caught through no fault of his own in an unholy mess. Silent, she nodded.

It was enough to feel the brawn of his arms, smell the familiar musk of his scent, hear the whisper of his breath against her skin. At last she pulled away, suddenly self-conscious of her wretched gown and tangled hair.

"They'll convict me just for looking like a witch," she said.

Robert caught her face in his hands. "Vanity is the least of yer worries, lass. He pulled the black band from his own hair and, reaching round, tied her mane of curls with it.

"Dinna worry now about how your hair is combed, lass. 'Tis in a sweet tangle and your skin is scented with the lavender of the floor. Your grandfather needs to know that his bonnie lass is still fiery. That will be better medicine, I wager, than any receipt in your Elspeth's stillroom book."

His voice vibrated through her. He was such a charmer. No wonder, as Lachlan said, the lasses fell over themselves for him. Only he could sweet-talk a lass confined to a wretched cell and make her feel desirable. How she loved him, though she'd not burden him with that admission now.

Catriona swallowed hard again. "Do you believe I am a witch and a saucebox and a wench?"

"A witch . . . never." He gave her shoulders a little shake. "As for the rest, it does no' matter now. But I promise you willna go to the stake. Do you hear, lass?"

"Your word as a Scotsman?"

"Aye."

She shut her eyes. If Robert believed in her, it had to be all right. Surely they'd find her innocent.

"Robert," warned Fraser.

"I'm coming," he called over his shoulder. "You must endure and have faith, lass."

"Aye, I can do it. You forget, Robert MacLean, I am of the clan Ferguson."

He reached for her face and tipped it up to his. He linked her hands with his and placed a kiss on her forehead, each of her cheeks, and then her chin.

Fraser's voice was urgent. "There's no time for tumbling the lass. You said only talk."

Robert was already feeling his way along the stones, searching for the release on the hidden door. It had stood for years without being opened. He prayed the mechanism had not rusted.

"You canna go that way, mon." Fraser sounded panicked.

Robert shook off his friend's arm. "This castle has secrets we've never known, Fraser. Did ye never talk to old Cameron?"

"Senile."

'Brighter than most of Lachlan's men." Robert tapped on yet another piece of stone and heard it echo hollowly behind him. He pushed, and the door gave way with barely a squeak. Bless whoever had had the foresight to slather it with grease last time it was used.

Fraser whistled low and ran a hand through his hair. "If Lachlan were to find this out . . ."

"He won't unless someone tells him, Fraser."

"Well, dinna think I'll give the bloody cur any secrets."

Together they moved through the opening, and as
Catriona stood watching, vanished somewhere in the stone
wall. Then she was alone again, almost as if Robert had
never come. Except there were lingering dewdrops on her
skin where he'd kissed her.

It had to be morning again, Catriona thought bleakly,
because once again she could hear the measured footsteps
of the guards coming to take her to the second day of her
trial. Waiting, she stood at the foot of the steps that led
up from the dungeon and tied her curls back with Robert's
ribbon. Somehow that small ritual gave her the courage to
endure yet another day of this madness.

It was, so the old people boasted, the first witchcraft
trial in the history of Glen Strahan, and most people did
not know what to do—except celebrate. Lachlan threw
open the castle gates to the villagers who came not only
to watch the proceedings in the great hall, but also to
feast. Lachlan ordered casks of ale to be cracked open,
and at least two score sheep roasted over fires in the outer
ward.

Looking hungry as well as curious, the villagers had on
the first day followed the scent of cooking meat to the
castle, and then, wrapped in woolen cloaks and plaids as
protection against the draughts, had crowded into the great
hall, sitting at either end, watching. Aye, it had been like
a sideshow event at a country fair, Catriona decided.

The door to her dungeon burst open and interrupted her
thoughts. There stood six of Lachlan's leering clansmen,
each wearing a protective amulet, each crossing himself
before touching her. Six strong men to handle one wee
female whose hands were bound in front of her, thought
Catriona as they led her outside and into the great hall,
the minister falling in behind them. She heard people catch
their breath when they saw her, and the superstitious
parted, making a path for her.

Slowly she moved forward to take her place in the
makeshift prisoner's docket—a straight chair facing a long

plank table. Alastair MacIvie, the corpulent sheriff of the local shire, whom even Catriona could see was a dull man of no more imagination or depth of soul than the bottom of his ale glass, sat his bulk beside her. Flanked by him and the quivering minister, she readied herself to endure yet more hours of this nightmare of a trial.

Lachlan had sent two of his ablest men to fetch the traveling justice, who as luck would have it had been holding an assize court in the farthest part of the shire from Glen Strahan. But the justice had wasted no time in coming, so Grizel had informed Catriona, adding that he was particularly well versed in ferreting out the black arts and believed in the supreme punishment.

Justice MacLeod, a man of severe countenance, sat now at the table facing her, flanked by Lachlan on the right hand and Robert on the left, facing the people of the clan MacLean seeking justice. And then, unexpectedly, the door to the great hall burst open.

Alexander MacLean, laird of Castle Fenella MacLean, chief of the MacLeans, stood in the doorway to his own great hall, his greyhound, tail wagging, pawing its master's knees. Except for the panting of the happy dog, sudden silence hung over the room.

"What is going on in my castle?" he demanded, looking at Lachlan as he spoke the words.

Lachlan half rose from the table. "You've returned ahead of time . . . 'Tis naught but a trial," he said with a weak wave of his hand at the justice.

"The king's court is in session," Justice MacLeod intoned, "and even the clan chiefs abide by the justice of the Hanoverian court."

Alexander's face flushed a darker hue, but his shoulders did not bend. His glance fell on Catriona, then on Robert, and back to Lachlan. "Ye brought this about?" he asked of Lachlan. Condemnation laced his words.

"The king's court is in session," said the justice with a bang of his gavel.

"Ye take a lot upon yerself as my heir," Alexander said loud enough for everyone in the great hall to hear.

" 'Tis justified." But Lachlan spoke in a whisper.

"All this over a woman?" Alexander fumed. "I expected a wedding, accepted a funeral, but no' a witchcraft trial. It's uncivilized."

" 'Tis justified," Lachlan repeated, his face florid.

"Can we no' disband this?" Alexander turned to the justice with his last request. "I want none of this in my castle."

The justice banged his gavel again. "Laird MacLean, I must beg you be seated. The proceedings have begun under the authority of His Majesty the King of England *and Scotland.*"

His features rigid with disapproval, Alexander strode to his chair, the one occupied by Lachlan. His grandson hastily stood up and offered his grandfather the seat. Alexander dragged it around to the head of the table and settled in to watch. Lachlan then rearranged himself on the bench and nodded at the justice, who rose his eyebrows impatiently.

Alexander, Catriona realized, was staring at her. And she wagered he had no intention of taking his gaze off her, the perpetrator of all this high drama in *his* castle.

Lachlan leaned forward, whispering to the justice the names of which villagers to call.

"Let the justice conduct the trial," Robert snapped, not taking his eyes from Catriona's face.

"Hold your peace, both of ye," Alexander said with quiet authority. "The justice presides, and after him, I do. Still." He looked meaningfully at Lachlan, who shrugged and slumped in his place.

One by one came the parade of witnesses to stand between Catriona and the justice. Everyone had something to say, from the farrier to the woman who had handed up a black bun to Robert on the day he'd arrived back in the village.

Their damning words rang over and over in Catriona's head, yet she tried to find a piece of charity in her heart for them. Alexander MacLean, after all, still ruled over the village in the feudal manner of old. Most of the villagers were in various ways beholden to Castle Fenella MacLean for their sustenance and protection.

Not even their obvious love for Robert could quell their fear of empty bellies, it seemed, for they cast fearful glances at Lachlan every so often. She felt so heartsick she couldn't concentrate and took in only bits and pieces of the testimony.

"Aye, ever since that redheaded lass came to the village me goat's been ailing," said an old woman. "Limps, it does, and barely gives us milk. The sickness started the very day she arrived back here. And as for the deaths, why I recall clearly the first body was found the very same day Angus gave us the news he'd called his granddaughter home. Practicing sorcery at a distance, she was."

"Didn't she come and give your son an herbal potion?" the justice asked after a prompting by Lachlan.

"Aye," the woman replied, "and now you mention it, that was when Jacob took a turn of temper."

Catriona hated Lachlan. It was the first time in her life she'd been certain she knew how to hate.

"The cow died the day after that fire-haired lass came to the village, and now our bairns are without milk," another man testified.

The evil did not bide in her, but in Lachlan, Catriona thought.

"I dinna have an affliction from the devil yet, but I can tell you this. It was God's truth that I saw that lass out after dark under the full new moon picking herbs . . . roots and berries that are poison."

It was a lie planted by Lachlan.

"Devil's work, I tell you. Now I'm no' that fond of English, but I'd ne'er want to see a young Englishwoman done in. Young Robert has always had a way with the lasses, had them wanting him, but when they resort to sorcery to provoke a man to unlawful love, then no, by God, we have to stamp it out. Lachlan is right when he says the devil has invaded her."

Lachlan and the devil. They should both be on trial.

"God's blood, but there's no denying the truth, for me own lad serves up in the castle as a sentry, and he says that the page told him that Catriona Ferguson pointed straight at Lachlan and laid a curse on him. That Frenchman says she cursed Robert MacLean as well on the journey up here.''

Catriona felt her head go light.

Lachlan had them all possessed with his lies and fear.

''She's possessed.''

Possessed.

''Possessed.''

Catriona did not realize she was holding her hands to her ears until a sentry yanked them to her sides again.

''The king's court calls Jacques Beaufort to testify,'' the justice intoned at last.

Her pulse raced. So, the quixotic Jacques had chosen to testify against her. She wondered what Lachlan had promised him in exchange.

The justice cleared his throat and looked queerly at Jacques's lace cravat. After dispensing with some legal formalities, he cut to the heart of the matter.

''Please if you will tell this court what you saw of the defendant engaging in black magic.''

Jacques's voice grew sober, as if it pained him dearly to have to tell the truth. ''I saw her change into a red deer, right before my eyes. She blew on a piece of thistle and poof, she was a deer. I would have swooned had I not been of stout French stock.''

''You lie!''

A great buzz went up in the courtroom as Robert, his visage fierce, stood and challenged Jacques.

''Och, now.'' The voice of the farrier's wife could be heard above the others. ''That display with Robert will seal her fate, it will. Why, she's obviously bewitched our beloved Robbie . . . Anyone can see that.''

The justice banged his gavel, and the crowd quieted, as if anxious to hear.

''Where did you see this happen?'' asked Robert, ignoring Lachlan's disgruntled look. ''I never left Catriona's side. Where was I when this happened?''

''Sit down,'' the justice yelled so loudly that his bald head grew as red as his face. ''You, sir, are no' trying the witness.''

At a precise motion of his lily-white hands, a pair of

sentries strode over and put restraining hands on Robert. He shook them off. "Answer me, Jacques," he demanded, "or I'll carry out the threat I promised in the manse."

With his profile turned to her, Catriona could see Jacques visibly gulp. *"Mon Dieu,* it was near a river where you and she had quarreled. She shouted at you and called you a Highland barbarian and cursed you in many tongues."

"A display of womanly temper, naught else," Robert replied, his voice harsh. "Her hot temper does not make her a witch. Mr. Beaufort exaggerates," he told the justice.

The justice smiled carefully at Robert and ran a hand over his bald head. "The court recognizes your personal concern in ferreting out the truth, given that the deceased was your betrothed. Nevertheless, we must proceed with questioning Mr. Beaufort." He swung his attention back to Jacques. "You did not spend every hour of the day with the accused, did you?"

Jacques spread his hands in a gesture of helplessness. "How could I? She changed into a blackbird occasionally. And besides, as the earlier witness tried to point out, any intelligent person knows that a witch need not be present at the place of her victim's misfortune. No doubt, this young woman simply *wished* the other ladies dead. Wished them dead from a distance. Everyone knows witches are capable of that."

"Dammit, there are no witches here in Glen Strahan." Robert was on his feet again, his brow thunderous. A buzz of excitement rippled through the spectators.

Lachlan favored them all with a cool smirk. "But, if not this woman, who so many have testified has a hot temper and knows the magic of herbs and has a way with animals and utters curses, then who else?"

"No witchcraft was involved. Look to some other reasons." Robert would have advanced on Lachlan and Jacques, but the sentries held him back.

Catriona sat perfectly still, not daring to move. A single tear slid down her face.

"Robert, ye disgrace the dignity of the MacLeans."
Alexander was on his feet, shaking. "Lachlan brings me
shame with his perfidy, and now ye, ye bring me disgrace
with your temper."

"Take Robert MacLean outside." The justice was
banging for order as pandemonium erupted among the
spectators, and Robert continued to shout and struggle
against the sentries restraining him.

"The trial is recessed," the justice announced peremp-
torily.

Catriona stood, heedless of the tears that continued to
slip down her cheeks, and waited for the sentries to take
her back to the dungeon. Alexander, laird of Castle Mac-
Lean, walked out, back straight, mien proud. Before following, Lachlan glared at Catriona, and she lifted her chin
proudly.

On her way out, she searched and found Robert. Their
gazes locked, his angry, hers despairing. He had promised
her—on his word as a Scotsman—that she would not go to
the stake. She wanted dearly to believe him, yet everything
seemed to be going against her.

By gloaming that same day, Robert slumped, exhausted
against the pear tree in the village, staring at the whitewashed thatch-roofed cottages and cursing Jacques Beaufort and his lies.

Though summer fruit ripened now, in his mind, white
blossoms of springtime sweetened the air. It was funny,
he mused, how the senses could trigger a long forgotten
memory: a pear tree on a windy day at gloaming.

How long ago was it Lachlan had pushed the little redheaded Ferguson lass out of this tree? Aye, she would have
been about seven. Her front teeth missing then. Red curls
flying about her, and her devoted dog yipping at her heels,
doing its best to keep up with her as she ran away from
Lachlan. The village bully even then, Lachlan was.

Now, while Robert watched, the cottages along the lane
gradually lost color and became shadows. For as far back
as he could remember, even before he'd left for St. Andrews, gloaming had fascinated him, that time of day when

the world was drained of color and became as simple to look at as black and white, until gradually even the white faded, and there was nothing left but black night.

These villagers, his old friends, saw life in terms of black and white, he realized. If ill times befell the village, there had to be an evil reason, and a witch was as good a person to blame as any. If only Robert could shed some light on the real reason Sarah Kendrick had died. Even if she had been murdered, he'd likely never prove it. Someone as devious as Lachlan, or Jacques, could have used any innocent castle servant to deliver a poisoned potion.

There was no time to worry now about the cause of Sarah's death. Only time to try to save Catriona. A movement on the lane caught his eye. Elspeth was coming, as arranged.

He remained where he was, leaning against the old pear tree and mulling over his options as he waited for the old woman to arrive.

It had finally occurred to him what his promise to Catriona would cost him. He'd thought, of course, when he'd promised her that she would never burn, that this farce of a trial would not go so far, that the accusations would be disproven.

But he'd been away at university a mite too long and had overestimated his own influence. In spite of his objections, the trial had proceeded, and now the verdict was a foregone conclusion.

He only hoped to God Catriona didn't know yet.

What was he going to do? Any open interference on his part would likely cost him his political ambitions. Yet, if he didn't interfere, Catriona would die.

How the deuce had it come to this? All he was supposed to do was escort a lass up to the Highlands.

Weary, Robert shut his eyes, trying to wish away the temptation to seek out Lachlan, wrap his bare hands around his cousin's throat, and choke the malice out of him.

Instead, Robert separated himself from the shadows and moved to join Elspeth.

She started to speak, but he put a cautioning finger to

his lips and drew her into the deeper darkness of a little alley and an eave. A village dog trotted up the lane. Then all was quiet, as silent as the shuttered cottages.

After a moment Robert bent down to Elspeth and, after whispering his fears, asked the old maidservant for words of wisdom.

"You realize, Robert MacLean," Elspeth said, "that you dinna need my advice. I believe ye've already decided yer course of action."

Catriona sat for a third day in the great hall, staring at the villagers, remembering the feel of Robert's arms about her, and, most of all, his promise.

By my word as a Scotsman . . . She would not burn.

Having heard all the witnesses, the justice ordered Catriona to stand as he intoned the verdict.

"I find Catriona Ferguson guilty of murder by witchcraft."

Distant thunder began to rumble in her ears, as if everyone were talking at once.

Guilty . . . *Guilty* . . . *Guilty.*

She stared straight ahead, her hands clenched into fists. This was a dream. Robert would come to her and take her in his arms and say it was all right.

By my word as a Scotsman. "It is the sentence of this court that Catriona Ferguson be burned at the stake." Thunder buffeted her back and forth. She wanted to run for cover before lightning struck. Trembling, she searched for Robert. Lachlan stood, his gaze triumphant. Grizel dabbed at her eyes.

Over and over, the words rang in Catriona's ears. Swaying, she felt the blood rush from her head and grabbed the back of a chair. Robert stood up then and, without a single glance at any of them, walked out of the great hall, his boots echoing on the stone floor.

At that moment Catriona knew the keenest despair of her life. Perhaps Grizel had been right and Robert was glad, after all, to see her pain. Was he more superstitious and vindictive than she realized? Had he lulled her with his comfort while secretly rejoicing at her suffering? A tight band pressed against her chest, and she couldn't think clearly.

Once again the sentries bound her hands with rope, but she didn't care. All she knew was that Robert's soft words and seductive hands and sacred oath played as false as Jacques's wolfish smile. Consummate politicians, the pair of them.

Jacques had damned her in court, and now Robert was going to let her burn. She knew only one word for how she felt.

Betrayed.

Chapter 16

❧◦❧

A t the midnight hour in a village beset with fears of witchcraft, one did not invite suspicion by dawdling. Robert moved quickly toward the stooped, cloaked figure that awaited him under the pear tree, and touched a hand to her shoulder.

Elspeth gave a little jump, then turned and peered up at him in the dark. "Startled me, ye did," she said crossly, then immediately lowered her voice. "Are ye certain ye can do this? If ye're caught—"

Robert placed another reassuring hand on the old woman's shoulder. "If we're caught, it means my skin as well, and I've become selfish about hanging on to what's mine. Never fear."

"And then what? Catriona's used to having me care for her."

He smiled. "Like it or no', she'll have to get used to me instead." He gripped Elspeth's shoulders more tightly. "The lass needs a platoon to keep her out of danger, but I promise to do my best. She'll be as safe as possible with only one man to keep watch over her."

"Ye exaggerate. If ye're the same man I got to know on the journey up here, ye can manage her."

He paused, debating whether to broach a rather nagging detail. "You have no fears for her virtue? No objections to us being together, a man and a woman unwed?"

Elspeth chuckled. "Do ye think because I'm an auld spinster lady that I'm prudish as well? If ye have to sacrifice her reputation, what price compared to her life?"

225

"Always the practical one, Elspeth." His low voice was wry. "I was rather hoping for a stern lecture forbidding me to touch her, but it appears I'm to be disappointed."

"Ye came to the wrong person for counsel, Robert MacLean," Elspeth snapped. "What ye ask is between ye and Catriona and yer conscience. I believe the lass has grown more than a little fond of ye, so let what happens naturally, happen. I could wish for worse for her. Only be gentle with her and above all, keep her alive."

Robert released a ragged sigh. The clever old woman, putting the decision and all the guilt on his shoulders. But there were other bridges to cross before he need worry about the intimate living arrangements. First, as Elspeth had pointed out, he had to rescue her.

"When?" Elspeth asked anxiously.

"Tomorrow night."

"What do you need?"

"Two horses. Blankets. A bag of dried food." As Elspeth nodded, Robert gave her specific directions on where to leave the bounty.

She nodded. "Aye, that place is secluded. I willna fail ye . . . or Catriona."

"There's one other thing I want," he said, "but I need it delivered to the castle. Douglas will meet you." He lowered his voice to a whisper because a dog was wandering by, and where there was a dog, there might be a master lurking in the dark, eavesdropping.

Elspeth gasped audibly when she heard his request, and Robert clamped a hand to her mouth. "Shh. Would you have us discovered?" With not a care to the high intrigue to which he was privy, the dog sniffed around the tree and then gave chase to a prowling cat.

"Ye dinna mean that," Elspeth objected when Robert released her. "Catriona's been raised a lady."

"You've practically given me permission to bed her, old woman. Are you going to quibble over a pair of breeches?"

"Aye. Ye're a man, and the garment was styled for yer anatomy. I'm thinking of her comfort."

"I'm well aware of the difference in our bodies, old

woman. I said I'd take care of her. Now will you get them for me? And a hat as well . . . to hide her flaming hair," he added, when Elspeth took a breath to object. "Elspeth, listen to me. It's far safer for a woman to roam the Highlands disguised as a lad. If she were recognized, any bandit could earn a pretty farthing for his tale."

Elspeth was silent, then agreed. "Is that all?"

He nodded.

She groped for Robert's hand. "Before yer run off to yer fancy post in England, promise to let me know when ye've delivered her somewhere safe?"

There was a long pause. "Aye, I promise . . ." He lingered a moment longer. "How fares Angus?" he asked.

"He can walk with help. He uses his golf club for a cane," she said, a smile in her voice. "But he pines for Catriona."

"I'll tell her."

"You have my prayers for a safe journey . . . and a clear conscience," Elspeth added.

Robert turned away. "You ask a lot, old woman," he muttered.

Catriona awoke to pitch dark. She had no way of knowing if it was day or night. Only silence kept her company. Black, thick, lonely silence. Dear God, the bandit woman Marcail had not lied when she'd prophesied Catriona would never leave these hills.

As for Robert, he was long gone. She knew that and decided it was just as well. For him to come now would mean his death, and she couldn't bear that. She yearned to see Angus, and despite their differences, to lend some comfort to him. One sentry had had the compassion to tell her that Angus was making a slow recovery, and for that Catriona was grateful.

At the top of the stairs the door creaked open. She heard a footstep. Then another.

By the light of a single taper, servants from the castle lugged down a wooden tub over which sloshed water. "You're to bathe," a toothless old woman said, "and then

dress in this.'' Laughing, she thrust Sarah's blue bridal
gown into Catriona's arms.

"No shyness, now, lassie," the old woman cackled.
" 'Tis on Lachlan's orders that ye be trussed up like a
pretty hen.'' She handed Catriona a bar of lavender-
scented soap and a new hair ribbon.

"You expect me to bathe wearing this chain?" Catriona
asked, lifting the heavy links of metal that bound her ankle
to the wall.

"And why not, lass? A bit more rust willna strike it
down with plague.'' Laughing to herself, the old woman
herded the other gaping servants out and left Catriona
alone.

Amazing, she thought. She never knew what to expect
next here. Strange custom this—more akin to the tradi-
tional wedding night bath. But then, if it was the custom
to burn witches at the full new moon, as Lachlan said, it
might also be the custom that they go to the stake freshly
washed. In any case, the sight of fresh water was so appealing that she cared naught for the reason. She'd already
slipped out of her tattered gown and into the tepid water,
savoring the first bit of luxury she'd known in days.

Too soon, the door to the storeroom creaked open again.
If the servants were coming to take her to the stake, Catriona was ready for them, her skin smelling of lavender,
the brocade wedding gown billowing out about her, and
her freshly washed hair piled in a damp knot on her head.
Considering she was about to die, she felt strangely calm.

Footsteps descended—one pair only—and she waited.

Suddenly, a second taper flared into life and there stood
Lachlan, his harsh features highlighted by the flame.

"Have you come to inspect me before I die?" she said,
trying to quell her trembling.

"You might say that," Lachlan said.

"I want to see my grandfather once before I die."

He shook his head. "Angus will live, unfortunately.
Isn't that enough to know?"

"I want to make my peace with him."

Lachlan shook his head, his smile patronizing. "The
laws for punishing witches are strict." After a pause, he

added, "Did you know it goes easier on witches who are no longer virgins?" There was no mistaking the leer in his voice.

Her heart slamming against her ribs, Catriona slowly backed around the ale barrels as far as the ankle chain would allow. Like the onslaught of a winter gale, the realization hit her full force. Lachlan was not here to taunt and inspect her. He had come to claim his rights as her betrothed.

Lachlan followed and picked up the chain, then jerked it and reeled her toward him as he might a salmon from the River Strahan. He placed a hand under her chin, and she promptly turned away. With taut fingers, he forced her face around, and holding the taper close, he studied her.

Her heart hammered in her ears. "You know I didn't murder Sarah," she said. "Why have you let all this madness happen?" Her plea ended on a stifled sob.

With a gloating smile, he reached up and fumbled for her ribbons and yanked her curls loose. "Whether you murdered Sarah does no' matter, my dearly betrothed. What matters is that you were intended for me and carelessly allowed yourself to fall prey to Robert's charm. A grave weakness on your part. An unforgivable mistake."

"Robert befriended me. Besides, he's . . . leaving for England."

"He took liberties with you."

"And if he did?" She lifted her chin defiantly. "I'd never wed you in any case."

Lachlan's eyes narrowed in anger, and she knew she'd risked too much. "Nor do I want a bride who is smitten with Robert . . . Whether he's here or in London matters not. Your heart would be with him instead of with me."

"You'd rather see the feud continue?"

"Aye, that I would, if I could avenge myself. Robert and you both betrayed me, and you both will suffer for it, one way or another."

She stood ramrod stiff with her hair tumbled about her shoulders. Very carefully, she drew in a breath. "Are you saying you killed Sarah?" Was Lachlan that twisted with jealousy for Robert?

His laugh sounded low and menacing. "You're the one who stands convicted for murder, Mistress Ferguson. You'll no' hear any confessions from the MacLeans."

Despite the hammering of her heart, her voice held a trace of pity. "Blackguard."

"Aye, I like a feisty wench. 'Tis all the more pleasure in taming her."

"No, you can't . . ." She screamed, backing away as far as the chain would permit.

Lachlan stood still. "Scream as loud as you want, my betrothed. The sentries will not hear you. I've sent them away."

She felt the wool of his plaid graze her leg when he pulled her close. Blindly, she tried to wrench away and stumbled to her knees on the cold stone floor.

Lachlan smiled at her vulnerable position. "I've no intention of harming ye, at least not yet. I want ye to live long enough to know the pleasures of a man. Robert has neglected to teach ye the finer points, I wager." He knelt over her.

Catriona's mind spun, and she twisted and writhed away—anything to avoid letting this man touch her.

In her panic, she barely saw the third figure who came out of the shadows, but she heard the blow of a pistol butt against bone and watched Lachlan's body grow slack and slip unconscious to the floor.

It took a moment for her to realize the uncommon gentleness in the hands that lifted her, the familiar feel of brawny contours. She smelled the scent of his skin, a mixture of heath and musk.

"Robert!" Tears mingled on her lips with the whispered name. She entwined her arms around his neck as if she'd never let go. His own arms closed around her, and for a moment, she knelt like that, time forgotten. Until she remembered how angry she was at him. She pushed away, knocking him off balance.

"What are *you* doing here?" she hissed at him. "I imagined that after you received your satisfaction in court, you'd have rushed off to see the English king and given him your *sacred* word as a *Scotsman.*" Oh, but she added all the sarcasm she could. "Well?"

Robert rubbed the welt on his head where she'd rammed him against an ale barrel and stood back up.

"I *had* to walk out of the great hall, lass, so no one would suspect what I plotted. You forget how many eyes watched us." He searched his cousin's body until he found the keys he needed.

"And now you think I want your help escaping?"

"Actually, Elspeth and Angus approve, if that makes it easier to accept, so you've no choice. I'll abduct you, if need be." Unlocking the chain from Catriona's ankle, Robert pulled her to her feet.

"Why did you come back like this after you abandoned me?"

"I never abandoned you," he said, leading her to the secret door in the wall.

"You did," she accused. "You walked out of that courtroom without so much as a final farewell. You would have let me burn."

"I wouldn't have, but I couldn't arouse suspicion about my plans or they might have moved you to another hiding place."

"You never said a word to me."

"I stand condemned of that," he said. "What's my sentence? Mayhap a day in the stocks would suffice and you can go to your fate."

She tugged back, as usual resisting his efforts to lead her. "Robert?" she asked hesitantly. "If Elspeth and Angus hadn't forced you into this, would you have rescued me anyway?"

He cast a nervous glance at Lachlan's unconscious form, wondering if he'd hit him hard enough to outlast this conversation. God's blood, but the lass was *still* unbiddable.

"Would you?" she asked again.

He turned back to her, thinking that women turned romantic and maudlin at the damnedest times. "They didn't force me. Catriona, do you mind if we discuss this later, when we're less pressed for time?"

"No."

"Now, listen, Catriona, I expect ye to be a brave Highlander."

She shrunk back. "You can't take me out of here. They'll kill you."

"Are you saying, lass, that they're going to outwit us?" he teased. "You, who nearly escaped from me I don't know how many times on the way up here?" Though his whispered words teased her, his tone promised he meant what he said. "I'm leaving this dank place, Catriona Ferguson, and I'm taking you with me."

She stood there, chin up, defiant and proud.

In one determined motion, he pulled her toward the back of the storeroom, where he shoved his shoulder against a stone wall until the secret door gave way. He tugged her into a narrow passageway and heaved the door shut behind them, and they were alone in the cold tunnel full of musty dust. He couldn't see his hand in front of his face, but he managed to find the stone he had left there and pushed it against the door, to seal it.

He felt Catriona moving away from him. "I can't see you, Robert."

"I'm here," he said and, reaching for her, ran a hand up her hip until he made contact with her arm. He took her hand in his and pulled her close. "Now, for once in your life stay where I put you," he ordered. Quickly striking a flint, he lit a taper.

With Catriona clinging to his hand, Robert tugged her along the passageway, following a path of footprints in the dust and batting away low-hanging moss. In moments, the path came to a dead end. Robert reached down to a bulging haversack that he'd stashed there and then pushed away some small stones and brambles. At the same moment, a rush of cold air extinguished the taper.

In the soft darkness, he told her what he wanted of her.

"But I can't change here, especially not into boy's clothes," she said with maddening feminine shyness. "And not in this tunnel. Lachlan might wake up and find me . . ."

Damn her, he swore, she wasn't going to turn into a prim and proper miss now, of all times. "You stripped off clothing the first three days of your journey up here. It's no different now, lass."

"Yes, it is. These are breeches."

"But," he countered smoothly, "considering the speed with which you ran away from me in a skirt, think how much faster you'll be able to move in breeches."

"I'm a lady."

"You could have fooled me, lass," he said dryly, and then his patience failed him. He pulled her to him. "By your life and mine, do as I tell you," he said through gritted teeth. Groping in the dark, he yanked at the laces of her mantua.

"Why can't I escape in this gown?" she asked. "It's lovely."

It seemed he would have to shock her into attention. "Because I've been wanting to take off your clothes ever since I saw you in your mother's overstuffed corset." She stiffened and he added a touch of understatement. "Besides, there's something more challenging about undressing a lass when her executioner is but a stone's wall away."

She spoke in a miffed voice. "Lachlan will find this dress lying here."

With practiced fingers, Robert kept on untying laces. "He doesn't even know about this tunnel."

"He'll turn the castle inside out to find me."

"But we'll be gone. Come on, wee thistle, dinna make this harder. It's difficult enough in the dark."

"I don't want to run away like this. I don't want to be hunted down by Lachlan."

"Unless you can suggest another course, we're running." As God was his witness, he was going to have to dress her in disguise himself. "After all the times you tried to run away from me, you disappoint me, Catriona Ferguson," he said, and pulled her close.

To balance her while he unlaced her bodice, he pulled her derriere close against his lap and thought wryly that if he'd known it would be practice for a rescue attempt, he'd have paid more attention to the clothing of the women he'd undressed in the past.

With the help of a shaft of moonlight, he caught fleeting

glimpses of Catriona's slim figure: the swell of a perfectly formed breast beneath a camisole when he peeled off her mantua; the curve of a hip when he stripped off her brocade skirt; the sight of a long, shapely thigh. Her lavender-scented skin looked like alabaster but had a softness not to be found in the smoothest statue.

"Hold still, lass, else I'll never find your arms." He thrust over her head a loose-fitting man's shirt, and with reassuring caresses, he moved his hands across her breasts, searching till he found the part of her anatomy needed to fill armholes.

He felt all thumbs and was too acutely aware that dressing a woman in boy's clothes was not among his more practiced accomplishments.

"Where do you think you're taking me?"

He was losing the train of his thought. "As far away as possible."

"You do realize you're pulling those breeches on me backward?"

He dropped them and raked an impatient hand through his hair. "I've no' served an apprenticeship as a maid, Catriona."

She took over then, and with efficient movements pulled the breeches up. He watched the subtle sway of her hips as she worked her way into them.

"May I see Angus before we leave?"

"No."

"But I need to—"

"He's mending. Walking a bit more each day with a golf club for a cane."

"Does he know what happened to me?"

He didn't know if he should tell her that Angus's fierce reaction to her imprisonment had triggered his seizure. "He asks after you, and Elspeth and I have reassured him we would rescue you. Can you imagine how angry he'd be if we risked recapture by stopping to visit him?"

She sighed. "Are we going to spend the night together or will this be a short journey?" she asked, tucking in the shirt.

"It will involve the nighttime." Oh, give it to her all at

once, so they could be out of here. "And all day, and all the next day and the next. I seem to be cursed with the duty of escorting Catriona Ferguson for ever and ever. Does that satisfy you?"

Fleetingly, he saw her face and knew she'd decided to forgive him. "And what about you?" she asked.

"I'll be dressed as a MacLean clansman, what else? That way, I will look exactly like one of the inevitable search party Lachlan will send after us."

"I see." She slipped something down the waist of her breeches.

He pulled her to him, which wasn't the wisest thing to do, given his frame of mind and the state of his body, but he'd have to be noble, as someone had once blithely suggested. "What are you holding?"

"My book," she said, turning away, but not before he had felt every curve and swell of her. "The Shakespearean sonnets . . . I'm taking it," she insisted, "even if I have to stuff it down these breeches."

His hands were on her waist and he discovered that she'd forgotten a detail. The breeches were slipping down beyond her hips. "You need to lace up. How the deuce did you manage so many costumes the day we left Edinburgh?"

"Desperation. And none of them were breeches."

Most of the women of Robert's acquaintance were well practiced at unfastening a man's breeches. He told himself to remember Catriona's unfamiliarity with the garment.

"There's a flap, lass, that you adjust before the lacing."

She jerked away from his hands. "I can do it myself." She fumbled with the unfamiliar ties before Robert caught her to him.

Modesty be damned. "There's no time to practice, lass." With both arms wrapped about her to hold her still, he deftly pulled the strings tight and fastened them into a knot. He heard a muffled sound—scurrying—in the tunnel, and didn't need Catriona's prompting this time to pray for luck. It was a rat. Just a rat. His hands lingered for a second on her waist as his heart pounded.

Beneath his hands he felt the frantic rise and fall of her

chest, the fragile feel of her. "There's no more time to tarry, lass. You'll have to put the cuarans on in the boat."

Hurriedly, Robert handed her the deerskin boots, then swept up her hair and slapped a Highland bonnet of blue onto her head.

"Robert—" She sounded frightened.

He clamped a hand over her mouth. "Can ye save the tears, lassie, till we're away from the castle? There's naught I can do to console ye now, else we'll be caught."

Nodding, she sniffled, as if gathering her courage.

They emerged from the tunnel and stood outside. Catriona blinked at the new moon shimmering off the loch. She was gulping in fresh air, as if savoring the smell of rain and the feel of cool grass against her feet. Nearby, a tiny boat bobbed on the dark water, shadowed by a cloudy sky in which the moon was now playing hide and seek.

Robert turned to look at her. She swiped at a wetness on her cheeks, and the sight wrenched something inside his chest. She looked so young standing there against the midnight sky that he had to think of something light-hearted to say.

"You won't fool anyone up close, but at a distance you'll pass as a Highland ghillie." Barely.

"Small comfort," she said in a wobbly voice.

He smiled. "Shall we have a race to the boat? Loser has to row."

"You'd best let me win then because I never learned how to row a boat in Edinburgh."

"That was shortsighted of your parents, wasn't it?" He wrapped his hand about her smaller one and tugged her down to the shore. As she climbed in, the boat wobbled, and she clutched the sides.

He tossed her one more item, her lavender cloak. "It's from Elspeth for warmth, but keep it hidden till we're well away from here." Robert shoved the bow of the boat, jumped in, and began rowing. Silently, they glided like a shadowy swan around the edge of the loch, ripples widening where the stern carved a path in the water.

They had gone about a quarter of the way around the body of water and Robert had just spotted their two horses waiting near a clump of fir trees in the burn when a shot went up from the castle, barely audible but formidable. The instant Catriona scrambled onto the shore, Robert set the boat adrift so no one would know where they had landed. Within moments they were mounted and riding, through the burn, up the fellside, heading south again, out of the Highlands.

It was Grizel, bearing a torch and accompanied by two servants, who found Lachlan on the floor of the keep and shook him awake. "You fool," she scoffed while her brother struggled to a sitting position. "You've let her get away."

"More fool you, Grizel. She was taken."

A sentry who was just coming on duty picked up the empty chain. "Milord, she's bewitched the castle. Turned into a bat and flew right out of her chains, she did."

Lachlan staggered to his feet and rubbed the back of his neck. His head ached. He snatched the chain from the servant and cuffed the fellow a good blow to his ears, first one side and then the other. "You simpleton. She's no bat. This has been unlocked."

"Beggin' yer pardon, milord, but coming down the stairs, I saw a bat. How else would a bat get in here, unless by black magic?"

"Mayhap a blackbird was what you saw. You know a blackbird was what flew up from the bodies of the lasses," suggested another servant.

"Simpletons!" stormed Lachlan. "Mind your tongues." He rounded on his sister. "Did you release her—as some twisted revenge on me?"

Grizel narrowed her gaze. "Why should I need revenge on you, brother? Have you deceived me? Have I not been the loyal sister?" Her voice rose hysterically. "And what thanks do I get? Blame because your witch escapes your lustful embrace?"

She ducked before Lachlan's fist could box her ears as well, dropped the torch onto the stones, and fled up the stairs. "One day you will go too far, Lachlan. Let your witch go. Isn't that what you wanted? To be rid of her and Robert both?'' She slammed the door in his face.

Lachlan picked up the torch and, helped by the two trembling servants, staggered up the stairs to the ward, across to the main floor of the keep, and up more stairs to Robert's bedchamber.

With the butt of a pistol, he pounded on the heavy oaken door. After an intolerable delay, a sleepy Douglas opened the portal a crack.

"Get Robert."

"Forgive him, milord, but he has passed out on the Scotch of Castle Fenella MacLean. He threatened as soon as the trial ended that he would drink himself to the dregs. Grief, ye ken.''

"God's teeth. Didn't he even learn how to drink down in Edinburgh?" Lachlan sneered. He shoved a foot in the door and stared across at the sleeping figure in Robert's bed. "My cousin is less and less the Highlander when it comes to holding his whiskey.''

"Mayhap someone from her grandfather's manor house rescued her," Grizel said, distracting him. "Who else would betray you but a Ferguson?"

Backing out, Lachlan pulled the door shut on Douglas and studied Grizel, who waited out in the hall, an annoying smirk on her face. She reminded him of an adder. Striding back out to the outer ward, Lachlan sent his servants to the outbuildings near the stables, where his clansmen slept.

"Wake the lazy dogs! I want their horses saddled in ten minutes."

While a sentry roused his clansmen, Lachlan paced. One by one, the men staggered from the outbuilding where they slept en masse. When Lachlan shot off his pistol so near the foot of one sluggish man that dust sprayed his foot, the others came running, plaids half wrapped about them, half dangling in the dirt, still unwound as blankets. They stood at motley attention.

Lachlan drew out a second pistol, loaded and ready to fire again. "Unless one of you sots desires me to test my aim on his leg, then do as I bid, and quickly.''

Within the half hour a small army of men bearing torches arrived on foot at Ferguson Manor and with quiet movements subdued the Ferguson guards who slept outside. Lachlan reserved for himself the honor of beating down the door with a log. The servants inside the house either hid or were quickly tied up. To Lachlan's disgust, both Angus and Elspeth were immediately accounted for—Angus in bed protesting loudly for a servant to bring him his pistol. A MacLean prowled his room, found the pistol, and tossed it to him—empty.

Then the MacLean clansmen spread through the darkened house, holding flares high and searching each and every room, binding and gagging stray servants, kicking over furniture, opening each armoire, each cupboard, and scavenging both attic and cellar.

With withering dignity, Elspeth stood on the staircase, encased in a woolen wrapper, her gray hair hanging in a loose braid. In one hand she held a branch of candles and in the other a loaded pistol that dared any MacLean to try and tie her down. On her face was written condemnation.

Lachlan lingered and stared up at the maidservant of his betrothed. "You dinna fool me, you wretched Fergusons. You know more about Catriona's disappearance than you're letting on. But dinna get your hopes up. My men will find her and have her back in chains. Nothing you do can prevent her death."

"Ye dinna know my Catriona, milord," Elspeth hissed. "Get out and take yer pillaging elsewhere. The Fergusons have had more than their share, and I wager ye've come here without Alexander's order. Alexander wanted a reconciliation, ye forget."

"Alexander wanted Ferguson property," Lachlan sneered, "and so do I. And don't forget, old woman, that my grandfather's honor is at stake." He fumbled with his pistol, loading it. "He arranged my betrothal, and I'll have his blessing to search for my missing betrothed. And don't tell me she flew off as a bat or as a blackbird, you old hag." Ignoring Elspeth's shaken expression, Lachlan turned and, leveling his pistol, shot out the candle that flickered in the entryway.

He stalked out, fuming, wondering if he should rouse the whole village and search the cottages, but he thought not. However the little witch had escaped, she was too clever to hide with the dull-minded villagers. He was riding back to the castle to plot a search into the Highlands when he spotted the little rowboat bobbing like a lost duck in the middle of Loch Aislair, the early dawn streaking across its deserted oars. He paused to study that boat. Could she have rowed herself away from the castle?

Impossible. Someone in the castle must have helped her. His suspicions narrowed on Douglas. He put nothing past the man, who was loyal to Robert to a fault. Back at the castle, he flung his reins to a groom and took the stairs to Robert's chamber two at a time. Again he beat in the door.

"Douglas," he roared. "Show yourself and answer for your actions."

But the chamber only echoed with Lachlan's voice off the rough stone walls, and a dawn breeze from the casement window fluttered the draperies about Robert's bed.

Lachlan stalked to the bed and kicked Robert's good-for-nothing egotistical form. "Wake up, cousin."

But his foot struck not muscle and bone, but only a pile of pillows and straw. In a sudden rage, Lachlan flung it all to the floor. Feathers and straw floated about him, clinging to his plaid.

"Douglas appears to be gone, milord," a trembling sentry informed his master from the doorway. "His horse is gone and his clothing. Shall we search for him further?"

"Blast Douglas! It's Robert I want." Lachlan cursed himself for being a fool. "Where's the sentry who was on duty tonight? I want him in chains for letting Robert take my betrothed."

As Lachlan's orders echoed through the castle keep, sentries shrunk from him. Let them cower, he thought. Mayhap they'd follow his orders next time instead of babbling about witches turning into bats. Damnation.

He yanked a pikestaff from the wall in passing. Let

them see which they feared more now—a witch or a piece of metal through their bellies.

His clansmen stood assembled in the outer ward, plaids wrapped neatly about them, dirks and pistols tucked in their belts. Horses neighed restlessly nearby.

Stony-faced, eyes cold, Lachlan stood seething at the door of the great hall. As he secretly surveyed his men, hand chosen for their loyalty to him, he planned his words of command. It must matter not that Robert was a Mac-Lean. He had betrayed his own family, and for that he deserved to be hunted down like a traitorous dog.

Grizel came up behind Lachlan in the doorway, her hands cupped about her pet lark. "So. Once again, Robert has outwitted you, brother." She laughed and opened her hands, and the lark fluttered on her palm and took wing into the gray dawn. "I wager you'll never find him, anymore than I'll find this lark."

He whirled on her and this time when his hand shot out, he did not miss his mark. He slapped her to the ground in full view of the waiting men. "Shut your mouth, woman. Robert will die for this, as he should have long ago."

His fury barely contained, he strode out into the breaking light of a gray, wet dawn to bawl his orders at his clansmen.

Chapter 17

Catriona peered out of the crude hunting shelter Robert had led her to and scanned the burn. Feeling a bit like an owl, she blinked at the light. There wasn't a window inside the decaying hut. Nothing but a dirt floor on which she'd spread their plaid, an ancient stone chimney, and silence.

From the way the light was fading, she guessed at least three hours had passed since Robert had vanished with their horses into the birch trees. How long did it take to plant a false path? Certainly Lachlan and his men must be far away by now. But if they weren't, if they'd found Robert and hunted him like a cornered stag, and he lay bleeding or . . . She couldn't bear to dwell on the possibilities.

She could not in good conscience wait here, huddled in a plaid with naught but dead leaves for companions. Wrapping her cloak about her, she ventured out. Yes, she was disobeying Robert's orders to stay put, but he wouldn't mind; not if some bandit held him captive.

Looking around to get her bearings, she decided to head for the stream she heard rippling in the distance. She knew Robert would have taken the horses there to lay a false track.

It was easy enough to find the stream, even easier to find the horses' footprints. Even the most cunning woodsman would suspect they had crossed the stream and had headed in the opposite direction from where Catriona had been hiding. It was a clever ploy. The only thing wrong was that Robert was still missing.

Slipping off her shoes, she rolled up the bottoms of her breeches and, ignoring the goosebumps breaking out on her skin, waded across the water. She was heading up the other bank, still barefoot, when brush crackled.

She stopped in her tracks, thinking it might be her imagination or her own footsteps. Again brush crackled, and she trembled, afraid to stand still and afraid to move. Before she could decide whether to run back to the hut, a figure in plaid swooped down on her and thrust the tip of a dirk against her ribs. Stifling a scream, she tried to run, but the stranger held her fast, and she swirled to see a leering man whose face consisted mostly of an unkempt beard.

"If you're earning your living as a bandit, you can take your dirk away," she said, trying to pitch her voice low and coarse like a village lad. "Someone's beat you to it and already stolen my locket."

"It's no' your locket I'm interested in, lassie," the fellow said, untying her cloak. "And your voice does no' fool me one bit."

It was then her gaze traveled down to his clothing, and she saw the red MacLean plaid. "I'm not—" She cleared her throat to pitch her voice normally again. "Not who you think I am."

"Now, now, 'tis a sin to tell a lie, lassie." The fellow lifted off her bonnet and smiled at her hair, which spilled down around her shoulders. "Well, if it isn't the grand prize of the Highlands. Lachlan willna want ye hurt now, so dinna move from me. Tell me, be ye still a maiden? Will Lachlan know if I also sample his fair lassie's charms?"

Chancing a look up at him, Catriona sucked in her breath. He wore his hair in a queue and beneath the hairline, the fellow's ears had been cropped. All that remained was a pair of scarred and crinkled holes.

Her look of revulsion did not escape him. He frowned and touched his hand to the mottled flesh. Grinning lasciviously, he said, "The English did it, lassie. I'm no' braw, I ken, but after dark, it does no' matter so much, eh?" He pulled her more tightly against him and ran a hand over the swell of her hips. "Breeches, eh? Make it hard on a laddie, dinna ye?"

Heaven was not going to help her this time.

"Who are you?" she asked. "I've never seen you about the castle."

"Sutherland's me name, lassie, and the reason you've no' seen me about is because I work in the stables. Then, too, you've been close to the dungeon lately, I ken."

"You're mistaken."

"Nay, I got a fair look at you during the trial. I was there the day they threw Robert out. He always was a lad of stubborn mettle, always insisting on the best horse in the stable. Used to groom his horse for him, I did. I liked Robert, but then, Lachlan provides my roof now, so it's his bidding I follow." He tightened his grip on her, and his smile showed the gaps in his teeth.

Catriona forced herself to remain calm. "If you liked Robert, then you'll let me go. Lachlan need never know." If she could stall for time, mayhap Robert would find her alive. "Have you seen Robert?" she asked carefully.

"Lost him, eh? Then aren't I the lucky kinsman to have found ye first?"

"My grandfather will pay more for me than Lachlan will," she said hastily.

The clansman's expression took on a hint of wickedness. "Aye, but what price on my life if Lachlan finds out? And I canna spend your grandfather's coin, lassie. The village is sorely lacking in shops, and I rarely leave the Highlands for Edinburgh. You'd have to offer me something more. A piece of land, a score of castle." The tip of the blade teased even closer to her breast.

"Your greed, sir, almost exceeds your cruelty. Fie on you," she nearly spat. She didn't dare move because of the dirk, but her words held venom.

His laugh was low and amused. "I've heard much of your temper, little witch. Tell me about you and Rob—"

Without warning, he sagged against Catriona, his hold on her arm slackening, his heavy weight causing her to stagger backward. Without her support, the man crumpled to the ground, and somewhere in the thicket a voice muttered what sounded like a French oath.

A stain of dark red oozed from the man's side and spattered Catriona's cuarans. She jumped back a foot and wrapped her arms around her, sickened at the sight of a dirk protruding from the man's back. She whirled in place, on guard for the unseen assailant.

"Who's there?" she asked.

A tall figure strode from a dark cluster of trees. "It is naught but me, your guardian."

Robert! He was alive. She took a grateful step toward him but stopped. The expression on his face was fierce. He did not welcome the sight of her. "Do I disappoint you, lassie?"

"Of course you don't disappoint me," she said, her voice tremulous.

"But you disappoint *me*, lassie." With that easy grace so unexpected in one so tall and brawny, he moved toward her.

"Do I?" Oh, his expression was as hard as a Highland crag, as forbidding as the blackest burn, and his eyes, his blue eyes, were merciless, and colder than the stream she had forded.

"You disobeyed me."

"But I'm not injured," she pointed out, glancing nervously at the body. Her thoughts were jumbled, her stomach churning. "I was worried about you. You took so long."

"I was being followed, hinny, as you can see. Not that you thought of that, I suppose." A muscle jerked by his mouth.

"No." She managed a whisper.

"A few more minutes and he'd have given up on me."

"Then everything's for the best." She scanned the bushes but saw no sign of their horses.

"Not quite. I just had to murder one of my own clansmen—" His voice was like ice slicing into her, and he advanced on her, a haunted look in her eyes. "I'm trying to keep you alive, Catriona, my lass. Why do you make that so damned difficult? Did you grow up thinking about no one save your own impetuous self?''

She shook her head. His anger hurt, and without warning her temper flared.

"It's difficult for you—a MacLean—to protect me?'' She watched him yank his dirk out of the man's body. Blood dripped off it and he wiped it on the man's shirt sleeve, then dragged the body into the undergrowth. Bile rose in her throat and everything crowded in on her at once. The funeral. The trial. Her guilt over Robert's kisses. The dungeon. Robert's rescue. And now a body . . . a bloody body lay at her feet. And Robert had the gall to *preach* to her? To suddenly turn sanctimonious on her? It was too much.

Fie on Robert! Fie on Lachlan! Fie on her grandfather! Fie on the entire feuding, inhospitable Highlands!

"You know I didn't ask to be here," she said in a strangled voice. "You're the one who dragged me away from my home in Edinburgh, who made me live like a barbarian in the middle of bandits and murderers, and put me in breeches and—'' She looked around and realized the horses were nowhere in sight.

The instant Robert reappeared she asked, "Where are our horses?''

"Gone.''

"Gone?''

"How else do you think I was able to plant a false trail?''

"I thought you were going to . . . well, use their footprints.''

Shaking his head, he smiled grimly. "I let them run off.''

Quick tears filled her eyes, tears of despair.

"It's rough country we'll be traveling,'' Robert said gently. "We can go as fast on foot and hide better without them.''

"But . . . on foot? Why didn't you ask me which way I wanted to escape? I might have—''

Before she could finish the sentence, he was stalking

toward her, an expression on his face she'd never seen before. Weary. Tender. Fierce.

"Because I'm the guide, that's why . . . You're upset."

"I'm not!" She backed up, still a little unstrung by the idea of being stranded in the Highlands with no horses. *"You're* the one who got mad first!" she accused. "But if *I* want to be upset, I've every right. How do you think it feels to be accused of being a witch? I wish I *were* one. I'd fly away to our horses right now and leave you to walk!" she cried.

It didn't help her temper one bit that a smile cracked his face.

"You and your fancy English alliances," she accused. "You're probably only rescuing me so you can prove to the English how good you are at stamping out violence in the Highlands." She backed into a tree, but paused only long enough to catch her breath before sliding behind it. She peered around the trunk. "Oh, aye, Robert MacLean can handle anything—even prevent such barbaric behavior as burnings at the stake. And then Lord Kendrick will forgive you for Sarah's death and . . . and . . ."

"Hell, lass, ye've got a bonnie imagination." With one fell swoop he moved around the tree, grabbed her, and slung her over his shoulder.

The giant lump in her throat threatened to choke her. "Put me down, Robert," she ordered. "If you've got trouble now, it's no more than you deserve for trying to consort with the English, as if bonnie Scottish lasses are no' good enough for the likes of you, so dinna be telling me who's the one with fancy notions." Angry as she was, she managed to mimic his brogue.

As he waded back across the stream with her, she pummeled his back. "Set me down."

"If you dinna lower your voice, I'll drop you right here in the stream."

A tear spilled onto his shoulder. "I . . . dinna . . . care. Drown me then and be d-done with it." Slumping against his shoulder again, she began to sob.

"Aye, wee hinny, that's all we need is tears." His voice showed no softening.

Not even her sobs slowed his step. She cried until finally she was spent of anger. She hiccupped against his shirt. Her eyes felt swollen, her hair tangled in her face.

Without setting her down, he walked with her into the hut. More gently than she would have expected, he eased her down onto the plaid. A few dried leaves crunched beneath them, then darkness enveloped them as the door closed. Darkness and Robert's warmth. Touching her forehead, he gently brushed back a strand of her hair. She turned her face from his touch.

"I hate you," she said in her most petulant voice, one calculated to make him feel guilty. Then she hiccupped.

"Aye, I dinna blame you, lass," he said, shifting himself so that he half lay beside her. To her consternation he began stroking her cheek. "I'd no' feel kindly toward anyone who threatened to throw me in the stream either, but you dinna ken how I felt when I saw you in the hands of Sutherland. It's the first time in my life I really wanted to kill a man." His voice sounded raw.

"Your knife could have hit me," she pointed out.

"Give me some credit, lass."

She felt him lean over her and then he kissed her lightly on the cheek. The gesture surprised her so that she turned her head. He caught her lips to his. The kiss was the touch of a feather against her skin, a warm touch that without warning deepened and suddenly caught fire.

For a long moment they lay like that, unmoving except for his lips brushing against hers, then deepening until her mouth throbbed, taunting a response from her until she kissed him back hungrily. They lingered together like that, savoring each other.

Catriona felt that same breathless feeling she'd known the night he'd first kissed her. She was Isolde, and Robert her Tristan. Of course, there was no magic potion to make her fantasy come true. But oh, Robert was alive and holding her in the dark, and she felt the most wonderful sensations pulsing through her—an ache in the very core of her that was growing steadily more fierce. As fierce as the restrained urgency of his hands and the rapid rise and fall of their chests.

As if startled by what had happened between them, he pulled up a fraction.

"I was so afraid," she whispered against his lips. "All afternoon I sent up prayer after prayer to God."

"You should have prayed that I would be able to keep my hands off you, lass." His voice sounded uncharacteristically shaky.

"I prayed, please, God, keep Robert safe, and I'll convince him to forget his alliances and—"

"God must have been listening, lass," he said, lowering his head to her lips again, "because I can't think of anything except you . . ." His words trailed off, but she didn't mind because he was kissing her again, the flame tugging them together, hot but gentle. He moved against her, and she felt the full length of him, hard with desire. Suddenly short of breath, she heard someone gasp and realized it was she.

Then there was nothing in her world but sensation. Though it was black as night inside the hut, she felt flooded with light. "Robert," she moaned with an intensity that surprised her. Even more surprising was the urgent way he molded her to him when she breathed his name. She felt his hardness pressing against her leg right through his plaid. She'd seen drawings of Greek statues in books—her father's books—and other lasses had boldly spoken of seeing men unclothed, but Catriona never had.

It was curious, but the way Robert felt against her leg and the drawings she'd seen in books did not quite match. She remembered once stumbling upon a coachman kissing the kitchen maid, and seeing the large bulge in the coachman's breeches. Later Elspeth had tried to explain it, but not very satisfactorily.

"Robert?"

"Mmm." He was pressing kisses to her throat, kisses that made her move beneath him, but she had to ask.

"If you were wearing breeches now, what would you look like?"

He leaned up on one elbow, puzzled. "What makes you ask that? Bookish curiosity or a compulsion to trade garments with me?"

"Both."

He pulled her hand down to his plaid, to the hardness beneath the fabric. "If I were wearing breeches, I'd be fit to burst the seams, lass. Why?"

"You feel different."

"From what?"

"From David."

He tensed and raised up. "David?"

"The drawings of Michelangelo's David."

He buried his face in her curls, and she felt rather than heard his laughter. "Catriona Ferguson, I thought your book reading was loftier stuff than drawings of unclothed men."

"I saw it by accident. Why do you feel so hard?"

"Because, lass," he said on a near moan as she innocently writhed beneath him, "it's the way of all men's bodies when they want to mate with a female." He pressed more feathery kisses to her lips until she felt an ache deep in the core of her, an ache that grew more fierce even while his kisses grew more gentle.

"And you want to mate with me?" she asked. In her books the men who mated always loved the women. Did he love her? Did she want his love?

Robert had forgotten how hard he'd been fighting his desire for this little red-haired thistle. If he'd been smart he'd have tumbled a wench at the castle before setting out alone with Catriona like this, but none of the other women had appealed to him. He'd not had any carnal desire—until just now when he'd touched his lips to Catriona's and it had hit him full force just how badly he wanted to slake his desire on her. Only her.

"Aye, I want to mate with you," he admitted. "Do you want to?"

"Is it like kissing?"

"Better. Lass, I canna stop. I need you," he said in a dark, compelling tone. He continued to caress her skin, savoring the feel of warm alabaster, and all the time his ardor grew increasingly painful with his need.

"No man's ever said those words to me before, that he needed me."

He moved over her, and his hardness molded to her soft places.

"It's all a jumble of sensations . . . Robert, please, I feel like I'm on fire," she whispered into the dampness of his woolen plaid. "I don't know what to say."

He tightened his hold. "Say 'aye' . . . or say 'I need you' . . . or say 'yes.' Your choice."

"Aye, Rob—" His tongue captured her unspoken word and he wrapped himself around her, as if he would fill her with sweet honey, that intoxicating it was. That fierce.

"Will you touch me back, lass?"

His kisses moved from her mouth to the delicate spot behind her ears, to the hollow of her throat. To her hair, her forehead, the bridge of her nose, her chin, and then there was a moment's hesitation before he took her lips again, this time with a fierceness that seemed to match the ache inside her. His hands slid up under the loose folds of her shirt and did exquisite things to her skin, leaving behind a trail of sweet, sensual tingles. She was aware of the musky scent of him, of wool, of the loam and leaves on the ground.

Gently, he peeled away her shirt and caressed her breasts until, to her shock, the nipples rose erect and ached with some secret torment. His hands were caressing her there while deep within her, the instinct to have this man's hard desire close inside her filled her, consumed her. Better than kissing, oh my. Before she decided never to wed, she'd better find out what she was missing.

She wrapped her arms around his neck and arched closer against him, and with an agonized moan, he buried his head against her shoulder. She did as he asked, touching his hair, shyly at first and then weaving her fingers through his thick mane and down across the muscles of his back.

With deft movements, he slid her body toward his greatest need, and she caught her breath. It was so natural to wrap her legs about him, but his desire pressed taut against her breeches, and she wasn't sure what to do about that, except let her heart go on pounding.

With a stifled moan, he rolled her sideways and lowered himself, burying his head between her breasts. At the same time she felt his hand move to her thigh, slide up the fabric of her breeches, and caress her in the very place that ached for his touch. The instant his hand stroked the fabric, she moaned, and then a red-hot blur of sensation consumed her so that she could barely speak.

"Oh, Robert . . . you don't know . . . Do you know what you're doing?"

He grimaced at her innocent words. Feeling her move beneath him, he knew too well.

And now fabric more impenetrable than a maidenhead stood between his desire and her innocence. He cursed his own doing. A virgin writhing in his hands, so ready for him that he could feel the honey practically dampening his hand . . .

"Whose idea was it to put you in breeches?" he said hoarsely.

"Yours," she answered breathlessly. "You said I'd be able to travel faster—"

"So I did." It was an effort to say the three little words.

"They're terribly inconvenient, aren't they?" she whispered.

Her understatement made something near his heart clench. He wanted to divest her of all her garments then and there, but he was painfully aware of her inexperience.

Lying his head against her breasts for a moment, he took a couple of deep breaths, steeling himself to go slower. Reminding himself that he was now her lady's maid as well as her savior, he reached for the tie at her waist. It would be so easy. One tug and it would come undone. He stopped resisting.

"Catriona . . ." he said, when he could trust himself to speak, but no other words would come. "Lass, lass," he moaned, cursing Elspeth for not forbidding this. Didn't the old woman know that where lasses were concerned, Robert and his conscience had made a pact to ignore each other? With a groan of longing, he moved his hand over her hips, riding with her shy hip thrusts. Catriona touched her fingers to the outline of his lips, and the simple innocence of the gesture finished him, absolutely rammed a battering log through his remaining resistance and shattered it.

With a curse and swift movements he untied the laces on her breeches and lifted her hips to pull them down and off so that she was naked. Desperately he tried to hold back the storm he felt climbing to a crescendo.

"Am I the first?" he asked hoarsely, half of him wishing she'd say "no" to ease his conscience, the other half ready to murder any man who'd touched her before him.

She nodded and tightened her arms around him. A gentleman would stop, but he was, he reminded himself, a rogue. Elspeth had given him license to be one, and he was no longer bound by a promise to his grandfather. *Just keep her alive.* Alive and arching beneath him.

"Rogues like me aren't usually the ones to deflower virgins, you know. Do you have any idea what comes next?"

She nodded against him. "Elspeth said it would hurt the first time, but she said it was a part of love."

Love. A black pall shadowed him, just for a moment. God, no, don't let her get love mixed up in this. Be a rogue. Take her gently, Elspeth said, but take her. Be a rogue, and when it was all over, hope she hated him for stealing her maidenhood, so at least she wouldn't love him. Anything but love.

"Catriona, lass, I need to be inside you. It hurts me not to be inside you. It's going to pain you when I enter, but be a brave lass. Soon enough it will feel braw for both me and you too. Do you understand?"

It was rogue talk, with no maudlin words to confuse the issue. All he was doing was slaking his desire. There was no love involved. "Do ye want me, lass?"

Catriona nodded. Oh, merciful heavens, how she loved him! In the dark she was aware only of the feel of his hand caressing the most private part of her until she nearly cried for mercy. He moved to cover her, and she curled close to his warmth. Still she felt his hand teasing her, tormenting her, and just when she thought she'd cry out from longing to have all of him, she felt him shift his weight, followed by a quicksilver stab of pain.

"Sweet, lass," he said on a moan, and with another gentle thrust he filled her, made them one. They moved as one, their hearts beat as one, they kissed as one. They moved together in what she guessed was the timeless rhythm of lovers—their hearts beating in unison, their lips touching, their bodies melding—until suddenly she reached a pinnacle of rapture she'd scarcely known existed. She cried out at the same moment that Robert shuddered and relaxed warmly against her.

Afterward, she lay in his embrace, trying to catch her breath, listening to the wild thud of her heart. A delicious weakness filled her, and she marveled at what had just happened between them. She wanted to ask Robert about it, but even more she wanted to savor the feeling of him close in her arms.

"Did I hurt you, my wee lass?" he asked, his voice husky.

"Only a bit. Not anymore. Do you know you fit inside me?" she added with wonder. "As if God planned it that way."

"God's a bully when it comes to writing Commandments, but when He designed bodies, He did impeccable work."

"Books never said it felt like this." Her books always talked about desire as a forbidden thing. Not a word about the sheer miracle of joining her body with his. Or about wanting to stay like this forever.

"Robert—?" He was pushing her hair off her face, his hands cool and strong.

She wished she were his. He had filled a part of her she had never known was there. She wrapped her legs around him as if she'd never let him go.

"Stay with me," she whispered. "Please . . . I don't know if it's proper, but can you hold me a wee bit longer?"

Robert hesitated. She didn't know what she was asking for, didn't know how long he'd desired her. He felt guilty as hell. Elspeth had told him to be gentle, not to treat her like a wench in a tavern, not to behave like a rogue.

"It's more than proper. You've a bonnie way of holding me. Do you ken how much I need you, lass?"

He felt the stirring in his loins again. He tried to find his sanity, but reason had vanished somewhere outside this sanctuary. God's truth, but she felt sweet moving shyly against him. The only coherent thought he had was one of surprise that he hadn't been able to control himself, that her innocence had not been enough to temper his aching need.

But he had desired Catriona altogether too long to be able to temper desire. Wise old Elspeth had no doubt guessed that once they were left alone this would be the inevitable conclusion.

"The books leave the best parts out, don't they?" Catriona said shyly.

"Hmm-mm." He stroked back a wisp of hair from her cheek. She was supposed to hate him for what he'd done to her, not rhapsodize about it. "What books might these be, hinny?"

She paused. "Tristan and Isolde and such stories."

"Ah . . ." There was a smile in his voice. "And what words of wisdom did these stories have to impart?" He wondered if she could feel him swelling inside her again.

"They hid. From the king's soldiers. For ever so long . . . oh, Robert, please."

"Then what happened?"

"Then the man and the woman hid out together, exactly as we are doing, and Tristan drank a potion . . ." Her voice trailed off.

To his surprise, he was nearly at the point of no return yet again. Books also never told her, he'd wager, that a man could grow hard with desire again so quickly or that this time when he moved inside her she would feel no quicksilver pain, only an exquisite rapture. He'd make certain of it.

He was looping a lock of her hair around her finger.

"How many times does a man mate with a woman before he's done?" she asked.

"That depends, lass."

"On what?"

"On how he pleasures her . . . It's no' so much when the man's done as when the woman's done."

He traced the curve of her face, lingering on her cheek. Her lashes fluttered against his hand. Then he let his hand descend, trailing a path down her body, feeling her tremble at each stop along the way.

"Imagine," he said, "the man is like the crags, always fierce. And the woman . . . she's the heather, biding her time to bloom." His hand found the most vulnerable part of her, and she gasped.

She reached up and kissed him, a butterfly touch, and he remembered his promise to make it gentle for her.

He loved her again—for all the times she'd tipped her pert face away from him on the journey up here. For all the times she'd talked like a saucebox and then turned innocent eyes on him. For the way she'd trusted him to undress her, to sleep by her. For the hundreds of hours of frustration he had endured. There was a sweet retaliation for each time he'd fought down desire earlier. A kiss, a caress, a touch. A wild explosion of pleasure. She cried out and convulsed around him, and he released himself into her, lost in pleasure. He couldn't be a gentleman in bed with her if he tried.

"You never finished your tale," he said after a moment, his head pressed against her shoulder while he collected his wits.

"What?" She sounded breathless. "Oh . . . next . . . Then, they hid some more, and then the book didn't tell anymore about how they managed to hide and what they did when they were alone at night . . . but it's all right because you've shown me, and it was far more wonderful than anything I've read."

Wonderful. Aye, it had been that, but he didn't want to admit it. Because easing his desire had never been so wonderful before. And he couldn't seem to slake his hunger for this chit.

At last, he pulled her close and held her, and with utter trust that amazed him still, she asked, "What are you going to show me now?"

"How to keep warm," he said with a smile in his voice,

his chest thumping oddly, guilty at playing the rogue while she talked of love.

He pulled her over and under his plaid, and she curled up close. His arms came up and pushed back her tangle of hair, and with a tender touch he moved his hands over her face, one finger tracing the line of her jaw.

He lay awake. He'd been shortsighted when he'd planned this escape with Elspeth. He'd congratulated himself for thinking of all he would need—horses, blankets, food, a haversack of clothes. Aye, he'd thought of everything except a chastity belt to keep Catriona safe from him.

Those breeches, as he'd proven tonight, were no' made of iron. Nor was he. He was a flesh-and-blood rogue who'd gone too long without a wench, that was all. Love, she called it, but she had her head full of fairy tales. Later, he supposed he'd have to explain the difference between her fairy-tale notions of love and the physical act of mating.

The last time he'd been here in this hut had been years ago when he and Fraser had sought shelter after hunting down a stag. The place had been decrepit then. Now, it barely provided shelter, just a fireplace and a floor on which to lay a plaid. He half wished for her sake he'd never found the place again.

He had no idea who else in the clan might have used this hut and might seek it out in their zeal to find Catriona. But he'd not worry her about that now.

"Robert?" She reached for him.

"I'm here."

"Don't leave me alone again tonight." She curled closer.

"No, I won't."

"Do you think we'll escape Lachlan's men?"

"Of course we'll escape them," he told her lightly. "How can you question it? You're the lass who almost escaped me on the journey up here—no, I haven't a doubt," he replied.

In truth, the journey ahead would be so fraught with danger he didn't have the heart to tell her that the odds of their escaping alive were slight indeed.

* * *

An icy draught entered the great hall followed by Jacques. It was late night, the witching hour, though Jacques doubted that Lachlan would be amused to have it called that.

No, Jacques had long ago learned to be more discreet, and so he would be now. With cautious steps he made his way across the stone floor toward the trestle table where Lachlan sat at one end, slouched in an oaken chair whose wooden arms resembled gargoyles, a cask of ale spilling onto the plank table where Lachlan kept refilling his tankard. The branch of candles had burned half down.

At the sound of Jacques's footsteps, Lachlan lazily looked up and scowled. "A visitor to the castle," he snarled in slightly slurred tones. "To what do I owe the pleasure—are you looking for any wench in particular?"

"Bonsoir," Jacques said, feeling his way into this conversation. "I desire a few words—"

"Spit it out."

"—about your betrothed."

Lachlan sneered. "If you intend to repeat the whispers that she has bewitched my own cousin and forsaken me, then save your breath." He gulped greedily and drained his tankard to the dregs. Slamming it down, he bellowed for more.

"Unworthy gossip," Jacques said. "Robert no doubt desired the lass himself. He's a man not to be trusted, as I found out myself on the journey up here." Jacques dusted a speck of lint off his sleeve and rearranged the lace ruff at his cuff.

As Lachlan slowly lowered his tankard, a flicker of interest lit his eyes. "You detest Robert?"

"He shows much arrogance, *n'est-ce pas?*"

"Aye."

"Especially toward you, the heir to this fine castle."

"What do you want?" Lachlan clearly grew impatient.

Jacques smiled, the easy smile calculated to show people he meant no harm. "To share your ale perhaps, as well as a proposition regarding the return of your betrothed." He pushed a strand of hair into his queue. Oh, to be back in France in civilized clothes and powdered wig. Still, he felt he was making excellent progress. So excellent that he could scarce believe his good fortune.

Unexpectedly, Lachlan slammed a fist onto the table. "I wish her to burn beneath me and then burn from the fire of a hundred faggots put to the torch."

"Naturally," Jacques agreed. "But first you need to find her. In fact, you surprise me. I would expect you to be out looking for her yourself, *monsieur.*"

Lachlan glowered at the veiled criticism.

"Perhaps, though, you are not wanting a confrontation with Robert?" Jacques couldn't help the slight taunt in his voice.

Shoving his empty ale tankard away, Lachlan eyed Jacques. "Why should I be out there slogging through the braes and fells when I have minions to do that part? I enjoy my creature comforts, my castle roof, my fire, and my ale too much to bother chasing Robert and Catriona personally. I am the heir."

"Indeed." And someday, Jacques, too, would have the luxury of letting others do his dirty work while *he* sat back and waited in comfort.

"Do you doubt the ability of my clansmen to track the fugitives?" Lachlan asked suddenly.

"Not at all," Jacques said, sinking down on a hard bench at an angle from Lachlan. "I only want to offer the benefit of my recent experience with Robert."

"Such as?"

"Alternative ways to find your little witch so you can both bed her and burn her."

Lachlan shot Jacques an appraising look. "You have a price, I assume. How steep? A sworn allegiance to the Stuarts?"

"Mais non, monsieur. I know better than to try to sway you—a loyal Scotsman. Though it is no secret I am sympathetic to the exiled king, I nevertheless trust that we are men of reason who can strike a deal when there is something to be gained for each of us."

"You ken what it is I want—the lass brought back here. Tell me about the gain for you."

Jacques paused, searching for a delicate phrase, considered Lachlan, then decided instead on the coarser approach.

"I want the buried treasure of Scotland. The crown for my king."

Lachlan's brows rose in surprise. "What makes you think I would know anything about that?"

"Your grandfather was a Jacobite who opposed Cromwell, n'est-ce pas?"

"So?"

"I have heard that the Regalia was buried somewhere—perhaps in a church in the last century. Perhaps in your castle. It is why I offer to bring the lass back, so that you will tell me."

"My grandfather and I dinna share everything. But this treasure—the crown you seek. You want it that badly?"

"Do you have another king in mind for it? You perhaps want it to end up in England for a lascivious Hanoverian to paw over?" Jacques's words dripped with venom.

Lachlan scowled. "Nay, but I want vengeance." He stood and paced.

"You are an honorable man who has been wronged," Jacques suggested in a smooth voice.

"I am a man to be reckoned with."

"But surely only a simpleton would doubt that," Jacques said, his smooth nod urging Lachlan on.

"My entire family needs to remember that I am heir."

"Surely not your sister as well," put in Jacques.

Lachlan smirked. "Grizel. That mealymouthed wench. I gave her her due already, only she's too much the idiot to know it." By now his voice was slurring beyond clarity, and as he paced, he staggered.

"You intrigue me, monsieur, but of course I could not pry."

"She would be too stupid to do anything about it even if she heard it to her face."

"You turned her lover against her?" It was an educated guess, based on his knowledge of the wiles of women's minds.

Lachlan twisted around to stare at Jacques. "How do you know?"

Jacques shrugged, trying to appear casual. His head pounded with the thrill that he might actually have hit upon a wicked truth.

"How do you know?" Lachlan insisted, drawing closer.

"Is that not what women most hate to lose?" Then after a pause, he added, "She speaks of a lost lover."

Lachlan smirked again, and his words were slurred, his eyes slightly glazed. "I did better than that. I killed her lover." With shaking hands, he refilled his tankard and gulped.

"A favor no doubt." By now, Jacques was practically trembling with excitement at this tidy piece of gossip. Dangerous words they were, for twisted around they could be used in his own favor.

"He was a Ferguson," Lachlan said, as if that explained all.

Jacques held his breath, waiting for the details, so transfixed that he forgot his ale.

Mon Dieu, to have killed his own sister's lover, a Ferguson, and to have lied about it. It would give Jacques more than enough information to bargain with.

"That debacle of a rebellion called the '15," Lachlan murmured. "Ian died defending the clan. 'Swhat everyone thinks." Lachlan looked off across the rafters of the great hall, as if speaking to himself. "You know what killed him? Scottish bullet in his back. Mine."

Jacques shivered. He had underestimated Lachlan, but better to know now than later.

"Your secret is mine," Jacques said at once.

"What secret?" Lachlan suddenly focused on Jacques as if trying to remember what he'd been talking about.

"Our business arrangement," Jacques lied hastily. "The location of the Regalia for the return of Catriona."

Lachlan thought for a minute, then eyed Jacques skeptically. "Why do you think you could bring her back rather than my own men?"

"I will hire a guide."

"My men can track as well as any guide."

Jacques smiled. "Your cousin Robert is a very intelligent man. I observed him in action on the journey up here. Your clansmen, you must concede, possess more brawn than brain."

"So?" Lachlan scowled.

"So it is my thinking skills that will enable me to find Robert and Catriona. I propose to find him by outwitting him."

With a scoff, Lachlan reached for a fresh tankard of ale and leaned back in his grandfather's great chair. "We shall see, Frenchman. But know this. I am smarter than either you or Robert. Robert is being hunted down like a wild stag, and you are no better than the dog I send after the stag."

Though he flushed slightly, Jacques managed to ignore the insult. Too much was at stake. "Very well. Do you send me after Robert and Catriona?"

"Aye." Lachlan waved a hand in dismissal. "Find her and bring her back—even if you have to drag her out of Robert's bed."

Chapter 18

Oh, Robert, what a beautiful creature.

It was near gloaming of the fourth day when Catriona spotted the red stag at the secluded loch and, with a finger to her lips, waved Robert over. Her protective instincts had given way to a more basic need. Hunger. As if by unspoken agreement, Catriona took the haversack from Robert and fell in behind him. If he could kill the animal, she knew it meant they could conserve the salted mutton and bannock he carried in the haversack. Besides his pistol, he had a rifle with him, but he needed to move into closer range. Before he could aim and cock the hammer, the stag looked up, twitched its ears, and bounded away.

"The wily old sot," Robert said under his breath. "We were no' close enough to scare him." He sounded more tired than disappointed.

Something moved in the bushes nearby, and Catriona laid a restraining hand on Robert's arm. When an old woman in dark blue homespun stood up, Catriona saw what had frightened their meat away, and she felt rather startled herself.

The woman was surprisingly close, but because she had been kneeling down and dressed in both a gown and a long plaid scarf of a dark hue, it had been understandably easy to miss her. Catriona tried to guess her age. The thin plaits of hair that hung past each shoulder suggested youth, but deep wrinkles etched her face, proving she'd seen many a bloom of heather. Over one arm she had draped a basket for the lichens she'd been gathering, and with her other arm she shielded her eyes from the last rays of light and studied her visitors.

Robert had warned Catriona before they set out several days ago that there'd be no gauging friend or foe, but now Catriona immediately forgot the admonitions and started forward.

"Wait, lass," she heard him say to her back, but she yearned so for a friendly woman to talk with that she kept slowly walking. What could he do? Get angry? When Robert got angry he ended up kissing her or . . . better. As a matter of fact, he'd been entirely too calm for the past three days. Calm to the point of treating her . . . well, the way all the university students used to. As if she were no more than a scrawny, gawky nuisance he had to be polite to.

Three nights ago in the hunting hut, she'd pleased him thoroughly. Instinct told her so, yet, for reasons only he knew, he'd not touched her since, and her body ached to have him closer.

Sighing, she gave her full attention to the strange woman.

Standing perfectly still, the old woman watched Catriona's approach, and nothing in her expression suggested either welcome or hostility. A few feet ahead, Catriona saw a little grave—a mound of dirt and a rough-hewn stone marker. The writing was in Erse. Catriona paused, reluctant to intrude on a scene of grief, but it was too late to turn back—not unless she wanted to arouse suspicion.

Robert moved so silently in the deerskin cuarans he wore that she felt rather than heard him come up behind her. There was unmistakable tension in his body, especially in the possessive hand he placed on Catriona's waist. The gesture startled her, coming after so many days of his not touching her, but she hid her surprise.

The old woman surveyed them a moment, then reached down to pick up a daisy she'd dropped and laid it on the little grave.

"What are ye seeking here?" she asked in heavily brogued English. "A fly cup or a night of shelter?"

"Do you welcome strangers?" Robert asked.

"If they're honest."

Catriona felt Robert's grip tighten and felt guilty that they were going to break one of the Commandments and lie to this innocent old woman. But what choice did they have? They couldn't admit that Catriona was an escaped witch, not if they hoped for hospitality.

"We're lost," Robert lied smoothly. "I'm one glen over from the trail, I fear." He then introduced himself with a false name, calling himself a Campbell no less.

"Annie is my name," the woman said, "and I'm auld, but no' a fool. What are ye running from?"

Catriona's heart lurched but Robert's hand tightened, a silent warning to remain calm while he finished his story.

"I ken what it looks like—but the truth is we lost our horses and the trail as well. 'Tis grateful we'd be if we could share your shelter for a night," he finished.

The woman nodded and eyed Catriona's breeches. "She's no lad. Why would ye dress her in Lowland garb?"

"Why do you think, old woman?" Robert draped an overly affectionate arm about Catriona. "To camouflage her from the other laddies who roam these Highlands. She's mine. Eloping with me. Her parents will disown her and throw her to the lepers if she weds the likes of me, but there's no help for it."

"Who are her parents?"

Robert's pause was barely perceptible. "David," he said unexpectedly, and covered Catriona's gasp with an easy correction. "MacDavid. But soon she'll be mine. All mine."

Annie surveyed Robert and then Catriona, who was still blushing at the charming tale. Robert really had a quite wonderful talent at the diplomatic turn of phrase. No wonder Lord Kendrick wanted his assistance.

"Take off yer bonnet, lass," Annie commanded, "and let yer hair down loose like a proper virgin."

Pausing only a second, Catriona swept off the blue cap and allowed the long curls to cascade about her shirt.

Annie stared at her. "Bonnie lass, ye are. My wee bairn that's buried over yonder had red hair like that. She would have been a blithe beauty too . . . Born and died the year of the Rebellion,'' the woman said wistfully. "About the age of this lassie here, she'd have been, no?''

Catriona nodded. Her heart went out to the old woman. It was Robert who posed the practical question. "What of your husband, Annie? Is he about?''

The woman's expression turned dour. "Died . . . in the '15. He never knew the bairn over there. I bore her here alone.'' Unexpectedly, she glared up at Robert, as if condemning him for being one of the male species. After a moment, though, her expression softened, and she pulled her shawl up over her head as protection from the mist that was fast falling in the little glen.

"It waxes late, and ye're no' here to listen to my grieving.'' She paused, studying them, as if deciding whether or not to offer her hospitality. "Come along,'' she said at last. "I'll see that bonnie lass gets a decent meal in her.'' She turned and led the way down a well-worn path from the gravesite.

Robert reached for Catriona's hand and, enfolding it in his, squeezed her fingers, a gesture that she took as a sign of trust. He would not leave her or let anything happen to her, she knew. He had promised, and ever since the night he had loved her, she had felt bound to him by an even deeper trust. Slanting a smile at him, she squeezed his hand in return and followed him down the path.

Past a stand of birch trees that crowded the loch's shore stood a half-hidden crofter's hut, blackened from peat soot. Even now a skinny plume of smoke trailed up from the chimney above its roof of heather thatch.

They waited while Annie lit a candle and entered her tiny dwelling. Catriona gulped at the spare surroundings. A narrow table. A settle. A pot bubbling over a fire in the center of the room. Straw blocked the wind from the single window, under which sat a weaving loom. Annie had left a piece of solid blue wool half woven on the loom, and the steamy cottage was a potpourri of many scents— dye, hanks of yarn drying from the ceiling, straw and animals from the byre adjoining the main room. But it was the acrid scent of cooking that gave Catriona a pang of homesickness, so strongly did it remind her of Elspeth and the good, pungent herbs of her kitchen in Edinburgh.

While Annie added peat and stoked the fire, Catriona peered into the small caldrons that bubbled over the hearth. Annie dropped another handful of lichens into one and stirred. Red dye . . . Catriona watched, savoring the companionship and homey tasks of another woman.

Arms folded, Robert leaned against the open door jamb, as if keeping watch on the glen from the doorway, and so it was Catriona who listened to Annie's lonely talk.

"I've been blessed with abundance in this glen," she said. "Not just lichens, but broom bark, bracken root—"

"Even whortleberries for blue dye," Catriona added, glancing over at Robert's formidable profile.

"Aye, near every color of the plaids is possible," Annie said, stirring. "The clans from many glens around come to me for their plaids and it has been so since the time of my grandmother. I would have passed the secrets of the plaids on to my own daughter." There was no mistaking the touch of bitterness in her voice.

Trying delicately to change the subject, Catriona asked what to her was the most natural question in the world. "And do you collect herbs as well?"

"Healing herbs?"

"Chamomile or feverfew. We have none with us and I—"

"Catriona." It was Robert's voice that interrupted. Without even turning, he said gently, "Come here and look across the loch. I think the red stag has come back."

Breaking off her talk, Catriona hurried outside and looked. Nothing moved except the summer grasses blowing against the rocks. As for the loch itself, the water was turning dark with gloaming, and the surface broke here and there in whitecaps. A bird skimmed the surface. Off in the distance, in the direction of Robert's gaze, she saw a tiny mound. He was staring at the bairn's grave.

Unexpectedly, he pulled her close in what at a distance would appear to be the embrace of two lovers. Except tiny worry lines appeared beside his eyes. "Dinna talk herbs or anything remotely connected to witchcraft, lass," he said in her ear.

Instinctively, Catriona nestled her face against the hollow of his neck. "But she's a good woman," she whispered against his throat, savoring the salty taste of him, this sudden closeness.

At her first breath, she felt his muscles tense, and he held her to him for a moment before whispering again.

"She appears to be good and honest, but we take no chances," he said. "The story of the trial in Glen Strahan could have traveled far by now. Do you understand?" he said so close to the lobe of her ear that she ached to mold herself to him.

"But every woman knows *those* herbs." She had to concentrate hard on her words, for Robert's rock-hard muscle, the masculine scent of him, nearly undid her.

Unexpectedly, he tweaked her cheek. "Och, here I thought I was traveling with the wench I met in the hunting hut, and it appears Catriona of the flinty tongue has suddenly taken her place."

She blushed at his reference to the joining of their bodies and at the undeniable evidence of his desire now. Yet though his voice and body were tense, he gave no other sign that this contact was affecting him. "Beware of your herb talk, hinny. Trust me."

With a reluctant nod, she pulled away, and Robert went in to offer Annie a present—the only thing he had to offer as far as Catriona knew—a pinch of snuff, courtesy of Lord Kendrick. Smiling gratefully, Annie took it and stashed it in a tin, then produced a meal of oatmeal porridge and oatcakes. Cream, butter, and milk appeared in abundance.

Catriona sat across from Robert and ate in silence while Annie continued to tend her caldron. Catriona kept looking up at Robert, trying to read what was in his face. Tousled hair, flecked gold by the candlelight, fell over his forehead, and dark shadows of worry etched the craggy lines of his face.

Trust me, he'd asked moments ago. Just a few nights ago she'd given her body, soul, and heart, as well as her life, into his keeping. He was, whether he knew it or not, the guardian not just of her life, but also of her heart.

Unimpressed by her romantic thoughts, a goat stuck its head over a partition separating the living quarters from the byre and began to chew on Annie's cloak. With a grumbled oath, Annie took a stick to shoo it onto its own side. "Get out. Good summer growth to eat all day, and ye're in here scavenging for hospitality." With an angry blat, the goat retreated.

Spinning back to her guests, Annie smoothed her gray braids and then went to work drying out the newly dyed red wool. All the while she managed to keep a surreptitious eye on her guests and maintain a steady stream of conversation, including directions on the best route to take out of this glen.

"Edinburgh, is it? And what is a fine Highland pair like ye going to do in the city? Ye canna live on love, ye ken?"

Robert looked up. "Details, details, Annie. Dinna tell her that. She may change her mind, and run off with some other Highland rogue."

Annie flashed a toothless grin. "Ye should keep the lass in the Highlands."

Catriona had a sudden fleeting memory of the bandit woman's curse: *Once ye've entered these hills, ye'll ne'er return to your own home alive. Unless you become an outlaw like us.*

She shook off the memory. Annie was not the bandit woman. Besides, that curse was not going to come true. It couldn't.

Catriona felt a sudden stab of loss. Soon, they *would* make their way out of the Highlands. Robert would go on to his diplomatic rendezvous with Lord Kendrick, and she might never see him again. Unexpectedly, as if he felt her watching him, he looked up and met her gaze. Deep blue his eyes were, like the fading sky at twilight.

Robert would do anything to regain the lost title for his old grandfather. Catriona's leg accidentally touched his beneath the narrow table, and she tried to remind herself that when she'd met him down in Edinburgh he'd been living a rogue's existence. But in their lovemaking she'd not thought him a rogue.

Abruptly pulling her legs away from his, she picked up her bowl and went outside to rinse it in Annie's dishpan. She lingered a bit to watch the sun fade. It was late, but the evenings held their light long at this time of year. Inside she could hear Annie babble on about how many of her kinsmen had escaped from this glen after the battle of Sheriffmuir. Like a man born to the role, Robert matched her political talk. At last, unable to stave off weariness, Catriona went back inside.

By the light of the dying fire, she saw at once the pallet of straw and heather that Annie had laid by the fire before vanishing behind a blanket strung over a rope. The pallet was barely wide enough for two—if they slept close. Catriona swallowed thickly, uncertain if she could endure another night of sleeping so close after having known Robert's fierce passion.

Though she saw the dark intensity of his eyes, his face by contrast held no hint of emotion. With her pulse thudding at her throat, she watched while he slowly unwound the plaid from his shoulders and waist and handed it to her, leaving him in only a loose shirt and his knee plaid.

"Sweet dreams, my jo," he said loud enough for Annie to hear and then he walked outside, leaving her bereft, except for the warm wool.

After washing in a basin of tepid water Annie had left for her, Catriona settled down on the mattress. It crunched each time she moved. Pulling the MacLean plaid over her, she prayed for sleep to come, but she couldn't relax. She'd grown used to Robert's comforting presence and sorely missed him. She prayed some more, but all her prayers went unanswered.

Too soon, his footfall sounded in the room and then the pallet shifted as he lay down beside her. Annie supposed them lovers, yet Robert never reached for her, and they might as well have a wall between them.

But then, why should the likes of Robert MacLean want a scrawny thing like her? she asked herself. She was surprised Annie had believed his half-cocked story about eloping. A golden-haired rogue and a red-haired thistle. What an unlikely pair. Tears welled in her eyes. *Oh, Robert, I didn't please you, did I?* she asked herself, desolation sweeping over her.

Beside her, Robert lay in an agony of throbbing need. If he could distract his mind from Catriona's sweet nearness, he might be able to sleep, but right now he'd wager on a long, sleepless night. And win heavily. Collect from every crony at the Crown and Mitre, he would.

She rolled over and faced him. "Robert?"

"So help me," he whispered, "if you so much as mention Michelangelo or ask about the name MacDavid, I'll get up and sleep in the byre."

"How often do men like to mate?" she whispered back.

Straw crunched beneath his torso as he rolled over to face her, so taken aback at the innocence of her question that it took all his willpower to ignore the blood surging to his loins and not reach for her. Instead, he forced himself to take a deep breath before answering. "That depends, lass. I told you, some men collect wenches like you collect books." Which might be a stark way of putting it, he thought, but there was no sense letting her build up romantic notions.

He sensed her hurt and confusion, and forgetting all his agonies, pulled her into his arms to hold her. "You need to sleep, lass," he said softly, "not consort with roguish types. Too much mating takes the curl out of yer hair, ye ken."

"You're teasing me. I hate being teased about my hair." She laid a hand on his chest, then her fingers splayed against his abdomen, and he thought he'd go mad from the sensation.

"You've a lot to learn about teasing, lass," he said hoarsely, and, covering her hand with his, slid it to a less flammable location. "If I promise to watch out for bandits, will you go to sleep?"

When he heard her sigh of resignation, he steeled his mind against it. "Yes, all right," came the tremulous reply, and he hated himself for both hurting and deceiving her.

But he'd made a vow, after seeing the grave of Annie's bairn, not to take her again. He'd been selfish that first night in the hut, risking a child in her when he intended to leave her eventually. On top of that, he felt guilty now, guilty because she thought he was taking her to Edinburgh and he'd not corrected her. Sooner or later, he'd have to tell her the truth, tell her that he intended to arrange exile for her.

Robert shut his eyes and feigned sleep in the straw, but instead of the rough bed, all he felt was Catriona's softness nestled against him. Silky curls fell over his cheek and drove him wild. And every time she moved, she curled a bit closer, touched a few more pulse points that inflamed his need for her. He needed her more than he wanted to admit, needed to touch her, enfold her, pour himself into her.

As the night mists moved over the glen, he lay awake, visions of Catriona filling his mind—a naive minx of too much temper and spirit for her own good.

In fact, he should have seen this coming the first time he'd kissed her. It hadn't turned out as he'd expected. Her body had moved too innocently against his, she'd smelled of dried lavender, and she had too much silk in her curls. And lately, he was noticing too often how the swell of her hips filled out the breeches he'd dressed her in.

He could feel those breeches now against his legs, and her soft face resting on one of his arms. Her chest rose and fell rhythmically beneath her shirt. At least she slept and wouldn't be plaguing him with any more questions, which meant he could put her out of his mind and sleep too.

He was still lying awake several hours later, wondering if he could stand Catriona's arm about his waist for one more minute, when the blanket hanging in the corner stirred as if from a gentle wind.

It was the old woman, Annie, who came creeping out. Instantly alert, Robert couldn't have said what time it was except that a bright moon still filtered in through the cottage window. With great care, he feigned the regular breathing of sleep. He sensed when Annie stood over them, watching, and heard when her unshod footsteps headed out the door. As soon as it creaked shut, he opened his eyes, his pulse thudding a warning of danger.

Immediately, he slipped from underneath the plaid and followed the old woman to the door, where, by the light of the full moon, he watched her hurry down a path and disappear into the mist.

He came back inside and stared down at Catriona, trying hard to remember a line from the Lord's Prayer. *And lead us not into temptation.* He bent low. It was temptation that made him kiss her awake instead of call her name. Her lips were pliant and tasted vaguely of sweet butter. Moving his hand around to cup the back of her neck, he pushed his hand through her hair. His kiss deepened, and with it, the ardor he'd held in check flared. Desperately, he tried to remember the next line. *But deliver us from evil.* Elspeth and Angus expected him to deliver her to safety.

He knew the instant she awakened, for her lips parted beneath his, and he was sorely tempted to deepen the kiss even more.

"It's still night," she said sleepily, then, more awake, she half sat up, blinked at him, and seemed to recall where they were. "What's wrong? Is Lachlan come?"

"The old woman has left the cottage," he whispered against her lips. "I dinna think we ought to stay till morning to find out who she went to tell about her guests. If she's heard about the witch of Glen Strahan, she's likely tattling about us right now."

"You want to escape?" Catriona said bleakly, her voice still a sleepy whisper.

"What I want is to keep on just as we are, lass," he replied dryly, "but we need to leave." He leaned back on his haunches, trying to get hold of himself, trying to ignore the pain of his own desire. When she sat up and rubbed sleep out of her eyes, he studied the straw more intently than if he were a connoisseur. *Deliver us from evil.* That was his task. He looked up to find her watching him.

"Now?"

He nodded. "And since between the two of us you have a vaster experience in plotting escapes, what do you suggest?"

She was already on her feet, reaching for the haversack and handing Robert both it and his plaid. "How many choices do we have?"

"None, lass, except to run."

A minute later, Catriona headed toward the path that Annie had said led to Edinburgh, but with a tug at her elbow Robert guided her west, explaining that they had to take a route that Annie would not expect. Later, he told himself guiltily, later he would explain to her that it was west he'd been intending to take her all along.

Robert knew she could keep up with him. He'd had to chase her once himself and knew what she was capable of. But he didn't know where they'd end up or how long it would take. Except for the meager contents of the haversack and the clothes on their backs, they had nothing.

And nobody they could trust.

Riding beside his guide, Jacques swore softly in French. Four days they'd been on the move, and except for the pair of riderless horses they'd spotted, the search had been uneventful. Robert and Catriona were proving to be exceptionally elusive, and if anything, the horse and pony were a nuisance, keeping them too close to the trails.

But Jacques would find Robert even if it meant backtracking through all those cursed mountains and lakes.

Arrogant Scotsman, that's what Robert was. Thinking himself superior just because he could wield a dirk and maneuver his way around this treacherous countryside. Jacques allowed himself a fleeting memory of Lachlan, warm and dry back in the castle, and made a vow. Someday, by all the saints, Jacques himself would have minions to do *his* bidding while *he* stayed behind wallowing in luxury. All he had to do was find Catriona and exchange her for the Regalia. Not even Robert was going to stop him.

And though Robert would probably scoff if he heard Jacques was chasing after him, what Robert didn't know was that Jacques had found himself a guide, a genuine Jacobite, a passionate, secret papist who lived right in Glen Strahan. Thomas had been so drunk on free whiskey and so enthralled with Jacques's tales of the king o'er the water that he had willingly volunteered to guide Jacques in exchange for a promise of easy gold.

"I can show you a shortcut out of this glen," Thomas offered now, riding by Jacques's side. "It's the route Robert likely took with the little witch. It could put us ahead of Lachlan's men," he offered hopefully.

Jacques shook his head. "Thomas, Thomas, we Jacobites are too wily to let ourselves be maneuvered."

"Sir?" From his pony Thomas looked up, confused.

Jacques drew in a patient breath. "I've told you before, my plan is to let Lachlan's men lead us right to the wench and her lover. Why should we do the searching when Lachlan's men are available to take the risks? Just keep us behind them."

Thomas's face fell.

"I'm not out here in Scotland to get shot at by Lachlan's clansmen, Thomas," Jacques said with practical-minded decisiveness, annoyed that this freckle-faced youth still wet behind his earlugs should question his judgment. He had hired a road map, nothing more.

"I prefer to be alive for future business dealings," he added.

Thomas nodded, for the moment convinced. "Aye, sir. Far the better plan, indeed, to let the others lead us to where Robert is taking the Ferguson lass."

Jacques nodded in approval. "And then we'll move in and snatch the little wench while Lachlan's men are still tethering their mounts and sneaking a dram, right, Thomas?"

"Two of us against so many?" Thomas's face showed his uncertainty.

Jacques scowled at his guide. "You'll not be a doubting Thomas, will you now? Faith, Thomas. We watch and wait for opportunity. With dull-witted men such as Lachlan's, opportunity always turns up."

They rode in silence for a few moments. "You believe

then that Robert is the lover of Lachlan's wench?'' Thomas asked, clearly intrigued by the possibility.

Jacques smiled to himself and decided to tell this green lad of the wiles of females. Reaching over to where Thomas sat on a shorter pony, he easily swatted Thomas on the neck with his tricorn, as if to wake him up.

"Trust me, my stout-hearted Thomas. I spent many a night observing them on the journey up here. I wager as certain as French brandy is potent that right now Robert has his hands on the wench.''

Chapter 19

When they finally emerged from the trees and saw the steep bank leading down to the river, they stopped in unison. Catriona, used to the Highlands now, knew without being told that there'd be no hope of wading across *this* river. Just listening to the rushing of the water far below the cliff told her that. Carefully, she edged toward the bank, then at the unexpected sound of voices in the trees behind them, Robert pulled her back, so quickly that she nearly bumped into him.

"What is it?" Instinctively, she clasped her hand about his forearm. There was something infinitely reassuring about the feel of masculine muscle. "Tell me, Robert," she said.

He put a finger to his lips. "I'm no' sure yet, lass."

Uneasy, she looked around, trying to see through the trees. "Is it MacLean clansmen?" she whispered.

He shook his head. "A soldier downriver. Who knows? An entire troop might be paying an afternoon call on us," he said, his expression glum. "Looking for anything from tea and scones to a dram." He put his arm about her and pulled her close.

"Soldiers in red? Dragoons?" Raw hope filled her voice. If it turned out to be English soldiers . . . She voiced her longing, praying it wasn't farfetched. "They might be able to help."

Robert shook his head and pointed behind her. She had been looking down at the raging waters far below them, but now looked up.

"That," he said, "is what's going to help us."

Turning carefully, Catriona followed his gaze to the decrepit stone bridge that spanned it. Her stomach clenched.

"It's a bridge." The wobble in her voice matched the architectural condition of the very old, unsound bridge.

Suddenly she knew who was in the burn. "It's soldiers coming to work on the bridge, isn't it?" The English had done so much work road building and bridge making in the Highlands that it was a logical deduction.

Robert nodded. "Most likely," and then he cursed their unfortunate timing. "Lazy red-coated garrisons . . . If the English could put in a day's work to match a Highlander's they'd have that bridge rebuilt by now so we could cross it without risking our necks."

"Mayhap you should have informed them in advance that you'd have need of it," Catriona suggested. As far as she was concerned, the English could have it, and she told him so.

"*We* need it, my jo, not the English. That's how we're going to get across this river."

"You'll climb up in a pulpit before I'll climb across that thing." Her voice sounded faint, and she couldn't for the life of her figure out why Robert looked so eager to go closer. Tugging her hand, he pulled her along to inspect it. Catriona, however, had eyes only for the wild river below.

The raging water, white with foam, flowed wildly through the Highland glen. The spray from its fury rose up to meet the low hanging mists and splashed over onto the opposite bank where heather and gorse bloomed in a riot of purple and yellow.

Suddenly Robert turned, face tense, and looked at the woods behind them, listening to a new sound behind them in the trees. As if an entire troop of men were singing. An English song, punctuated by the thud of marching feet and snapping brush.

"Can you still climb the Highland crags the way you told me you used to when you and your grandfather roamed Glen Strahan?" he asked, his voice low but urgent.

"That depends . . . on where you want me to climb.

I'm not going to cross that bridge." She looked at the bleak expression on Robert's face and knew her fate. "No, Robert, please." She backed away from his arms.

He was already shaking his head. "Lass, half the soldiers are bribed. By Lachlan mayhap." He let that sink in before adding, "Believe me, an English dragoon is going to look with suspicion on any Scots who appear to be fleeing for their lives." Taking her hand, Robert moved swiftly toward the crumbling bridge.

She tugged back. "Oh, no, Robert, please, it's at least as old as Rome and looks so . . . so slippery." Half of the stones had fallen away, leaving a narrow trellis, narrower than any trail he'd guided their horses along. She walked around a lonely cluster of fading bluebells. "I can't," she said faintly.

"There's no time for reluctance, lass."

"Why don't we simply hide in the woods until they leave?" she suggested.

He made a scoffing sound. "Because we don't know how long they'll stay, and I wager there's enough of them that one would trip over us. Besides, sooner or later, we *have* to cross this river."

She felt her knees turn to broth. He was right, of course.

"Could we say a prayer first?"

"Your prayers are too long."

Robert didn't bother to argue further. He simply untied the strings of her cloak and after easing the garment off her, stuffed it in the haversack.

Numb with fear, she grabbed his wrists and looked up. "You won't let me fall?"

He gave her a quick shake. "Catriona, dinna lose your mettle now. In another five minutes that first soldier will be here to start work on this bridge and then we'll have to hide like trapped animals waiting to be taken alive."

She cast another nervous glance at the bridge. It was as high from the water as the top floor of an Edinburgh townhouse was from a lane. "It's too far down. I can't walk across it. I can't."

"We've trekked up the stiffest braes, lass, and you ne'er told me you feared heights," he accused.

"You never asked me."

His fingers dug into her shoulders. "Catriona, as God is my witness, you have to. It's our only hope. Dinna turn into an English miss now. Ye're my Highland lass. Say ye can do it. Say it."

"You go first."

He apparently took that as an affirmative and as they moved toward the bridge, he reassured her. "Walking a bridge is like trust, Catriona. You dinna look to the left or right, dinna look for the wee creatures like wounded hares, dinna check to see where your enemies are. Look straight ahead and follow in my footsteps."

A red squirrel scampered through the rocks in a noisy rush. In the distance, she heard the clear sound of voices. His meaning finally sank in. English soldiers would show no more mercy to a Scotswoman accused of witchcraft than Lachlan would.

"Ready?"

Drowning was perhaps no more awful a way to die than burning, she decided and nodded.

"There's a braw lass. I may not have learned to part the waters down at university, Catriona, but I did learn that there are times when one must have faith in oneself. Did you no' learn that in any of your father's fancy books?"

"Bridge architecture never held my interest in particular."

"Aye, well, Michelangelo and all those other artists canna help you here, I fear, lass."

She took a deep, steadying breath and looked at him, his face fierce with determination, his lithe body already clambering up on the rocky structure. Grimacing, she took his outstretched hand and climbed up with him.

The sound of tramping horses' hooves and soldiers' voices grew closer as she positioned her feet one in front of the other and said a prayer that something more than habit held the pile of stones together . . . and that they would get across before the soldiers emerged from the forest cover. She kept her eyes on Robert's back, on the exact place between his shoulder blades where a tiny leaf from a birch tree clung like a guiding light. Every few steps bits of stone shifted and pebbly chunks fell away. Down below her she could hear the raging torrent of water and almost feel the mist from it kissing her skin. Her heart beat in her ears, but slowly she eased her way across, her arms stretched out for balance.

A breeze took her hat by surprise and lifted the little circlet of blue wool right off her head. She reached up for it, but it was gone, and her hair spilled down over her shoulders. Out of the corner of her eye, she saw the hat fall straight down toward the river, and then a wave of dizziness shot through her. The next thing she knew she was straddling the narrow ledge of stone, head down, hair tangling in her face, arms clinging for dear life.

Robert, with sinful agility, jumped off onto a patch of heather first and turned back for Catriona. Trembling, yet reluctant to break her tenuous balance, she scooted herself along, wondering how the birds managed their wobbly perches with such grace. Carefully, she pulled herself back up to her feet, but remained crouched as slowly she inched her way the remaining distance.

On the other side of the river, someone barked out a military command. She teetered and looked down. Raging white currents beckoned and she felt herself go dizzy again.

"Look at me," Robert ordered, his voice barely loud enough to be heard above the roar of the current. "Look at me and jump. Hurry, love, before he sees you."

Shutting her eyes, she said a prayer for mercy and flew in the direction of Robert's voice. She felt the impact of flesh against muscle and then she was falling forward. They landed together, sprawled in the heather, he on his back, she at an awkward angle across his torso, her hand grasping the inside of his thigh. Gently he extricated her fingers, pulled her up, and ran with her up over a small hill. On the other side, they fell to the ground, protected by both the hill and the clumps of heather.

"Bravo, lassie," he said and, pulling her up to face him, punctuated his jest with a light kiss. The kiss deepened, and she felt a fire igniting. Like two parts of a whole, they clung and kissed, still breathless from their stroll across the bridge.

Another command cut through the air, and reluctantly she dragged herself up from him. "Robert, we've got to go on."

He pulled her back down on top of him. "We'd do best to stay right here and hide till they distract themselves with their labor," he pointed out. "Ye dinna think they're brave enough to cross that bridge, do ye?" He molded her into his own contours. "Besides, I'm uncommonly comfortable beneath a rather bonnie Highland lass and fancy biding in the heather with her."

"Will you stop, Robert? They'll hear us."

"Then you'll have to find other ways to distract my words, lass," he said, and his mouth claimed hers again.

If she had bewitched him, then he had bedeviled her, and she could scarce breathe at times for thinking of his hands, practiced and sensual, moving over her body.

They both seemed to gather their wits at the same time. She rolled off him and they lay quietly, side by side, not talking, only listening. She could hear his breathing, heavy and uneven, over the muted sound of raging water. Muted because her pulse throbbed so wildly in her ears. If she had any thought at all before she drifted under the spell of exhausted sleep, it was the wonder that a man and woman could meet as strangers and by some mysterious process grow to this sweet snare of bondage—something far beyond friendship. All mixed up with bodies and minds and souls, it was. Only God could explain it.

Even with her eyes shut, she saw Robert, and the thought made her heart beat faster, her body burn with a want that she marveled at. Far away, she could still hear soldiers calling out commands. Robert reached for her hand. She lay there dreaming that he was leading her by the hand inside the walls of Edinburgh, and she was home at last.

When she opened her eyes, he was gone from her side, but almost immediately a shadow blocked the sun and she sat up to find him kneeling over her, water cupped in his hands. She sat up and drank. It was not a lot and it trickled through the cracks between his fingers and spotted her shirt. Holding his wrist, she licked the last of it from his palms and then buried her face in his hands. She started to pull away, and his hands framed her face.

"Thank you," she whispered.

"If you thought that was good, wait till you taste the fine claret at our next stop," he teased.

She fought back a lump in her throat. "I'm scared, Robert."

His smile held a rare tenderness. "Ye're a bonnie bridge climber, lass." Like a sorcerer he produced the haversack and pulled out her cloak for her. With all the panache of a gentleman in an Edinburgh parlor, he wrapped it around her shoulders, tied the bow, and then gave her his hand as if leading her to the dance floor.

"Lachlan's going to find us, isn't he?" she asked.

He looked back at her, tempted to hold her, but didn't dare risk it. "I've always bested Lachlan, and I will this time too," he said fiercely.

"But *if* they find us, will you die too?" she asked.

Robert pulled back and, tipping her face up to his, looked into her liquid gray eyes. He saw reflected back some of his own sudden uncertainty. Until now, he hadn't thought of receiving his own death sentence. The possibility was there after all. He didn't trust himself to deepen the discussion.

"I won't let them find us. Now we'd best march on ourselves." He turned and led her up the fell, walking low so the troops would not see them.

It was late afternoon before Robert stopped to rest, mostly because he could feel Catriona lagging. He took her high within the hills, then down into a tiny glen, a secluded place. Catriona dropped into a patch of just blooming heather, stretching out on her cloak, her breeches and shirt molded to her by the breeze. He took in the delicate thrust of finely formed breasts and the gentle swell of feminine hip and had to turn away.

He busied himself finding peat for a fire, then, in a small copse of pine, he set a primitive snare for any animal that might wander by and provide them with food. He hoped the Highlands would not be frugal with its hospi-

tality. When he returned, the mists had fallen low and the
fire sputtered. Frustrated, he swore at the damp rocks that
ringed the peat. But it wasn't really the fire that angered
him, and he knew it. Catriona was on her feet, coming
toward him, looking like the very heather itself wrapped
in that lavender cloak, and all the memories of their journey to the Highlands rushed back at him.

The first time he'd seen her, wielding a candlestick . . .

The chase through the field until he caught her . . .

The books she stuffed in her clothes . . .

When she walked into his arms, it seemed as natural as
breathing. When his arms went around her, that seemed
natural too. She came just to the tip of his chin, and her
wild red curls, tangled and damp, felt like raw silk.

They stood, arms about each other, staring at the fire.

"Robert, how did Sarah die? I mean, that's not a diplomatic secret like where the Regalia is hidden, is it?"

He threw aside a last piece of peat and sighed tiredly.
Slumping against a rock, he reached for her, pulling her
against his plaid, nestling her close against him. He pulled
up her hood and tucked loose curls inside it.

"I don't know, love. I only know it wasn't because of
anything you did."

"Then why do you believe in me when no one else in
the village does? Not one soul . . ." Her voice cracked,
and tears filled her eyes. "I grew up there," she managed.

"Lass, 'tis not you who's at fault." He pulled her as
close as possible, and felt her muffled sobs against his
shoulder. Lord, he'd been hoping they could make their
escape before the shock of everything that had happened
to her turned to emotion.

"There's one thing ye must ken about the village, lass.
The people are moved by fear more than by thinking. Now,
you and I . . . we've had the thinking given to us with all
those wretched books."

She gave a muffled half laugh, half cry.

"It's true. Wretched they were, those years of book
learning, but from them I've learned that life has many
questions and for every question there are many answers.

The villagers have no answers to turn to except fear . . . and fear has no reason, no logic. Do ye ken?''

Nodding, she pulled away.

He stood there, unable to move, wanting to go on pressing his lips to her alabaster skin. He put a hand to her shoulder and let her curls tease his skin. "Your hair," he remarked, "is like a dangerous flag. You should leave your bonnet on."

She smiled ruefully. "It fell off."

At once, he stiffened. "Where? Why didn't you tell me? If the English find it—"

"It fell off on the bridge. I imagine it's long since drowned."

Despite her reassurance, he looked around at the Highland scenery, then shut his eyes and for the first time since he'd met Catriona said an honest prayer, silently to himself. *God in heaven, don't let the English find that little blue bonnet, and if they do, let them think it's been lost by anyone else. By rights, no one should associate it with Catriona. Give us that reassurance, Lord. Amen.*

He looked at her, at the fear in her eyes. "You're probably right," he said gently. "No one will ever find it."

The breeze pushed the hood of her cloak down, and with a casual gesture, he reached around and pulled it back up for her.

"A fine pair of runaways we make. You leave a trail of clothes wherever we go, and me, I canna even start a simple fire to cook our supper."

"Supper?" she said hungrily.

"Whatever walks into my trap, lass."

She reached into the pocket of her cloak and pulled out a tiny book. "Here," she said, handing it to him. "If you need to, you can use this for kindling. It might help." She pushed it into his hands.

"It's your Shakespeare," he said quietly.

"I've no time to read at the pace you set, it seems," she said lightly. "Someday I'll get another."

She turned on her heel and left him with the book, and once again he bent to the fire. This time he made it glow, and by the time she came back he had a small blaze going.

He could only pray again that none of Lachlan's men were nearby, because without food and a bit of warmth, he and Catriona could not keep going. Risks. One after another after another. But he'd known that that's what this journey held when he stole Catriona out of that dungeon.

"Your snare worked," she said. Without belaboring the subject, he went and did what had to be done. A while later, he returned with the skinned hare skewered on a branch and laid it across the fire. Catriona averted her face.

"Here now, lass," he said softly, "I thought you were hungry."

"It's different. This was a hare . . . like the one I healed."

He feared she was losing her mettle and—unable to abide another moment of her stoic look—walked over to her.

"I thought we'd come to an understanding about God's wee creatures . . ."

She nodded, but kept her face down. He sat beside her and pulled her against his shoulder.

After they had eaten and the fire burned low, her spirits seemed to improve.

"What do we do next?" he asked.

They could talk or sleep. Now seemed as good a time as any to tell her of his plan, but—uncertain of her reaction—he spoke in generalities.

"It's important that you know in case anything goes wrong."

"In case we get separated, you mean."

"There was a time not so long ago when separating yourself from me, lass, seemed to be your dearest wish." His voice held an ironic edge.

Nodding, she glanced up and caught his smile. "How long will it be until we get to Edinburgh?"

Ironically, *she* had forced the issue. Now that she'd asked the direct question, he could not avoid the honest answer.

"We're heading for the west coast of Scotland," he confessed softly. "To the Buchanans' castle just outside a wee coastal village named Three Caves. There I'm going to arrange passage for you to . . . to France and then—''

She was on her feet, her face incredulous. "You can't mean it. You would send me alone—''

"I have an escort in mind from the Buchanans' castle."

"But . . . but where would I live? What would I do?"

"I was thinking of Paris. You speak French well enough to serve as a language instructor in some fine household. I have contacts—''

"You mean to tell me," she interrupted, slanting a baleful look at him, "that you've thought it all through without even asking me? I suppose you're even going to loan me money to hasten my departure. Good English money?"

Her words hurt more than if she'd slapped him. "You canna go to Edinburgh, lass, and you know it. Leaving Scotland is the only safe thing to do."

Her gaze bore into him and her hands were clenched. "I don't care. I want to go back to Edinburgh." Whirling, she stalked away.

In a few quick strides he caught her and pulled her back around to face him. Damn, but he wasn't up to handling her hysterics.

"For the love of God, lass, you've been convicted of murder in Scotland. You've no choice but to go into exile. Do you understand me?"

He stopped. Her anger gone as suddenly as it had come, she was staring at him now as if the full extent of her predicament had suddenly sunk in.

"I'll never see Scotland again."

"Who can see into the future, lass?" He turned away and raked a weary hand through his hair. He had to avoid the trapped look in her eyes.

"After you meet Lord Kendrick, what will you do?" she asked.

He stiffened at her question. "I intend to try and regain the peerage that is rightly my family's. I'll go to England to see the king, if need be."

"And after that?" There was an edge to her voice. She was being betrayed. Abandoned.

"I'm no' the heir, hinny," he said softly. "That has always limited what I am allowed to do. There is nothing for me in Glen Strahan, so I will seek my fortune elsewhere. That, too, is the way of the world."

"Why are you not content to teach at university like my father—or be a simple shepherd?"

"Why are you not content, lass, to be a simple weaver of cloth like Annie? Or go to Paris and take a position?"

"Because I don't want to."

"And you think I want my lot? Had I been heir and my family titles not stolen, I might be content. But I am not, and I dinna see life in terms of shepherding sheep forever."

"Or shepherding runaway lasses either." By now her voice trembled.

"That too." As he remembered the way she had melted in his arms moments earlier, a liquid heat began to course through him. If he wanted to, he could pull her back into his embrace. She was so obviously infatuated with him—and momentarily vulnerable—that he could easily slake his rising desire on her.

He saw the hurt and betrayal pooling in her lovely gray eyes and felt infinitely weary. Not bodily weary, but weary of fighting off his roguish impulses.

"For now, all I want is to help you get away." What else was there to say? She knew he had a future with Lord Kendrick, knew of his need to regain his family titles. But at the moment he was miles away from that life.

"We were discussing a village called Three Caves," he continued. "Named after the caves along the coastline. It's a safe place to book passage on a ship." He tipped her chin up and wiped away the single tear that slipped down her cheek. "Don't cry. I'd rather you lose your temper again. Don't cry, hinny."

Sniffling, she squared her shoulders. "Will you visit me if you and Lord Kendrick come to Paris on business?"

He paused. "Aye."

She nodded and bit her lip. "Go on then. What else do I need to know?"

He felt as if a band were tightening around his chest.

The idea of Catriona alone in Paris was not what he wanted to think about. Hastily, he changed the subject. "I want you to remember that the caves where we'll end up are deceptive."

"So are you," she said.

He grabbed her shoulders. "Hear me out now, Catriona. These caves are narrow and dark at the sea, but they open up inside to a cavern big of a church. Long ago, an entire clan perished in such a cave. They hid out from their enemies and were outsmarted when the enemies blocked the narrow entrance with peat and fir boughs . . . and set it afire."

Catriona raised a horrified hand to her mouth.

"Aye, they hoped to smoke them out. Instead the clan all died, suffocated by smoke."

"Why are you telling me this now?"

"I want you to know what to expect." And talking kept him from pulling her into his arms.

Her tremulous smile had a strange effect on his breathing. "And I made the ultimate sacrifice and let you burn my last book."

"Not quite." Letting go of her, he reached into the pocket of his jacket and handed her the volume of Shakespeare. Slanting him a puzzled look, she took it, ran her fingers along the gilt edging, then rippled the pages, watching the light play off the gold. The question in her eyes demanded an answer.

He shrugged. "If I canna start a fire without resorting to the help of an English bard, I'd be a sorry excuse for a Highlander, and I've not been in Edinburgh that long—" He broke off, wondering if the mention of her former home would set off another storm within her.

She lifted her chin and put on a brave face. "Where do we go next?"

"I spotted a little cave a ways back in the hill," he said quickly, broaching the other subject he'd put off. "It's dry."

"What more do we need? Warmth, food, and a bed."

Uneasy with the way she spoke of sleeping in terms of "we," he simply jerked his head in the direction of the tiny cave. "It's just beyond where the snare was. Will you want it to yourself? I can rest out here just as well." Probably better, he added to himself.

"There's only one plaid, Robert."

"And two of us." He swallowed, his throat dry and aching.

"I expect then we'll honor the tradition of Highland hospitality and share," she said lightly.

He nodded and watched her walk off toward the little cave.

Briefly, he thought of staying outside, but moments later, he gave in, telling himself it wasn't right to leave her alone. In the dark, he had to feel for her, and she rolled over on the bed of pine boughs and reached for him, making it all too easy for him to gather her into his arms and bury his face in her silken curls. Sensual threads pulled him to her.

He began to kiss her throat, her chin, slowly moving his way by feel up to her lips, which parted against the onslaught of his desire. Tenderness, that was her seductive weapon. Tender innocence. He kissed her gently, almost reverently. Differently from any way he'd ever kissed a woman before. She was no tavern wench, he reminded himself again. Softly, her mouth moved beneath his lips, and he gathered her closer against him.

"Do you still want me, Robert?"

It was the naivete of her question that brought him to his senses. For the hundredth time since he'd met her, he felt like the selfish rogue he'd oft been accused of being, and he moved away, fighting the heat that coursed through him. With a stifled moan, he rolled off her before passion swept them away again.

She sat up. "Robert, what is it? Was that wrong to ask?" She reached for his sleeve.

He wanted to pound his fist against the wall of the cave. He was afraid that if he looked at her he'd be lost. "We canna go on like this, lass. We've no right." With a gentle movement, he pushed her hand away. "Do ye no' see that, lass?"

When he turned to tuck the cloak around her curves,

his hand brushed one of her breasts, and she stayed his hand. She felt soft beneath his weather-roughened fingers.

"No," she said on a wobbly note. "I don't see. What did I do wrong?"

He paused. "You had the misfortune to meet me, lass— to have a grandfather who had the bad sense to ask me to be your guardian."

"Tell me the truth."

"The tale does go round that I have been bewitched," he said, and touched her face. Her lashes fluttered against his hand. The air was thick with the scent of pine and damp loam. Outside, the Highland wind moaned through the treetops and a fine rain fell steadily.

She was silent. He really was going to have to explain it to her.

"In a few days we'll be separated, Catriona. I canna send you into exile encumbered with more trouble than ye've got."

She was silent, thinking that over.

"Elspeth explained something to you about bairns, didn't she?"

When she nodded, he breathed a sigh of relief and kissed her on the chin. "Sleep, lass."

That night, wrapped in her cloak, Catriona lay awake, while outside in the fine falling mist, Robert, stubborn man, lay just beyond the cave in a tent fashioned from their one plaid. She listened to the rain drum softly against the wool. He would have slept in the rain even if she'd not forced him to take the plaid. Stubborn, stubborn Scotsman. Just like her grandfather, she thought with a bittersweet lump in her throat.

Real life, she concluded that long cold night, was not at all for her as it was in the books. In books the heroes loved without stopping to think of practical worries. But it seemed to Catriona that of the few men she'd loved— Grandfather, Father, and now Robert—each in the end, in different ways, had rejected her. That should have been the bandit woman's curse:

The men you love will reject you, Catriona, each and every one of them.

* * *

Alexander MacLean, golf club tucked under his arm, strode across the castle ward to where old Cameron sat against the stables, his gnarled fingers mending a pony's harness.

When the MacLean stopped, his greyhound stopped as well, wagging its tail at the sight of Cameron, who looked up, eyes wary.

"A fine morning it is, milord."

"Indeed," agreed the MacLean. "The castle is at peace. Grizel weaves, my heir sleeps late, and the clansmen roam the Highlands, searching for the Ferguson lass. Aye, 'tis unusually peaceful for a change."

Cameron eyed the club. "Golfing, milord?" he asked with distinct skepticism.

Alexander MacLean had never golfed with the enthusiasm of Angus Ferguson. For one thing, the rocky perch on which his castle stood did not lend itself to golf holes. "Angus Ferguson invited me to golf on the property that by rights should be MacLean land. The old goat is too tough to remain in bed and insists on recovering from his seizure."

"Will you best him at golf, milord?"

"I am the chief of the MacLeans. When we were lads, did I no' beat everyone at sport?" At Cameron's respectful nod, Alexander added, "I suspect he wants to ask me what Robert did with Catriona."

"A mystery indeed."

"Indeed." The MacLean ran a hand over his stubbly chin. "Cameron, I have bided awhile down by the loch, by the outside of the castle tower."

Old Cameron let the harness fall to his lap and looked up. " 'Twas just yesterday, it seems, ye and I played there as lads," he replied.

"So it seems. As we vowed, I never told my sons or grandsons about that tunnel. There was no need with sieges at an end. Yet, I wonder, Cameron, if that could be the way Robert took the Ferguson lass out of here?"

Old Cameron met his chief's gaze with an unwavering

stare. "Why would you think Robert could do that, milord?"

"The rocks near the secret door have been disturbed, recently, and inside—"

"You didna open the tunnel door! Begging yer pardon, milord." He bent his head to the harness.

The MacLean's face split in a smile. "I am the chief, and if that were no' reason enough, I am auld enough to do whatever I please, and the devil take the consequences, aye, Cameron?"

"Aye. Age gives one courage."

"I was thinking that while I bided there, Cameron . . . if I were to break the pact and give out the secret, which one of my grandsons would ye suggest I tell?"

Cameron's hands were still, and he looked up. "I am no' the laird of the castle. 'Tis no' for me to decide."

A twinkle lit Alexander's eye. "Though Lachlan is heir, in my judgment, it is Robert I would entrust with the secret of the tunnel. Do ye no' agree, Cameron?"

"Aye, milord," the gnarled old man said with barely a pause.

The two men looked each other in the eye. "And if Robert were to take Catriona out through that tunnel," the MacLean went on, "Robert would care for her well, I believe. Angus will doubtless ask," he added.

Cameron squinted up at the MacLean. " 'Tis my feeling that Robert cares for the lass, milord. He'll care for her well . . . unless, of course, MacLean clansmen find them."

Alexander pursed his lips. "As to that . . . I had to allow Lachlan to spend his anger, but if I know Robert, he'll outdistance his own clansmen."

"Aye, Robert always was the swiftest."

Alexander nodded. "I shall go and talk with Angus now," he said. "Later, ye and I shall tarry over some ale and recall the old days when we played gallant to the bonnie lasses, eh? Do ye recall those days, Cameron?"

"Well indeed, milord." Cameron flashed a wrinkled smile at the MacLean, who smiled back fondly.

"Robert favors you, milord," Cameron said. "More and more."

"Indeed, that he does. A shame he is no' my heir."

And off the MacLean went, whistling, his greyhound at his heels.

Chapter 20

R obert spotted the mountain cat, tawny and sleek with hunger, down the fell, and said a quick prayer that Catriona, walking ahead, would not notice. Scared she'd be for certain, with all sorts of false notions that a mountain cat might attack and make a dinner of her. Unlike men, these four-footed beasts much preferred to slink and hide from people. He fervently hoped Catriona would believe that.

Nay, it was the two-footed beasts they had more to fear from. Robert had a feeling a two-footed danger was following them, though he'd not told Catriona yet.

For the past few hours, he'd seen suspicious signs when he'd glanced back from the crest of hills—the glint of sunlight on metal, flocks of birds startled into the air. Worst of all, he thought he saw silhouetted against a hilltop the shape of a horse and rider. Whether it was a random traveler or someone dangerous to them, he had no idea. But ever since, he'd led Catriona along lower ground.

He'd have walked on were it not for the nuisance of the mountain cat and Catriona's exhaustion.

Apparently catching sight of them, the cat bounded off in a taut stretch of muscle, disappearing in a cluster of spindly Caledonian pines. Robert should have breathed easier, but it was the unseen danger still out there that worried him.

Robert took Catriona's arm and pulled her along. If she noticed that he'd hastened the pace, she said nothing.

Until they stopped outside a hut.

Catriona peered inside and wrinkled her nose. "No one's crossed this threshold since before last Hogmanay, I wager."

"Superstitious, lass?" Robert asked, one eye on the landscape for the odd traveler. The altitude here was so high that the climate nourished little—nothing except a bit of bracken and lichen and nettles.

Anxious to get inside, Robert slipped an arm around Catriona's waist. It was a deliberately casual gesture, but it felt just right to him, like the warmth of summer after a bleak winter. Suddenly a squirrel scampered around the side of the little hut.

Catriona pressed close to Robert. "I'm accused of being a witch, so I've a right to take on a few superstitions, don't I?" she said. "And I say this place may not hold good luck."

She attempted to jest, but he knew her light tone was forced. Ever since the night at Annie's, Catriona hadn't trusted any cottage, even an empty one. In fact, she'd been pretending ever since Annie's to be valiant and brave when he knew she was probably terrified every second. Again he thought uneasily of the danger signs he'd seen behind them.

"Lass, 'tis summer and the heather blooms and even God's wee creatures like squirrels bide in this hut . . . I say it offers a night of safe shelter." He turned her in his arms. "And as for luck," he scoffed, "why will ye no' give yer escort some credit? Mayhap 'tis my skill that's kept us safe, lass." He, too, was deliberately striving for a light tone.

"That doesn't signify," she said. "Even the best escort needs a bit of luck now." Sweeping up a dark pebble from the rocky ground, she pressed it into Robert's hand. "To keep luck with us," she told him.

He stared at the pebble, striving for patience with the lass.

"Our luck's running high as the River Strahan in spring," he lied easily. Grabbing her hand, he tugged her inside, and they stood in the dim hut while their eyes became accustomed to the dark. The place was draughty, and the scent of peat pervaded the place. But at least it offered a temporary haven from predators—both four-legged and two-legged.

Ashes from the rock fireplace blew about, and from the corners hung spiders. Catriona batted at them with an old broom she found behind the door. She swatted the wall, and peat crumbled down to the dirt floor. "It's no sturdier than the hunting hut," she said in a small voice.

"But furnished," Robert said bracingly. If you could call furniture the crude pallet atop a bed of pine boughs. Or the spindly chair, little more than pieces of crude wood tied together with rope.

A while later, they sat by a small fire watching nettle broth brew in the rusted kettle they'd found.

" 'Bubble, bubble, toil and trouble,' " Robert said, his voice hoarse and soft. "Now a *real* witch could transform that brew into something more potent. Something intoxicating."

"Mayhap you underestimate my skill at brewing." Catriona dipped their single mug into the kettle and offered Robert the first sip. "The evidence, milord. I await your verdict."

Robert took a swallow. "It's no' whiskey, lass. I'm afraid I have to find you innocent of all charges of witchcraft."

A tentative smile tugged at her mouth. "Grateful I am," she said softly, "even if that does leave you without a dram."

"Then I'll just have to seek other diversions." He fastened his gaze on her while he continued to sip the brew.

That they could even jest about the horror back in Glen Strahan was amazing to him, but if it kept Catriona distracted from their plight, all the better.

"We'll escape safely?" she asked unexpectedly.

He allowed his gaze to linger on the fine way her womanly shape molded to the breeches and shirt. It depended on what she wanted to be safe from, he thought, and at once felt his body stirring at the innocent sight of her. She bent over the fire, and he was beset with all sorts of images and memories.

Her softness pressed against him on the floor of the manse . . . the shy stirrings of her first kiss . . . the way her curls blew about her shoulders like raw silk . . . tempting him to all sorts of roguish impulses. Aye, bewitched and beguiled him, she had.

"Robert . . . ?"

He realized she was standing there, waiting for him to reply.

He looked up at her face, shadowed and uncertain. "Aye, lass," he replied gently, "but wrap yourself in that cloak and dinna tempt the rogue who escorts ye, else ye'll no' be safe inside this hut."

It was impossible to see if she blushed, but he did see how the angry intake of her breath moved her shirt against her breasts, and the sight created a stir within his loins.

"There was a time when you made jest of me for wearing too many clothes," she said smartly.

"Catriona, for God's sake, put on the cloak."

Without arguing further, she reached for it. For a few moments he stared at the fire. He was weary, so weary, and knew he could find forgetfulness from all his troubles in Catriona's arms. But he felt her fragile trust in him—a slender thread bonding them, like the warp and woof of a finely woven plaid. What could he do to keep her distracted from outside predators, to keep himself distracted?

Robert watched her stand up and tie on her cloak. Before it fell down around her legs, he noted how the breeches clung to her—a fetching sight indeed. That lavender cloak might hide her womanly curves, but it did nothing to assuage his desire.

He half-wished he were back in the Crown and Mitre, with no greater worry than which wench to favor with his attentions. Rogues like himself had no business trying to be noble, he tried to tell himself. Yet the curiosity he felt toward her wouldn't go away. It wasn't just a physical pull, but a need to know more about Catriona, the person. His gaze moved up to her face. She was watching him.

"Tell me, lass," he said. "Why is it Angus banished ye to Edinburgh so long ago? Ye've never told me."

Her eyes widened in surprise, and she edged closer to

him. "Because I saw the Regalia being hidden, that's why." She stared down as if pained by her confession, then up again. "But you know I never saw the Regalia," she said. "Your grandfather and mine just assumed I did."

He ached to hold her, to lend comfort, but thought better of it. Comfort could lead too easily down less innocent paths.

"Times were dangerous then," he said. "Men of ruthless ambition held power, greedy men with much to lure them into desperate acts."

"Is the Regalia worth all that?"

He nodded. "They say the crown is alluring indeed. Gold and crimson. As many pearls in it as stars in the sky. The scepter is silver, with a globe of crystal and topped with pearls. And the sword of state—the scabbard, they say—is covered with crimson silk velvet."

"Fit for a king . . . go on, tell me more," she urged. Shadows from the fire played across her skin.

He was silent, one knee drawn up on the chair in a deceptively casual position.

"Aye, fit for a *Scottish* king," he said at last. "Well, lass, long ago when Cromwell was running about, all these regal trappings were hidden, ye ken. In Castle Dunnottar and then smuggled out and hidden in a kirk. Oh, but the English garrisons had a fine time searching for it."

Catriona's gaze did not once leave his face. "And if someone moved it to Castle Fenella MacLean for a while and I saw it being moved, the Jacobites might want to murder me," she said with sudden comprehension. "My grandfather was so angry with me, and at my father and mother." Her voice caught.

She stood close beside him, so close he could feel her pain and her warmth, smell the heather of her hair. He'd just given himself a severe lecture on the dangers of touching her, but before he could resist, he reached over and tucked an errant curl behind her ear. His hand lingered on her face.

"Only Angus can tell you what really happened, lass. But mayhap you were sent away for your own protection, no' out of anger."

"So Angus claims."

"Then 'tis Angus ye must get the whole truth from someday."

Pretending restlessness, he moved away from her. Given the smallness of the hut, there wasn't far to go. In a moment she moved beside him and covered his hands with her own. The touch nearly took him to his knees, and he had to ask her to repeat herself.

"Do you know where the Regalia is now?" she asked, as if he were some neutered university professor instead of a flesh-and-blood rogue with naught but physical needs on his mind.

With supreme willpower he ignored the lure of her touch. The fire crackled, sending sparks into the darkness. "Rumors persist," he managed at last, "that it's been stolen by the English. Others say the chest's been locked away and forgotten. I expect only the spiders and mice know where it bides now."

"You mean you're not going to tell me." She sounded betrayed, and her hand fell away.

"Let's just say that in this regard, I'm the superstitious one."

She thought that over, then said, "Jacques searches for it, you know."

Robert felt his gut clench at the mention of the Frenchman. "I suspected he was up to no good—even before his damning words at the trial."

"Imagine it," she said after a moment. "Jacques. Like a Viking looking for plunder. And I thought he was an artist. Once upon a time, he seemed so charming."

"Charm can hide many motives," Robert observed.

Catriona laughed mirthlessly and poked a stick into their little fire. "Well, I hope he never finds it. In any case, why would he want it?"

"For the same reasons men in the old days wanted it," Robert replied. "Power. Glory. The same things a lot of us seek."

In a way, Jacques and he had one thing in common—using others to obtain a coveted possession. Robert could explain to no one—not even Catriona—how fer vently he dreamed of restoring the MacLean peerage. He ran a weary hand over the stubble on his face and chanced a look at Catriona.

Sitting there in the flickering firelight, her lashes dark against her pale skin, she hugged her cloak about her and resembled a child waiting for a bedtime story.

"Now you tell me some stories," he said, desperate for continued distraction. He sank onto the edge of the crude little bed, hoping she'd keep her distance.

But no. With guileless enthusiasm she came at once and perched beside him, legs drawn up like a lad. "A."

"What?" He looked at her, thinking the broth must have letched him, either that or the swell of her hips in those breeches.

"It's a game my father used to play," she explained. "The first letter of the alphabet. You tell me the first thing that comes to mind. Like A for Aristotle. Except let's think of foods that we miss most. Now you go first."

Totally at ease now, she didn't seem to notice the sound that Robert distinctly heard—some rocks falling outside the cottage. He prayed it was naught but a squirrel or the wind. He pulled his concentration back to her innocent game.

"Go on then," she said.

"Ale," he said, half listening for more suspicious sounds outside. "Your turn," he said easily. "B."

"Bread . . . and berries . . . and barley. Your turn. C."

"C?" He leaned back, the better to appreciate Catriona's animated face and the way her breeches molded to her. "Claret. Remember, I told you at our next stop we'd have the finest? And D is for dram. A long dram." He shut his eyes and swallowed hard. How he needed a dram.

"And G for greedy."

"E is next," he pointed out.

"I know that," she said, "but you took two letters. I wanted to order dandelion wine." She hopped off the pallet, and he was so busy congratulating himself in keeping his hands off her that he didn't fully realize her intention.

"There's a wee clump of dandelions right beside the

door, you know. I'll add it to the nettles, and we'll pretend it's . . . brandy? Would that taste good?"

She opened the door.

"Catriona, wait . . ."

Pausing at his words, she turned, half in and half out of the hut.

The screech of a wild animal echoed down the chimney of the hut, and nearly shook the sod off the ceiling. Like a giant gnashing his teeth, the cat screamed again.

"What is it?" Catriona cried.

For a second he focused on her hands. She was gripping the door so tightly that he could practically see splinters dig into her little hands.

"Dinna move, lass," Robert said, and reached for his pistol.

With Thomas's snores for company, Jacques Beaufort lay on the soggy ground, ruing the day he had befriended the exiled king. It had seemed such an easy way to power and glory. Now, living in these wild Highlands, Jacques had, not regrets exactly, but certainly second thoughts.

Had he remained in France living his luxurious life, he could at this moment be lingering in the bedchamber of a perfumed courtesan, taking his pleasure beneath a gilt and flame chandelier upon a bed of the softest goose feathers.

Instead, his cravat and the lace ruffs of his sleeves were hopelessly limp and soiled. His bones ached from too many nights spent on hard dirt. His sword needed polishing. His boots needed soles. He would not be surprised if he caught the ague before this expedition was concluded.

Finding Catriona Ferguson, however, would prove to be far more profitable and pleasurable than any fever, and despite the drizzle, he cheered at the thought of the price she would bring him. Not mere francs or farthings, but solid gold. A golden crown fit for a king. *Mon Dieu,* who was Jacques to complain over a little rain now and then? If the Jacobites could organize their supporters and reclaim this place, Jacques might sit at the right hand of a king.

With a sudden jab of his elbow, he poked Thomas in

the ribs. His Jacobite guide snorted awake, with a flailing of arms and legs, rusty curls on end.

"Anxious to leave then, eh?" Thomas said on a yawn.

Jacques scowled at the fellow. "How can you sleep like that?" he complained, envious. "A MacLean clansman could slit your throat, and you'd know nothing till the devil ushered you into hell."

"Nay, Jacques. We Jacobites will gather in heaven. But I wouldna fret so. They wouldna slit my throat. I am from the village of Glen Strahan. *Your* throat, now that is another worry, for you are a foreigner." He sliced off a piece of mutton and offered Jacques some on the tip of his knife.

"Breakfast?"

Jacques reached gingerly for the nasty-looking meat. Better this than starving. "We are going in circles," he complained. "Can you not hasten the chase?"

"But, sir, you said you wanted me to follow Lachlan's men. Then, too, your horse lacks the surefootedness of my pony . . ."

"Yes, yes." He'd heard enough about the superiority of Thomas's pony to last him a lifetime.

Thomas stood and stretched. Except for the shift he wore, he was as naked as the birds. Shaking out his plaid, he lay down on it and wrapped it about him in the Highland fashion, fastening the pleats of fabric with a leather belt and lastly sticking in a dirk and pistol.

Disgusted by the barbarity of these Highlanders, Jacques bit off a chunk of meat and moved to ready his horse.

"What is your advice for today, Thomas?" he asked at length.

"As you say, you are paying me only to guide, not to make the decisions, Frenchman."

"But of course. Just be certain you do not lead us into any mountain wildcats."

"If you have faced Lachlan, Frenchman, you can face down any animal the Highlands has to offer."

"A pack of brawling crazy men, the lot of you," Jacques said, mounting his horse.

The men rode off through the mist. *Mon Dieu,* I crave a French pastry, Jacques thought. Both in my stomach and in my bed. He envied Robert traveling with the pretty red-haired wench and wondered if the Scotsman had taken advantage of his good fortune.

"Dinna move, lass," Robert repeated, loading the pistol. The damned mountain cat, that's what it was, hungry and prowling around after squirrels. He could see its eyes, like the glow of twin tapers, gleaming in the dark somewhere behind Catriona.

Robert reached over her shoulder with the barrel of the pistol and used her shoulder to prop it up. He and the mountain cat ought to be able to settle this like reasonable males. Make a pact, he thought, and if the thought was whimsical he didn't care. Whimsy was always preferable to panic.

Aye, he'd offer the cat the mountain. Half the mountain. Prowling rights everywhere except around this hut. In exchange for the ransom of Catriona and a few dozen nettles each day, the cat could still be king of the mountain. A fine arrangement, if Robert said so himself.

The cat growled again, and all Robert's instincts told him that this time he'd waited too long to talk the situation over. Only a brute show of force would get the beast's attention.

The pistol fired somewhere above Catriona's shoulder, and she flinched, then fell against Robert, while the wildcat took off in a bounding leap into the higher reaches of the barren fells.

Robert kicked the door shut. Catriona laid her cheek against his chest, her heart pounding, begging him for comfort.

"I hate your Highland scenery," she cried.

"Lass . . ." The tension no sooner left him from the wildcat encounter than his body hardened again—this time in response to her softness.

"Take me to Edinburgh." She looked up at him, tears in her eyes. "Do you hear me? Take me back to where I came from. I don't want to go to Paris. I want to go home."

"We're almost there, lass," he said hoarsely. "After

this last mountain, the path drops down steeply to the coast.''

"Your word as a Scotsman?''

He nodded.

"I was happy living in Edinburgh, you know.'' She sniffled. "I had nothing more to worry about than where my next meal was coming from. The creditors may have prowled round our door, but at least they kept their claws sheathed. Elspeth and I were getting on just fine. We lived like gentlewomen.''

Robert wasn't so sure he could agree with her. She had been no gentlewoman when she'd threatened him with a brass candlestick. His mouth twitched at the memory, and a wild tension gripped his body.

He managed to remain standing while she clung to him. Later, he could not have said when comfort veered into desire. It might have been when she moved instinctively against him, melded them together even as they stood there fully clothed, he in his plaid, she in her breeches.

"Take me to Edinburgh,'' she said softly. "Please . . .''

He gathered her closer against him. "I canna grant all your wishes and keep you alive too, lass,'' he said hoarsely. "Do ye think I'm a wizard? I've told you before that keeping you alive is a full-time task.'' He dabbed at her tears.

"Then keep on holding me.''

"God did no' create men just to hold lasses in comfort.''

She glanced down to where their bodies were straining to join. "Do you ache for me?'' she asked with surprising guilelessness.

"Lass, ye dinna know the half . . .''

"Robert, don't let go . . .'' To his complete undoing, this innocent lass shyly arched against him and slid her body up and down.

He groaned into her hair. "Lass . . . I canna be noble forever. God did no' intend that.''

"And I'm not about to be brave forever. Just hold me. Need me.''

Oh, but his body was giving new definition to the word

"hold." Gently moving against her in response, he reassured her of his desire. With supreme effort, he pulled back, breathless. With luck, he had one reprieve left in him, one last argument.

"You're going to be safe, lass. The cat's gone. I'll sleep by the fire."

She pressed her face against his chest. "If you leave me alone tonight," she informed him, "I'll tell every last one of your friends at the castle we'll soon reach that you showed me the pictures of Michelangelo's drawings. And Leonardo da Vinci's. And every one of the Greek gods."

"Goddesses too?" he said, unable to resist. He leaned down and brushed her mouth with his. "The Buchanans think I'm a rogue in any case, hinny."

Arching against him, she touched the back of her hand to the contours of his face. "Robert, stay beside me. I don't want to be alone, and you make me ache for you."

He couldn't resist a smile. "Now, lass, ye dinna want the world to know you're saying bonnie words to a rogue like me." He stared at her, unable to move away.

In the distance, the mountain cat screeched, and again Catriona clung to him, so tightly that there was no beginning or end to the pairing.

"Hold me," she whispered, arms locked around his neck, body molded to his, breath warming his skin. "I'm scared."

"You ought to be scared," he said, carrying her over to the pallet and lying down with her. "Scared of me, hinny." The lure he'd been resisting was too great. The need burning his body had consumed his conscience. He began kissing her throat. "You dinna know what ye ask, lass, do ye?"

The question was rhetorical, for already he was tipping her chin up and had found her mouth again. As one hand moved between her thighs, his other began unfastening her waistband.

Catriona knew exactly what she'd been asking for—respite from all their fears, but more . . . the haven of his embrace. And now it was hers. All at once, there was no danger anywhere, only Robert's hands skillfully playing

across her body, his kisses feverishly claiming her throat.
His tongue sought hers and slowly, sweetly, taught her
new pleasures until her entire body felt liquid and warm
and safe, and all the while the lithe contours of his frame
molded against hers.

Reaching for the hem of her skirt, he slipped the garment off her. His hands cupped her breasts, savoring their
silken fullness, and then his lips moved up her throat again
to her mouth, and without breaking the kiss he rolled her
onto her back.

She lay there naked, shimmering in the scant firelight,
watching his gaze move over her in a kind of worship.

"Robert," she said shyly, "I ache so when you touch
me. Do men feel the same way?"

"Oh, God, lass, have a mercy."

He didn't take time to unwind his plaid. Before he could
free himself, shyly she joined his hands and pushed the
fabric out of the way and gazed upon him with wonder.

"Catriona—" He could barely say her name. Gently he
reached between her legs, and if there was any nobility
left in him at all, it showed in the supreme gentleness with
which he slid his hand up her inner thigh.

"Robert!"

"Shh."

"Oh, Robert, it's a sin to feel this."

"Nay, 'twill be heaven, lass, for you as well as me."

"Robert . . . oh!" She arched beneath the gentle rhythm
of his hand. "Oh, no."

"Aye, lass, some pleasures feel like sin, but the good
Lord made it that way."

"Sin—"

"Sweet—"

"Oh, God."

Robert removed his hand and, entering, gently made
them one. Immediately, a wholeness of spirit suffused him,
a spiritual beauty he'd never known before. He took his
time, savoring the feel of her arching beneath him, and
then all his feelings reached a crescendo. "Catriona, my
jo . . . *M'eudail* . . . *m'eudail* . . ."

Thrusting tenderly, he filled her ever more deeply until

he felt her tremble beneath him. And then he filled her more deeply still. She was the tide drawing him to her, fiercely, inexorably. Together they rode the rhythm of the sea, until together they convulsed and shattered, crashing upon the shore . . .

"Heaven, it is. Did I no' explain that, lass?" he whispered into her hair. He held her like that until she slept.

Later, when she awoke and recalled all that had passed between them, Catriona nestled close by Robert. Outside somewhere she knew the mountain cat prowled the gloaming and the Highland mists moved in on them as well, but lost to the pleasures of Robert's touch, Catriona mercifully blocked out everything else. He'd needed her. Oh, aye.

Long into the night, Catriona lay there, divested of all her clothing save the cloak and Robert's plaid. Her thighs were damp from the joining of their bodies, the most private part of her still sweetly throbbing.

Oh, Robert, she thought, Robert, with his rogue's charm and diplomatic words. He knew how to soften the stark blacks and whites of the world to muted shades. He took the night and made it seem like sunrise. A wall between her and the glare of hate, he was, and she loved him for it.

She smiled in the dark. If they'd gotten as far as L, she wouldn't have had to stop and think of a word. Love.

Chapter 21

$\sim\!\!\sim\!\!Q\!Q\!\sim$

For Robert, morning brought acute frustration. He had rid them of the cat only to be confined now by fog and . . . desire. They'd bided here too long in each other's arms. Now the fog was too thick to permit them to travel.

After their meager meal of nettle broth, there was nothing left to do but look at Catriona while she plaited those long red locks. He paced the cottage, stopping every few minutes to stare at the wee lass who'd made him yield to temptation.

She was driving him crazy, and by midday he'd figured out why. He feared he needed her in ways that could be dangerous to his future as a rogue. Aye, that was it. They'd bided here too long with naught to do save lie abed.

Now she sat in that rickety little chair, lost in thoughts of her own. From across the silent cottage, he watched her out of the corner of his eye. Her slender arms and legs poked out of the lavender cloak, which she'd draped over herself for extra warmth.

Robert paced a few more times, then raked his fingers through his hair and over his stubbly beard. He stopped and studied her again, all wide eyes and tumbled red hair. Desire rose in him at the merest sight of her. But he didn't need her. After this journey ended and he'd helped her to exile, he'd be the carefree rogue he'd been when he met her down in Edinburgh.

For the rest of the day, Robert paced while Catriona stoked the fire until it died down. Then Robert would go outside for chunks of peat or more branches from the dead

tree alongside the hut. He would kneel and stoke the fire
back up, while Catriona paced. Then he would stand, a
signal that the fire was going full. Without a word, they
would trade places. She would stoke. He would pace. And
then the cycle repeated itself.

By afternoon, for the hundredth time, Robert cracked
the door and inspected the fog. Curse the Highland
weather. Curse this lass for making him need her so. He
picked up his pistol, loaded it, and poked it out the door.
He pulled the trigger and shot into the fog, as if he could
scare the mist away. The shot echoed off the rocks, but in
his head all he heard reverberating were the same words
over and over. *He didn't need her* . . . And he busied
himself reloading the pistol.

He looked back at her where she sat huddled in the
chair, her eyes shadowed. In a few moments, she dozed
off, and he covered her with the plaid, noting as he did
that she looked enticingly vulnerable. With the back of his
hand, he couldn't resist brushing a wisp of hair from her
cheek, and another, regretting that life could not be al-
tered to suit a man's wants.

He paced some more and tended the fire. When he next
looked at her, she was awake and watching him. She
blushed and slanted a shy look at him, and all the inti-
macies they'd shared came back to him. He'd never felt so
tender toward a woman. It had to be a mistake to let himself feel that way.

"Robert," she began in that soft voice as she stretched,
"why are you pacing so? You'll wear a circle in our wee
floor, and there's nothing we can do about the mist or . . .
anyone who might be following us. I can watch the fog if
you wish to rest a bit—"

Without warning he slammed a hand into the earthen
wall. Peat crumbled down and spilled onto his boots.

"Robert, what's wrong?" She frowned. "I-I'm sorry I
cried so last night about the mountain cat."

In a moment he had closed the distance between them
and was pulling her to her feet and backing her into the
sod wall of the hut.

"Do you think that matters, a woman's tears?"

She shook her head. "No," she whispered. "Not with you."

Her face crumpled, and something twisted in him.

Then he was kissing her, as he would a tavern wench. His mouth was slanting across hers as he boldly allowed his body to mold itself to her soft contours. If she were a common wench, she would saucily reach around and run a teasing finger down his plaid, and after long moments of bawdy pleasure, he might set her aside, deciding she didn't suit his fancy. But the instant his lips touched hers, he knew Catriona did suit his fancy. Too well. And this despite her lack of teasing.

Like the innocent lass she was, she turned pliant in his arms, a response more potent than the practiced movements of all the wenches he'd ever known. His traitorous body told her only too well how much he needed her. With a groan, he slid his hands up under her shirt and cupped his hands about her breasts. She moaned softly as his fingers found and caressed them to tautness.

Despite his intentions to the contrary, he could not take her as casually as he would a wench. His kiss softened; his lips caressed hers. He didn't grasp her so much as cherish her. He'd intended to have her against the wall. Instead he swept her up in his arms and carried her to the bed. There he lingered over her, savoring her innocent responses to his every touch. Finally, when he could bear it no longer, he reached for her breeches, and the saucy minx, to his surprise, reached for his plaid.

"I wager that somewhere in your list of rules it says that rogues never, ever let women beguile them." She spoke the words wistfully.

"Nor do they spend time being noble, gentlemanly, or mouthing sweet words."

And then they were naked. He slid into her, meaning to take his pleasure quickly, but again he lingered. Why was it that every time he touched her, it never ended as he intended? Beguiled? she had asked. He'd never been beguiled in his life and wasn't about to let some tart-tongued minx do so now. But he had to admit he enjoyed being with her, inside her, prolonging the oneness for as long as possible.

Aye, he could linger long over her, and did. Especially when she wrapped her legs and arms around him and drew him ever deeper into her, hardly moving, savoring each nuance of feeling, each slowly budding pleasure . . . until she pressed more urgently against him and he responded, thrusting, thrusting. Her ragged breath came fast and hard against his neck. She moaned. When finally she cried out his name, his own release came quickly, fiercely.

Long afterward, separated from her, he still felt restless . . . confined . . . and guilty. He'd used her shamelessly . . .

He rose from their bed and paced outside to listen for clansmen.

He paced inside and stared at Catriona, telling himself that tonight he would not touch her. Not ever again.

But when the day crawled on to its end, and darkness fell, all his resolution crumpled and he took her into his arms. Alone in the night he could admit to his need. Not by day, not to her face, but in the night he was lost to her . . .

For two days and two nights they lived in that cottage, held captive first by a wandering mountain cat and then by a low fog, but most of all by desire.

By the third morning, he'd told Catriona every tale he knew and some he'd invented.

He'd stoked at least two dozen fires.

He'd discharged his pistol blindly into the mist.

He'd nearly shoved his hand through the peat wall.

He'd repeatedly made love to her.

Nothing worked.

He still wanted her. He still needed her constantly.

All that was left to do was pace and let his beard grow . . . or rejoin her on the bed.

Now he was losing patience with everything, including the unfamiliar ache in his chest whenever he practiced words of goodbye to Catriona. God seemed determined to thwart his career as a rogue.

"What are you thinking about?" she whispered from where she lay on the bed.

"What do you think?"

She looked at him and sighed. "The mountain cat has gone on to find someone meatier than me, hasn't he?" At least she fervently hoped so. For half a day now they'd heard nary a growl from him. Only the fog kept them here, both a blessing and a curse.

A blessing because of the time they'd shared in each other's arms.

A curse should Lachlan's men happen on this hut.

Life had never seemed more precious to her, or more to be savored.

He turned to the fire, and Catriona lay there remembering his sweet words of the night before. "I canna slake my thirst of ye, bonnie lass. I need ye."

But all day he had moodily paced, making her afraid of what he was thinking . . .

Outside, the cat suddenly screamed from a distance.

Catriona started and sat up "He's probably just hungry," she said valiantly. "Like us." Rolling over, she looked at Robert. "Where are you going?" she asked anxiously as he stepped toward the door. It wasn't that she needed him to continue kissing her every night. It was that she needed him to stay alive. And he gave every appearance of a man going to do battle.

"I'm going outside to shoo away our feline friend. I dinna want him around here when the mists lift."

"But—" She was terrified of being left alone. Scooting off the bed, she stopped him the only way she could think of—by picking up his pistol and holding it away from him.

His face fierce, he rounded on her and with a shaky hand tried to yank the weapon from her. "We've bided here too long."

"I understand. You're a rogue, and you're wearying of me, is that it?" she asked shakily.

"I'm a rogue who does no' care to be found in the arms of a lass if Lachlan's men come upon us." That was as close as he'd come to telling her the truth . . . or to sharing his worry about the unidentified follower.

With a boldness that surprised him, she clung to his arm, trying to hold him inside. "Don't go out, Robert."

"Well, lass, when it comes to mountain wildcats, I dinna need yer help."

"But I need you . . ."

"I dinna need *you,*" he said. "Do you understand?" Grabbing his dirk, he stalked out into the mist and slammed the door behind him.

Catriona stared at the door. Despite the sweet things Robert did to her body, he didn't need her for anything else. He'd made that clear enough. But she needed him: his strength, his courage, his brave words, even his angry words.

I dinna need you.

It seemed she'd have to learn to live without him.

When, after a reasonable interval, he didn't return, she knew he must have been lying. Perhaps, after all, mountain cats did, indeed, eat people. She heard the crunch of rocks outside the hut, and her pulse beat faster. Anxiously, she eyed the pistol that lay on their little bed.

Pray God she didn't have to use it.

And then she heard his footsteps approaching the door. She leaped up off the chair and pulled open the door.

"Robert, I thought—"

The rest of the words froze unspoken.

A sorry-looking wild man of a MacLean stood staring at her, a lascivious grin on his face. Though his ears had not been lopped off like those of the fellow they'd encountered way back at the hunting hut, this one had a long crooked nose and a scar down one cheek.

"Lass, will ye invite me in to bide awhile?"

"Where's Robert?"

"Ye'll no' need Robert anymore."

Out of the corner of her eye, she saw Robert then . . . lying unmoving on the ground.

No! Pure, raw rage coursed through her. Without thinking, she had the pistol in her hand and before the ugly, filthy man could blink, she pointed it and squeezed the trigger.

Her eyes were shut, and so she had no idea if her aim

had been worth anything until he fell heavily at her feet. She didn't let go of the pistol. Her fingers were melded to it. Slightly sick, she pressed her face to the dank wall and let the tremors shake her.

Robert! She wanted to scream the name, but dared not. She had no idea if this man was alone or if fifty more waited to grab her. Dropping the useless pistol, she stared out at the mist.

Flattening herself against the hut, she made her way around the dead man.

"Robert," she whispered. Oh, how she wanted him to come walking out of that mist and take her in his arms. But it wasn't to be.

He was lying on his back, looking as dead as the man she had just shot. She ran to him and dropped to her knees. *Please wake up, Robert. Please . . .*

He moaned but didn't stir, and she pressed her face to his chest.

"Oh, Robert, don't you know there's nothing about you I don't need, no matter your fancy speech . . . and . . . and you need me whether you're admitting it or no'," she finished.

He mumbled then, his golden hair tousled like a lad's. "Catriona . . . lass . . . mine, my jo. My jo. Catriona . . . bonnie *bhoidheach* . . ."

Her heart turned over at the sweetness of his words, the same words he'd used when his body filled hers. But fie on pretty words. She wanted Robert awake and alive, taunting her unmercifully. Robert, the rogue with the Highland charm.

Long minutes later, when he'd still not opened his eyes or moved, she folded her hands around his and began to pray out loud.

"Dear God, if Robert survives, I'll never lose my temper again, not once, so help me . . ."

The third time through the words, God answered. At least it seemed so, it had been so long since she'd heard the reassurance of a deep voice. But of course it was Robert who spoke her name. She looked up. He was regarding her intently through half-opened eyes.

"How many promises have you made to God?" he said in a clear voice. "You're going to be too busy remembering them all to ever have a thought for me."

"You're awake."

"Aye."

Tears welled. "I thought that—that awful man . . . Oh, Robert, I killed him . . ." Her voice broke.

He levered himself up and, pulling her to him, held her.

"I thought he—he hurt you . . . or killed you." She turned her face into his chest where his heart beat strong.

Stroking her hair, he said softly, "He gave me a good blow when I wasn't looking. I was about to get up when I saw you point the pistol. Not certain of your aim, lass, I lay low."

As the meaning of his words registered, she pulled back. "You mean, you heard—you listened in on my prayers just now?"

"Every word," he confessed. "A rogue's an unprincipled lout, lass."

Still he held her to him tightly, and she clung back. He was alive and holding her, and while they were stranded here, he was hers.

"You're a stubborn man, do you know that?" she said shakily.

"Makes for the best survivor, hinny," he said in a shaky voice. "Now shall we hide the body and go? The fog's lifting, and more MacLeans will be coming, I wager."

Within the hour, as if God had waved a wand, the fog finally lifted, and they could see for miles into the distance. Far across the mountains, Robert detected men on horseback.

Catriona was already lacing on her cuarans for the long walk ahead and without a word handed him a walking stick she'd broken from a fallen tree. "You might need this," she said.

"I might," he said, and their eyes met, other messages left unsaid. Their time together was over. They must continue on.

* * *

Scowling with undisguised envy at Thomas's surefooted pony, Jacques cursed his own slower horse. "If only you'd told me about this terrain, Thomas, I'd have made myself look the fool and taken one of those ponies."

"We've lost time," Thomas acknowledged, "but you did want to stay behind Lachlan's men."

"They are still going in circles. We're on a wild goose chase. Even I, ignorant of Scotland's geography, can mark the sun's position and tell that. Besides, look at them ahead of us on a clear day like this, riding in the open across the hills where anyone could spot them. Robert will elude them forever."

"You are considering setting off on our own?"

"Do you know where Robert will take the wench?"

"No. It would be a gamble to leave Lachlan's men and strike out on our own, but I know where he has friends."

"What about Edinburgh?"

"Alone, she would head there, but Robert is wilier than that. He will keep her better hidden. This castle I'm thinking he'll go to is in a remote location. I'm only trying to outwit Robert, mind—"

"Outwitting Robert is what I have every intention of doing. What are our odds, do you wager, that this castle is where he takes her?"

"Fifty-fifty."

"Take me to this castle, Thomas. I've always been lucky at gambling. *Mais oui,* we'll outwit him yet."

Through most of the day, Robert and Catriona trekked across the Highlands. In and out of glens and burns. Up and down the fells. Over a stretch of wide flat heath covered with purple heather. It was a restful place, but they stopped only for the briefest time at a loch of cold water. With his dirk, Robert whittled Catriona a walking stick from a broken birch bow, and she valiantly matched his steps.

"How much longer?" she asked periodically.

"Are you anxious to be rid of your arrogant Highland guide?" he teased.

"You're walking as if the devil were at our heels, Robert."

For a long minute his blue gaze lingered on her.

The devil *was* at his heels, he thought dourly. Sensual devils plagued him, and Catriona was bewitching him. Their brief idyll in the hut burned itself in his memory: Catriona's red curls close to him in sleep, her soft voice crooning to him. Despite his better intentions, words of endearment had slipped from his mouth in the throes of passion.

Again they stopped to rest and he broached the subject. Rather abruptly, not at all the way he would approach a delicate diplomatic matter.

"I gave in to temptation when we lay together in that hut. It won't happen again."

Catriona froze into immobility, growing numb with pain. She forced lightness into her soft voice. "I didn't mind. I became very tired of waiting for the fog to lift, and you were a most warm place to rest my head."

He paced back and forth in front of her. "Catriona," he explained, anxious to do away with any misconceptions, "ashamed I am to admit it, but I've a roving eye for a lissome lass. If I was slaking my desire, I said bonnie words to you—"

Quick tears glittered in her eyes, and she bent her head and plucked a little stem off a gorse bush.

"Dinna fret so, Robert MacLean," she said. "You behaved as the perfect rogue. You ceased calling me 'hinny.' Most of what you said was in the Erse tongue, therefore I could understand but little."

Robert flinched. Of course. Some of his most wooing endearments were in Erse. "Do you recall any of the words?" he asked carefully. Perhaps he'd pleasured her so much that she'd paid no attention to his words.

She looked up. " 'My jo.' I cannot pronounce the others. You do not talk so clearly in your sleep, I fear."

In his sleep! If it came to muttering endearments in his sleep, she'd no doubt heard them all. Catriona, my jo. My dear. And no doubt *boidheach* and *m'eudail* as well. Pretty and winsome and darling . . . Hell. What were the odds that she was even more learned than she claimed and had studied more than a bit of Erse?

"What else do you remember me saying to you?" He leaned against a rock, feeling as if the wind had been knocked out of him.

Smiling, she shook her head. "That you didn't need me. You distinctly told me you didn't need me at all. In English. That was shortly before I fired the pistol at that ugly clansman sent by Lachlan." Her chin was thrust out defiantly.

As if he needed reminding. He stood up and reached for his walking stick.

"You needn't worry so, Robert," she said. "We shared a bed for a couple of nights, bided close for warmth, drank the same nettle broth, and together fought down a mountain cat and a burly MacLean, who as you said when you piled rocks over him should have met his just reward years ago." She got up and tied on her cloak. "And on top of all else, you can rest assured I won't carry your bairn."

If any of the women he'd laid with had conceived a bairn, he'd never known it. But it worried him no end that Catriona might go off to exile with his seed in her belly. "How do you know?" he asked.

"I'm barren. I'm certain of it."

At first he was nonplussed, then a smile tugged at his mouth. She was such a mixture of naivete and forthrightness. "Barren," he scoffed. "You're too young to ken such a thing. Too . . . untried."

She shot him a bemused look. After their days together in the hut, "untried" was not exactly the word for her.

"Nevertheless, I'm barren," she lied, "so now you can take me to your caves and leave me with a clear conscience to pursue your fabled title," she snapped. "And I hope you live happily ever after with it."

He frowned. Actually, he didn't know what he wanted. But he didn't believe for a minute the nonsense about her being barren. It was a tale meant to slake his conscience and nothing more.

"Is that what you want, lass?"

"Yes," she lied again, and picking up her stick, walked

on. At least it was what he wanted to hear, and she could no longer continue this painful conversation. She set off ahead of him, forcing him to follow.

For a long while they walked in silence. She was the first to see movement in the trees ahead.

Reaching for Robert's hand, she wrapped her fingers in his larger grasp and looked up at him, worried.

Robert pulled Catriona down behind a large boulder and peered around the edge of the rock as a pony came into view. A pony!

She started up, but he dragged her back, close between his legs, and wrapped his arms about her so tightly that she couldn't move. "Bide a bit," he whispered against her ear.

She was pressed against his shoulder. "We need that pony," she said softly. "Robert . . . listen. When I was little Angus showed me a way to steal a pony, and the owner would be none the wiser . . ."

He set her away from him, a look of disbelief on his face.

"Well, it's done all the time," she insisted. "We sneak up and cut the harness. One of us takes the rein—I wager it's just made of hair—and then . . ."

"Have you forgotten the lesson of Annie?" he asked. "Worse, this pony probably belongs to one of Lachlan's men." His hand went to the hilt of his dirk.

No, she thought. Surely after all they'd been through, they wouldn't be captured so close to the end.

Huddled there between Robert's legs, she pressed close to him, feeling his heart beat through his shirt.

"And who's talking of stealing my pony?" a masculine voice boomed from behind them.

Robert was on his feet so fast that Catriona was hard put to scramble to her own feet. She glanced around the copsehalf expecting the entire clan to surround them with pike-staffs and broadswords drawn. She stood, tense, wait-ing, knowing this was the end of everything.

"Robert." The stranger smiled and, to Catriona's surprise, extended his hand in greeting. His voice held a note of familiarity.

It was strange, Catriona thought, how they stood on social amenities. She'd have expected to have her hands bound by now. The stranger was, after all, garbed in the red tartan trews of Lachlan's own men.

"Fraser Robertson," Robert said, his voice glum. "I'm sorely sad it's you who's found us."

"Come, mon, ye dinna think I'm going to take you back to that dungeon, after all you went through to get the bonnie lass out?"

"Fraser!" Suddenly Catriona recognized this man. "You're the sentry who helped Robert sneak into the dungeon to see me." Here was a friend indeed.

Catriona moved close to Robert, so close she could clutch a hand to his arm, and for the first time, Fraser cast an appraising glance at her, then looked back at Robert. He held out a package.

"Looking peaked you are, Robert. Ye need this lassie to put a wee bit of color in yer cheeks."

Robert pointed his dirk at Fraser, who sighed.

"Now, now," Fraser said, "I dinna blame you for holding that dirk to me, despite the fact we've known each other since boyhood. But running and archery and hunting together years ago carries little weight set against the lass's life."

Robert glowered. "Are there others with you?"

Fraser shook his head and shoved a hand in the belt of his lean waist. "Naught but my dependable pony. Take it as a gift. To help you move faster. And take this food." He thrust the package into Robert's hands. "A gift from Mrs. Drummond in Glen Strahan, who wishes you well."

Robert looked wary, and Catriona could guess why. Despite Fraser's earlier help, more than one kinsman had betrayed them lately at Lachlan's bidding. Even though Fraser did not act like a man about to move in and capture them, Robert was beyond trusting anyone. And Catriona trusted only Robert.

"There's an old adage that says to beware Highland clansmen bearing gifts from Lachlan."

"Ah. As for Lachlan, when he sent us out on the hunt for the lass, I took the opportunity to leave for good. I'm heading for Fort William on the coast and then the Canadian territories. Had enough of Lachlan's way, I have. And you? Where are you going, Robert?''

''Away.''

''To be sure . . . Away from the madness, eh?'' Sighing, Fraser pulled out a pipe and played with it in his hands. ''See here, Robert, I'm no' keen on having that dirk slip from yer hand. If you want to put it to use, then saw off a bit of tobacco for me.'' He held out a bag. ''After that, I'm for making a fire and biding awhile to smoke my cuttie—''

''And let the others move in on us? We'll go hungry,'' Robert declared.

''Suit yourself.''

''Take the food, Robert,'' Catriona whispered, her mouth watering. She'd lost count of the days, but it must have been close to a week since their last decent meal.

Robert's face was dark and hard. ''Why do you want to give up an animal in the middle of the Highlands and go about yourself on foot?''

Fraser smiled. ''My own Highland hospitality. Now, I'd be much obliged if the bewitching lass would trade me her walking stick for my pony. Her name's Brownie. Here then.'' He led the animal back by the reins. ''The others are headed south, and that's my solemn word. They'll no' find you, that I ken.'' Fraser cast an appraising eye on Catriona and back to Robert.

''Go on, lass, this stubborn Highlander ye're with is no' going to believe me. You take the pony wherever ye must, and with my good wishes.''

''You'll be on foot then,'' Catriona said.

''Aye, but 'tis no' so far to the coast, and I'm no' in the hurry you must be. Besides, I canna take my pony to the New World. Go on with ye, now.''

''You're certain?'' she said, glancing at Robert for his approval. She dearly wanted the pony.

''Aye, I'm certain.''

Like some Highland sorcerer, Fraser walked away and disappeared into the light mist. His footsteps whispered on the forest floor, a twig snapped, and then he was lost in the gorse and the woods were silent. Catriona stood spellbound.

"I believe, Robert, that he means it."

"We'll know soon enough," he said, looking around, his posture tense, as if waiting for other clansmen to appear.

None showed himself.

Catriona moved up to stroke the pony. "Blessed beast. God's best invention," she said. After a man's gentle kiss, that is, she thought. Brownie nickered, and Catriona laid her face into her mane while Robert moved up to take over the reins.

"And we don't have to go to all the work of stealing the pony . . . Oh, Robert, she's beautiful. Just like one I had many years ago."

For the first time she began to believe that they might elude Lachlan and escape the Highlands.

Chapter 22

Dunsmuir Castle was like a dream come true. Perched on a cliff high up above the sea and possessed of fanciful turrets and towers, it resembled a fairy-tale picture. It had been the residence of the Laird Buchanan for many generations and bore the distinction of being the castle in Scotland that had seen the fewest battles. Though harsh winds from the sea discouraged vegetation, inside the sheltered courtyard, gardens and fruit trees flourished in abundance.

Buchanans of all ages lived here, all on good terms. Robert had become acquainted with one of the Buchanan sons at university and visited here often. From the sheep's eyes that all the Buchanan daughters made at Robert when they rode into the castle ward, Catriona guessed that more than one of them hoped to marry him.

They certainly wasted no time in whisking *her* away to a private chamber so that they could have Robert to themselves. Catriona could hear them now, their voices floating up through her open window, giggling and simpering and saying Robert's name. Well, let them. Catriona would enjoy watching her Highland rogue worm his way free of the attentions of so many women. She gave her own attention to her toilette.

There were many luxuries in her chamber in which to indulge. A lavender-scented bath. A glass of mead. A dish of comfits. Indeed, she was licking the sweet residue of one more comfit off her fingers a while later when Robert came to escort her to the dining room.

"I'm not ready," she apologized.

His eyes flicked over her, taking in her half-dressed state. She wore the blue gown that her hostess, Lady Buchanan, had loaned her, but the bodice needed fastening, and there was a tartan sash still to arrange over her shoulder. And perhaps a ribbon or two was needed to secure the errant curls that kept slipping out of her plaited hair.

Robert stepped into the room and shut the door. He kissed the corner of her mouth, right where a last residue of sugar clung temptingly. Blushing, Catriona pushed him away and reached up to fasten her hair.

"You taste good," he said. "Comfits?"

"Mmm-mmm."

"Lavender scent?"

"Yes. What else do you notice?"

"You look different in a gown, lass. You know, you remind me of another lass I met recently. She was much scrawnier and meaner tempered than you, of course, but she filled out a pair of breeches in a bonnie way."

Catriona wrapped a ribbon about her plaited hair. "Do you think I'd know such an immodest female?"

"Doubtful, lass. This one hangs about up in the Highlands with roguish sorts. In bandit huts and castle ruins and wet caves. Can work a pistol on a surly henchman, and they say the mountain cats fear her. Ye dinna know her, surely."

"She sounds like a perfect wench. The sort rogues consort with."

Robert paused, then reached around to pull the laces on Catriona's bodice. "Oh, she can be," he said in a husky voice.

While he worked the lacings on her bodice, she leaned into the solid wall of his chest. When he finished, they stood there, her head against him, his hands wrapped around her.

"I won't need to know how to curtsy, will I?"

"Lass, these are the Buchanans, not the king."

"I know, but it seems so odd to be decked out in fripperies after the way we've lived—" Abruptly, she cut herself off, trying to push away the pain of the thought that her time alone with Robert was nearly at an end. Exile would follow, she had to keep reminding herself. And Robert would be going to London.

He chuckled softly against her ear. "Have the Highland laddies no' been teaching you the finer points of social behavior then?" he asked, his hands lingering beneath her breasts. She watched them move in and out with her breathing. Her Highland escort had taught her the finer points of kissing, of how a man's body and a woman's body came together, but now was not the time to remind him. Hastily, she turned out of his embrace.

"I have no' had lessons in how to curtsy, milord, not since my mother taught me," Catriona said, and strolled to the window.

Following her, Robert brought the plaid sash and swung it over her left shoulder, then with a dexterity that spoke of practice he fastened the brooch at her shoulder, his lean fingers both warm and nimble. Catriona couldn't help re-calling the night he'd dressed her in breeches, and she wondered with a pang of jealousy how many women he'd undressed and . . . well, the thought hurt too much to contemplate. It was enough to feel his hands warm against her skin where he pushed the brooch through the sash.

He stood back to view the result. "Much more appeal-ing than when ye were burdened with five dresses, lass."

Looking at him, standing there in his freshly brushed plaid, she swallowed hard, making no secret of her ad-miration. "You look most fine, Robert Duncan Mac-Lean."

Robert was indeed a braw Highlander. Sandals laced up his legs, and his plaid belted at his waist, fell in loose folds about his torso. His dark gold hair glimmered in the candlelight, his jaw was as smooth-shaven now as a hard-ened crag, and his eyes shone as blue as the lochs on a sparkling day. He looked raw and tensile and masculine, and she blushed to think of the nights she'd spent in his arms, when he had been her only protection. She was suddenly desperately afraid of losing him.

"Lachlan's men cannot get in here, can they?" she asked.

He shook his head. "Malcolm Buchanan is my friend. I've explained the situation, and if any of Lachlan's clansmen come prowling about asking after me, they'll be thrown out like a pack of skulking dogs. It's almost over, Catriona. Trust me."

It's almost over. Oh, Robert.

There was tenderness in his eyes, and, hugging her to him, he whispered close to her ear, "You're safe, lass."

As if the urgent force of a magnet pulled them together, she melted against him, and for a moment his arms tightened around her. "Nothing can happen here." His words were reassuring, but not the rising desire she felt tugging at them. She knew that in one way she wasn't safe. Not from Robert, she wasn't safe, and indeed a lot could happen here—if Robert went on holding her.

With a fierce look, he pulled away first. "We're dallying," he said brusquely, "and the Buchanans expect us in the great hall for supper. Tomorrow we must make an early start. 'Tis a hard trek the last few miles, and I'm trusting ye'll no' take it in your bonnie head to run away at the last moment." Holding out his hand, his expression a bit more taut, he gripped her fingers.

She shook her head. Run away? To where? The Buchanans' great hall? To whom? The Buchanan laird? That was as far as she could think.

Moments later, the entire Buchanan family swept them in to supper, and in the confusion Robert and Catriona became separated. At the far end of the long table, surrounded by fine china and crystal and many Buchanan kin, Catriona felt both lost and overwhelmed. She'd lived such a simple life the last days and had had Robert near for every need.

Across from her a freckled-faced Buchanan male close to her own age sat staring at her as if besotted. Catriona almost looked over her shoulder, wondering about the lass who had so entranced the lad, then realized it was she and introduced herself. Blushing, the boy stabbed at his turnips, missed, and wounded the table. Catriona giggled. She was enchanted by his attack of shyness and asked him about himself. John Buchanan, it turned out, had just come down from university in England. Fascinated, Catriona peppered him with questions about the difference between an English university and a Scottish university.

Glancing down at the other end, Catriona noted that Robert seemed to have not a moment to reminisce, surrounded as he was by lovely dark-haired Buchanan females, none of whom made a secret of her appreciation of his manly attributes. The lasses at this castle, from the lowest maids to the finest ladies, were fawning about him, captivated by his rugged charm. Such an exciting, elegant life, in even greater abundance, awaited him in England once he rid himself of her.

By this time next week, he could be in London, at the very least in Edinburgh, taking up his duties as assistant to the secretary of state for Scotland, Lord Kendrick. Their host, Laird Buchanan, had been quick with the news that Lord Kendrick had snared his coveted appointment. Now the Englishman would certainly need Robert as liaison to the Highlands.

Everything Robert yearned for was going to come true, while Catriona went off in disgrace. Suddenly she didn't think she could swallow a bite. After all these days of near starvation, of living on nettle broth, now the abundant food held no appeal. Not the bread. Not the grouse. Not the venison. Not any of the sweets or wine.

Not even the bashful attentions of John Buchanan. Even so, to distract her melancholy thoughts, she forced herself to ask him about his favorite studies.

"Philosophy. St. Augustine. No question about it."

" 'Hope is a waking dream,' " Catriona supplied somewhat absently.

"Quite. You like him too, then?"

"Very much."

Suddenly she was acutely aware of her wild red hair, her too pale skin, her unattractiveness compared to the lovelier Buchanan ladies. This time next week, where would she be? Languishing on a ship bound for France. Lurching along in a coach bound for Paris. Lonely. Condemned. Unloved.

Somewhere nearby a pipe began to play, sad at first and

then fast-paced, and they moved away from the table. The pipers' tune turned more lively, and the guests danced the reels and jigs. Catriona danced with her host and felt the color bloom in her cheeks, her spirits rise somewhat.

Out of the corner of her eye she looked for Robert. He was not dancing but standing and talking to flirtatious Buchanan women.

Someone spoke, and Catriona turned. It was freckle-faced John. He complimented her on her hair and gown.

"You flatter me," she said, trying to deflect his praise.

"I f-found it difficult to eat from the effect of your beauty," he stammered sweetly.

"Indeed, the turnips were quite good, though," she said, and they laughed briefly. "Though, actually, I should prefer the punch, I think."

John nearly tripped over himself in his haste to fetch Catriona some punch and, handing her a goblet, stammered again how lovely she was, how the blue of her gown reminded him of bluebells.

"Please, miss, but I would be the happiest man alive if I could have the honor of partnering you for this dance."

Catriona smiled and set down her punch, then gave John her arm. He ducked his head as if he found a spot on his jerkin most fascinating.

"I should be delighted to dance with you, John," she said, charmed by the young man's obvious infatuation, appreciative of how he took her mind off her own woes. Truth be told, she found the attention flattering, for she had never had a season in Edinburgh and so had never known the attentions of any young men except the ones who had teased her at university.

John, as it turned out, was a remarkably lithe dancer, who blushed to hear her compliment him.

"It would be the greatest pleasure to partner you again on the dance floor, Miss Ferguson," he stammered. Catriona was further charmed. She'd never had this effect on any man before.

Unexpectedly, Robert was at her elbow, scowling darkly.

"Pardon me, but the lady has promised me at least one dance," he said, glowering at poor John, who retreated like a cowed pup in the face of Robert's forbidding presence.

"He's too young," Robert said, leading Catriona to the bottom of the set. "Why, he couldn't set a snare for an ant, let alone keep you alive on the run."

"He's from England."

"He's too foreign then."

"From university."

"Too bookish then. I wager he doesn't know how to start a fire."

"He only wanted to dance."

"He never took his eyes off you all through dinner."

Catriona stared at Robert, dumbfounded. Why, she hadn't even been aware of him watching her . . . and now he sounded jealous. Of a younger man. A shy one at that. As the music began, her color rose higher. Dancing with John had been a pleasure, but dancing with Robert quickly became agony. They briefly touched hands and then moved away in the steps of the dance. A brief touch again. And again. When he moved in close, she felt as exhilarated as if she was racing her Highland pony across the heath, her red hair flying out behind her. When he moved away, she was lost. She wanted to scream from frustration.

"Take me away, Robert," she pleaded. In truth she was weary, and he seemed of a like mind. He escorted her with unaccustomed haste to their host to say their farewells.

John Buchanan looked crestfallen, and Catriona said a special good-night to him, while Robert stood waiting, looking fierce and forbidding. Her heart caught in her throat, she loved him that dearly. But there'd be no telling him that. Mayhap he wouldn't discover it till it was too late, and the time for them, like memories, was fading in the mist.

Well, she for one was tired of might-have-beens. All her life she'd wondered about what might have been had she never been sent away from her Highland home. If she'd hugged Angus one more time long ago, would that have prevented . . . No, the time for those regrets was gone.

But there was still time to do something about Robert. She was filled with a new determination.

Robert Duncan MacLean would not cast her off as easily as her grandfather had, or if he did, he'd remember her all his life.

She wasn't sure what she would do, but she'd let feminine instinct guide her now.

As they made their way up the winding castle staircase to the upper floor, neither of them spoke. Longing was there, tugging between them, weaving its spell about her, as if the fairies were spinning a web. She didn't think she could say good-night without crying, and she'd done enough of that on this journey.

They arrived at the door to her chamber. She deliberately fumbled with the latch, forcing him to open it. A mere thank-you would have sufficed, but Catriona wanted something more ample in the way of last words.

"You were saying something about the Highland laddies teaching me how to curtsy?" she said softly. "I should like you to show me, in case we ever meet in a diplomatic reception. With me going into exile," she said brightly, "you never know where I might end up. Wouldn't that be too ironic if we should cross paths in the same country someday? Of course, I would be the witch lady in exile and you the diplomat who—"

"Stop." Robert's expression was strangely taut, his body tense, as if poised for a skirmish.

"Perhaps," she said helpfully, "you are hoping we shall never meet again? If so, you've only to say the word, and I'll forget you ever said you'd come and see me in Paris. If I see you, I shall pretend not to know you. And should I curtsy dreadfully, you can say I look like someone you used to know, but claim no knowledge of me." She didn't think she could keep her smile much longer.

The scent of dried heather hung in the room, heavy like her heart. Please do something, Robert, she silently begged. Please either leave me this instant or kiss me.

"Did you enjoy meeting the Buchanan ladies?" she asked.

" 'Tis no' the Buchanan ladies who tempt me, lass."

"Then what does?" Catriona asked, turning those vulnerable gray eyes up at him.

Robert realized he was sorely short of patience for idle chitchat. Grabbing her elbow, he steered her inside the chamber and slammed the door behind him. Silently, he followed Catriona as she glided across the room to the candle and lit it with the tinder.

As he watched the play of candlelight on the flame of her curls, the tension in his loins increased. Her hair, tangled from the jigs and reels she'd danced, glowed like wine in a crystal goblet. He knew he should leave and leave now, but, God help him, he wanted her more than she knew. He'd actually allowed it to annoy him when that puppy of a Buchanan lad had tried to turn her head.

She toyed nervously with a silver-handled brush.

"In case there's no time or privacy tomorrow, I should now like to thank you for helping me," she said. For some reason, her words sounded wooden, not at all like those of the Catriona he'd grown used to. Suddenly the brush slipped from her hands and clattered to the floor.

Robert retrieved it and turned it over in his hands, watching how it glinted in the candlelight. After he handed it to her, he watched her unplait her long hair into a mane of curls. She pulled the hair over her left shoulder and began to brush. At the bottom of the curling sweep of hair, his hand covered hers and, taking the brush, he continued the task, brushing until without thinking he lifted her hair and kissed the back of her neck. Her skin felt like silken honey beneath his lips.

She turned and touched his face sadly. "It's our last night together, Robert."

"Do ye think I needed reminding, hinny? I thought you didn't care, judging by the way you allowed young Buchanan to flatter you."

"Are you jealous of a shy young man like him?"

The silence hung between them, charged with feeling.

He pulled her into his arms and kissed her . . . just to show her how foolish he found her question. She pressed against him and kissed him back, and time hung suspended while he tasted her lips again, long and deep to make up for all the nights he would not have her. Her hand lay flat against his chest, and slowly she slid it up his jacket until her fingers curved around his neck.

In the past, Robert had always been the one who decided when he wanted a lass. Now for the first time, he felt a vulnerability, a loss of control. He blamed it on the intimacy they'd shared. The release from danger. His petty jealousy. All combined in a heady explosion of desire.

He intended to break off the kiss and leave her there to sleep. But she tasted sweet. Of wine. Of heather. He became intoxicated by the taste of her lips, which provided a far headier dram than anything he'd sipped downstairs. Head swimming, he only knew he wanted her.

"Catriona, lass," he murmured thickly, "send me away now before it's too late, before I canna leave." He broke away, trying to hold back because of her inexperience, but he had waited too long to retreat.

And when she pulled him more closely to her, he found himself kissing her hair, her eyes, her throat, tantalizing her, feeling her turn to liquid gold in his arms.

He unlaced the ties of her bodice and slipped it off her, doing likewise with her skirt, letting the fabric fall into a blue puddle at her feet. Burying his face against the cool skin between her breasts, he let his lips glide across the silk of each perfect breast until the rosy tips stood vibrant in his palms, and he could feel the aching pleasure he'd brought to her in the way she clung to him. Only then did his touch move down her body, taunting her, chasing her desire now here and now there, not stopping until he reached the most vulnerable core of her. Through his plaid, he felt his desire straining for release.

Standing before him, Catriona kissed him on the lips and spun a web of fairy kisses down his neck. She reached for the brooch on his plaid and, to his surprise and pleasure, divested him of his Highland garb slowly, one piece at a time, as if intent on prolonging this wild agony. He did away with his belt himself, and then Catriona slowly unwound the plaid until it too fell to the floor, and she gazed at his fully aroused body in the candlelight.

Aching to possess her, he swung her up in his arms and

kissed her. He was still kissing her when he gently laid her upon the tester bed. They melted down into the softness of a velvet counterpane and, parting her thighs, Robert came into her at once. Swift and fierce his thrust was, as if he had waited too long and would not be denied a second longer.

He filled her soul as well as her body, Robert did, and this kind of oneness Catriona had never thought to know. Instinctively she moved beneath him, arching up to meet him.

"Lass, dinna do that." His ragged command held a rare tenderness.

"I can't help it. Robert, I can't. It's a bonnie pleasure."

His mouth covered hers, his words against her lips warm and soft. "Ye had best lie still, lass, else I'll take my pleasure before ye've known the half of yours." He kissed her, slowly, exquisitely torturing her with the velvet touch of his tongue. He was taunting the inside of her mouth in a kind of shadow play to the mesmerizing thrusts of his hips, moving inside her at first gently and then more boldly in the most ancient dance between man and woman.

Desperate for release from the tender torment, she moved her lips down his throat, tasting the wild wind on his skin and then, like a Highland storm's sudden onslaught, the tension broke and in a fierce skirl of desire, their passions collided.

Again and again.

And each time it did they answered the desire, dancing to some instinctive song within them. The candle had guttered down when, finally, wrapped in Robert's plaid, Catriona nestled close against him, arms encircling him. If this had been a battle, she had not lost. As long as the memory of this night held, she would never lose him.

From Dunsmuir Castle, it was a fair walk to the village of Three Caves on the coast. Because Robert wanted no one to follow them, he had left their pony with Laird Buchanan and insisted they travel by foot. The elderly female servant who had agreed to accompany Catriona in her exile was packing a trunk full of clothes and would join them later. Robert had tried to convince Catriona to wait at the castle as well, but she would not be parted from him.

"I should be hanged for taking a beautiful, lissome lass into a rough sea village," he said.

"I'm not afraid. I want to be with you."

Halfway there he stopped. "We can't take the chance. I know a place where you can wait in seclusion—and safety. I dinna want any seaman to lay eyes on you."

She didn't argue. It only mattered that she savor every last moment with Robert.

The ocean wind blew cold. Clutching her lavender cloak about her for protection, Catriona bravely followed through the heath until it sloped down and at last met the sea.

When Robert pointed ahead to the tiny fishing village, Three Caves, where he would secure her passage on a ship, she swallowed back the lump in her throat. When he told her they'd have to settle for whatever ship they could get, she stared at him numbly. For all she cared, it could be a pirate ship to the Fountain of Youth. What did it matter where she went? She wasn't like Robert, who could choose his fate, who thanks to Lord Kendrick would no doubt find himself another politically expedient marriage of alliance the instant Catriona's ship had cleared the horizon. They walked steadily down to the sea.

At last they stopped and, for the first time, she saw the entrance to the cave in which he planned to have her hide and wait. It was no more than a narrow crawlspace with waves washing against it, and she felt as if she were being swept out to sea, utterly lost. She momentarily panicked.

"I should go with you to the village, I think, in case there is some choice about boats," she said.

He shook his head and set about clearing the opening. "I've told you why you can't. I won't have every seaman in the tavern set his sights on you. Besides, how do I know someone isn't waiting there now in case the wee witch of Glen Strahan shows up?"

Her heart sank. She had to plumb the depths to find her courage. "You mean they know about me? All the way down here?"

He nodded. She remembered his earnest talk with their

host last evening and the easy way she'd been able to draw him away. Had he made love to her to get her away from the people? From the talk?

"Well, I never thought when Elspeth first taught me how to crumble feverfew that I'd end up being an infamous exile," she said in a small voice, kicking at a seashell with her toe until she'd given it a hiding place behind a rock. "I rather preferred being anonymous like all the grains of sand." Kneeling down, she carved her initial in the wet sand with her finger. A wave moved in and washed over it, but the letter's faint outline remained.

"Edinburgh was crowded," she continued, "but at least I could dispense herbs side by side with the oyster vendor and not be noticed. I got on there just fine, temper, red hair, and all."

Robert stood up and turned to look at her.

"Catriona, lass, trust me. I'm trying to do what's safest. I'll arrange for a fishing boat to meet us here after dark," he said.

Her heart pounded in her ears. "Promise you'll be back? I know an old legend about a roguish sort, like you. He got tired of his woman and tied her to a rock and waited for the sea to come in and drown her."

Robert pressed his cheek to hers and silently shook his head. He didn't say a word, just held her like that for the longest time, until the frothy waves stopped lapping against her feet.

"The tide's going out," she said softly. "It must be time to weigh anchor."

"Just about," he said, and his voice cracked. "I suppose you'll want the finest stateroom I can book."

"I told you—a pirate ship will do fine. If you book me on a smelly fishing ship, I shall get seasick for sure. Then again, witches aren't supposed to be fussy, I don't suppose."

His smile was whimsical, slightly sad.

She reached up to press a hand to his face. "Don't be sad, Robert. No one could have done more for me than you did, and I promise not to shout at the captain or run away from the ship, or any of those silly things you hated.

And someday, you know what I'd like to do? Write my
memoirs. Except I'd make you the hero, not the rogue,
whether you like it or not.''

All she could see was his gilt-flecked hair, his head was
that close to her, so she wasn't sure if he was laughing at
her, but his shoulders shook perceptibly. ''Robert, I've
been waiting a very long time for a chance to escape from
you. Are you going to arrange passage for me?''

He lifted his head.

She'd never seen a rogue with tears in his eyes before
and didn't know what to say now.

With a finger to his lips to signal silence, he laced his
fingers through hers and led her inside the narrow opening
of the cave. Shadows and darkness overwhelmed her, and,
walking through wet sand, she clung to his hand. He lit a
tallow candle, and to her amazement she saw that once
they were inside the narrow opening the space widened
into a cathedral-like cavern, filled with majestic columns
of rock. They found a dry ledge for her to wait on, and
he wrapped a plaid about her and gave her extra candles
that he'd brought from the Buchanans.

''I'll be back,'' he whispered against her lips, and then
brushed a speck of sand off her cheek. His hand lingered
on her face, and then he walked away.

Bleakly, she watched the darkness swallow him. It
wasn't the same without Robert. Nothing ever would be.
Wrapping the plaid more tightly, she hunched up and
looked around her.

Like a clock ticking away the hours, water dripped off
the rock ceiling and echoed in a multitude of pitches.

Drip. Drop. Seconds. Minutes. Hours.

Robert was taking so long. What could he be doing?
But she didn't dare go looking. She'd promised.

Holding up the tallow candle, she imagined this was a
fairyland and the shadows on the rocks were fairy god-
mothers, the symphony of dripping water a serenade.

When at last she heard childlike voices echoing off the
rock, she sat up, wary and then glad. Children from the
village coming to splash and romp with a barking dog.

Delighted to pass the time with local children, Catriona climbed down from the ledge.

With a high-pitched bark, a spaniel splashed through the narrow aperture and pulled up short, wagging its tail, waiting for its masters.

"Hello there," a childish voice called.

"Hello yourself," she called, and caught her breath. Her own voice had sounded high-pitched and childlike. To her horror, she realized too late that the cave's vaulted ceiling distorted the voices. That meant . . .

Too late, she blew out her candle.

"You've a visitor, Catriona."

They knew her name.

Another candle flickered to life out of the darkness. Standing there, legs straddled like a buccaneer's, were none other than Jacques Beaufort and young Thomas from Glen Strahan. Jacques pointed a pistol at her while his normally deep-pitched voice greeted her in a childish echo that reminded her of a macabre nightmare.

"Chère mademoiselle. I've been so looking forward to seeing you again. Robert is remiss in leaving you alone, but I shall be more careful as I escort you back to Glen Strahan."

She started to protest, but he cut her short.

"Lachlan, your anxious bridegroom, has been most worried about you."

Chapter 23

By the time Catriona, her hands bound in front of her, arrived in sight of Glen Strahan days later, she was too exhausted to protest. A keening wind skirled through the late summer air, whipping her red curls about her face.

Heartsick though she was, she had to give Jacques credit for behaving like the perfect gentleman—all French charm behind his wolfish smile, asking constantly after her needs.

Did she wish to rest? As if the Highlands were a palace chamber.

Did she wish to eat? As if the bannock he and Thomas gave her were a rich sauce from the table of the French king.

Did she wish to sleep? As if she could dream of anything but Robert.

What must he have thought upon coming back to find the cave empty? That once again she'd run away from him? No, impossible, not after all they'd shared. In her heart of hearts, she knew he'd guess she'd been stolen away and he would come after her. But a worry nagged at her heart: Why hadn't he already caught up with her and Jacques and rescued her once again?

Her welcome in Glen Strahan was far different from that when she'd arrived with Robert. At first sight of her, the Grants stared, openmouthed, and crossed themselves. Other villagers ran and slammed their cottage doors. Still others remained inside and peered from behind their shutters.

Only two people braved the lane to smile in encouragement—Agnes Drummond and her wee lad, to whom Catriona had once given an herbal potion.

Riding beside Catriona, Jacques tipped his cocked hat in greeting to Agnes and said in French, "*Mais oui,* my Highland heathens, the red-haired witch is back. Bewitched your Robert, she did indeed."

Catriona grew angry at his mockery. "Leave them be," she said. "They are simple people, but they are my people."

With a shrug, Jacques commented idly, "You defend those who pass judgment on you?"

"Agnes Drummond had the courage to defend me. It was Lachlan who passed judgment on me and forced the villagers to his way of thinking."

"Quite so," Jacques agreed amiably. "Your own loving betrothed," he taunted.

"He is jealous of Robert to the point of madness."

Mrs. Drummond was running alongside Catriona's horse and now held up a beseeching hand to her. " 'Tis good to see ye, miss, back safe. I believe ye're an angel, I do. My own lad, my little Peter, owes his life to ye." Her gaze slid to Thomas. "Worthless lad, selling yer loyalties as if they were no more than bones for the meanest dog."

Under her withering scrutiny, Thomas flushed as red as his hair.

Catriona looked down at the woman dressed in homespun and felt gratitude for the kindness she was sure she could never repay. Humble words were all the woman had given her, but to Catriona right now they meant more than all the crowns and gold in the world.

"Is Peter well now?" she asked. "No more coughs?"

Agnes wrung her apron between her hands. "Oh, aye, he's been fit as a fiddle, and I-I wanted to thank ye." She moved along with the pace of the horses. "Only dinna tell Lachlan I spoke to ye, miss. Please . . . my husband needs the work at the castle stable."

"Of course I won't tell," she reassured Mrs. Drummond gently, and by then Jacques was tugging her away down the deserted lane.

Jacques and Thomas escorted her past the turn to the castle for her execution and she glared up at the gates where a wooden stake stood waiting for her execution.

"Where are we going?" she asked, surprised when Jacques turned the other way and took the road leading around Loch Aislair.

"To the crags behind your grandfather's manor house. You can bide with Thomas in the heather until I settle my business with Lachlan."

"He *paid* you to come and find me?" she asked, incredulous.

Jacques flashed a cold smile. "Unlike Robert, I do nothing without fair recompense—not even escort fair damsels."

Given other circumstances, she'd have slapped him and run, but the heart seemed to have been wrung out of her. She supposed Robert was right and she'd had her head in fairy tales for too long, but she did feel hurt that he'd not ridden after her like a knight to her rescue. Squaring her shoulders, she rode on in silence.

A wave of the nausea that had plagued her all day quivered through her. She carried Robert's bairn; she was so sure of it that she didn't need Elspeth to confirm it.

In silence the party completed its journey, and too soon she found herself in a rocky alcove by Loch Aislair, halfway between the castle and Ferguson Manor. So near to home and yet so far. She plunked herself down on the rocks and favored Jacques with a baleful glare.

"Welcome home, *mademoiselle,*" he said, bowing with all the subservience of a scraping hostler. "You shall, of course, be under arrest—the arrest of the English courts—for murder by witchcraft."

"What authority do you have?" she accused.

"Thomas here is my authority," Jacques replied with typical panache.

Young Thomas squirmed. He'd not yet lost the flush of guilt he'd felt when Agnes had taken him to task.

"*Oui*, Thomas the good butcher will have authority over you, and should I be delayed for any reason, Thomas will know exactly what to do with you." So saying, he started to draw Thomas aside.

"Fie on you and the English," Catriona said to their backs. "You're naught but a blackguard, not worthy to grovel in Robert's shadow."

"Doubtless, *chérie,*" Jacques agreed, turning briefly and making no effort to conceal the amusement in his eyes. "But as I already explained, such a life as mine yields greater rewards than trapping furs in the New World."

Disgusted, she swirled away to her rocky seat.

Returning to her side, Jacques reached down and tightened the ropes on her wrists. He reached for her hands to kiss them, but she snatched them away. Waving Thomas over, he ordered the village butcher to remove his dirk from his waist and slice off a flame-colored curl.

Thomas's hand shook. Craven butcher, thought Catriona. Bandits had more mettle than he did.

He moved in closer to guard her while, with a wave, Jacques rode off. Already Catriona's mind was plotting. Someone would find her. If not, she'd outwit Thomas and escape. She had to. She'd die before she'd allow Lachlan to touch her again.

In the great hall of Castle Fenella MacLean, a silver vase of drying heather stood on the long plank table amid a platoon of empty wine and whiskey bottles. At one end, alone, captain to this silent army, slumped Lachlan, the very person Jacques wanted.

"I brought your witch back for you," Jacques said, placing the lock of Catriona's hair next to a puddle of whiskey. "In the end Robert left her to her own devices, like some shipwrecked waif."

Lachlan pushed a congratulatory bottle toward Jacques and turned his attention to the lock of red hair—a single curl—that was now floating in a puddle of Scotch.

"I suppose with typical French deceit you are hiding her somewhere?"

"The obvious choice until we settled our account."

Lachlan looked up from under his eyebrows, a sly half smile on his face. "What account?"

Jacques's hand closed around the whiskey bottle. "Come, come, surely the grandson of an honorable chief cannot have forgotten his promise to me."

From somewhere outside the castle, a wail cut through the still air. Lachlan visibly started.

Jacques looked mildly curious. "What is that?"

"A foretelling of death in the Highlands, Frenchman," Lachlan explained. "The Caoineag. She had wailed all night, and at the river Grizel says a ghostly figure washes a shroud."

Afraid to question Lachlan further, Jacques shook his head and reached for a glass. He truly was in need of a dram. Once more the wail, a sound somewhere between pain and tears, wound like invisible mist through the great hall.

"If I were you, I would make haste to leave."

"Not yet." Jacques looked at the unsteady hand with which Lachlan poured himself more whiskey. "Unlike you Highlanders, I am not superstitious, only practical."

Behind him, footsteps shuffled and he turned to see Grizel, dressed in homespun yellow. About her shoulders she'd carelessly tossed a shawl of dark colors, and her lank hair fell loose. She was barefoot. He'd never seen her looking more unkempt, or less hospitable.

"So you have brought back the little witch of Glen Strahan," she commented without expression. Turning to her brother, she asked matter-of-factly, "Are you going to bed her or burn her?"

Draining his whiskey, Lachlan eyed her with annoyance. "Go outside and tell the Caoineag to stop her wailing."

Seating herself, Grizel picked up her tapestry and stabbed it with a needle. "I canna stop her, Lachlan. Mayhap Grandfather will die tonight and you will become chief at last. Mayhap Ian will kill the last Englishman and—"

"Grizel!" Half rising from his chair, Lachlan spread his palms flat on the table, as if his nerves were stretched taut. "Ian is dead. You remember, don't you? He died in battle long ago."

Jacques's eyebrows rose at the obvious lie. For the first

time, he actually felt a bit uneasy, alone with these two. But a bargain was a bargain.

From outside came again the eerie wailing of the Caoineag, and Grizel idly poked her needle at the wooden bars of the empty lark's cage.

Silence stretched between Jacques and Lachlan, and, mumbling something about walnuts, Grizel laid down her tapestry, pulled her cloak tight, and shuffled outside.

"Come, come," Jacques said to Lachlan, a note of uncertainty in his voice. "You will not insult me and tell me you have forgotten. You promised."

Lachlan stood, a sneering smile on his face. "Do you think that a promise to a Frenchman means aught to me? A promise to a kinsman, mayhap. But you harbor vain and foolish hopes if you think I would reveal the whereabouts of the hidden Regalia to a foreigner."

"But—but you gave me your word, as grandson of the chief of clan MacLean." Jacques felt momentarily at a loss. "In France, a man's word is his honor."

"This is not France," Lachlan shouted. "I may despise the king's law, but if you think I'd hand over one of Scotland's treasures to you, you're as addlepated as my stupid sister Grizel—still besotted with her dead Ferguson lover," he finished in obvious disgust.

Jacques saw that he would have to remove his gentlemanly facade and fight for his due with bare knuckles if necessary. Even among thieves and murderers in France, a code of honor existed. "I outwitted Robert and I shall outwit you!" he said. "I thought we could do business, *monsieur*, but if that is not possible I have my own means of getting what I want."

He stalked out, determined to tear this village apart, if need be, to find the Regalia.

The first thing he stumbled upon, however, was Grizel, just outside the door. She knelt down on her haunches and rocked back and forth. She looked positively tetched, he thought. Muttering about this Ian Ferguson, some long-lost love . . . Ah, yes.

A memory of an earlier conversation with Lachlan came back to Jacques. Lachlan had admitted killing his sister's beloved Ian. It would serve Lachlan right if Jacques told Grizel the truth about what a murdering lout her brother was.

"Grizel," he began, "I have news about Ian that may pain you, but help you understand why your lover left you . . ."

She looked up, at once still and alert. Oh, *oui*, he thought, this would be a fine revenge on Lachlan, and afterward, if Grizel would exchange information, Jacques might find the Regalia . . .

"I know why he left me," Grizel said. She plucked a wild thistle that grew by the door and now sat there crushing its purple bloom. The eerie wail of the woman of death could be heard in the background.

"Ian Ferguson took another lover," she said sadly. "Lachlan told me so."

Jacques knelt beside her. "Lachlan lied to you. Your lover never betrayed you. He was a faithful Ferguson."

When Grizel looked up, confusion in her eyes, he continued with ruthless relish. "You see, Lachlan murdered him—"

"You lie!" Grizel stood up suddenly, hands clutching her plaid while she swayed back and forth, a look of profound disbelief on her face. The bits of thistle fell to the ground. "You lie!"

The air around them seemed charged, heavy as before a storm. Jacques stood also and continued, whispering in a low rumble directly into her ear. "I am a man who speaks the truth. Lachlan killed Ian and blamed it on the English. A Scotsman—your own brother, no less—killed your lover."

Grizel seemed to shrink before Jacques's eyes. And in her face, the pain of betrayal slid over her plain features. She smiled, sadly, wistfully. Yet her eyes remained blank. And then she began to tremble. She hugged her arms about herself as if for protection. "Ian . . . Ian," she said, as if searching for the ghost of her lover. "Ian, is it true?"

"Go and ask Lachlan if you do not believe me. He boasted of the deed to me. Now, in exchange for this information, will you tell me where the MacLeans hid the Regalia?''

Grizel's eyes glittered with tears, and Jacques had to repeat his request. As if coming back from a long distance, she focused on him. She frowned.

"Grizel? A secret for a secret," he prompted.

The tears fell to her cheeks. "For many years I have kept Lachlan's secrets, but no more. Always it's been under the floor of the wee kirk." Her voice broke.

Grizel took a step forward, almost as if she would fall prostrate into Jacques's arms. She looked back at the door to the great hall. Then at Jacques. And again at the door. The sad glaze never left her eyes, and suddenly she picked up her skirts and ran off, disappearing around a mist-shrouded corner of the castle's outer ward. "No more!" she screamed, her wail of pain echoing with that of the Caoineag's.

Jacques shrugged. He had done his part. Now was his chance to see if her words about the Regalia's whereabouts were correct.

"Where is she? I want to know who's taken her, do you hear me?"

Lachlan heard Robert growling like a wounded cat, heard his voice coming closer and closer, and with a ragged release of breath, rolled off the naked kitchen wench. First it was Jacques, now, mere hours later, Robert. Damnation. Such a tedious nuisance was this woman Catriona. Tossing a plaid over his naked form, he reached for the key to his chest full of private papers.

If it came to a contest of physical force, Robert could likely best him, so Lachlan pulled out the letter he'd received from Lord Kendrick in England. Actually, the letter had come for Robert, but after Robert had abducted Catriona, Lachlan had felt it his prerogative to read Robert's mail, lest any pressing business needed attending. Aye, this letter would be his trump. This and as many lies as he could quickly concoct.

Mere seconds later, Robert barged into the bedchamber, his face an icy mask, a dirk flashing in his hand.

Lachlan pressed a hand to Meg's thigh to stay her from fleeing. "I am no' done with you, lass."

"Where have you locked Catriona away this time?" Robert demanded, advancing on Lachlan with predatory menace.

"Jacques has her."

"Liar. I passed Jacques at the wee kirk. He was alone."

"Why should I know anything about Catriona Ferguson?" Lachlan said with flagrant superiority. " 'Twas no' my men who brought her back."

Robert held murder in his eyes, and Lachlan began to unfold the letter. Rushing on, he added some lies to his earlier words. "There is no use threatening me, your own kin. Can I help it if she has decided to wed me after all?"

He savored the incredulous expression on Robert's face for a few seconds, then said, "Oh, dinna look so surprised, cousin. What did you offer her? Naught but exile, so I hear."

Moving to the window, Robert leaned over and stared out at the castle ward. "What did you offer?" Lachlan goaded. "Sending her off somewhere, I wager. Given such a fate, what would a hunted young woman choose? The only marriage available to her," he answered with logic.

"I offered her safety," Robert countered, turning on Lachlan. "You offered naught but a witchcraft trial and the stake." His eyes were glacial.

To be safe, Lachlan assumed his most abashed expression. "But it was that Frenchman who told the villagers all the tales about sorcery and witchcraft and stirred them into a frenzy. He'd do anything for his own gain. Meanwhile, Grandfather and I have had a talk, and I've reconsidered the wisdom of burning Catriona. After all, Sarah was but an English."

Walking around the bed, Lachlan ran a languid hand down the kitchen wench's blanketed shape. "Do you think I'd have been so heartless with Catriona had I not been forced into the trial?" He asked his question of the kitchen wench. "Do you, Meg?" he prompted, tugging at her plait of light brown hair.

Wide-eyed, the maid managed to shake her head.

Immediately, Lachlan's gaze went to Robert. "You see, Meg knows me well enough."

"That does no' explain the murder."

Shrugging, Lachlan sighed, deliberately rueful. "True, Robert," he admitted sadly, strolling to the narrow window and looking out. "No one's more aware of that than I, but mayhap it's better left unsolved. Send Jacques away and let it all die down. A good diplomat like you would no' want to inflame Scottish-French relations, now, hmm?" All the time he lied, he counted in his mind the number of men stationed around the borders of the Ferguson land, waiting to nab the little vixen should she steal away from Jacques and run onto her grandfather's property.

"You are undeserving of the MacLean name, let alone the honor of being heir," Robert said quietly.

When Lachlan turned to face Robert, he'd managed to put a pleasant expression on his face. "Are you jealous? There's no need to condemn me. I'll be gentle with Catriona because, above all, our grandfather's dream of ending this feud must be realized."

"You're lying."

"About what? That she returned with Jacques? The entire village saw her come. I hear her mother was fond of the amusements of the French court. No doubt the daughter too will let her head be swayed by the false charms of a roguish Frenchman, unless I rid the glen of him and wed her soon."

"You lie, Lachlan," Robert repeated, shaking his head. "She was captured and brought back against her will."

Feigning sadness, Lachlan shook his head. " 'Tis regrettable, Robert. I know how much you longed to return the title to our family, but after this . . ." Outside the castle walls, practically below the window to Lachlan's chamber, the old woman Caoineag wailed. She'd not wailed so close to the castle since the night a few years ago when that pious nuisance, Robert's mother, had died. Lachlan strode over and slammed the window shut.

Turning back, he saw Robert's fists clenching and unclenching, his body tense, looking as if he might lunge at any moment for Lachlan's throat. A most unnerving discussion this was becoming. Time to end it. "Here . . . a letter from Lord Kendrick, come while you and Catriona were . . . uh, gone. You canna call this a lie." Lachlan thrust the parchment at his cousin, who snatched it away and crackled it open.

Lachlan watched Robert briefly scan the contents, waiting till Robert's face turned ashen.

Of course Lachlan had the words practically memorized and could recite to himself the message.

. . . *warned you about association with the murder of an Englishwoman, but harboring a convicted witch . . . If this information should find its way to court, I shall never obtain the post of secretary of state and you can banish all thought of serving under me as my liaison to the Highlands . . . and as for regaining titles . . .*

Recalling Lord Kendrick's succinct writing style, Lachlan smiled, glad all over again that he'd thought to write Lord Kendrick and tell him that his trusted confidant, Robert MacLean, had abducted a witch.

With Robert fully distracted by the news that his diplomatic hopes were in a shambles, Lachlan reached across the bed for the wench.

"Troubling news, cousin?" Lachlan asked, before settling himself against Meg.

Robert shook his head as he tried to make sense of the letter. Obviously Lachlan had wasted no time in informing Lord Kendrick of Robert's actions regarding Catriona. There was no depth, it seemed, to Lachlan's perfidy. And this return letter had been written some time ago, obviously before Lord Kendrick had obtained the coveted appointment.

Robert didn't care.

He didn't care whether Lord Kendrick wanted his services. Nor did he particularly care whether he got the family title back. It was given freely, that would be one thing, but he'd no longer toady to Lord Kendrick for them.

But even that wasn't all.

Leaving Lachlan to his wench, Robert crumpled the letter in his hand and, striding out, slammed the door behind him.

His only thought was for Catriona. Was it possible she had been feeling so desperate for a solution that she'd decided to settle for Lachlan rather than face exile? Impossible. Not the lass he'd come to know and . . . aye, come to love.

He loved her. They belonged to each other, like the rose and the thorn, like the heather and the mist, like the braes and the fells. Without her he felt half empty, he realized. He could still recall vividly the first awareness of his desire. She'd been standing by a raging river, her flame hair and lavender cloak blowing in the Highland breeze. And the first moment of love? It must have been when he first laid eyes on her.

His boots clicking on the stones, he took the steps two at a time as he made his way to the great hall. Already his mind was filled with possible hiding places. He knew Glen Strahan and its nooks and crannies better than Jacques. On the other hand, he could simply accost the lily-livered Frenchman at the wee kirk, if he was still there snooping around, and wring his neck if he didn't reveal where he'd left Catriona. Robert couldn't get to his horse fast enough.

But the instant he entered the great hall, a pair of soggy-looking men, one skinny, one rotund, stood and blocked his way.

Chapter 24

〜〜◯◯〜〜

"**W**hat is it?" Robert brusquely pushed the be-draggled strangers out of his way.

"We've trekked all the way from England. Messengers from the king's court."

Unimpressed, Robert favored them with a nod. "Congratulations. Not all English can withstand the ardors of the journey." He reached to the table for his cocked hat.

He was halfway across the great hall when he realized the messenger, a pale, skinny man dressed in the English fashion, was chasing after him.

"Wait, please. Are you not Robert MacLean? Lord Kendrick described you in great detail. He was right. You favor your cousin. Like flip sides of a coin, you two are. Your face is honest, his counterfeit. Amazing."

Robert paused. "What do you want of me?"

"I've come all the way from London with a personal message." He bowed low, displaying a bald spot in his thin hair. "Oliver Godwin at your service."

"I've already received the message. Lachlan was kind enough to save the letter," Robert said in a dry voice. Amused by the look of confusion in the man's face, he resumed walking across the great hall.

Within seconds, he heard Oliver Godwin's steps running behind him again.

"Begging your pardon, but my instructions were to place *this* missive in no other hands but your own, especially not the hands of your kin. I was told most specifi-

351

cally *not* to let Lachlan MacLean hear the message from the secretary of state.

The secretary of state?

"For Scotland?" Robert asked, turning to look at the foppish Oliver Godwin and his mud-spattered manservant. Unlike Lachlan, Robert had already heard from Laird Buchanan of Lord Kendrick's appointment. That meant this message was of a more recent date than the tactless words Lachlan had handed him.

"Secretary of state for Scotland?" Robert repeated, his curiosity truly piqued now. He turned and stalked Mr. Godwin until he was close enough to stare down at the freckles on his bald spot.

"How long have you been waiting?" It did not escape his notice that Lachlan had not seen fit to tell him he had a visitor.

"I've only just arrived," Mr. Godwin said with an apologetic wave at his manservant's muddy apparel. "Grueling trip, I must say. Lord Kendrick has his work cut out for him." As he spoke, he reached into his coat pocket, pulled out a piece of parchment, and handed it over.

Robert ripped open the seal and quickly scanned the contents, curious what Lord Kendrick wanted to chastise him for now.

Oliver Godwin was obviously privy to the contents and was now elaborating. "Blasted lucky dog, that's what I call any Scotsman who can work so closely with Lord Kendrick. In the Hanoverian court yet." Oliver Godwin wet his lips and continued in a rush. "He told me to convey personally his regret over the dreadful misunderstanding in the first letter and pray forgiveness. Dashed it off in the heat of the moment before realizing that if your cousin Lachlan passed the news on . . . Well, Lord Kendrick decided not to believe it all, especially that witchcraft nonsense." He took a quick breath and finished, "He deeply regrets the hastiness of those words."

So that was it, Robert thought. After Lord Kendrick had obtained his coveted appointment, he'd reconsidered his anger at Robert. While Robert stood there impassively, Mr. Godwin gushed on.

"And Lord Kendrick said to tell you the marriage he's arranged this time would set many an English lad to envy. It's with a far more politically powerful family than the Kendricks. Mind, there'll be no dragging the bride to the Highlands to wed. They'll want you to hasten to London for a proper English ceremony.''

In the company of gaping castle servants, Robert listened to these glad tidings but felt not a speck of joy. All he could think about was Catriona. He missed her that dearly and was too worried for her to bide any longer with this coxcomb.

"My father wed my mother for love," he said, reaching again for his hat. "As, I believe, my grandfather did my grandmother."

Mr. Godwin blinked myopically. His smile was tolerant. "A romantic notion that few practical people can indulge in. Come now, Robert—"

"Mr. MacLean is how I'm known among Lord Kendrick's circle.''

The messenger cleared his throat and lowered his voice conspiratorially. "Lord Kendrick needs you for the Highlands. As I've just told you, your future with the new secretary of state stretches before you, rich and well-rewarded, full of profit.''

Unaccountably, Robert thought of a Bible verse from divinity class. *For what shall it profit a man, if he shall gain the whole world and lose his own soul?*

He was being offered everything he'd ever wanted—except now his wants had changed.

And it was Catriona for whom he ached. Yearned for. Needed deep in his soul.

Was it too late? Had he already traded away his soul? Not yet.

Mr. Godwin, who'd apparently been watching the play of emotion on Robert's face, now wore a bemused expression. "She was a tasty wench?" he guessed.

Robert shoved the man aside and headed for the door.

He felt as if his entire life force had been stretched out on the rack and the devil himself was turning the screws.

"Here now, where are you going? You've not given an answer to Lord Kendrick."

"Move aside. I need to find someone."

"You can't ignore an offer like this, not after all the trouble Lord Kendrick went to on your behalf. You owe him something."

Robert turned on Oliver Godwin, ready to pounce on the next obstacle in his path. At once, the messenger and his manservant shrank back against the wall of the great hall, and the servants hushed, staring. Let them stare. Lord Kendrick and his messenger were naught but bothersome mongrels nipping at his heels and whining about England when he had larger matters on his mind.

"Dammit, I endured a difficult journey to bring that personal message to you," Mr. Godwin said, his bald spot reddening. "You at least owe *me* something for my trouble."

Robert slapped on his cocked hat and flipped the fellow a farthing. "For your trouble."

The rotund manservant lunged for the coin, scooped it up, and bit into it. "It's a real one, all right."

"Is this all?" Oliver Godwin shoved the coin away.

"No, not all." Seized with sudden and perverse inspiration, Robert grabbed this bothersome little Englishman's arm and hauled him out into the castle ward.

"Where are you taking us?" Mr. Godwin demanded when they were all mounted on horseback.

"To the wee kirk," Robert said, and deliberately avoided elaborating. If he was wrong, it would be a waste of time, a delay in finding Catriona, but if he was right, it would be worth it.

Within the half hour, Robert in company with Oliver Godwin and his manservant tethered their horses outside the wee kirk and approached the door, which hung slightly ajar. From inside came the unmistakable sounds of human grunting, accompanied by the groan of wood being pried loose from nails.

Followed by the messenger, Robert stepped inside and scooped up a rusted length of metal; he needed only one look to identify it as the rim from an old coach wheel, which someone had used as a lever on the floorboards. He looked down into the hole in the floor and smiled. He'd guessed right.

There stood Jacques, his lace ruffs torn and his hair, draped with a spiderweb, hanging loose from its ribbon. Perspiration actually beaded his handsome brow. He was leaning over a dusty chest, catching his breath.

Robert tensed, while, beside him, the messenger looked at what, at first glance, could be taken for a simple grave robbery. "What the deuce is this?"

Jacques looked up at Robert, and they took each other's measure.

"I crawled under here," Jacques said, "and found the chest under the altar and pushed it all the way through the mice and spiderwebs to this hole, and I'm taking it."

"Ah, but I found you before you opened it, Jacques," Robert pointed out.

Jacques's eyes narrowed. "It's the Regalia. I've no doubt," he gloated.

"Je regrette." Robert turned to the messenger. "He's a Jacobite spy. You may take him back to Lord Kendrick, with my compliments, and tell the good secretary of state for Scotland that the capture of Jacques Beaufort is a wee something in exchange for his trouble."

"I'm not going to London," Jacques said in disgust. "I'm going back to France . . . to wealth and power."

But Robert had already knelt down close to the splintered hole in the floor and aimed a pistol at Jacques's head. "Where's Catriona?"

"You have a single-minded purpose in that wench, *n'est-ce pas?"*

"Where?" The pistol shook visibly.

Jacques gulped. "If I tell, you will let me keep the Regalia?"

"You don't even know if it's in that chest, you greedy toad." And then Robert handed his pistol to Oliver Godwin, and in one lithe motion reached over and grabbed

Jacques by the hair. As he dragged him out of the hole, Jacques's coat ripped under the arm, and finally he was sprawling on the floor of the wee kirk, panting like a beached fish.

At once, he tried to get up on all fours, but with a swift thrust of his boot, Robert pushed him down and shoved a foot against his throat.

"Good God!" muttered Oliver Godwin behind them.

"Listen well, Mr. Godwin," Robert said, "and dinna turn fainthearted on me now. You'll want, I'm sure, to give Lord Kendrick a full accounting." For a long moment he glared at Jacques, who squirmed beneath his boot.

"A long time ago, Frenchman," he said in a low voice, "I told you that if I found out you'd come to Scotland for anything besides whiskey and sketches, you'd be wearing a necklace of red home. Now, what is your choice for the necklace, Frenchman? Pistol or dirk?"

Jacques managed to push up his hips, but Robert pushed him down again. *"Monsieur,* please . . . I . . . I . . . will . . . leave," Jacques sputtered, clearly conceding defeat. He squirmed out from under the heel of Robert's boot. "Regrettably, it appears as if my sojourn in Scotland has come to a precipitous end. If I say *adieu* and go with the Englishman . . . ?"

"You may take your neck with you. Naught else." Robert grabbed a piece of rope that had bound the chest and motioned a quivering Oliver Godwin to bind Jacques's hands. Only then did they help the Frenchman to his feet.

"Such a barbaric place," Jacques muttered.

"No place is barbaric," Robert corrected. "Only its people . . . Now, tell me, how did you know where to find this chest?"

"Grizel told me," he said. "The only hospitable MacLean in the entire village."

Clearly hungry to see the contents of the chest he'd uncovered, Jacques craned his neck toward the floorboards.

"And Catriona?"

"Hidden in the hills behind the manor. Thomas has instructions to take her to the castle should I be delayed by more than half a day. By now she is probably back in

Lachlan's embrace. A fitting punishment for all you MacLeans for not letting me take what is rightfully the Pretender's.''

This taunt was the last straw for Robert. With a quick flash of his dirk, he made good on his threat and, grabbing Jacques by one ear, neatly marked his throat. A red line, a scratch, just deep enough to draw drops of blood. "A souvenir of Scotland," Robert said in disgust.

Screeching like a fishwoman, Jacques began begging Oliver Godwin, who was turning paler by the moment.

"My cravat. Take it. Staunch the blood." He held up his fingers to display a pale smudge of red. "Don't let me bleed to death," he pleaded, pressing shaky fingers to his throat. And then he knelt at the feet of a clearly shocked Mr. Godwin.

"Cease, I pray," Mr. Godwin said. "Lord Kendrick must be insane to want to serve up here," he muttered in an aside to the ceiling.

"Help me. I can pay you well," Jacques pleaded to him.

Robert scoffed. "You infant. 'Tis naught but a scratch," after which Jacques slumped in a near faint.

"Get him out of here," Robert said, and the messenger hurried to summon his manservant, who had waited outside with the horses.

The Frenchman's words about Catriona's fate rang in Robert's ears. The castle. A fist clenched inside Robert's chest. Lachlan mustn't get his hands on Catriona.

By this time, Jacques, though still whimpering, had recovered enough to walk out to his horse.

The sound grated on Robert's temper.

"Go!" Robert said. "All of you. English and French. Get out of my glen and never set foot here again."

Jacques glared back while, with his bound hands, he dabbed at his neck with his cravat. "Despite your curses, be assured, I shall return someday at the side of the true king."

"You'll be wallowing in an English prison at the side of a common pickpocket before that happens," Robert called back. He mused with perverse pleasure on what would be Jacques's worst punishment: never to know whether the chest did, indeed, contain the lost Regalia.

Oh, Robert had no doubt that it was the lost treasure, and later there'd be time enough to arrange to have it escorted back to its rightful place in Edinburgh. He moved a few floorboards back into place, enough so that the floor appeared to be untouched. Sabbath services were some days off, but women would be in to clean, might even notice that the floor had been torn up. Robert could do no more than trust it would bide safe for a wee bit.

Mounting his horse, he watched Jacques, hands bound, ride off toward his just reward in England. Robert headed for Castle Fenella MacLean, one thought consuming him. If Lachlan had touched Catriona, he'd murder him.

"Kill him, I will," Elspeth said upon hearing the news that Jacques had returned. "He did no' have Catriona with him?"

"Nay, he was riding alone among the crags, heading back to the village," Angus said. "Not an hour ago."

"He'll know about our Catriona. He's no' come back for naught. Catriona did no' deserve this kind of homecoming, Angus. She feared ye, ye ken, and now the village fears her."

Angus turned away from the window. "And why would she fear me?"

"Well, how would ye remember a grandfather who'd sent ye away unloved? Who blamed a child for Jacobite doings?"

Blinking rapidly, Angus chewed on his lip. " 'Tis no' as she thinks."

"Then how is it?"

"I didna want to send her away, and no MacLean could make me give up my own beloved granddaughter. 'Twas her mother who was selling Scottish secrets."

"Her mother? Go on with ye. I was her maidservant. Fastened her into her gowns until the day she died."

"And how do ye think she came by so many French gowns? No' by the purse of my son."

"Ye mean . . ." Elspeth felt sick at heart.

"I mean, 'twas a weakness. A need for fripperies that drove her to sell secrets. The MacLean found out and came to me. When he took a dirk to Catriona, I knew the time had come to send the family away. 'Twas my daughter-in-law I banished," he said softly. "But I had to let Catriona go with her mother . . . I had no choice there." His voice choked.

"If ye want Catriona's love back, ye must tell her."

"Aye . . . but a man hates to plant hurtful words in a child's head about her own mother . . ."

"Catriona is no longer a child, and I wager she'll understand her mother's extravagant ways better than ye think. 'Twould be a blessing to tell her."

Angus nodded.

"Now I'm going out to find her."

"Take care, Elspeth, for yer own life."

She nodded and slid a knife inside the folds of her cloak. "I'm auld, and there's naught I wouldna do to avenge the MacLeans for how they hurt my Catriona . . . especially Lachlan MacLean."

Lachlan sat drinking in the great hall when the door creaked open, letting in the infernal wail of the Caoineag. After he glanced around, his face relaxed.

"So it's you again. Come back to argue some more? My replies will be the same." He drank his cup of whiskey to the dregs. Nothing in life pleasured him quite so much as letting the last drop of good whiskey roll on his tongue. Nothing, that is, except nursing his hatred of all Fergusons.

"Well, speak up. Have your say and be gone."

He reached for a nut to crack in his fist, and tiny bits of shells scattered over the half-finished tapestry and on the long plank table.

There was no reply.

"Fine then, if you dinna choose to speak, sit down and drink with me."

Idly, Lachlan watched the play of shadows on the wall. The wailing of the Caoineag had so unnerved him that in a rare show of extravagance, he had lit all the candles and positioned himself between them and the wall, so he could watch his own shadow.

"You heard me," he growled. "Cease pacing and sit. You unnerve me as much as that wailing woman."

Out of the corner of his eye he saw the shadows flicker and glanced again at the wall. Above the seated shadow of himself, a higher shadow loomed, the dark outline of an upraised hand, and in it a dirk.

Both the shadow and Lachlan moved at the same moment. As pain overwhelmed him, the last sound he heard beyond his head thumping to the table and the drip of blood on the planks was the Caoineag wailing her prophecy of death.

Chapter 25

❦

They had sat waiting in the rocky alcove above Loch Aislair for only a short time when Thomas, who admittedly disliked idleness, drew a pair of dice from his sporan. To Catriona's annoyance, he had the temerity to rattle them in his hand, spill them onto the ground, and immediately scoop them up, Highland dust and all, and then begin the ritual all over again.

"Care to play, lass?" he asked as casually as if they were in a gaming hall. "Passes the time better than counting the Highland rocks."

"With my hands tied?" she said.

Shaking her head, Catriona stood, scanning the crags and wondering how fast she could run over the rocky terrain with bound hands. And if she could escape without running into a MacLean sentry. If Robert were with her, he'd say she could.

Aye, lass, there's a bonnie bridge climber . . . Aye, lass, there's a braw Highland lass . . .

But Robert wasn't with her now. She had no one but herself and her own courage on which to rely. Behind her, the dice clicked together in Thomas's palm and then clanked against a rock. The leaden sky could no longer contain itself, and scattered raindrops began to fall, dampening Catriona's hair. Thomas shook a fist at the sky and cursed it for raining on his sport. Polishing the dice on his sleeve, however, he simply turned and began rolling them into a little dry recess in the rocks.

His back was practically turned to her, and Catriona took a few steps away.

"Dinna try to leave, lass," Thomas said at once. "My eyes may look occupied on the dice, but I'm watching ye."

Her shoulders slumped. She couldn't—wouldn't wait here like a pawn in a chess game, or let Jacques trade her to Lachlan. Just the memory of Lachlan's cold lips made her shudder in revulsion.

Then out of the corner of her eye, she saw a movement down by the loch. Someone was wandering along the rocky shore of Loch Aislair, a woman in a Highland gown of ancient design. It was light-colored, gathered at the waist, the fabric looped loosely over a belt and falling to her bare feet. Instantly, Catriona's hopes soared. If only it were Elspeth, her gentle maidservant.

Closer and closer the figure came until Catriona could hear the whipping of the woman's skirts in the wind, like flapping wings. Whoever it was would help . . . unless it was a villager who still feared her as a witch. Oh, please, couldn't it be Elspeth? And then she heard the cry, a single, keening moan that soon became a word . . .

"Ian . . . Ian. Where are ye? Ian . . ."

Grizel.

If Catriona felt disappointment, she shoved it away. Grizel may have taunted Catriona while she'd been imprisoned, but that was in the past. At least Grizel didn't fear her as a witch. And if approached in a spirit of humility, Grizel was capable of giving comfort and sympathy . . . even help. Catriona watched her approach, not wanting to alarm her by calling out too soon.

Thomas was occupied with his dice, and so Catriona had a moment to watch Grizel. Why, with a smile, Catriona mused, Grizel could actually be attractive. If only she'd plait her hair instead of letting it hang loose. Such a shame she was so lonely . . . If it were up to Catriona, she'd send Grizel away to Edinburgh where there would be more people to meet and she could keep her mind in the present. Maybe even find a man to wed. She'd be so much happier.

"Grizel," she called suddenly, and Thomas started to attention. Now that he didn't have Jacques's bravado to back him up, she'd wager he would not have the courage to wield his dirk on a defenseless woman, much less on two of them.

"Grizel, I'm over—"

Thomas clamped a hand to her mouth, the scent of rain on his skin filling Catriona's every breath. With his other hand, he squeezed her waist, and she winced where the sharp corners of the dice dug into her ribs.

Then Grizel looked up and stopped in her tracks, staring. Catriona held up her hands, mutely pleading. All Grizel had to do was see the rope binding her wrists.

Grizel smiled sadly and veered toward Catriona. As she picked her way over the rocky shore and steadily ascended the crags, she stopped here and there to find a foothold. Thomas snorted. "If you think Grizel MacLean has the muscle to rescue you, ye're daft, lass," he said.

He released Catriona so suddenly that she stumbled and fell against the sharp crags. The impact of skin against rock made her wince.

Summoning all the strength she had left, she looped the rope on her wrists around a sharp tip of rock and used it to lever herself back up to a sitting position, then finally stood. Thomas leaned back against a crag and watched. He fished a cuttie from his pocket and began tamping tobacco into it. Disgusted, Catriona raised her arms and pressed her scraped arm against her face. It hurt so. She looked again for Grizel.

Grizel had paused in her tracks, like a wary doe about to run.

"*Please* . . . Grizel," Catriona called. "Please help me."

After a moment, Grizel began clambering onward again. "Robert is back, ye ken . . . Have ye no' seen him?" she called from the bottom of the crag.

Clearly Grizel wanted Catriona to know that Robert had not ridden immediately to her rescue. But, despite Grizel's veiled taunt, Catriona's hopes rose. "Back in Glen Strahan?"

Oh, merciful Lord, Robert was back. He would come to find her . . . if only he would ride out to Ferguson Manor and pass this way. He had to wonder why she'd disappeared from the cave.

"Where, Grizel?" she called back into the wind. "Where did Robert go?"

Grizel's fingers went to the round silver brooch at her neck. Again she gave a sad little smile. "He and Lachlan argued at the castle."

At once worried, Catriona shook off Thomas's restraining hold and moved as close to Grizel as she could. "Argued? About what?"

A pause. "I dinna know . . . but Robert was angry enough to kill Lachlan." With one finger, Grizel traced an imaginary line around the brooch. "Ian is waiting for me."

Oh, Lord, not Ian again.

"No, wait. Grizel, tell me why Robert would be so angry. What did Lachlan do? Did he . . . did he cause Sarah's death?" If she was ever to save herself, she'd have to convince the villagers of her innocence regarding Sarah Kendrick.

Grizel's fingers grew still. "Nay . . . why should Lachlan have killed Sarah?" She smiled. "Now, Robert—he'd have the better reason, eh? Poison his English bride-to-be so he could steal another lass from Lachlan? Does he desire you enough to do that?"

Catriona recoiled from the bitter words. "No. No, he doesn't." Desire her he might, but he would never kill to have her. Grizel was taunting her, playing with her emotions. "I don't care if Robert desires me," she lied. "Please help me. Either go get someone or come up here yourself."

Quick tears stung Catriona's eyes, so that when Grizel moved toward her it was like an apparition.

Random thoughts washed over her. Robert had returned but had gone straight to his castle instead of searching for her. Mayhap he cared more for his future with Lord Kendrick than he did about finding her . . . then again, may-hap he assumed she'd run away from the cave . . .

No! Surely he knew her better than that by now. Surely he would be trying to find her, to offer her exile, to reassure himself she was safe from the stake, wouldn't he? Or if he were weary of rescuing her and wanted to go to Lord Kendrick, wouldn't he at least say farewell before he left her to her own devices?

Frantic, she watched Grizel clamber over the last rock separating them and saw that Grizel had cut one of her bare feet. Blood trickled across her arch.

"You know," she said when Grizel finally faced her, "you're not safe roaming these hills alone." Grizel's shawl had fallen off her hair and lay over her shoulders in a careless fashion. Her dress, Catriona noted, was yellow and white stripes, the skirt rather short, the fabric at the belted waist more voluminous than Catriona had realized . . . and stained. Poor Grizel.

"Isn't this where the two lasses were found dead?" Catriona asked uneasily. "In the rocks outside Glen Strahan?" She cast a nervous look at Thomas.

Thomas only shrugged and said defensively, " 'Twas no' my doing, so you can rest on that account."

Grizel had tilted her head, and the sad little smile was there again. "Aye, the lasses died somewhere near here. 'Twas where Lachlan used to take them to slake his lust on them," she added in the same voice with which she'd once comforted a weeping Sarah. "Thomas will let me untie you." It was then that Catriona allowed herself to look down at Grizel's hands.

From the folds of fabric at her waist, she was removing a dirk.

A dirk smeared red with dried blood.

Catriona felt her own blood drain to her toes, rooting her to the spot.

"Almighty saints," Thomas said, and backed into a crag.

When Catriona could breathe again, she looked from the dirk back up into Grizel's eyes and recognized the smile as one of madness.

"Grizel . . ."

Face to face with the murderer of Glen Strahan she was, and she could scarcely form words.

"Grizel . . ." The name was a whisper.

"Always I've done Lachlan's bidding," Grizel explained calmly.

Backing away, one step at a time, Catriona heard her own voice as if from far away. "No . . . that can't be." And now, if the blood on Grizel's clothes spoke true, someone else lay dead in the village. Catriona's back hit a jagged crag and she was forced to stop. Grizel stalked her, dirk at her side.

Thomas stood aside, crossing himself over and over. "Saints preserve me . . . Holy Mother of God and all the saints preserve me . . ." His eyes were as big as a dying cow's.

Slowly, the tip of the dirk moved toward Catriona's ribs who held her hands in a position of prayer. Suddenly, Grizel thrust the blade under Catriona's wrists and began to slice at the rope, as gently as if she were severing a tapestry thread. Catronia's wrists were chafed and raw before the deed was done, and finally with a last thrust the knife sliced through. The rope fell to the ground, and Grizel pulled the dirk away, holding it close to her breast, like an amulet.

Heart thudding, Catriona flexed her wrists. Her head whirled dizzily. Thomas was running off along the crags in the direction of Loch Aislair, and now Catriona and Grizel stood alone. Suddenly Catriona felt a ruthless need to stay alive.

Her best hope would be to talk to Grizel, if possible, to convince her to walk back toward the castle. She would pretend that Ian was still alive. "Will you walk with me back to the castle?" Catriona asked as casually as possible. "I'll help you look for Ian."

"Ian is waiting for me," Grizel said in a monotone voice.

"Yes, he is," Catriona said. "Walk with me," she begged. "Just you and me," she added softly. "Together we'll find Ian Ferguson . . . Come, walk with me."

There was a bright sheen to Grizel's eyes. "That's what I told the lasses before I gave them poisoned wine. I invited them to walk . . ."

Involuntarily, Catriona put a hand to her throat and willed herself not to run. Had she known for certain how fleet or slow of foot Grizel was, she would have tried to run away, but she dared not. Grizel, she sensed, would panic, and then who knew what she might do?

Her pulse pounding, Catriona put one foot in front of the other. To her relief Grizel fell in step. As long as they could keep moving, step by step in the direction of the castle, the village, people, maybe she would be all right.

Without Catriona having to ask anything, Grizel began to talk as if they were a pair of villagers on their way to market. "I killed them for Lachlan. They tired of him, and Lachlan is my brother. They were easy to poison—just as Sarah was. It was so easy to blame you."

"What did you poison them with?" Catriona trembled.

"Belladonna. Most deadly, you know."

"Yes, I know. But whyever would you want to blame me?" Catriona asked in as normal a voice as if she were bartering over a piece of mutton.

Grizel smiled beatifically. "Lachlan was jealous that you were besotted by Robert. He wanted Robert to suffer . . . both of you for letting your desire have its way."

"Lachlan assumed too much."

"Even if Robert kissed you, that would be enough. Lachlan is jealous of Robert and his easy ways with the lasses."

Catriona flinched. His easy ways. Roguish Robert. But now was not the time to dwell on her feelings for Robert. She had to get Grizel back to the castle. Walking side by side along the shore of the loch, rocks crunching beneath their feet, wind blowing through the wild thistles, they might have been two simple lasses out for a stroll. All the time, however, Catriona's mind screamed: *Tell me, Grizel. Tell me who has died this day.*

They'd covered half the distance.

"But the other lasses. They had naught to do with Robert," Catriona said.

Grizel laughed. "Nay, they both told Lachlan that Robert was a bonnier lad, and he bade me avenge him. Once I poisoned one, he began to blackmail me. And I had to do his bidding over and over . . . Lachlan is clever, so clever—but I am more clever than he thinks. I shall never do his bidding again."

"Of course not."

"Unless you give away my secrets."

Suddenly nauseous, Catriona stumbled over a rock and caught herself. She wanted to fall to her knees and wait for Robert to find her. She wanted to run, but didn't dare. Hugging her arms about herself, she tried to quell her shaking, and then with an effort, she made herself speak normally.

"Don't be afraid," Catriona soothed, wiping rain off her face. "I won't tell on you. Besides," she said lightly, "I've already been convicted for the murder of Sarah, so you see no one else can burn for it—not even Lachlan. Only me."

Stooping down, Grizel plucked a thistle and carried it with her. "I love Ian Ferguson—only Ian."

Catriona pushed damp curls off her forehead. Grizel's mind seemed to exist in a time and place of its own. "I know Ian Ferguson is my kin, and a braw Ferguson he was—is," she amended.

"Aye."

They walked in silence.

Catriona's cousin Ian Ferguson had died when Catriona was but an infant. There was naught left of him but two entries in the family Bible—a date of birth and a date of death.

But this she knew: Ian Ferguson had been a hero to her family, the heir to all things Ferguson until his heroic death at Sheriffmuir. The Fergusons had always believed Ian died in battle. Proudly. Heroically.

Grizel kept droning on. "I thought Ian betrayed me," she murmured, tears slipping down her face. "Lachlan told me so," she continued, looking up at the dark sky.

"But Lachlan lied. Lachlan shot Ian because he didna want me to wed with the feuding family, and I'm sorely sorry now that I did Lachlan's bidding."

Somehow Catriona still managed to put one foot in front of the other, but her mind reeled. Angus must never know about Lachlan's treachery. The shock might kill him.

Still Catriona felt a scream rising inside her. Whose blood did Grizel wear? Angus's? Robert's? Oh, God, the possibility was beyond thought. Would Lachlan have bade Grizel kill Robert? Not Robert. Please, she couldn't bear to think that this might be Robert's blood.

The rain had let up, but the air around them seemed charged, heavy as before a storm.

"Lachlan will never make you harm another soul," Catriona said.

"No . . . because now he's dead too."

Lachlan dead? Unexpectedly, Catriona slipped on a wet rock and nearly fell. Catching her balance, she continued on. The two women were approaching the castle from behind the village. A dog began to bark beneath the village pear tree.

A man pushing a cart looked up and saw them. He pointed, and a woman followed his gaze. Screaming, she dropped her pail and milk spread in a puddle in the dirt.

" 'Tis Grizel . . . covered in blood," the woman babbled. The man started to run, and without warning Grizel fled, weaving in and out among the village buildings.

The keening wind vied with the moaning Caoineag, and whipped Grizel's tangled dark hair about her face. Her eyes burned fever bright as she approached the villagers. Rubbing her palms against the blood on her gown, she held them up to one villager's face and then another.

"Lachlan is dead," she repeated as proudly as a child. "Would you make black pudding of his blood?"

At the sight, Agnes Drummond turned and pressed her face to her husband's chest.

A few awestruck villagers and castle sentries stood back at a distance, witnessing this morbid confession.

"Poison was too good for Lachlan," Grizel said in an emotionless voice. "I wanted to see him bleed the way he caused my heart to bleed for Ian . . . Ian, my jo . . ." Her voice broke, and again she took off running, dropping the bloody dirk.

"Catriona," a voice called.

She looked up. Then she, too, ran, for at that instant she'd spotted the one person in all the world who could make things safe and right.

Robert. On the village lane, he stood tall and braw, a study in barely leashed passion, his blue eyes snapping with inexplicable emotion, his golden hair wind-tousled.

"Robert . . . oh, Robert. Oh, Robert, you won't believe this. It's . . . it's . . ." Before she could run all the way, he had caught her in his arms. She fought for words.

He held her to him, cradling her head against his chest. All warnings were swept away in the dark tide of feeling that consumed her. "I told ye to wait in the cave, red thistle," he murmured close. "Instead . . ." He kissed the side of her forehead where her hair blew loose.

For the longest moment, Robert held her, cradling her head to his chest while around them gathered a ring of curious villagers. Catriona didn't care if God Himself watched. Robert was alive and holding her and they were together again. She felt the steady thud of his heart beneath her face.

Too soon, she was jerked from her haven as the villagers vied for Robert's attention. One after another, they clutched at him, pointing after Grizel and beseeching him in panicked voices.

"Grizel's been bewitched," they cried.

"Not bewitched," Robert said. "If there's been evil done, it's been by Grizel's own hand, and not because of some witch's spell. There'll be no more talk of witchcraft in this village."

Fiona Grant, tears running down her face, nodded. "Robert is the heir now, and his word must be obeyed."

Catriona stared up at Robert's strong, fierce profile. Tentatively, she touched his arm. "Is it Lachlan then who is dead?" she asked, needing to hear it from his lips.

As he nodded, she shut her eyes, the full horror of Grizel's madness closing in on her.

"Catriona, dear heart, 'twas Elspeth who found him," he said.

Overwhelmed, she pressed her face to his shirt.

Fiona Grant grabbed Catriona's skirt. "When it comes to the time of the full moon, we will set the first torch to the faggots. But we shall burn Grizel in place of this one."

"Never!" Robert shouted, the word vibrating through Catriona's heart as he spun her away from the villagers. "Never, not as long as I or my children or my children's children live." With those simple words, Robert decreed an end to the hysteria.

A long pause followed while the villagers mumbled among themselves.

Heart pounding, Catriona stayed still in Robert's arms, clutching his muscular back. His shirt was wet from the rain, and her fingers slid against the fabric, while all the time his voice vibrated through her. *His children,* she thought. He had no idea how soon it would come to pass that he would be a father. Nor would he ever know . . .

Suddenly, from between two huts, a tiny figure zigzagged out. Gently, Robert untangled Catriona and handed her over to Elspeth, who had run toward them.

"Lass, lass, ye're coming home with me now," said the older woman.

Gratefully, Catriona let herself be led off. "Oh, Elspeth, I was so afraid it might be Robert's blood on Grizel's knife."

"There now, Robert's safe, ye see. He'll stay safe. Ye dinna think a braw man like that would come to harm?"

For a long moment, Robert stared after Catriona, shaken by the exchange of words he'd overheard. Catriona had worried that he might be dead? And then his attention was drawn to the village lane leading up to the castle where Grizel made her crooked progress. She headed for the castle's inner wall.

"Robert!" The people turned to him as one. If anyone could subdue Grizel, it might be Robert with his words of reason.

Panicked villagers chased Lachlan's murderer. Sheriff MacIvie staggered out of the great hall, looking as pasty and useless as raw bread dough. Colin Grant lunged for Grizel, but she dodged past him, eluding one man after another until she reached a flight of stone steps that led to the castle ramparts. Like an insect, she clambered up.

Only Robert and Colin Grant dared follow. The rest of the village men hung back, their reluctant wives and sweethearts clinging to them.

Farther and farther along the narrow parapet Grizel darted, until Robert went dizzy watching her. It was impossible to keep up with her nimble feet, but he saw the sawtoothed gap in the ramparts ahead of her and expected her to lose her courage. But instead, the blood-covered figure leaped right over the gap, her cloak spreading to resemble a bat's wings. She stumbled on landing, and a gasp rose from the spectators below. Still on she went, nimbly dancing along the narrow stones.

Reaching the chapel tower, she found a toehold in the rugged stone and began to climb, while the wind blew in, whipping her bloody skirts about her.

Robert and Colin Grant stood on the rampart, their breathing ragged, watching Grizel work her way right up to the top of the parapet of the tower. It jutted out over Loch Aislair, and Robert had an icy foreboding of what was to come. He tried to gain a toehold on the tower, but Colin pulled him back.

"Dinna be daft, mon."

"Ian . . . Ian." Grizel looked around, as if searching

for the ghost of her lover. "Ian, my jo," she called. "Ian, I'm coming for ye."

With those words, she leaped, like a frantic blackbird launching herself off a cliff. For a moment it seemed as if she might actually be able to fly before she plummeted, down, down into the dark loch below. The water scarcely rippled as she broke the surface and disappeared from sight.

"The murderess of Glen Strahan," Colin Grant whispered, and doffed his cap. "May God have mercy on her soul."

A search party from the village found Grizel's body washed ashore the next day. Catriona wept.

Before the dirge of the pipes skirled through the glen in memory of Lachlan and Grizel, the humbled villagers assembled in the outer ward of the castle to pay their respects and pledge their fealty to Robert. Doffing their caps to Catriona, they each recanted their earlier testimony at the trial. Then, one by one they knelt and placed their hands in those of first Alexander, the laird, and then Robert, the new heir.

Touched though she was by her own tributes of apology—a sprig of dried heather, a posy of lavender, an offer to brush her new pony—for Catriona the service was an ordeal, and she left the funeral feast early, while Robert was still surrounded by villagers. She was too sick to stay longer, and by now Elspeth had figured out that Catriona carried Robert's bairn.

"He'll know soon enough," Elspeth said once they were back in Catriona's room in Ferguson Manor.

"Not if I return to Edinburgh. Is there a portmanteau about the manor house? I have no books to take, so I only need something small. If I hurry I can travel back in a coach with one of the funeral guests."

"And I suppose I must promise never to tell Robert ye carry his bairn? What kind of foolishness is this?"

"Knowing Robert, he would wed me out of duty, but I could never bear to have that."

"Lass, there's naught wrong with duty." Elspeth pressed a cool towel to Catriona's forehead. "After all, he's given up his dreams of London to assume the duties of an heir."

Catriona waved a dismissive hand. "That's not the same thing. Because he turned Jacques over to the English, he's regained his family's title, so there's no need for London."

Elspeth soothed Catriona's curls back from her forehead. "Have ye forgotten the risks he took to save ye from the stake, Catriona? Why did ye no' tell him ye carry his bairn? No one can help ye like Robert can, methinks. Ye need him, hinny."

Catriona's eyes blurred with tears as she pictured the hard planes of a masculine face. Deep blue eyes. An exquisite mouth, one that gave pleasure and demanded response. Robert's hands, roaming over her skin, enticing her to exquisite heights. She leaned back, recalling the first day she'd ever laid eyes on him in Edinburgh. A man so beautiful that a naive, foolish lass like herself had not been able to resist falling in love. If she shut her eyes, she could smell the rain upon his shirt, feel the thud of his heart beneath her face, the strength of his arms around her.

"Yer thoughts are elsewhere," Elspeth guessed. "Thinking of Robert MacLean, eh?"

"He's far too roguish for my tastes. Besides, he has his pick of the village lasses far and wide."

"What of *his* taste in lasses? Mayhap he cares for ye more than the others."

"Pish," she scoffed. "He was going to send me into exile. Why should I fall at his feet because he is now the heir? And I will not bribe him with his bairn."

Shaking her head and clucking her tongue, Elspeth handed Catriona a chamomile brew to soothe her. "Ye mean ye'd rather die than tell the man ye love him. Tsk, tsk. Catriona. Ye're a more cowardly lass than I took ye for. Either that or proud beyond reason. 'Tis no' the way to tell a man ye care, hiding away from him."

"Exactly, and he's never to know." She took a sip of the brew.

Hands on hips, Elspeth glared at her charge. "Ye're as stubborn as Angus, did I ever tell ye that?"

Catriona glared back. "Only a thousand times."

Chapter 26

A week later, Catriona was packed and ready to return to Edinburgh. She had only to wait for transportation, and no one seemed anxious to lend her a horse or a guide. That meant waiting for someone to come into Glen Strahan by coach. Undecided about whether to tell Robert she was leaving the village, Catriona went instead to pay a farewell visit to Mrs. Drummond. She stayed to tend her sick lad, Peter, who suffered from the ague again. For the better part of the night Catriona sat up with him, helping his mother, until at last the fever broke.

Only in late morning did Catriona give in to her fatigue. Resting her head against a chair back, she recalled, unbidden, the days she'd spent with Robert in the mountain hut, captive to a mountain cat and the Highland fog, but most of all to passion. Days and days alone with Robert. Years and years ago, it seemed now. Since the pipes had played the last funeral dirges, she'd not seen him, and though she tried to tell herself he was occupied in reorganizing castle affairs, a tiny frown line worried its way between her eyes. For she couldn't help imagining all the village lasses fawning over him, vying for the position of lady of the castle.

Abruptly she stood up, chiding herself for being a silly chit, for letting daydreams consume her. Little Peter was better. It was time to leave.

As thanks, Agnes Drummond grasped both of Catriona's hands in hers and blessed her. She handed her a small basket of pears, ripe ones from the tree by the kirk, and waved Catriona off as she stepped into the misty morning.

Halfway down the path that followed the shoreline of Loch Aislair to Ferguson Manor, she saw someone waiting for her at the MacLean-Ferguson property line.

"Robert." Her breath caught. Had she wished for him to come to her so much that she was imagining it? Drawing closer, she saw his breeches molding his thighs, his shirt sleeves rippling in the Highland breeze. And not even Lowland dress could hide the braw Highland crags of his face, and when she walked closer yet, she saw how his eyes reflected the blue of the lochs and how his hair was flecked with gold.

She looked up, trying to keep her expression composed. Soon, mayhap even today, she'd be on a coach heading south.

"Where are you going?" Reins in hand, he led his horse while he fell into step beside her.

"To the manor house," she said, balancing the basket of pears on her hip.

"That's no' what I mean. I saw Angus—"

"What were *you* doing at the manor house?"

"Looking for you, lass. Instead I found your portmanteau in the hallway."

"Oh, that case full of clothes?" she said lightly. "Don't worry, I'm not hauling books through the Highlands. There'll be plenty in the Lowlands."

"I didna inspect the contents this time, Catriona. For all I care, ye can pack yer grandfather's entire house. You ken what I'm asking." His voice sounded raw.

She swallowed hard. "Edinburgh." Her reply was barely a whisper. "I'm going back to Edinburgh. I can be a governess there as easily as in Paris."

He didn't answer immediately, but walking beside her, not touching her, he looked straight ahead. "Ye've a bad habit, lass, of running off when I'm no' looking or before I can find the words," he observed quietly. "I'd have come sooner but for the deaths."

"I understand. This is a fine enough time to say fare-well."

Laying his arm on hers, he stopped her. "But I don't understand, lass. Why when you're the heiress to Angus do you insist on going back to Edinburgh? There's naught to run from now."

"It's where I belong. Angus explained some family matters to me, and we've made our peace."

"That easily?" Robert asked gently.

"Of course not. He had to tell me that my mother at one time sold secrets to Jacobites, that she was a . . . a spy . . ." Her voice broke before she rushed on. "And here all these years I thought it was I who'd done the spying. Actually, I spied on your grandfather's castle, but according to Angus that's not as great a sin as . . . my mother's. In any case, I have his blessing." She pressed her lips shut, afraid her voice might break.

Oh, Robert. She snatched a glance at his face, all the while aware of the pulse beating in his wrist near her hand. The dark pull of sensuality tugged at her, tempting her. Her fingers pulsed from the longing to reach up and caress away the lock of golden hair that blew over his forehead. But if she so much as touched him once more, she might be lost, might tell him of his bairn that grew within her. With just one sentence she would make him hers. But if there was one thing she didn't want, it was his offer of a dutiful alliance.

Unable to bear more, she pulled away and turned to walk on, her cloak billowing out behind her.

"I'll escort you back to the manor," he said easily and, after vaulting into the saddle, reached for her and lifted her, basket of pears and all, up onto his horse.

"Ye belong to the Highlands, lass," he whispered against her hair.

Sweet rogue. She was aware of his hand just beneath her breasts and was certain he could feel the rapid pace of her heart. "I told you, there's naught for me here . . ."

Behind her, he went perfectly still.

"I belong in Edinburgh. Besides, you're the one with pressing duties as the heir. And now a title as well."

"Which I got because a fiery red-haired lass helped me expose a spying Frenchman," he reminded her.

Her entire body ached with the effort it took to speak. "Will you return to Edinburgh?"

He took his time answering. "Someday."

Of course, and by then she would be an aged spinster— with a child who favored Robert, a child she would raise to be heir to Ferguson Manor.

As soon as they arrived at the old manor house, she handed the basket of pears to a waiting groom and slid off the horse. "The master has found a coach to take you to Edinburgh, miss," the groom said. "It's waiting in the village." He set her portmanteau down smartly beside the pears.

"So soon?" she said quietly.

"Ye've been waiting all week, I was told, miss," he said, a twinkle in his eye, then discreetly left.

"I need to go in and say my farewells then," Catriona said to no one in particular. But she didn't move.

"Catriona." Raw longing laced Robert's voice.

"We became allies, Robert, and it hurts, I imagine, when friendly alliances go their separate ways."

She could have sworn he flinched.

He reached for the leather portmanteau.

"No, don't—"

She grabbed for it too, and the next thing she knew all her chemises and petticoats and nightdresses were spilling out onto the heather.

Kneeling, she stuffed everything back in while Robert stood quietly watching. She snapped shut the case, leaving the lace trim of a chemise dangling out.

In one swift motion, he pried the case from her. She managed to hang on to only a strip of lace, which neatly unraveled into a long thread when he tossed the case toward the door of the manor. He turned back and studied the strand of lace connecting them. Tugging gently, he reeled the silly little strip of lace frippery until he stood next to her, touching her hand.

The seconds ticked away in silence. She wanted him to grab her, kiss her, tell her he loved her. But that was, as Elspeth would remind her, the stuff of foolish dreams.

A quick glance at the house confirmed her suspicions. The servants, from Mrs. Burns to the groom, were peering out the windows. Angus and Elspeth were there too. This had gone on long enough. Snatching the ball of lace, she walked with purpose to the door of Ferguson Manor.

"I can guess why you've come . . . I think," she said.

"Oh, now ye've the sight, eh, lass?"

Reaching for her portmanteau, she looked back at him over her shoulder. "Already the villagers gossip." The words came shyly. "Robert MacLean will want the Ferguson properties. What better way than if he and the Ferguson lass form an alliance? She'll do as well for one MacLean as for another."

"They say that, do they?"

Solemnly, she nodded.

"Village gossip." He was striding toward her. "A lass can get into trouble listening to village gossip."

"Well, it's not your bother. I'm only telling you to explain."

"Ah, but it *is* my concern, lass. I'm the rogue who's had to keep you out of trouble while my castle falls apart in my absence."

"That won't be necessary anymore. I'll leave you in peace in your castle."

A smile played on his mouth. "What if I don't want to be left in peace in my castle? And if, as the villagers gossip, I wanted an alliance, what would you say?"

She glanced at him, gauging his mood. His expression was perfectly serious. He wasn't going to jest with her, not now.

"I don't want an alliance, not between MacLeans and Fergusons." She stared down at her toes.

"Did I no' beguile ye then, lass?" Like honey his words were, and then he tipped her chin up and made her look at him. "A rogue's task, you see, is to beguile the lass," he said whimsically, and she saw the smile in his eyes.

Deciding to play along, she said shyly, "You're very good at beguiling lasses. But, Robert, the lasses like to sometimes beguile the rogue . . . and you don't want to be beguiled."

Embarrassed by her forthright words, she turned to run inside the house, but with a quick movement, he stretched an arm across the door frame. Almost at once, she felt his hands on her shoulders.

"No, you don't, lass. You canna run away from the one diplomatic speech I may get to make in my life. Hear me out, ye will."

Somehow she kept on breathing. Somehow she ignored the tug of his touch and refrained from turning into his embrace. His words came low and close to her ear.

"After I left you at the caves, I knew at once how sorely I missed you, but I'd never planned to love any of the lasses, not forever. I was sorely tempted to book passage with you and give up the rogue's life. I had a dram with the sailors to think it over. Only I took too long to decide. When I got back to the cave, you were gone, and I was sure I'd let you down."

"You don't have to explain or apologize, Robert." It seemed that no matter where she ran, there was no escaping his sweet words. She got as far as a little bush of heather in front of the manor when he caught up with her again and, pulling her round, gathered her close and kissed her, the way the wind kissed the heather against the earth.

At last he let her go, his breath hard and deep. "What I'm trying to tell ye, lass, if ye'll quit running from me, is that ye've beguiled me."

And before she could run away from *those* words, he slid his hands down the length of her body until he was down on his knees and pressing his face to her stomach.

"God help me, Catriona, but I've been an arrogant, selfish man, chasing glory when all I really want is you."

Taken by surprise, she opened her mouth and stared. "I've beguiled you?"

He looked up. "Even before Lachlan died, I sent Lord

Kendrick's messenger packing. Even then, I'd made my choice. So you see, e'en were I no' the heir now, I'd be loving you and asking ye to wed with me." He took her hands in his and kissed them.

With dawning comprehension came her slow smile. It started inside her heart and spread across her face. Oh, how she smiled, enchanted by her fallen rogue.

"Lass, I dinna want an alliance. I want yer love." Looking up at the top windows of the manor house, he shouted, "Ye hear me, Angus Ferguson? I dinna want yer scrabbly land. 'Tis yer granddaughter I love, and I want naught else."

There was a medley of sounds as casements were suddenly slammed shut, and then Robert and Catriona turned back and stared at each other.

"Why, Robert," she said in surprise. "Robert, you said yourself that marriages of alliance are the way of the world."

"A man's got a right to change his mind, after all, doesn't he?" He looked up at her with stark longing.

"Yes, Robert." All she wanted was for him to kiss her, to go on holding her, to let her melt against the hard length of him. And then he explained in words meant only for her and the moors and the wind: "I love you, lass," he whispered, pressing his face against her belly. "I've been loving you ever since the start, and though I never guessed I'd wed for love, it's what I'm asking for."

"Oh, Robert . . ." Her smile widened. She ought to tell him that right where he pressed his face his own bairn grew, but she decided to savor all the fanciful words for a while longer. There would be time enough . . .

He rose and cupped her face, never taking his gaze off hers. "Would you wed me for love, lass?"

He pulled her close, and she felt the pounding of his heart.

"Say it, Catriona. Aye or nay?"

"Aye."

"Over and over, so I can memorize the sweet sound of it."

"Aye, Robert . . . I said 'aye.' I'll wed you and no one else."

Pressing her cheek against his neck, she felt his arms come up around her, his lips close against her.

The Highland winds buffeted the basket of pears and tipped it over. Ripe pears fell at their feet, but Catriona paid nary a heed. Robert's kiss was that fierce, it was.

And one last window up in the house slammed shut.

Epilogue

⌢⌢⌢⌢⌢⌢

"**A**ngus is a frightful name to give a wee bairn," Alexander grumbled. "Ye should have the decency to lose this golf match and let the bairn be named after me. The name Alexander Angus shows the proper respect for the father's family—which, after all, holds a peerage."

"A great-grandchild of mine named Alexander?" Angus Ferguson shuddered in mock horror. "There's no' been one in the Ferguson family yet. Angus Alexander is the most braw name."

Alexander MacLean whacked the ball, then lowered his golf club and shielded his eyes to follow the flight of the golf ball. When he saw where it landed, he turned to Angus.

"Yer granddaughter's taking an uncommon long time in whelping that bairn," he muttered.

Angus frowned. "Dinna be blaming her. It was *yer* grandson's doing." His hands tightened on his own golf club. Truth be told, if he didn't hear some news soon, he'd likely snap the cherrywood stick in two.

Alexander MacLean strode over to the scrubby patch of rust-colored heather and dug around for his ball.

"Well?" Angus demanded, hands folded over his club for support as if it were a walking stick. Angus was feeling stronger now that spring was here, and his feisty words proved it. "Where'd the blasted feathery land?"

"Smack in the middle of a patch of heather," confessed Alexander with a sheepish face.

384

"Then ye must hit it from out of the heather." Before Alexander could object, he added, "This is my land and we play by my rules."

This is *our* land," Alexander countered. "My grandson wed yer granddaughter and that makes the rules common."

"The plague it does. Play by yer own rules. See if I dinna win despite yer cheating."

Alexander hit and whiffed, and Angus lit his cuttie.

Afternoon had faded to gloaming by the time Robert joined them.

As one, they turned on him.

"Well?" Angus demanded. "Will ye wipe that foolish grin off yer face and tell us the news?"

" 'Tis a bonnie lass," Robert said proudly. "A wee red thistle just like her mother." He went on to announce the proper lady's name she'd bear.

"Margaret Mary!" the great-grandfathers echoed and, dragging their golf clubs behind them, headed for the manor house to see for themselves. In spite of last year's illness, Angus managed to beat Alexander to the door of the upstairs bedroom.

Catriona was leaning back against the pillows, cradling her newborn daughter in her arms, but at the sound of Angus's thundering footsteps, she looked up. Suddenly, Angus felt for all the world like a shy pup. Tiptoeing in behind Robert, he crept to the foot of the great canopied bed and beheld his smiling granddaughter. Catriona gazed down at the object of her affection—her daughter, Angus's great-granddaughter, gnawing on a tiny pink fist, her red-haired head peeking out of a plaid.

Catriona crooned to the bairn. "Lady Margaret Mary Ferguson MacLean, may I present you to your great-grandfathers, and may they live to see you wed a prince."

"A prince," Robert said, doubt in his voice. "A braw Highland man would suit me better."

"A prince of a man is what I meant, of course, daughter. Though your father may keep forgetting, there *is* a difference between a prince of the realm and a prince of a man."

Angus wondered if he'd ever in his life smiled the way Robert was. Robert reached down to stroke wee Margaret's cheek and kissed Catriona in full view of them all.

Clearing his throat, Angus moved forward to pay homage to the new wee lass who reigned in Glen Strahan. Aye, he reminded himself, taking his great-granddaughter in his arms for the first time and displaying her to Alexander, love was king and always had been so. Only fools forgot.

Author's Note

Highland Scotland of the early eighteenth century was a place of isolation and fervent superstitions. The punishment for murder by witchcraft remained burning at the stake until 1736. It was a place, too, in which clans held divided loyalties—some to England; others (Jacobites) to the exiled Stuart court.

According to historical sources, the Royal Regalia of Scotland (crown, sword, and scepter), is possessed of a romantic history. Hidden at one time in the seventeenth century in Castle Dunnottar to protect it from Cromwellian forces, it was secreted to another hiding place under the floorboards of a Scottish church. Eventually recovered, it was again locked away in a chest after the Act of Union in 1707 and essentially forgotten. Missing for more than a hundred years, the dusty chest was finally discovered in Edinburgh in 1818 and, under orders of the Prince Regent, pried open. Today, the Regalia is on display in the Crown Room at Edinburgh Castle.

The idea of a real treasure missing for over one hundred years intrigued me so much that I could not resist putting the Regalia on stage in my story. If I took liberty with the historical facts of the Regalia, it was solely to enhance the dramatic impact of my story, and I trust the reader will understand and, most of all, enjoy.

All references to "the Rebellion" in this novel refer to the Battle of Sheriffmuir, 1715, during which the Old Pretender, James Stuart, attempted unsuccessfully to reclaim his throne and after which many participating Highland clans suffered various punishments, some so severe that, as a result, some Highlanders declined to participate in the 1745 rebellion.

Avon Romances—
the best in exceptional authors and unforgettable novels!

DEVIL'S MOON   Suzannah Davis
76127-0/$3.95 US/$4.95 Can

ROUGH AND TENDER   Selina MacPherson
76322-2/$3.95 US/$4.95 Can

CAPTIVE ROSE   Miriam Minger
76311-7/$3.95 US/$4.95 Can

RUGGED SPLENDOR   Robin Leigh
76318-4/$3.95 US/$4.95 Can

CHEROKEE NIGHTS   Genell Dellin
76014-2/$4.50 US/$5.50 Can

SCANDAL'S DARLING   Anne Caldwell
76110-6/$4.50 US/$5.50 Can

LAVENDER FLAME   Karen Stratford
76267-6/$4.50 US/$5.50 Can

FOOL FOR LOVE   DeLoras Scott
76342-7/$4.50 US/$5.50 Can

OUTLAW BRIDE   Katherine Compton
76411-3/$4.50 US/$5.50 Can

DEFIANT ANGEL   Stephanie Stevens
76449-0/$4.50 US/$5.50 Can

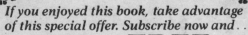